Amidst a rising tide of poachers, three unlikely eco-warriors take a stand to save endangered Eastern Gray Wolves—even if it means the slow slaughter of their captors.

Deep in the woods of Jackson, New Hampshire, an ancient evil lurks. Armed poachers patrol a secret enclosure, holding captive a pack of majestic Eastern Gray Wolves. But three unlikely eco-warriors are determined to free the wolves, embarking on a dangerous mission to end their torture. With courage and conviction, Shawnee, Mayhem, and Jacy Lee march onward, even if it means risking their own lives to take down the poachers and restore freedom to the wolves. It's a battle between justice and injustice, and the eco-warriors are determined to win—no matter the cost.

But what if something even more evil lurks in those woods? What if Shawnee's not ready to answer the cry for help?

RESTLESS MAYHEM
Mayhem Series, #6
Sue Coletta
Author Copyright: Sue Coletta
Publisher: Crow Talons Publishing
Cover Art: Elle J. Rossi (evernightdesigns.com)
Editor: Staci Troilo

This story is a work of fiction. The names, characters, places, and incidents are products of the author's imagination. Any resemblance to actual events, locales, or persons, living or dead, is entirely coincidental.

DEDICATION

May the warm winds of heaven blow softly upon your house.
May the Great Spirit bless all who enter there.
May your moccasins make happy trails in many snows.
And may the rainbow always touch your shoulder.

ACKNOWLEDGMENTS
The heartfelt message in the dedication is a Native American blessing.
Special thanks to all my consultants and sources who added realism to Restless Mayhem:
NHdeeds.org
Warpaths2Peacepipes
Angel Eyes & Angel Eyes 300
Angel Fire
Hanksville.org
NavajoPeople.org
NRDC.org
Tony Hillerman Portal
LegendsofAmerica.com
Openjournals.bsu.edu
Discover Navajo
Hanksville.org
NHMU.Utah.edu
FirstPeople.us
Pachamama.com
Native-American-online.com
Justice.gov
Balladeer's Blog
Backstory.org
International Wolf Center
NWCG
Native-Languages.org
Wolf.org
TohoFit
Ya-Native
Indigenous Ability
NativeJewelrylit.com

RESTLESS MAYHEM

Indian Country Today
WikiHow
Cornell.edu
National Geographic
Omni Mt. Washington Hotels & Resorts
Carve Me a Bear
Notes from the Frontier
NMAI Magazine
WolvesWolves.blogspot.com
Wolf Haven International
AAA Native Arts
GrandfatherSpirit.com
OneLittleAngel.com
NavajoCodetalkers.com
Miramar Beach Dental
Slife.org
Wolf Conservation Center
Stanford University
DanceFacts.net
Ncbi.nlm.nih.gov
LindsayWildlife.org
Bigorrin.org
Very Well Health
TwinRocks.com
Limacello Kitchen
Defenders of Wildlife
UMass.edu
NativeAmericanConjure.com
Aihc1998tripod.com
MorningChores.com
Feena
Treehugger.com

Family Cookbook Project
Outside Online
StudentsThesis.universiteltleiden.nl

To Bob, Bobby, Kathy, Berlyn, Scarlet, Joey, Dad, and Frank: Thank you for remaining my loudest cheerleaders. The endless hours spent at my desk—headphones on, music cranked—can't be easy on you, yet you (almost) never complain. Love you all!
To Sandi & Amiel, thank you for the blessed Hands of the Most High and the Native cross. I cannot express how much those sculptures (and you) mean to me.
As always, thank you, God, for blessing my life in unimaginable ways.

RESTLESS MAYHEM

RESTLESS MAYHEM
Mayhem Series, #6
Sue Coletta

Crow Talons
Publishing

Chapter 1

M*onday, 3:20 a.m.*

As I faded into a peaceful slumber in the back bedroom of Mr. Mayhem's log cabin in Jackson, New Hampshire, a hair-raising shriek startled me awake. I jolted upright. In the window, burning red eyes peered through a deluge of blackness, the background silenced by an eerie stillness, the stench of death seeping through the screen.

Oh. My. God. An icy tongue licked up my spine. *Shicheii's* right. We woke the beast.

I leaped out of bed. Sprinted down the hall, my bare feet slapping the wide-pine floor. Up the stairs, I clamored. Braked at the top. Who should I wake? For days, my grandfather, a Diné Medicine Man with unlimited spiritual power, warned me and Mr. Mayhem that our so-called "mistakes" could reanimate an ancient beast from its dormancy. So, waking *Shicheii* probably wasn't the best idea. But the last time I woke Mr. Mayhem, a cunning warrior steeped in mystery and mystique... Well, let's just say it didn't go well.

If he and I hadn't left two dead poachers in the forest surrounding the property, I wouldn't have to make this decision. But those burning red eyes weren't going away on their own. I had to do something, tell someone about the creature lurking outside my window. Those eyes didn't belong to a normal animal.

With no other alternative, I padded into Mr. Mayhem's dark and quiet bedroom. Even though this felt wrong on so many levels, I crept closer.

Steps away from the bed, Poe—his freakishly human crow companion—cracked open one eye, and I swear that bird chuckled under his breath, no doubt thinking, *Good luck, asshole.* Spirit Crow slept next to him, her brilliant white plumage glistening in the moonlight, delicate feet tucked under her body on the tribal blanket. Almost scentless, a slight hint of citrus surfed the air.

Moonbeams cascaded over Mr. Mayhem's face and bare chest. Out cold, a deep sleep like last time. Uh-oh. From several feet away, I cleared my throat.

He didn't budge.

A little louder—not too loud or I might wake *Shicheii* in the bedroom next door—I cleared my throat a second time, my insides screaming for me to leave.

Nothing. Not even a twitch of the eyelids.

Shit. I couldn't call out without alerting my grandfather, but approaching Mr. Mayhem without fair warning could turn deadly fast. If touched, his first reaction was to attack, so nudging him was out of the question. Learned that little tidbit the hard way, and I certainly wasn't in a hurry to do it again.

Down on the floor—out of reach of swinging fists—I crawled toward the bed. But my knee hit a squeaky floorboard, and in a flash, he pounced, flattening me, unbreakable hands squeezing my throat, cutting off airflow.

"It's me," I choked out, waving my arms, hoping to avoid death. "Stop. Please...it's me..." Fogginess swarmed my head, distorting his face more and more until he became almost unrecognizable. My arms fell limp. Crumpled on the wide pine floors, my world faded to black.

A cold wet cloth dabbed my forehead, cheeks, and down my neck, bringing me around. It took me a minute to figure out where I was or whose long hair swept across my bare shoulder, my nightshirt twisted and tight.

"*Shicheii?*"

Mr. Mayhem said, "No."

"What happened?"

"Well, I thought you'd learned not to startle me awake, but apparently, you needed a refresher. Take tiny sips." With one hand under my head, he pressed the rim of a glass to my lips. "For the life of me, Cat, I cannot figure out why you would enter my bedroom in the middle of the night, announced and uninvited."

Long story for why he called me Cat instead of Shawnee. Basically, over the course of our long history—most of it terrifying—he and his wife, Kimi, gave me the nickname because of my past work as a cat burglar. Also, shorter and easier for Kimi's BCI technology to type. She didn't die from the ALS, by the way. A skinwalker murdered her. But her soul reincarnated into the breathtakingly beautiful Spirit Crow.

He pulled the glass away and sat me upright. "If you have misconstrued any of our interactions—"

"What? Ew." Flashing a splayed hand, I turned my head. "I'm gonna stop you right there before this gets weird. That's not at all why I'm here."

With one palm pressed to his heart, he audibly exhaled. "Oh, thank goodness."

"Seriously? Why would you even think—?" I batted away my question. "Y'know what? Let's agree to scrub the last few seconds from our minds."e

"Works for me."

"For me, too, believe me." While I straightened my nightshirt, Mr. Mayhem sat back on folded legs, shirtless, with a sheet draped over his bare lap. "Are you, um—?"

"Cautious Cat, I was asleep." His tone hardened. "Alone. In my bedroom. What I wear, or choose not to wear, is my business."

"Right. Sorry." Clearing my throat for real this time, I crawled to my feet. "I gotta show you something—now."

"Can it wait till I put pants on?" The raised eyebrows showed his frustration.

"Oh. My bad. Absolutely." I turned my back to allow him privacy, but he ordered me to wait in the hall. Probably best.

A few minutes later, he strolled out of the bedroom with his hair pulled back in a low ponytail—elastic bands evenly spaced down the length—dark strands resting in front of one shoulder. Barefooted and shirtless, birdshot pellet wounds scattered from elbow to chin on one side, he wore pressed and pristine jeans. Think he'd wear sweatpants? Oh, hell no. Even at home in the middle of the night—early morning, whatever—the man dressed to impress.

Without a word, he gestured toward the stairs, urging me to go ahead. In the kitchen, he followed close behind as I veered down the hall to my room in the back.

The moment he stepped through the doorway, he glanced right and left. "Why are half the kitchen dishes in here?"

"Never mind the mess. Look." I thrust a finger at the window. "We woke the beast."

He hustled over, peered into the darkness, then whirled back to me.

"Well," I said, "did you see it?"

"What exactly should I have seen, Cat?"

"Burning red eyes." I flung out my hand. "They were right there."

"Come." He beckoned me closer. "Nothing is out there. Look for yourself."

With a quick peek through the screen, blackness shrouded the backside of the property. "Maybe it's hiding?"

"Let me ask you this." He raised praying hands to his lips. "How did this... discovery... come about?"

"Well, this strange noise startled me awake. Kinda like a bloodcurdling shriek, only worse. When I glanced out the window, these burning red eyes stared back at me."

"Did you leave your bed at all?"

"Not till I fled to get you. Why?"

"So, you were still in bed, under the covers, when you saw the red eyes?"

"Yeah."

"All right, then." He sat at the foot of my bed. "Is it possible—and please let me finish before you respond—is it possible that perhaps you did not fully wake before spotting what you claim to be eyes?"

I firmed a fist on my hip. "No."

"No? It's not possible?"

"No." I crossed my arms on my chest. "I know what I saw. That thing was out there."

"I admire your confidence—I really do, Cat—however, we discussed the beast shortly before bed. As such—"

"I didn't imagine it, if that's what you're sayin'."

"If you'd let me finish..." He shot me a steely eyed glare. "I was about to say we all went through a lot over the last few days. Perhaps this was your mind's way of compartmentalizing. Lucid dreams bring order to the disorderly. They decrease anxiety while awake. The sense of control we feel while lucid dreaming we carry with us in our waking life. The trick is learning that you are, in fact, in a dream, thus shaping the story and the ending any way you wish. Think of this as a good thing, a gift."

Certainty waning, I plopped down next to him. "You really think I dreamed it?"

"I do."

"But it felt so real."

"Lucid dreams usually do."

"Huh." Could I have imagined it? I bolted out of the bedroom so fast I guess it's possible.

When Mr. Mayhem rose, I latched onto his arm.

"Where're you goin'?"

His gaze shifted from my hand to my eyes, and I let go. "Why did you wake me and not your grandfather?"

"I didn't wanna worry him."

"Because you had doubts about what you saw?"

I stared at the floor. "I guess, yeah."

"Chin up. The blood of our People runs through your veins. It's well after three now." A breathy exhale drove home the message that he'd rather crawl back into bed. "I suppose I could make tea."

"Cool." I sprang to my bare feet. "I'll help."

For a moment, he studied me before shaking his head. "All right, Cat. You win. There's something we should discuss, anyway. Not in the kitchen, however. Your grandfather needs his rest."

"Where're we gonna talk, then?"

"On the porch." After dropping that bomb, he strolled out the door.

Outside? An invisible cattle prod jabbed me in the gut. What if I hadn't conjured the beast in a lucid dream? What if it's still out there, waiting for the chance to attack? We'd walk straight into a no-win situation without weapons to defend ourselves. Easy prey. But I couldn't argue with Mr. Mayhem after he agreed to stay up with me. And we couldn't chat in the kitchen. *Shicheii* did need rest. Medicine Men poured a lot of themselves into their work. Absorbing everyone's problems took a toll if they didn't also practice self-care.

After Mr. Mayhem reheated *Shicheii's* homemade wild tea on the stove, herbs wafting from the saucepan, I followed him out to the porch. In my usual chair—the log wall safeguarding my back—I curled my hands around the hot mug. Made from clay, my grandfather handcrafted the serving set on the reservation years ago, each mug and the honey pot adorned with four Sacred Colors of black, white, yellow, and blue.

A Sacred Fire blazed in the yard. Timber crackling, a lone orange spark leaped beyond the circle of white stones, campfire smoke wafting in the mild summer air. In the center of the table, Mr. Mayhem lit the wick of a fat candle. Not only did the candle represent the Central Fire, the heart of a Hogan, but it aligned with Polaris, the North Star.

In front of me, he slid the honey pot. "Ladies first."

"Thanks." Chivalry was alive and well in his world. "Don't mind if I do."

I swished the dipper through the honey, drizzled a heap of sweet nectar into my wild tea, then slid the pot over to him. Leaning back in my chair, I surveyed the wooded landscape for anything out of the ordinary. Tree frogs chirped in the trees. A great horned owl hooted and barked. Moonlight trickling through the leaves, the forest amplified the cry of predators and prey. But no smoldering red eyes anywhere. Maybe I did dream it.

"Thanks for stayin' up with me."

Sipping his tea, he basked in the peacefulness. "My pleasure, Cautious Cat."

"Should I have woken *Shicheii* instead?"

Firelight sparkled in his gray, almost translucent eyes. "You tell me."

"Well, I mean, other than almost being strangled to death—for the second time, in case we're keeping score—I think I made the right decision."

A smirk lurked on his lips. "You think, or you know?"

"I made the right decision." Honey tap-danced on my tongue, *Shicheii's* special tea filling me with love. "Wanna talk about your"—I flashed air quotes—"*reaction*? It's an area you really should work on. Just sayin.'"

The smirk morphed into a chuckle. "Touché." A brownie point flipped my way. "Do you feel more relaxed?"

"Definitely. Whaddaya wanna talk to me about?"

"Are you familiar with the term 'wolfdogs'?"

I clawed back my bangs. "Werewolves?"

"No. Wolfdogs. They're a hybrid of Gray Wolf and domestic dog." He leaned forward, hands clasped around the mug. "Years ago, around the time when the white man drove our People off ancestral land, they also hunted the Eastern Gray Wolf to extinction throughout all six New England states. Wolves still traversed through Canada. Any animals who dared to breach the border, poachers captured. More recently, poachers bred domestic dogs with captive wolves."

Scumbags never ceased to baffle me. "Why?"

"A wolfdog pup sells for a minimum of ten thousand dollars on the black market. Prospective buyers, however, do not realize the dangers of cohabitating with a wild animal. When the adorable pup balloons to two hundred pounds and predates on pets or attacks family members, wolfdogs are often shot in the head and dumped."

"Wow." Gobsmacked by this news, I jerked away from the table. "This is still happening?"

"It is, yes. New Hampshire has become a dumping ground for wolfdogs. Protection for these animals is nonexistent. One side claims they're domestic dogs, the other side knows they're not. According to the white man's law, it is illegal to sell wolfdogs, but no one enforces the law. It's a gray area. And so, these beautiful animals fall through the cracks."

"Wait, wait, wait." I teed my hands, those words unfathomable to comprehend. "Y'mean, no one protects wolfdogs? Like, absolutely no one?"

Mr. Mayhem rocked his head no.

"Then we have to."

A grin emerged through the candlelight. "I was hoping you'd agree."

After a quick sip, I set down my mug. "Got a lead on a seller?"

"Do the names Chip Worthington and Curran Rothschild ring a bell?"

I slapped the table. "Shut up." In case he misread the expression as disrespect, I covered with, "I mean, shut the front door. How do you know?"

"Apparently, Misters Worthington and Rothschild played middlemen for the business, introducing prospective buyers to sellers. I found mention of their activities in one folder from his safe."

Last weekend, Mr. Mayhem butchered Chester "Chip" Worthington into pieces after finding a plethora of taxidermied crows in his home office, along with elephant tusks and stuffed lion and zebra heads, among others. Disposing of him wasn't the best time I ever had, but if ever there was a guy who deserved to die, it was Worthington. A rich, entitled asshole who bought his way through life, even if it meant the slaughter of innocent animals so he could display the busts on his trophy wall. Curran Rothschild—also dead—was one of his so-called associates.

"Who runs the business now?"

"That's the question, isn't it?"

While sipping my tea, I grappled with why no one protected these animals. What's wrong with people these days? Had society become so jaded and self-centered that we just accepted the mistreatment of Mother Earth's Innocent Ones, as long as it didn't affect our way of life? I sure as hell couldn't. Neither could Mr. Mayhem, or he wouldn't've told me.

"When do you wanna start?"

"Well, first, we need to inform your grandfather. We'll need his help with the animals. However, the conversation might sound better coming from you." When he paused, I agreed. "Do you plan to tell him about your lucid dream?"

"Meh. I don't think it's necessary. Why worry him?"

"That was my feeling, as well." He leaned back in his chair, ankles crossed in front of him. "Then it's settled. After sunrise, morning prayer, and cleaning up our earlier mess—the disposal of Mister Underwood and his friend—we'll gather intel."

Great. Just what I wanted to do before breakfast, get arm deep in human remains. Again.

Chapter 2
*"Coyote is always out there waiting,
and Coyote is always hungry."*
—Navajo (Diné) Proverb

4:30 a.m.

Empty mug in hand, Mayhem headed into the cabin for a refill. Jacy Lee strode down the stairs, his gray hair already combed into two long braids. "Would you like a cup, dear friend?"

"Yes please, Cheveyo. Thank you."

Not many could get away with using Mayhem's legal name—he much preferred the anonymity of his epithet—but he'd known Jacy Lee since he was a young boy.

"Is Mourning Dove still asleep?" he said, using Shawnee's traditional name.

"She's on the porch. Your granddaughter and I both rose rather early this morning."

Smiling, he said, "How nice."

When Mayhem passed him a mug, Jacy Lee strolled out to the porch. Before joining them outside, Mayhem dashed up the stairs and into his bedroom. "Good morning, my loves."

After stretching his wings, Poe flew to his shoulder. Spirit Crow perched on his forearm, and he tucked her close to his chest, his heart overflowing with love from her delicate touch. Many did not possess the wherewithal to comprehend their unusual relationship—that a human soul cast from its flesh through violence could reincarnate, as his beloved wife Kimi had and now embodied Spirit Crow—but their ignorance of the unknown could never break their bond.

Downstairs, when he stepped out to the porch, Poe and Spirit Crow took flight, soaring around the yard, basking in the predawn dimness, two awe-inspiring beings flying in synchronicity.

Jacy Lee said, "Cheveyo, would you mind playing the flute for morning prayer?"

"I'd be honored."

"Super. Thank you." Jacy Lee laid a gentle palm on Shawnee's hand. "How was your tea, child?"

"Delicious as always, *Shicheii*. Mind if I have another?"

"Not at all. Help yourself."

As Shawnee passed Mayhem to get to the door, he hushed, "Make it quick. Morning prayer starts in a few minutes."

"Got it."

At the table, Mayhem dragged the dipper through honey. "Did you sleep well?"

"Funny thing." Elbows on the table, the mug hovered in front of his lips. "I could have sworn I heard my granddaughter's voice in your bedroom early this morning."

Lying to an elder rubbed against all his beliefs. Thus, instead, he sidestepped the truth. "Huh." While he mulled over how to explain, he sipped his tea, honey and greenthread—a member of the sunflower family—rejoicing on his palate.

"Was she in your bedroom this morning, Cheveyo?"

A direct question deserved a truthful response. "Yes. A lucid dream startled her awake, and she needed to talk it through."

His lifelong friend seemed hurt. "Why would she go to you instead of me?"

"I'm afraid only she can answer that question. She may have stumbled into the wrong room."

"Perhaps." His brow furrowed. "What did she dream about?"

"The details aren't important." If he learned she'd seen the eyes of a Wendigo, he might panic. "The point is, she experienced a lucid dream. Meaning, you've had a profound effect on her life. She's learning and flourishing because of your influence."

"And yours." Jacy Lee's cheeks dimpled. "Perhaps I should add a little sweet gale to her nighttime tea."

Hand-picked in the Algonquian wilderness, sweet gale was usually found by the tribe near lakes or running water. This delightful herb had delicate earthy, low notes with fruity, fresh, and lively floral and honey undertones that aided in digestion and helped initiate lucid dreaming.

However, after Shawnee's reaction this morning, it may not be smart to add this herb to her tea. "Are you asking for my advice?"

"I am."

"In that case, I would hold off on the sweet gale until you've explained lucid dreaming more fully. The experience frightened her."

"Oh, dear. Thank you, Cheveyo. I'll hold off, then. Though it is an exciting new path for her."

Mayhem winked. "Indeed, it is, old friend."

The screen door slapped open, and Shawnee strolled out to the porch in the thick terrycloth robe from Thorn Hill Inn. When she sat, her brilliant emerald eyes shimmied in the firelight, her gaze ping-ponging between them. "Why do I get the feeling I just interrupted something? Were you two talkin' about me again?"

"Don't be silly, child." Jacy Lee smiled at her. "Have I told you how proud I am of you?"

"Only every single day. Hey, um, *Shicheii*? Need to talk to you about somethin.'"

"Will it keep till breakfast?" The subtle hint showed he was ready to welcome the day.

"Absolutely."

After Mayhem drank the last drop of tea, he darted into the cabin, brushed his teeth in the en suite bathroom upstairs, slung a button-down shirt over one shoulder, slipped into knee-high moccasins, then grabbed the flute by the door on his way out. Meeting Jacy Lee in the hall, he followed him down the stairs. Shawnee waited in the yard.

In front of the northeastern horizon, he blew through the flute's mouthpiece while Jacy Lee recited the opening prayer in Athabaskan, the native tongue of Diné People.

As Mayhem played harmonizing notes, Jacy Lee sang to the Holy Ones. For the first time, Shawnee joined in, singing the phrases she recognized, silent for the foreign ones. All three united in the present moment as Father Sky brushed the horizon with muted pinks and violets. Every five minutes, more transformations took place—the colors brightening and rising and spreading outward like the barbs of a feather.

While the Sun rose—a big and brilliant fireball of orange—Mayhem played louder, stronger, holding each note in celebration. Jacy Lee's words cut straight through the harmony of the flute, his everlasting devotion to the Holy Ones fully displayed.

Once Father Sun relaxed into the sky, Mayhem lowered the instrument. Filled with a positive mindset for the day, he led his lifelong friend and Shawnee back to the porch.

As Mayhem held open the screen door for Jacy Lee, he said, "I need to steal your granddaughter for about an hour to straighten out that mess we talked about last night."

Shawnee whirled around. "Now?"

Mayhem ignored her.

"Understood, Cheveyo. I'll get breakfast ready for when you return."

"Perfect. Thank you." His gaze traced Shawnee up and down. "Is that what you're planning to wear today?"

"What's wrong with sweats and a T-shirt?"

Too many responses fled through his mind, but he pushed them aside and swept a hand toward the stairs. "After you, Cat."

When she strode to the Caddy, Poe swooped her head, running his talons through her raven hair. She screamed like a little girl. Poe sailed high out of her reach, and her tresses nestled back into place, cherry highlights glinting in the sun. Admittedly, Poe still harbored some resentment. Understandable. Crows did not take kindly to capture or assault, accidental or otherwise. Poe landed on Dad's shoulder, nuzzling his feathery crown into the crook of his neck, begging to tag along.

"All right, buddy." He opened the driver's door, and Poe flew inside, landing on the driver's seat, hopping up to the middle console. "Mind your manners, you two." He slipped behind the wheel. "We have to work to do."

Even after his warning, Poe and Shawnee tossed dirty looks back and forth, the tension growing thick. Would the animosity between them ever end?

Chapter 3

6 a.m.

So far, so good. After a few side-glances between us, my upper lip twitching with disdain, Poe stared straight out the windshield like a good little doobie. Daddy's boy. Mr. Mayhem pulled down the dirt road to the back of his property and parked. When he got out, Pissy Pants rode his forearm.

Over the Caddy's roof, I said, "Why didn't Spirit Crow come?"

"She'd rather stay close to home with the others. They've grown attached to her."

Most of the massive, one-hundred-strong murder dispersed back to their territory after the immediate danger of crow hunting passed, but many still remained at the cabin.

"Does that mean she's stickin' around for a while?"

"She has no choice." Mr. Mayhem strode to the back of the vehicle. When he waved his foot under the back bumper, the trunk opened on its own. "At least until she regains full strength."

"Cool. I mean, not that she's still, y'know, healing, but I love having her around."

"As do I, Cat. As do I." While rummaging through the trunk, he grabbed a lawn 'n leaf bag and the foldable spade. "Care for gloves this time?"

"Um, yeah." I flashed a quick sarcastic smirk, and he jerked back, his gray eyes focused on my mouth. "What?" The back of my hand wiped my lips. "Why're you lookin' at me like that?"

"You forgot to brush your teeth this morning."

"So?" My tongue rolled back and forth across my teeth. "I'll brush 'em when we get back."

"It may be too late for that, I'm afraid."

"What?" In the side mirror I flashed my teeth—all the enamel stained bright red like I'd morphed into some sort of blood-sucking monster. "Oh, my effin' head." I slapped my forehead. "You guys were serious about that?"

"Never have we lied to you, Cat." Staring at my teeth, a smirk lurked right below the surface.

Think Poe would hide his laughter? Oh, hell no. That punk threw his head back and cackled. Friggin' psycho. I should've let the trophy hunters stuff his sorry ass.

"If memory serves," Mr. Mayhem said, "your grandfather and I both explained how our People dye wool rugs with greenthread." The chief ingredient in *Shicheii's* wild tea. "Did we not?"

"Well, yeah, but—" Scrubbing my forefinger across my teeth, I glanced into the mirror again. "How long are they gonna stay like this?"

"Till the dye wears off, I suppose. It's difficult to say how long that may be."

"No, really. I'm dead serious. How long till they're white again?"

Ignoring me, he dug through a duffle bag in the trunk. For what, I had no idea. Probably more supplies to scrub decomposing human remains off the forest floor. Oh, joy.

"Lemme get this straight." Balled fists flew to my hips. "You're sayin' I gotta walk around like this, with blood-red teeth? Nothing I can do about it? No secret potion for *Shicheii* to whip up? No herbal remedies to counteract the effect?"

"Hence our forewarning." His dismissive hand waved like it was no big deal, and I was overreacting to a minor disturbance. "It's a lesson we all had to learn growing up." A chuckle escaped his lips, joyful tears filling his eyes. "Think of it as a rite of passage."

"For the record, I don't find the humor in this at all."

"Noted." Reining in his emotion, his lips jiggled like he was about to laugh his ass off, and my upper cheek twitched in protest. "Now, if we're done here"—he pressed the lid of the trunk closed—"we really should get a move-on before the wildlife indulges on Mister Underwood even more."

"Fine." I unfolded the spade, my tongue in constant motion across my upper and lower teeth, concentrating on the areas that showed the second I parted my lips. "Let's just get this over with."

As we strolled through the dense forest, Poe waited several yards ahead for his father to catch up, flew ahead again, then waited, as though he'd turned this excursion into a game.

When Mr. Mayhem veered down a narrow path toward where he'd tied Underwood to the tree for safekeeping, I followed close behind, the two of us strolling single file. At the end of the trail, he stopped dead, his head turning left and right.

I peered over his shoulder—the tree stump bathed in blood. "Where the hell did he go?"

Mr. Mayhem approached, with me on his heels. "Hm."

"Hm? That's all you gotta say?" I flung a hand at the base of the tree. "Underwood's gone, for fuck's sake!"

"Look, Cat." His tone turned ruthless. "I understand you're upset, but that vile language is not helpful."

Poe cawed from a high branch. When my gaze crawled up the tree, blood splattered in my eyes, nose, and lips. "I'm blind!" I ran my forearm across my face, but it didn't seem to help much. Every time I cracked open my eyes, the unbroken forest had a reddish hue. I gagged. Gagged again. And again.

"Get ahold of yourself." Mr. Mayhem wrangled my flailing hands under control. "You are *not* blind." With a loud exhale, he bent my head back and poured bottled water over my face. A bandana patted dry my skin. "There. See? No reason to panic."

"Thanks." Now with clearer vision, I stepped back a few feet and glanced up at the branch. Someone had wedged a mangled Mr. Underwood—what was left of him, anyway—in the crook of the tree between a thick branch and the trunk. Didn't the Wendigo stash food in trees? "You don't think my dream was real, do you?"

"Under normal conditions, I may give your lucid dream more weight. Here, however, I'd say it's unlikely."

"But not impossible?"

"Nothing is impossible, Cat."

"Are you willing to bet our lives on it?"

"Please don't weaponize my words. Frankly, it belittles us both." Two fingers pointed at a blood trail on the bark, with long bare marks from where the bark fell off by something rubbing against it. "The creature you speak of possesses supreme supernatural strength. Thus, it would not need to *hoist* Mister Underwood up the tree."

"Oh." Good point. A Wendigo could probably carry him on its shoulder. Did they even have shoulders? "Okay, well, if the beast didn't stuff him up there, who did?"

"The most likely suspect is a mountain lion."

Speechless, all I managed was, "Wow." The metallic sweetness of blood churned my stomach acids, the incessant buzz of insects wearing my nerves raw. "Maybe that's a good thing. Since the mountain lion obviously plans to come back for him, he did us a favor."

His eyebrows squished together. "How so?"

"Whaddaya mean? Underwood belongs to the mountain lion now, right?"

"Wrong. We cannot leave Mister Underwood up there. Did you learn nothing from your grandfather's reaction last night?"

When *Shicheii* got a whiff of decomposition in the woods, he panicked, leaping to the conclusion that a Wendigo lurked nearby. Hence why I couldn't tell him about my dream. Mr. Mayhem came clean and told him the truth. Well, enough pieces of the story to calm him, anyway. The funny part was, Mr. Mayhem really didn't kill Underwood. All he did was tie him to the tree. The wildlife did the rest. Karma bit back, he'd said. A trophy hunter killed by the very animals he hunted? In hindsight, it's hard to argue against that logic.

"But you just said—"

"Regardless of how you misinterpret this scene, Cat, our objective hasn't changed."

"Right. My bad." Fuck. Could this day get any worse? Scratch that. It probably could. "Suppose you want me to climb up there."

"I'll handle it." Mr. Mayhem strode to the back of the tree—careful not to get bloody—and scaled the clean side of the trunk. Once he reached the branch, he called out, "On three. One... Two... Coming down."

The second Underwood's mangled remains struck the earth, it hit a massive crimson pool at the base of the tree, and arcs of blood showered over me like Carrie on prom night.

"What. The. Fuck!"

Cackling like a lunatic, Poe tossed his head back.

"Shut up, you freak o' nature! It's not funny!"

Spotless, Mr. Mayhem jumped down to the ground. One look at me, and he said, "Ooh, that's unfortunate."

A wave of nausea rose in the back of my throat, and I folded in half, my hands cupped on bent knees, spitting and choking, saliva dripping off my tongue. Vomit sprayed from my mouth until I dry heaved, my stomach twisting, clenching like a fist.

Mr. Mayhem rubbed my back. "Breathe, Cat."

"I can't." I dry-heaved, acid lurching up my throat.

"Please remove that word from your vocabulary. Warriors do not crumble under pressure. We thrive. Perhaps you're simply not cut out for this."

In a flash, I straightened. "What're you sayin'?"

"I rushed you before you were ready. And for that, I apologize."

"No, you didn't." With the back of my forearm, I smeared the blood off my face. "I'm fine. All this blood just threw me for a sec." I shoved down the nausea boiling my stomach acids. "I can do this, I swear."

"Look at yourself." Rocking his head, he waved a hand up and down my body. "You're a disaster. Did you not hear me call out to you?"

"Yeah, but I didn't know what you meant."

"If you don't understand my instructions, ask me to clarify and we can avoid these situations in the future."

"Understood." Chin slightly dipped, I threw him the sad puppy dog eyes. Desperate times called for desperate measures.

"Follow me, please."

He trekked up an embankment then down the other side, snaked around trees, zigzagged to a small pond in the middle of nowhere. Lily pads filled the murky water, a green glaze floating on top. When he rotated toward me, he didn't speak.

Gulp. "I take it, you want me to go in there?"

One slow nod of confirmation.

"Are you coming in?"

"Why, pray tell, would I? I am not the one covered in blood."

"So, like"—I hesitated, insides screaming for me to disobey—"just jump in, clothes and all?"

Another nod.

"No problem," I lied. "I got this." I pinned back my shoulders and inched toward the edge. With my arms held chest high, I waded into the water. "Other than the green slime, the water's not that bad, actually." Before I dunked my head, I glanced back at Mr. Mayhem, now seated on a boulder with Poe on his shoulder. "I, uh, probably shoulda asked this sooner, but—besides frogs—do other things live in here?"

A slight grin.

"That a yes?"

Glimpsing the Sun, he rolled his hand. "We need to move this along, Cat. Your grandfather is expecting us, and we still have work to do."

"Okay, okay, I'm goin.'"

Pinching my nose, I dunked under the water. When I shot back up, Mr. Mayhem rose off the rock, staring beyond me into the woods.

"Don't. Move."

Frozen in place, my whole body stiffened, my gaze pinned on his expression. Stoic, he focused straight ahead. Even Poe didn't dare budge.

What the hell was behind me? And how close was it?

Chapter 4
*"We must protect the unprotected,
care for the uncared for, and speak for the voiceless.
We must give all animals a chance to live a life."*
—A. D. Williams

6:25 a.m.

Agorgeous two-hundred-pound male mountain lion—the cat of forty names—stood in silence, his complete focus on Shawnee. Thankfully, she was not aware of his approach. If she turned back, without question she would panic. Sudden movements triggered cougar attacks.

In slow motion, Mayhem raised his arms to shoulder level, extending his hands toward the North and South. After waiting a beat to gauge the animal's reaction, he reached for the sky.

"We're no threat to you." To scare off the cougar, his loud and firm tone resonated through the forest. "Run along now, handsome. It's time for you to leave." When the big cat refused to obey, he raised his voice even more. "Go. Now."

The mountain lion's intense stare narrowed on him. Tawny eyes shifted down to Shawnee, still trapped in the pond—easy prey—then rose to Mayhem, standing on higher ground.

"You heard me." Without breaking eye contact, he lowered—nice and slow—and collected two decent sized rocks. "Go. Now."

The mountain lion still didn't move.

Mayhem threw the first rock over the animal's head. Close enough to make an impact but far enough away so he didn't misread the message as an attack. The second rock he threw closer, intentionally missing the big cat by inches. The cougar bolted in the opposite direction.

"He's gone." He waved Shawnee to shore. "Come on out, Cat."

"Oh, thank God." She dragged her waterlogged sneakers from the pond. Drenched, her entire body quivered. "What was it?"

"We may have found the culprit whose been feeding on Mister Underwood."

"Great. A maneater. Perfect." She shook out her hair before following him up the embankment.

Once she caught up, Mayhem used this opportunity as a teaching tool. "There's an Apache legend about a fox and a mountain lion that you may find helpful."

Before continuing he paused for acknowledgment. "Fox could not find food for so long of a period he grew weak and thin. While on a journey in search of sustenance, he met Mountain Lion. Mountain Lion took pity on Fox and said, 'I will hunt for you, and you shall grow fat again.' Fox, of course, agreed, and the two friends traveled to a spring, frequented by various animals. Mountain Lion told Fox to keep watch while he rested. If Fox saw a dust cloud arising from the approach of other animals, he was to wake Mountain Lion."

With Shawnee's full attention, he headed down the path to the bloody tree. "Soon, Fox noticed a dust cloud caused by a drove of horses. He woke Mountain Lion, who said, 'Just observe how I catch horses.' As one animal went down to drink from the spring, Mountain Lion sprang, fastening his fangs in the horse's throat, clawing its legs and shoulders until the animal fell at the water's edge—dead. Mountain Lion dragged the horse up to the rock and laid it before Fox. 'Stay here, eat, drink, and grow fat,' he said. But Fox thought he had learned how to hunt horses by watching Mountain Lion kill one animal. And so, when Coyote came along, he volunteered to bring him a horse. Fox sprang on to the neck of the horse as Mountain Lion had done, but rather than bring the animal down, Fox became entangled in its mane and died."

Shawnee said, "And the moral of the story is?"

"What do you think it means?"

"Was Mountain Lion still there when Fox died?"

"Not important."

"Kinda is."

"Explain."

"Well, if Mountain Lion deserted him and he had to fend for himself, then Fox had no choice but to try."

How could she misinterpret such a simple message? "If you remember, Mountain Lion told Fox he would help him fatten up, so why would he forsake him?"

"He wouldn't."

"Correct."

"Then Mountain Lion is still there, and Fox tried to kill the horse on his own, anyway?"

In a breathy voice, he said, "Yes, Cat."

"Okay, now we're gettin' somewhere." Shawnee stopped at the bloody tree, whirled toward Mayhem. "Am I Fox?"

"You tell me." He slipped into black latex gloves, shook open the trash bag, and handed it to her. "Hold it steady, please."

With her face turned to one side, she held the bag far away from her body. "Fine. You made your point."

"And what point would that be, Cat?"

Shoveling what remained of Mr. Underwood into the bag, he had to give Shawnee credit. Never once did she complain, even when bodily fluids splashed on her bare knuckles. Nonetheless, she remained silent. Perhaps she was still mulling over the meaning behind the old Apache legend. Impressive. For once, she didn't jump on her first response.

"No rush. Let the story simmer in your mind. When you're ready, let me know." Mayhem hoisted the bag over one shoulder. "Let's drop this off at the Caddy before taking care of the unnamed poacher."

She snatched the spade off the ground. "Want me to rinse this somewhere? I can jog back to the pond real quick."

"No time." He redistributed the weight on his shoulder. "There's another gallon of water in the trunk. Be a dear and grab that empty jug before we leave, please. Plastic and the environment do not mix."

Head down, her gaze stayed with the remnants of Mr. Underwood. "What about all this blood? Are we just gonna leave it?"

"Bodily fluids contain nutrients. As a large mammal like a human decomposes in the forest, its breakdown transforms the soil in several ways."

Poe flew several yards ahead as Mayhem headed deeper into the forest with Shawnee, their legs moving in unison. "Briefly, the body's necrobiome—all the bacteria that lived inside the mortal shell—replicates like wildfire in the absence of an immune system. This necrobiome mixes with microbes in the soil. Plants benefit the most from the high levels of nitrogen. Visiting animals, like the cougar, may also contribute with urine and feces. All of that notwithstanding, the soil's microbial community will change, and with it, the animal community, as well."

"That's a lot more than I needed to know."

He chuckled. "Perhaps."

At the Caddy, he duct-taped the twisted end of the bag, then passed Shawnee a fresh gallon of water to rinse off the spade. Once he deposited Mr. Underwood's remains in the trunk, he dried the spade with a rag that he'd burn in the fire at the cabin, along with his latex gloves.

Gaze tracing her up and down, he stated the obvious. "You're still soaked."

Normally, she caught on quick. This, however, was not one of those moments.

"So?"

He whistled for Poe and only clicked the key fob once. By the time he swung open the driver's door, his loyal companion landed on the roof.

"Thank you for your promptness." He extended his forearm, and Poe stepped aboard.

"Click it again." Shawnee tugged on the passenger door handle. "It's still locked." Mayhem ducked into the driver's seat with Poe, and she knocked on the glass. "I said it's locked."

Mayhem lowered her window a few inches. "Head due West. We'll stay right alongside you."

A look of betrayal crossed her face, her arms swinging wide. "Seriously?"

"The poacher should not be far." Anticipating a colorful response, he pressed a button on his armrest, closing the passenger window. Still, her voice rang clear.

"This is total bullshit."

Mayhem pulled away, periodic glances at the rearview mirror.

Shawnee flung up her hands, her head rocking side to side. Clearly outraged, she chased the Caddy, arms pumping to increase momentum.

He derived no genuine pleasure from her unfortunate circumstance. However, the pig skin leather seats stained much too easily for her to accompany him in wet, slimy clothes. Besides, adversity built character. Easing up on the gas allowed her to catch up. As promised, he drove alongside her, even though she refused to acknowledge his presence.

When he lowered the driver's window, Poe cackled from the console. "Not nice," he admonished. "Cat, I understand you're upset, but—"

She flashed her palm and jogged ahead. But then, she stopped and whirled back. A look of confusion crossed her face.

Mayhem slid the shifter into Park. With one leg out the door, he rose. "Is there a problem?"

"Yeah. Where's the body?"

"Perhaps it's down farther?"

"Not with all this blood, it's not." She scanned the forest floor. "Think they came back for him?" Meaning, the other poachers who'd hunted crows on Mayhem's land last weekend—a direct threat to him and his loved ones.

"It's possible, I suppose." Mayhem reached for Poe, who climbed onto his forearm. With a fluff of the chest feathers, he said, "Search."

Poe leaped into the air. Every ten seconds or so he cawed, alerting Dad to his precise location at all times. A few minutes later, he landed on the hood. One shake of the head meant he did not find the dead poacher.

"All right, then." He glimpsed Father Sun rising higher in the cloudless sky. "Thank you, buddy."

"So..." Shawnee stalled. "Now what?"

"Now we head back to the cabin."

"What about..." She jabbed her head at the trunk. "Y'know."

"We'll have to dispose of Mister Underwood after breakfast. Your grandfather's waiting." He dragged a freshly laundered blanket from the backseat and held it out for Shawnee. "Would you mind terribly?"

Loud exhale, and she snatched it from his grasp. "Fine, but I'm not sitting on the floor again."

"Fair enough. Thank you." He and Poe ducked into the Caddy while Shawnee wrapped the blanket around her algae-covered sweatpants and T-shirt.

One could hope the poachers had returned for their man rather than the alternative.

Chapter 5

7:15 a.m.

Strolling into the cabin, I greeted *Shicheii* in Athabaskan. "*Yá'át'ééh.*"

He reached to frame my face in his palms, then froze. "You didn't brush your teeth this morning, child."

"Oh. Yeah, I forgot."

A grin arched his lips.

"You gonna laugh at me, too?"

"Of course not." He kissed my forehead. "Why don't you clean up before breakfast."

"Okay." As I strolled toward the bedroom in the back, I called over my shoulder, "Breakfast smells amazing, *Shicheii.*"

While I changed, they chatted in the kitchen, but I couldn't unscramble their muffled voices. Whatever they discussed couldn't be good because by the time I joined them at the table, my grandfather had a palpable somberness to him, his hands folded in front of him rather than passing around the eggs and pancakes.

"Honey," he said, soulful brown eyes sedating me, "Cheveyo and I think, if this is truly the destiny you wish to fulfill, that you would benefit from training."

Mr. Mayhem clarified, "Apache warrior training."

"Really?" Energy shot through me. "Awesome."

To silence me, *Shicheii* flashed a flat palm. "I've given Cheveyo my blessing to train you in the same way his mentor trained him as a young boy. Beginning with the basics. Should you accept his generous offer, you will be his apprentice until you've successfully completed four trials. To prepare for these trials, you must learn many, many things about survival, about nature, about becoming one with the environment, and whatever else Cheveyo feels is important for you to learn. He has full control of your training. I, of course, will be here for spiritual council, but you will be his apprentice, not mine. I need you to understand that."

Not sure what he meant, but I agreed anyway.

Mr. Mayhem added, "Should you choose to accept, all the whining and complaining ceases today. I will not go easy on you."

Warm blueberries encircled my head, my stomach growling and empty. "I know."

"Do you? I doubt you realize what you're agreeing to. Neither of us will think any less of you should you decide to back out. Now's your chance."

"Not backing out. This is what I want. I need this—right?—to become who I'm meant to be?"

Two heads nodded back at me.

"Then I'm in."

"I'm so proud of you, honey." *Shicheii* dished out a pile of scrambled eggs with cheese—one of my favorites—then passed me the platter of blueberry pancakes.

"The two advantages that will serve you well"—Mr. Mayhem scooped fresh fruit onto his plate—"is you're agile and in great physical shape. That said, training will push even those attributes to the breaking point."

Uh-oh. Didn't like the sound of that at all.

"Had you trained with Poe," he continued, "you'd be better equipped to handle the first lesson. Alas, our focus was needed elsewhere."

"Where is Poe? He loves *Shicheii's* cooking."

In between bites Mr. Mayhem raised a closed fist in front of his mouth. "He loves his mother more."

Fork teeth slid across the china as we pigged out.

After popping a melon cube into my mouth, I cheeked it. "What about the wolfdogs?"

Shicheii's gaze bounced between me and Mr. Mayhem. "Wolfdogs? I thought you ran into a mountain lion."

"We did." Cheesy eggs slid down my throat. "Remember when I asked if I could talk to you about somethin' before sunrise?"

"I do."

I filled him in about wolfdogs, and how New Hampshire was a dumping ground for them. But instead of responding to me, he chatted with Mr. Mayhem as though I'd left the room.

"Will this new venture interfere with her training, Cheveyo?"

"Not at all." He forked into the stack of blueberry pancakes, maple syrup cascading off the sides. "The two will go hand in hand quite nicely."

At first, *Shicheii* seemed reluctant. "The people who enslave wolfdogs must be dangerous."

"Jacy Lee, we talked about this, did we not?" The fork froze in his hand. "For her training to work I need you to loosen the reins a bit. If that is not something you can do, then there's no point in moving forward."

"I understand that, Cheveyo, but she is still my granddaughter. It's my job to worry about her."

"Understood. However, you vowed not to second guess me, regardless of potential dangers. Did you not? I need you to trust that I have her best interests at heart."

"You're right." He patted the side of Mr. Mayhem's arm. "I'll help any way I can."

As if they'd settled the matter, my new mentor said, "Thank you." Then focused on me, the fork still hovering above his plate while I devoured a buttery croissant. "Your training begins today. Before we get started, do you have questions for me?"

I had many but chose not to voice them. Probably best. "No." I sucked melted butter off each finger. "Oh, by the way, I understand the legend. For now, I may be Fox, but I won't stop till I'm Mountain Lion."

With a slight nod of acknowledgment, a smile emerged. "In the far corner of my bedroom you will find a brown-leather satchel. Inside, there is more appropriate attire. I'd planned to leave it with you while training with Poe before those plans went array."

I set down my fork. "Want me to change now?"

"Finish your fruit first. You'll need the added vitamins they provide."

I wolfed the rest of my breakfast, smiled through a packed mouthful, and raced up the stairs. The last outfit he bought me for this type of thing kicked ass. Seemed wrong to change in Mr. Mayhem's bedroom, so I dragged the satchel into *Shicheii's* room and laid it on his bed. Stripping down to my thong and bra, excitement spiraled up my spine.

After changing, I strode down the stairs in knee-high moccasins, buckskin pants and matching halter, with a choker of bone and black stones and an armband of silver and turquoise.

"You look so beautiful, Mourning Dove." *Shicheii* hugged me. "One final touch." He clasped long, hollow, wooden beads around my neck, securing the bottom band in back, each bead carved with Spirit Animals.

"Did you make this, *Shicheii?*"

"No, honey. Your mom did. She spent hours carving those beads."

Tears tumbled over the rim of my eyes. "I don't know what to say." My fingers brushed across the carvings. "I'll make you proud, *Shicheii.*"

"Aww." With my face framed in warm palms, he kissed my forehead. "You already do, child."

Once he released me, Mr. Mayhem approached. "The stones of the choker are called Apache Tears. Each stone has a lump with an uneven coating of perlite from being pried or dug up. Formed by rhythmic crystallization that produces a separation of light and dark materials into spherical shapes, they are a form of volcanic glass called obsidian. If you hold the Tears to the light, you'll note their translucency."

"Cheveyo"—*Shicheii* rested his hand on Mr. Mayhem's back—"why don't you share the story behind it, so she realizes what a special gift this is."

"Good idea." Vision locked on the stones, his fingertips walked across my choker, a frown tugging down the corners of his lips. "After the Pinal Apache made several raids on a settlement in Arizona, the Cavalry and volunteers trailed the tracks of the stolen cattle. At dawn, the white men moved in. The Apache were so confident in the safety of their location, the Cavalry caught them by surprise. Grossly outnumbered, nearly fifty of the seventy-five Pinal Apache lost their lives in the first volley of shots."

The way my Caucasian ancestors treated Native Americans wrecked me, the heart sinking in my chest. How do you even reconcile something like that? *Shicheii* said we shouldn't judge the many by the actions of some, but I still grappled with how and why it happened in the first place.

"Rather than die by the hands of white men, the rest of the tribe retreated to the cliff's edge then leaped off," Mr. Mayhem continued, shredding my soul even more. "Within a short distance from the base of the cliff where the sands were white, Apache women gathered, and for a moon they wept for their loved ones. They mourned, keening over their loss, for not only had their seventy-five brave warriors died, but with them died the great fighting spirit of the Pinal Apache. For years afterward, those who ventured up the treacherous face of Big Picacho in Arizona found Apache skeletons or viewed the distant sun-bleached bones wedged in the crevices of the cliffside."

This story tore the heart from my chest and stomped on it, my chest heaving against the swell of tears.

"Their sadness was so great, and their burden of sorrow so sincere, the Great Father imbedded the Apache women's tears into black volcanic stones. When held to the light, the black obsidian reveals the translucent tear of the Apache. The stones are said to bring good luck. Whoever owns an Apache Tear will never have to cry again, for the Apache women have shed their tears in place of yours."

Mr. Mayhem thumbed away my sadness. "They also balance one's emotional nature and protect the wearer from being taken advantage of. As an amulet, an Apache Tear stimulates success in business endeavors. The stones produce clear vision and increase psychic powers. Black obsidian is also a powerful meditation stone. The purpose is to bring light to that which hides from the conscious mind. They also dissolve and purify suppressed negativity. One caution, however. Apache Tears may create somewhat radical behavior as new positive attitudes replace old, negative, egocentric patterns."

A warmth filled me deep inside. "This is a big deal, huh?"

"Yes, very. While training, remember what you're fighting for—remember *who* you're fighting for—and why." He tapped my armband. "This is platinum and turquoise, worn for protection."

"I'm honored that you're willing to mentor me. Thank you. I won't let you down."

Stroking my head, his gray eyes softened. "I know, you won't. Ready to get started?"

"I'm ready."

"Follow me, please."

He strode out to the porch then down the stairs, and I followed close behind. In the middle of the yard, he and I stood close, the toes of moccasins separated by less than two feet of dirt.

"I am what I am," he said, and I repeated the line. "In having faith in the beauty within me, I develop trust. In softness, I have strength. In silence, I walk the higher realms. In peace, I understand myself and the world. In conflict, I stay calm, cool, collected. In detachment, I am free."

As I echoed his words, he leaned closer, piercing gray eyes staring into my soul.

"In respecting all living things," he continued the warrior prayer, "I respect myself. In dedication, I honor the courage within me. In eternity, I have compassion for the nature of all things. In love, I unconditionally accept the evolution of others. In freedom, I have power. In my individuality, I express the God-Force within me. In service, I give of what I have become. I am what I am—eternal, immortal, universal, and infinite."

Mr. Mayhem tore off his shirt and unbraided his hair, and I wasn't sure why, but the look of concern on my grandfather's face worried me.

Shicheii passed him a bottled water. "Remember how much I love you, Mourning Dove."

Before I had a chance to respond, Mr. Mayhem told me take one chug of water and hold it in my mouth. "Do not swallow that water. At the end of this exercise, I will expect you to spit it out in front me, and it better be there."

To show him I understood, I nodded.

"I'll run with you this time to show you the trail you'll take every morning. Pay attention. I will not show you twice."

When I nodded a second time, he shot across the yard like a bullet left an automatic pistol, and I ran at full speed to catch him. Man, was he fast. The ends of his dark hair, silver strands sprinkled within, and flashes of skin were often the only way I could tell where to turn or when to stay straight. An overwhelming urge to swallow the water hit way earlier than I'd expected, my sinuses draining of mucus as my body overheated. From not having the ability to breathe through my mouth, my pace slowed. Oxygen reduced from only nose-breathing, especially with my mucus on overdrive, suffocating me from the inside out, moccasins clamoring through leaf litter.

You wouldn't think a mouthful of water would do damage, but it made even simple tasks, like breathing, much more difficult. Didn't matter. I had to push through it, even though every muscle in my body begged for me to stop.

Lightning-fast, Mr. Mayhem scaled a steep hill. Then stopped. Sight glued to him, I scrambled upward, my hands groping for something to grab hold of, my moccasins slipping down the rocky terrain. I stopped. Inhaled through my snotty nose. On the exhale I regained enough control to make it to the top.

"Did you swallow the water?"

I shook my head no.

"Do you want to?"

Yes was definitely the wrong answer, so I wagged another no.

"Do you want to quit?"

I rocked my head in an emphatic no.

"You can, you know. I won't think any less of you."

After another nonverbal no, I swept my fingers across the Apache Tears, then down to my mother's beads strapped to my chest.

"All right, then. Let's proceed." He raced down the other side of the cliff-like hill a lot faster than I expected, and I chased after him, my gut instinct screaming for me to rest.

While he zigzagged around trees—quick flashes of skin and hair ahead of me—I almost lost track of him till Spirit Crow soared in to show me the way, her angelic wings flapping almost in slow motion as I hauled ass. At the V in the trail, they both vanished. The forest embraced them in its arms, shielding them from sight. I slowed, my head swiveling left and right, but I had to keep going or I'd fail the first exercise.

Accelerating to a full-on sprint, I lowered my eyelids for a split second, the blood of my ancestors pumping through my veins, steering me to the right. Halfway down the rocky trail, I caught a flash of skin and hair, and I worked harder, ran faster, my heart drumming, rattling my ribcage.

Around the next bend, Mr. Mayhem stood with Spirit Crow on his shoulder, his bare chest sheened with sweat, but not breathing heavily at all, like he was born to run.

Once I caught up, I folded in half, hands cupped on bent knees.

"Did you swallow the water?"

I wagged my head no.

"Do you want to?"

Dear God, yes. I'd do anything to swallow this water. But rather than admit it, I rocked another no.

"Do you want to stop?"

I patted the choker, and he grinned. With the gentleness of raising a feather to the heavens, he lifted Spirit Crow, and she leaped into the air, angelic white wings flapping in harmony with the environment, her breathtaking beauty on display. This time, I was ready when he took off. I still fell several strides behind, the water making it nearly impossible to breathe, snot running over my upper lip. But at least I kept track of him.

After he looped around the entire acreage, he cut through the woods near the main drag. With the cabin in range, I gave it everything I had left and careened through the tunnel of trees, fringing the sides of the dirt driveway.

By the time I reached the middle of the yard, I stopped in front of him and spat out the water, inhaling a deep breath through my mouth.

Mr. Mayhem rocked his head in disappointment. "You just failed."

"Whaddaya mean? I didn't swallow one sip." I thrust a hand at the puddle in the dirt. "Look. It's all there."

"Did I instruct you to release the water?"

Fuck. "No."

"Then you failed the exercise."

Inside, I called him every name in my arsenal, but I couldn't show it, or he might stop mentoring me. And that, I could never allow. Not yet. Not until I discovered how much I could endure.

"You're right," I said, steadfast. "I failed you. I failed myself. Worst of all, I failed all those who came before me."

Eyes thinning, Mr. Mayhem grunted his approval. "Moving on." He strode back into the forest, and I followed close behind. When he stopped short, I almost crashed into him but caught myself at the last second.

With a deadpan expression, he rotated toward me. "Take three steps forward. And look."

And so, I did. "Look at what?"

"Everything. Then you'll never have to ask."

I surveyed the woods. Pine scented the warm summer air. Prey animals scurried through crunchy leaves, our presence scattering them in all directions.

"Please list five distinct things within your environment. Do not limit your scope to sight. Utilize all your senses—what you hear, what you smell, what you feel on your skin, what you taste on your tongue. Understood?"

"Yes."

"Begin."

I closed my eyes. "Wood thrush to my left." I reclined my head. "Poe's hovering above me, a coolness on my back from the force of his wings. Wildflowers are blooming in front of me, their blossoms releasing hints of a floral sweetness."

"Very good. Take three more steps forward."

Again, I complied.

"List five additional things within the environment. You may not repeat anything from your previous list. Begin."

Each time I moved forward, I bet this exercise got more difficult, but after failing the previous challenge, I had to shelve my misgivings and ace this assignment. "Thick bark of an ash tree to my right. Sticky pine needles beneath my feet." I closed my eyes. "The faint hooting of a sleepy owl. Moisture in the air, humidity. Chipmunk rustling through the leaves to my right."

"Nice. Three more steps forward, please."

The minute I stopped I parted my lips to list five more things, then shut my mouth. He didn't tell me to start yet. What if he changed the exercise?

"Why did you not speak, Cat?"

"I'm waiting for instructions."

"Very good." Mr. Mayhem grinned. "List five more things within your environment. You may not repeat anything from your previous list. Begin."

"A tuft of fur caught on a branch straight ahead."

"Be specific."

"The fur looks course. It's dark brown or black." My gaze shot to him. "Bear fur."

"Correct. Continue."

"A feather from Spirit Crow entangled in the branches of the bush to my left." I glanced over my shoulder, but he showed no reaction. "Two blue jays munching on..." I squinted, my sight narrowing on the birds. "Hm, not sure." I paused, rephrased. "Two blue jays eating to my right. Hawk whistle in the distance. Crows all cawing at once, angry voices."

"Excellent. Take three more steps forward and list five more things within your environment. You may not repeat anything from your previous list. Whenever you're ready, you may begin."

Well, I was right. Each time I moved forward I had to work harder to find new items to list, but this exercise forced me to experience the environment in ways I never expected. Once I fully committed to the assignment, I discovered all the things I missed on an average day. Like most people, I'd glossed over and glided through so much of my life and skipped the most important parts, the breathtaking beauty that surrounded me. *Shicheii* had taught me a lot, but Mr. Mayhem forced me to probe even deeper.

And I learned this undeniable truth. My connection to the Natural World—the same connection living in all of us—was the secret superpower of my People, of all Native Americans. If folks stopped for just a moment—put away all the electronic devices and luxuries of the modern world—and experienced nature in all its wondrous ways, they'd marvel at what they discovered.

At the end of an hour, Mr. Mayhem slung his arm over my shoulders and led me past the Sacred Fire, smoke spiraling into the air. "Brava, Cat. You excelled at that exercise."

Pride exuded out every pore. "Thanks."

Once we reached the cabin, *Shicheii* met us on the porch with a serving tray and set three mugs of wild tea on the table, along with the honey pot. "How did she do, Cheveyo?"

"Failed the first exercise, passed the second."

Clawing a hand through my wind-swept hair, I dropped into my chair, praying my poor performance with the endurance test didn't upset *Shicheii*. The last thing I ever wanted to do was disappoint him. I parted my lips to apologize, but he wasn't done speaking.

"What's your assessment thus far?"

"I'll know better tonight." Mr. Mayhem swirled the dipper through the honey. "I want to see how she reacts to being stalked as prey."

Startled, my eyes flashed wide. "Say what, now?"

"Since you did so well with the awareness test, tonight you'll become prey."

A gulp lodged in my throat. "Who's the predator?"

"Me." An evil little grin arched his lips. "And Poe. And various other partners."

"Can Spirit Crow be on my team?"

"You have no team," he said, as if I should've known. "You're the prey."

Like for real? Uh-oh. What happened if he caught me?

Chapter 6
"There is no greater agony than bearing an untold story inside you.
A bird does not sing because it has the answer.
It sings because it has a song."
—Geronimo, Apache Warrior

Noon

After a brief respite with Jacy Lee, Shawnee bustled inside to scrub her flaming red teeth while Mayhem instructed Poe on how to move forward. "Don't get too carried away, little mister. Feel free to torment her. However, ideally she should survive the exercise." He stroked the crown of Spirit Crow. "Darling, I realize you want to protect Cat, but you are also cognizant of the stakes. Are you not?"

Her head bowed.

"She won't always have you around to fall back on, and it's imperative for her to learn how to fend for herself in the wild. Thus, I am asking you to pick a side for this exercise. Whatever side you choose, you cannot influence the others."

"Cheveyo's right, child. As much as we may want to help, we cannot micromanage from the sidelines."

Spirit Crow hopped closer and nuzzled her cheek against Mayhem's bare chest, feathers tickling his skin.

"Thank you, my love."

"You will first train her on how to avoid capture. Correct?"

"Of course." Mayhem rose from the chair. "Now, if you'll excuse me, I need to freshen up before my teeth also change color."

Jacy Lee laughed. "She learned that lesson the hard way."

"That she did, my friend." Chuckling, he patted his elder's shoulder. "She won't be making the same mistake twice."

After brushing his teeth and hair, he strode down the stairs and into the kitchen, where Jacy Lee stood in front the kitchen chair, painting Shawnee's face, blessing her with the power it held. With the tip of his finger, he drew crow feet under each eye—a V from the corners of her eyes with a solid line at the base—for protection. Black was a living color worn for strength.

"Hope you don't mind, Cheveyo."

"Not at all. She'll need the blessings from the face paint."

Jacy Lee lifted her bangs and covered her eyelids up to each eyebrow in dark green, with a smudge under her bottom lashes. "To help with night vision later," he told her, then dotted each earlobe in the same color. "For endurance, harmony, and healing power." After drawing three red lines from the middle of her bottom lip down and under the chin, Jacy Lee dotted them in white. "Red for war, strength, blood, energy, power, and success in defeating the enemy. White for peace." He glanced over his shoulder, but Mayhem did not react.

If Jacy Lee felt safer adding spiritual symbols to his granddaughter's face, then so be it.

A thick band of blue he finger-swiped from her temples to her hairline. "For wisdom, confidence." Jacy Lee zigzagged a black thunderbolt across her forehead. "For power and speed." He added jagged streaks of blue and black down each arm. "To represent our family."

Shawnee squinted at her grandfather. "Weren't they white last time?"

"Yes, to help with mourning your parents. Blue and black are our family's traditional colors." Jacy Lee drew Sprit Crow on the back of one hand—Shawnee's Spirit Animal—a golden eagle on the other for courage, wisdom, and strength from the mighty hunter's connection to the Creator.

When he stepped back, Mayhem dipped his finger in yellow and added a dot to the end of the left collarbone at the base of her neck. "You'll have to earn the second dot."

She gazed up at him, her eyes filled with hope. "Last time I had two, remember?"

"I do. However, we needed you in the right frame of mind. From here on out, you'll earn your symbols like the rest of us. No more freebies, family symbols notwithstanding."

"Understood." She hesitated. "Hey, um, aren't you gonna wear face paint?"

"Would your enemy give you their playbook in advance?"

"Oh. No, they wouldn't."

He rather enjoyed the precise responses she gave lately. "Correct." Resting a hand on Jacy Lee's shoulder, he said, "Would you like to join us for the training exercise?"

"Very much. I'll clean up and meet you out there."

"Perfect. Cat, follow me, please." Mayhem held open the screen door. Shawnee strode out to the porch then down the stairs, where she stopped, waiting for him. Rather than join her, he waved her back up the stairs.

"Sorry." Her shoulders sprang to her ears. "Thought we were starting in the yard."

"Because that's what I wanted you to think. Let me explain something. When we become predictable, we create an unintentional pattern that the enemy can foresee. Predictability often ends in death."

A continual nod of the head. "Got it."

Mayhem sat cross-legged on the deck boards and patted the spot next to him. Lowering, Shawnee mimicked his movements. "Look for your reflection."

"Where?"

"Everywhere."

After a few moments, she scratched the back of her head. "But there aren't any shiny surfaces."

"No?" Focused straight ahead, he cupped the sides of his eyes. "Move just your upper body to one side." After Shawnee did as instructed, he said, "You leaned to the right."

"How'd you—?"

"I watched your reflection." He pointed at a flawless orb weaver spider's web in the corner of the railing. "Her silk strands reflect sunlight, moonlight, and shadows."

"Wow." Mouth agape, she glanced over each shoulder before shielding the sides of her eyes. "Let me try."

Mayhem leaned to the left.

"Did you move?"

If he responded, his voice might give him away.

"Can you do it one more time?"

Mayhem straightened, then leaned left.

"Left."

"Correct. Let's try it again." This time, he leaned backward.

"Hm. I had you, then lost you."

Sitting upright, he waited for eye contact, but she didn't drop her hands. "What does that movement tell you?"

"I'm not sure."

"Fair enough. This time lower your hands. Since I'm seated beside you, you should detect my movement in your peripheral, but I want you to concentrate on watching how my shadow reacts in the web."

Once her hands topped her folded knees, he reclined, his bare spine flattened against rough wooden decking. He hesitated to give her time. Then inched upright.

"Your shadow disappeared, then progressively got bigger and bigger. Lemme think. That means, you leaned all the way back, then back up."

"Very good."

"Not for nothin' but that takes some serious core strength while sitting with your legs crossed."

A flush skipped across his cheeks, and he chuckled. "Thank you."

Jacy Lee settled on the other side of his granddaughter. "What did I miss?"

"We're focusing on finding reflective surfaces, *Shicheii*. I just watched his shadow move in the spiderweb."

"Oh, isn't she lovely." He leaned toward the spider. "Hello, beautiful. Orb weavers are especially brilliant with their—"

Mayhem warned, "Jacy Lee."

"Story for another time, child." He patted his granddaughter's knee. "Concentrate on your lesson."

Mayhem rose. Asked them to face each other, cross-legged, with their knees touching. Once they repositioned, he squatted next to Shawnee. "Do you see your reflection?"

"Where?"

"Look at his eyes. You're right there in his corneas."

She leaned closer. "Oh. My. God. I am."

Mayhem gently turned Jacy Lee's chin toward the Sun. "Now where's your reflection?"

While staring at her grandfather, she waved her head back and forth to detect movement. "On his cheek."

"Excellent. Warriors must be aware of everything. We must be awake. Every detail is interesting, every detail important. You never know when one of those details could save your life. There's an old Comanche teaching that's apt. 'Don't get caught looking for leaves in the trees in Autumn. Those leaves are on the ground.'" Since the meaning was obvious, he didn't bother to ask if she understood. Instead, he thrust a pointed finger at the yard. "Do you see where you spat out the water earlier?"

"Yeah."

"Go there, please."

When she bustled into the yard, he snatched the water bottle off the table and followed. Behind her back, he squirted a line. "Where's your reflection now?"

Shawnee stared straight down at the dried puddle of dirt in front of her moccasins.

"Where's your reflection, Cautious Cat?"

Squinting, she leaned forward even more. "Umm..."

"Why are you only looking in one spot?"

"Because you told me to."

"Did I? Or were you subtly mislead?"

"You asked me to find my reflection."

"Correct. Did I tell you where to look?"

"No." Straightening, her widened gaze scanned a young sapling that stood ten feet away, rocking her head from side to side to detect movement. "There I am." She jutted a stiff finger at the tree. "I'm on that leaf. Second branch up from the bottom, third leaf in from the end."

"She's right." Smiling, Jacy Lee crinkled his nose. "She's a natural, Cheveyo."

"I'm not saying that wasn't impressive—good job, Cat—but she also missed the most obvious place to find her reflection."

"Did I?" Shawnee twirled from side to side. "Where?"

"I understand that, Cheveyo. Looking deeper and farther, however, is an advanced skill that will serve her well in the future."

"Perhaps, but not if she misses the obvious."

"Found it." She pointed at the Caddy parked twenty feet away. "I'm on the front quarter panel."

Amazed, Mayhem and Jacy Lee both turned.

"Right again. Told you she's a natural."

Mayhem threw up his hands.

"Thanks, *Shicheii.*"

"Cautious Cat," he said, firm and harsh, "when you hear hoofbeats, think horses, not zebras."

"Unless you're in Africa, right? Because then it really could be zebras."

Staring into her eyes, Mayhem clamped his hands on her shoulders. "Focus. Where is your reflection?"

"In your corneas."

He slammed his eyes closed. Waited a beat, petting the beast within, then spun Shawnee toward the driveway. "Without turning left or right, where is your reflection?"

When her gaze crawled up the trees, Mayhem swiped a whiplike branch off the ground and snapped her ankle.

"Ow." Finally, she skimmed the earth, her head cocking at the wet streak by her moccasins. "There I am. In the puddle."

"Yes!" He blew a strand of hair off his face. "All right. Clearly, you've mastered depth perception. However, if you overlook the details that are right in front of you, all the depth perception in the world won't save your life. What if I severed your Achilles tendon? How would you escape?"

"Are you mad at me?"

"No. I am not angry." To slow the flood of frustration threatening his resolve, he paced in circles. "If you let a black bear or cougar sneak up on you tonight, you could die."

"Cheveyo's right, honey." He played with strands of her hair. "You need to be more aware of your surroundings."

"Perhaps we should do a dry run. Any objections, Jacy Lee?"

"None. I think it's a great idea."

"For this exercise," he told Shawnee, "you and your grandfather will work together. Let him guide you on how to protect yourself as prey. Otherwise, you may die. Okie doke." He clapped his hands together. "Remember the rules. You cannot trust anyone, except Jacy Lee."

"Got it," she said, but he doubted she grasped the full meaning.

"Super. Let's meet back here in two hours. Unless I find you first, of course." He winked. "Questions?"

Shawnee raised her hand.

"Speak freely."

"I left my watch in *Shicheii's* room. Can I run back and get it real quick?"

"Forget the luxuries of a modern world, Cat. Society has forced us to use timepieces. However, humans were never meant to keep exact times. We lived within the confines of seasons, light and dark, and our own body's rhythms, which are not the same from day to day or year to year. We rolled with the ebb and flow of nature, daylight and moonlight, and with the flow of seasons." In case his message wasn't clear, he pointed at the sky. "For this training exercise, Father Sun is all you'll need." He cocked his head at Jacy Lee. "Have we not taught her Indian time?"

"I thought we had, Cheveyo."

"Were our teachings unclear?"

"Not to my knowledge, no. Would you like me to refresh her memory?"

"If you wouldn't mind, old friend."

"I'd be happy to." By the time Jacy Lee refocused on his granddaughter, her mouth had fallen open. "Raise your arm and bend your wrist." He demonstrated by raising a flat hand toward his face, and she mimicked his movements. "Perfect. Now, get your thumb out of the way and stiffen your fingers so the top edge of your index finger aligns with the bottom of the Sun." When Shawnee followed his instructions, he praised her. "Very good, child. Now, while keeping your thumbs out of the way, bring your left hand under your right."

Shawnee positioned her hands. "Like this?"

"Perfect. See all that space below your bottom hand?"

"Y'mean, the space above the horizon?"

"Yes, exactly. While keeping your left hand steady, stack your right hand beneath it. If you still have space, continue to stack lower and lower. We'll be counting the number of hands from the Sun to the horizon."

"What about the fingers that fall below the horizon?" Shawnee held the pose. "Do I count them, too?"

"No. Count only the digits above the horizon."

"Okay, then"—she stacked and re-stacked her hands—"seven hands and two fingers."

"Perfect. Then there are seven hours—seven hands—and thirty minutes left of daylight. Each finger equals fifteen minutes. And that, my sweet child, is Indian time."

"Wow. So cool."

Before Jacy Lee began a new lesson on an unrelated topic, Mayhem cleared his throat. "Now that we've settled the time issue, I shall return to the cabin and wait awhile to give you a chance to acclimate. Then I'm coming for you, Cat. Do *not* let me catch you."

Visibly, she gulped.

"Come, child." With his fingers woven with hers, Jacy Lee hurried her into the forest.

Mayhem waited a few moments before whistling for his hunting partner. When Poe shot out of a nearby conifer, magnificent ebony wings fluttered down to his forearm perch.

"Thank you for your promptness." Quick fluff of the chest feathers for morale. "Ready for a little fun?"

Ca-caw!

Chapter 7

1:03 p.m.

Once *Shicheii* and I trekked deep enough into the wilderness, he let go of my hand, and I chased after him as he zigzagged around trees and leaped narrow streams. Not nearly as fast as Mr. Mayhem, but still impressive for a man of his age.

Surrounded by thick forest, he stopped and whirled back to me. "Use your observation skills to spot reflections. Don't search for yourself, though you should stay aware of places Cheveyo can use as a mirror. Your primary goal is to spot predators. I don't want to frighten you, honey, but I'd be remiss if I didn't warn you that Apache warriors are freakishly impressive hunters. They train as young boys and girls, far younger than you, and become masters of their environment, of speed and stealth, of awareness and observation, along with a host of other skills in their arsenal. How do you think Cheveyo received his epithet?"

My heart stopped mid-beat. "Y'mean—?"

"Yes. Cheveyo enjoys changing the story's origin from time to time, but the truth is, he earned the epithet because of his skills in battle. Where and when that battle took place isn't important. My point is, very few could go head-to-head with the Mister Mayhem persona. And that's who will hunt you tonight."

Fuck. I'd been on the wrong side of Mr. Mayhem, and lemme tell ya, it wasn't pretty. He almost killed me more than once. "*Shicheii,* what's he planning for after he captures me?"

"That I don't know, honey." Careful not to smudge my blessed symbols, he framed my face in his palms. "The best course of action is to not allow him to find you. Hiding is not losing if it saves your life. Focus, Mourning Dove. You can do this." He held a finger to his lips—*no more talking*—then scanned the thick wooded terrain.

Using leaves as side mirrors, he directed me off-trail, our moccasins silent against the earth. With my mind on high alert, acutely aware of my surroundings, I pointed at the black pinion feathers of a crow in the distance.

Cheeks dimpling, *Shicheii* nodded, then drew back into the shadows, undid his long braids, and used his hair to mask his face. A blue jay soared by us, chattering about something. Did Mr. Mayhem have him on the payroll, too? He said I couldn't trust anyone, including animals. I hooked an arm at *Shicheii,* and he followed me to the South end of the property, where I spotted a dugout—perfect place to hide. But when I pointed it out to *Shicheii,* he rocked his head in an emphatic no.

In my mind, his voice resonated.

Black bear den.

Poe let out a screech that raised all my tiny neck hairs at once. *Shicheii* motioned for me to close my eyes. With a hand dead center on my chest, his touch steadied my breathing. When I opened my eyes, I raised my chin and brushed my fingertips across the Apache Tears then down the Spirit Animals Mom hand-carved into the wooden beads. The turquoise armband tightened when I flexed to scale a sturdy maple tree for a better vantage point. Below me, *Shicheii* monitored ground level.

Peering through multiple branches, thick with leaves, the ends of Mr. Mayhem's hair dangled high in a canopy.

Gotcha.

I climbed down to the lowest branch, jumped to the ground, my knees bending, absorbing the dismount. A mourning dove flitted down to the soil, and I gasped. But when I turned my head to tell *Shicheii,* a bullet of brown swooped in, nailing the mourning dove with such immense power an explosion of feathers flew in all directions.

Hawk. Huh. Maybe I could use him to my advantage. Crows and hawks were mortal enemies. If he's hunting here, Poe and the others must defend their turf. Ipso facto, if they're preoccupied, they couldn't track me and *Shicheii*.

Reading my mind or deciphering my body language—hard to tell which—my grandfather switched to silent communication.

Now you're thinking like a warrior. Use the environment to guide you, Mourning Dove.

We hugged the shadows, waiting for the crows to pursue the hawk. A chorus of angry caws stirred a cloudless sky while my grandfather gathered sticks and dead limbs, stacking them against a large bolder. He mouthed, "Decoy."

Smart. I see how this works.

If a predator couldn't detect its prey, the prey won. The best defense was camouflage. Animals who knew how to blend into their environment lasted the longest. If the predator didn't notice its prey, the prey avoided having to outrun or fight the predator. Background matching worked best. *Shicheii* once told me about the Eastern Screech Owl who hid during the day by matching the color and pattern of tree bark. Disruptive coloration broke up the shape of its body and made it harder to spot because it didn't fit the shape for which the predator was searching.

I could do the same. Because I sure as hell couldn't go head-to-head with Mr. Mayhem.

And so, with the crows in hot pursuit of the intruder—*thank you, Mr. Hawk*—I bundled dead leaves and pine needles off the forest floor as quietly as I could, freezing at the points when my activity got too loud. When *Shicheii* noticed what I was doing, he jumped in to help, piling the leaf litter in the shadows, smoothing out a flat surface thick enough for me to hide beneath.

Once all the forest debris was in place, he showed me how to slither under the blanket of leaves. Sticks and discarded branches covered me, including my face, my eyes peering through thin slivers. In my head, *Shicheii's* voice rang clear.

When he comes for you, use your face paint as camouflage by lowering your eyelids.

With that bit of expert advice, he vanished into the surrounding area.

Confined under the forest floor, my heart worked overtime, blood sluicing through my veins, my gaze shifting left, right, and up at the trees, searching for a glimpse of Mr. Mayhem. But I couldn't find him anywhere. Nor could I spot *Shicheii.* Even without the benefit of face paint, they both blended into the fabric of the forest.

If I didn't steady my breathing, Mr. Mayhem would sniff me out. So, I closed my eyes and recited the warrior's prayer while envisioning how Mr. Mayhem appeared speaking the same words, words he lived by each and every day.

I am what I am. In having faith in the beauty within me, I develop trust. In softness, I have strength. In silence, I walk the higher realms. In peace, I understand myself and the world. In conflict, I stay calm, cool, collected... I am what I am—eternal, immortal, universal, and infinite.

About fifteen feet to my right, someone—or something—stepped on a stick.

Crunch.

I cracked open one eye. Oh. My. God. My breath stalled.

A massive mountain lion paw stepped into view, followed by a second.

Dear God, don't let him find me.

The cougar stalked closer.

Lowering my eyelids, I didn't dare breathe, didn't dare move. Inside my head *Shicheii's* voice resonated.

Great Spirit of us all, you have made her body strong. Please fill her with your wisdom, so she'll know right from wrong. Let her see herself as others also see her, so she'll know if her character agrees with how you say it should be. Let her be slow to anger, yet so quickly to forgive. Grant her patience, O Great Spirit, so a happier life she can live. Teach her fairness so honor she can bring to you; with fairness you will judge her life when her days are finally through. When war must be waged, give her the strength and courage of the bear. The cunning and endurance of the Wolf, so she can push her enemies back to their lair.

When I opened my eyes, the tail of the mountain lion swished into the thick wooden terrain in the distance. And I exhaled.

But then, moccasins struck the earth in front of me. When I glanced up, Mr. Mayhem was squatting in front of me, his gaze deadlocked on me.

"I wonder"—he tapped a stiff finger to his lips—"what you would have done if he found you."

Out of nowhere, *Shicheii* appeared. "I would have put him to sleep for a while."

"Hello, Jacy Lee." He grinned. "What if he returns tonight? Your granddaughter won't have you around to protect her."

"Then we better teach her how to protect herself." *Shicheii* extended a hand to me, and I latched on, crawling to my feet, leaves and debris falling off my back. "Come, child. We're done here."

"Okay, but *Shicheii*, I failed again."

"You did not fail." He plucked sticks out of my hair. "You outsmarted a mountain lion. Isn't that right, Cheveyo?"

"Indeed, she did. However, the exercise was to outsmart me, not the cougar." Mr. Mayhem focused on me. "How do you think you did?"

My chin dropped to my chest. "I failed."

"Correct. Though using the hawk to lure Poe and the others away was a brilliant move. That is the type of thinking I'd hoped you would develop. That is precisely how to use the environment to your advantage. And that was a technique you thought of on your own, without the help of your grandfather. He guided every other move you made. But the hawk, dearest Cat, came from you. It came from within. Stand tall and proud. Instinct is something I cannot teach. You either have it or you don't. And you, Mourning Dove, have it in spades."

Emotions heaved my chest. "I do?"

"You do."

Pride radiated off my grandfather, his soulful brown eyes pooled with tears, visibly touched by our exchange. "Thank you, Cheveyo. As a mentor and a man, your kindness knows no bounds."

"Hey, um." Inconsistencies flitted through my mind. "How'd you know about the hawk? I saw your hair way off in the distance."

"Because that's what I wanted you to see. In reality, I was right there"—he pointed to the tree above my hiding spot—"watching every move you made."

"Seriously? But the hair—"

Big smile. "Mull it over on the walk back. When we reach the cabin, if you can tell me how I misled you, I'll give you partial credit for the exercise."

Shicheii parted his lips to speak.

"Jacy Lee," Mr. Mayhem warned, "do not help her."

"I was merely going to point her in the right direction."

"No. She must puzzle it out on her own, or she fails." His voice showed a hint of aggravation. "You know this."

"I do, Cheveyo. My apologies."

Right then, Spirit Crow fluttered down to my shoulder and rubbed her feathery cheek against mine. "I love you, too. But he's right. I need to do this on my own." She faced front, but didn't leave her perch, her delicate talons cool against my skin as I trekked through the forest with my two greatest allies.

When we neared the edge of the property, I slowed, my mind whirling with possibilities. Silent, we crossed the yard, past the spot where we prayed as the Sun rose in Father Sky, past the Sacred Fire that offered blessings to the Holy Ones during the night, past where we constructed the lodge before each spiritual sweat. And I realized, our culture and traditions were all based in faith. Without the Holy Ones' guidance and protection, our People wouldn't thrive, wouldn't have survived the torture and destruction caused by the white man—not my dad—and I wouldn't have gained the passion that drove me now.

At the foot of the porch stairs, Mr. Mayhem stood with his hand on the railing. "It's time, Cat. How did I mislead you?"

"You intentionally left strands of hair on a high branch before climbing down from the tree. That's why I only saw the ends. You masked the knotted end with the canopy of leaves."

His eyebrows arched. "Correct. Nicely done."

"Thanks."

"This calls for a celebration." *Shicheii* bustled up the stairs. "Do we have time for tea, Cheveyo?"

"A quick one. Then I need to steal your granddaughter for about an hour for an errand we intended to run after breakfast."

Shit. I forgot all about Underwood. Mr. Mayhem's trunk must be rank by now. Guess who probably had to clean it.

Chapter 8
*"By awakening the Native American teachings,
you come to the realization that the earth is not something
simply that you build upon and walk upon and drive upon
and take for granted. It is a living entity.
It has consciousness."*
—Edgar Cayce

3:30 p.m.

After pulling out to the main drag, Mayhem passed Shawnee a cell phone. "Download the data, please. And be sure to remove the SIM card when you're through."

"Where's the PC?"

"Backseat."

Shawnee wedged in between the bucket seats then settled back in the passenger seat with the computer on her lap. "Whose phone is this?"

"Mister Worthington's."

Blinking eyes stared back at him. "You've had this the whole time?"

"Before you swell with self-righteousness, I found the phone this morning in one of the file folders that you still had not gone through."

"Oh." She plugged one end of the charging cord into the phone, the other end into the USB drive. "Once I turn this on, it'll start transmitting a signal. You know that, right?"

"If you do not possess the skills to bounce the signal elsewhere, then wait... one... minute..." He turned down a heavily wooded trail. At the end, he parked beneath a thick canopy of leaves. "Now, you may proceed. These mighty oaks and conifers should provide enough shelter to mask the signal."

"For the record, I do have the skills to bounce the signal. Just sayin.'" Lines of code scrolled up the screen as her fingers raced across the keyboard. "Gimme one sec to check the data, make sure I got everything."

Resting his elbow on the middle console, he propped his chin on a loose fist. "While you're in there, search for wolfdog activities. We either need an address of where they're being held or a buyer."

"That might take me a while." Once she's downloaded the data, she slid off the backing of the cell phone, took out the battery, and unplugged the SIM card. Tossed all three on the floor by her moccasins. "It's safe to drive."

After a quick glimpse of the floor, he pulled back, thick cords stiffened in his neck.

"What's the look for? I'll pick it up when we stop."

"I don't disrespect your personal property, do I?"

"You rummaged through my room for the files."

He cocked an eyebrow. "At least you weren't sound asleep in bed at the time."

"Okay, okay, I'll pick it up." She gathered the trash off the mat. "Happy?"

"I am. Thank you, Cat."

"Can I put the phone in the glove for now?"

"Yes, you may." Mayhem slung an arm around the passenger seat and reversed down the trail, backed into the road, and slide the shifter into Drive. "Once we dispose of Mister Underwood, we'll need to sterilize the trunk."

Her gaze stayed glued to the computer screen. "And by 'we', you mean me?"

"I do, yes."

"Kinda figured."

"Think of it as part of your training. War is ugly."

Shockingly, she handled the news rather well. Much better than she had before.

At Jackson Village Cemetery, he drove under the wrought-iron archway, winding down the roads to the back of the cemetery, near that vile building called the Crow's Nest. Parked far enough away to avoid unwanted attention.

"Keep working." He gripped the door handle. "I shan't be long."

"Are you sure you don't need my help?"

Mayhem swept a hand up and down her body. "With the face paint, body paint, and stained teeth, you may be more helpful by staying out of the public eye. Wouldn't you agree?"

"You just had to bring up the teeth again, didn't 'cha? Geesh, you know I'm sensitive about it."

"Did you brush before we left the cabin?"

"Shit." Her forehead fell into an opened hand. "They're never gonna be white again."

Sniggering, he slid on black leather gloves and swung his legs out the door. With the trash bag slung over one shoulder, he stalked the wood line, hugging the shadows around the perimeter of the cemetery. From the sidelines he'd spot potential obstacles before potential obstacles spotted him.

No sentinels masqueraded as the landscaping crew today. Interesting.

Once he padded closer to the side-by-side buildings, he scaled a nearby tree. From up high, he scanned the cemetery for potential witnesses. The cemetery, however, was quiet today, which made sense. On Mondays, many folks returned to their nine-to-five jobs, dreading the day ahead rather than reveling in the fact that they woke that morning. Shame more didn't appreciate nature's bounty. Without a fiery passion driving one to succeed, what was the point?

Mayhem jumped down, slung the bag over his shoulder again, lugging the body to the Crow's Nest. The eviscerated remains of Mr. Underwood would now act as a warning to the animal trafficking organization. An announcement that read, "Prepare, Entitled Ones, for I am the storm you've feared. I am Mayhem. And I'm coming for you next."

Using the key he borrowed from the sentinel who violated Shawnee—the vile pig didn't live long enough to brag about it—Mayhem deposited the bag right inside the door then re-engaged the lock. Simple-minded folks risked their security by not changing the locks after a break-in. Shame, really. A little forethought went a long way. Mayhem strode across the grass, weaving in between headstones until emerging on the road near the Caddy.

When he slipped behind the wheel, Shawnee's head popped up from the computer screen. "That was fast. Where'd you stash Underwood, an empty grave?"

Mayhem started the engine. "Did you find an address?"

"Yeah, but it's in Bretton Woods."

"Buyer or seller?"

"Seller."

"Perfect."

"Do you know where Bretton Woods is? It sounds vaguely familiar for some reason."

"Bretton Woods is best known for their popular ski resort." He shifted into Drive. "It's about forty minutes North on three-oh-two. Let's check things out before involving your grandfather." Pausing, he glanced her up and down. "Hm. Shall we run back to the cabin first so you can freshen up and change clothes?"

"Um, yeah. Obviously."

"On second thought, you'll be fine." One hand riding the steering wheel, Mayhem drove out of the cemetery. "The address, please?"

"All it says is Old Cherry Mountain Road. No house number."

"Because there is no house. As I told you, most people are not kind to wolfdogs. Far from it. Prepare yourself for what we may find." Speaking aloud but more to himself, he plotted a strategy. "Though the drive may take forty minutes, this will not be a quick excursion. Old Cherry Mountain Road winds through a thick forest for many miles." With no vehicles behind the Caddy, he used the opportunity to bang a U-turn. "We need to head back to the cabin for Poe. He'll be able to guide us."

Whining, Shawnee tsked her tongue. "Does he have to come?"

"Do you have a better idea?"

"What about a drone?"

Mayhem heaved a sigh. "Why are electronic devices your go-to resolution for most situations?"

"Um, 'cause they're helpful."

"They can be, however, relying solely on electronics is not healthy. The human brain is a muscle that requires exercise. If the device does the lion's share of the work for you, your brain remains dormant. Thus, does not flex." Mayhem glanced over to ensure he had her full attention. "If you were guarding a covert facility, what might you be more apt to stay on the lookout for—a mechanical drone or a crow that seamlessly blends into his environment?"

The arms crossed on her chest. "Fine, you made your point."

"Thank you. I realize you and Poe have had your differences. Nonetheless, you two will need to find a way to work together. Think of this trip as a solid step forward on common ground."

"Just so *you* know, I hate this idea with every fiber of my being."

"Noted." He veered down the long, dirt driveway. "Perhaps it's best if I break the news to your grandfather."

"Works for me." She grabbed the door handle. "I won't say a word."

When Mayhem climbed the stairs behind Shawnee, Jacy Lee pushed open the screen door.

"Cheveyo, I wasn't expecting you back so soon." He embraced his granddaughter. "Are you hungry, child?"

"No, thanks, *Shicheii*. I gotta go brush my teeth."

Slight chuckle. "All right, honey. Be careful not to smudge your face paint."

"Yeah, about that—"

Before she insulted an elder, Mayhem said, "Leave it."

Shawnee's mouth clamped shut, her moccasins hustling through the cabin.

Still on the porch, Mayhem braced open the screen door. "Is Poe with you?"

Jacy Lee stepped aside to reveal Poe and Spirit Crow on the kitchen island, bill-deep in a wooden bowl. "They wanted a little snack after the business with the H-A-W-K."

"Understandable." As he approached, Spirit Crow raised her head. "Hello, my love." He stroked her back. "I need to steal Poe for a few hours."

Juices drooled out Poe's mouth when his gaze shot to Dad, his chest feathers soaked from gorging on cubed cantaloupe, honeydew melon, and berries, pulverized blueberry coating the tip of his bill.

"Must you ingurgitate? It's atrocious to watch." He heaved a sigh. "Please preen your plumage. Look at your mother. Not even a dribble."

When Shawnee strolled up the hall, an overnight bag dangled from one shoulder. "Figured I'd prepare this time."

Jacy Lee's gaze shifted between them. "Are you two headed somewhere?"

"Your granddaughter found a lead on where they're holding the wolfdogs."

A smile brightened his face, dimples siding his cheeks. "All on her own?"

"She sure did."

"What about her training, Cheveyo?"

"We'll be back in a few hours. She cannot train properly in daylight, anyway." He hesitated. "I hadn't planned on muscling in on your time until we found an exact location, but if you'd like to join us, you're more than welcome."

"That may be difficult." Jacy Lee's gaze flitted to Spirit Crow, his voice lowering to a whisper. "She shouldn't travel just yet. Would you mind if I stayed here?"

"Not at all. Thank you, sweet friend. I appreciate all you're doing for her."

"Of course. She's family. You will keep me updated, won't you?"

"Will do." Mayhem patted his shoulder. "Thank you again." He headed up the stairs to pack a bag, then hesitated again. "We may not be back in time to dine with you. Is that a problem?"

"Not at all, Cheveyo. Spirit Crow and I will be fine."

By the time he'd returned to the kitchen, Jacy Lee had thrown together a bag of essential oils, balms, healing teas, and salves. When he passed the first-aid kit to Mayhem, he whispered, "I'll make sure she doesn't leave the property." Meaning, Spirit Crow.

Four thousand pounds lifted off his shoulders. Even in human form, strong-minded Kimi answered to no one, least of all her husband. That personality trait never left her, even when she transitioned to Spirit Crow. It may have even worsened.

Hopefully, she'd learned her lesson the last time. If she followed him and Shawnee, she might not survive another round with poachers.

Chapter 9

6:09 p.m.

For the entire trip North, Poe stood on the middle console, glaring at me. Friggin' psycho needed an attitude adjustment. When Mr. Mayhem pulled down a dirt trail off Old Cherry Mountain Road, nothing but thick forest surrounded us.

Swiveling in my seat, my gaze ping-ponged from window to window. "We're parking here?"

"For now, yes."

"What if someone calls the cops?"

"Then we'll deal with it. Never allow *What-ifs?* to rule your life. Problems will arise from time to time. Remember, Coyote causes chaos, but you cannot let him win."

For the Diné—my People—Coyote was a trickster who thrived on chaos. He was also a star called Canopus, but he wreaked havoc in the sky, too, by tossing a blanket full of crystals into the atmosphere, scattering stars everywhere instead of placing them one by one in an orderly fashion. Basically, when things couldn't get more perfect in life and then something, or someone, disrupted it, that was Coyote at work.

After trekking through the woods for a good mile, Mr. Mayhem told Poe to search for the wolfdogs. "Please be careful. Your winning personality may not be enough to persuade the local murder to allow you to encroach on their territory."

Poe leaped off his arm and took flight but stayed low since he was in an unfamiliar landscape. Like a caged animal, Mr. Mayhem paced back and forth, his full attention on the treetops. Once again, he risked the most precious beings in his life for the greater good. That must take a toll.

Even I worried about the little bastard. "What happens if he runs into the local murder?"

"Crows do not take kindly to trespassers."

"What's that mean? They could kill him?"

"First offense is usually a broken wing. However, if he still refuses to leave their domain, he becomes fair game."

Those words jabbed my side. "How could he leave with a broken wing?"

"On foot. All the while being targeted from above."

"Shit." My heart raced even faster. "Poe and I might have our differences, but I don't wanna see him hurt."

"Nor do I, Cat. Nor do I." He thrust out a hand. "Look."

Poe soared toward us, landing moments later on Mr. Mayhem's forearm, his chest heaving with adrenaline.

"Problem?"

Poe dipped his bill.

"Did the local murder spot you?"

No reaction, his sight deadlocked on his dad.

"Did you locate the wolfdogs?"

Still no reaction.

"Show me."

Poe leaped off his arm perch but stayed right in front of us while we trampled over fallen logs and around trees. I scanned the area, but everything seemed copasetic. No idea what upset him. Poe circled back and landed on Mr. Mayhem's shoulder, signaling with a warning call that this was the spot that concerned him.

"I don't get it." I spun left, right. "What's the problem?"

"Look up."

A massive nest hovered above us.

"The home of sharp-shinned hawks. That explains the lack of crows in the area." Two fingers fluffed Poe's chest feathers. "All right, buddy. Let's allow them space." Mr. Mayhem headed back the way we entered the forest, and I followed behind.

Not for nothing... a drone wouldn't worry about a few hawks. But no, God forbid anyone took my advice.

"Cat," Mr. Mayhem warned.

"Yeah?"

"Lose the attitude, please."

"How'd you—?" Stupid question. I stopped trying to figure him out and concentrated on getting through the thick and rocky terrain.

Once we arrived at the Caddy, I settled into the passenger seat. The dashboard clock read 6:40 p.m.

In case it wasn't obvious, I said, "It'll be dark soon. When's sunset?"

"You tell me."

"Alright, I will." I held a flat hand under the sun, stacked another beneath it, and two and a half fingers dipped below the horizon. "One hour, twenty minutes, give or take."

"Correct." He grinned. "Nicely done, Cat. Are you hungry?"

"Starv—" I caught myself, unwilling to listen to his speech about me not suffering from starvation again. "I mean, yeah, I could eat."

"All right, then. I took the liberty of reserving us a three-bedroom suite at the Omni Mount Washington Resort."

"Three bedrooms?" The breeze from the open window slapped the air freshener, and black coconut tickled my nostril hairs. "But we only need two."

"When your grandfather joins us, he will also need a place to rest. Will he not?"

I tried to scratch without smudging my face paint, my nose wiggling back and forth. "Is..." I waved at my nostrils, the overpowering scent watering my eyes. "Is that new?"

"Pardon?"

How could he not smell that?

Beady eyes filled with judgment, Pissy Pants glanced me up and down, and I stuck out my tongue.

"Cat—"

"Yeah?"

"Please don't antagonize him."

"I'm not. I was just—" I scratched the back of my head. "So, has *Shicheii* ever slept at a hotel before? He's such a homebody. I can't picture it."

Focused on the road, Mr. Mayhem chuckled. "In all honesty, he'd much prefer to camp. Over the years, I've tried to spoil him with upscale restaurants, but he wants no part of it. When we travel back to our homeland, he insists on camping along the way."

I brushed dirt off the leg of my new buckskin pants. "He's not wrong. Mother Earth provides everything we need."

"She does. However, through various life experiences—both good and bad—we gain knowledge and a wider view of the world. After all, how do you defeat an enemy you know nothing about? We cannot, unless we walk in their footsteps and experience their world. Only then will vulnerabilities reveal themselves."

"Makes a lot of sense, actually."

"Stick with me, kid." When he winked, Poe screeched as though I was stealing his father's attention. Mr. Mayhem had to stroke his head to get him to chill the fuck out.

That's when the gravity of the situation dawned on me. "Where's Mister Personality gonna stay?"

"With us, of course."

"With us?" My eyeballs almost rolled out the sockets. "Whaddaya mean, like, he's staying *in* the suite?"

"What would you propose I do, leave him in the Caddy?" A touch of sarcasm laced his tone, even though it seemed like the perfect solution to me.

Regardless, I knew better than to fall into that trap. So, instead, I said nothing. Safer that way. My bedroom door better have a lock to keep the freakshow from clawing my eyes out while I slept. Without Spirit Crow to keep him in line, who knew what he'd do.

"Are we sleeping there?"

"Not tonight. We'll work in the suite, try to narrow down the location. Then you have a training session later at the cabin."

"Right. Yeah. I forgot. I'm the prey."

Chuckling, his gaze never strayed from the road. "Oh, Cautious Cat, you amuse me."

When Mr. Mayhem turned on to Hotel Drive, the road angled up at a steep incline. The massive resort stood at the end, looming over mountain ranges, wildflowers, and periodic trees fringing the steep cliff out my side window. The ivory building curved like a smile, with two massive towers at each bend. A magenta-red metal roof capped the top and front entrance, and two flags at the peak of each tower wafted in the breeze, periodic brick chimneys speckling the roofline.

Elevation popped my ears as I swiveled toward my mentor. "I can't walk in there dressed like this."

"Correct. You cannot. The suite comes with its own private stairwell." He parked around the back. "I'll check us in, get the room key, then meet you and Poe at the stairwell door."

"Are you fuckin' serious right now? The wounds are still fresh from the last time you left me alone with him."

"Watch your language." Piercing gray eyes narrowed on me. "And your tone." After holding my gaze for an eternity of minutes, my knee bouncing on its own, the hard lines of his face softened. "What choice do I have? Neither of you can stroll through the lobby in your present condition. As it is, you must be very careful not to show yourself, or you may frighten the other guests. Even if they could look past the face and body paint, the blood-red teeth make you unforgettable. And that, dearest Cat, could prove disastrous if this mission goes south."

I clawed back my bangs. "Why do you always gotta bring up the teeth?"

Rather than respond, he flipped down the visor in front of me, and I flashed my pearly reds in the mirror. Not sure how it's possible, but somehow, they got even darker.

"Behave yourself," he told Poe before shutting the driver's door behind him. Through the glass, he pointed out the stairwell door, where me and Poe would meet him after he checked in. "I'll text you when I'm on my way. Stay put until then." When I nodded in agreement, he strode around the side of the building to the front.

"Mind scooting over for a sec?" I asked Poe. "I need something from the backseat."

Mr. Personality's beady eyed glare never left me as he took his sweet time, inching back to the driver's seat. Once he got the hell out of my way, I snatched my overnight bag off the backseat and rummaged through it for my phone.

"Look. Can't we just call a truce?"

Poe's haughty stare never wavered.

"I'm not talkin' about forever, but we need to push the pause button. At least till we get up to the room. Whaddaya say? I'm game if you are."

No reaction.

"Fine. I didn't wanna play this card, but you forced my hand. If you won't do it for me, then do it for your dad. He asked for our cooperation."

A slight dip of the head.

"Thank you."

Raising one leg, Poe bill-tapped his gold ankle band.

"Yeah, yeah, I know the clock's ticking." I mumbled, "Friggin' freakshow."

While waiting for Mr. Mayhem, I scrolled through all my missed calls and text messages. I lost count of how many times Levaughn tried to get ahold of me. A shitload, that's for sure. Lieutenant Holt probably told him I took four weeks of vacation time—I'd built up six from all the overtime—but I hadn't gotten around to returning his calls. Nor could I explain why I needed to leave the state over the phone.

How could I tell him I was heading to Alaska next week with Mr. Mayhem and *Shicheii* to prevent the slaughter of polar bears? He'd think I lost my ever-lovin' mind. When I ran home to pack for the trip, Nadine—my BFF, who's crashing at my place to take care of my fur-babies, Berkley and Katie McGuire—would undoubtedly slam me with questions, too, and had also called about a hundred times. I didn't feel like dealing with either of them yet. I had to stay laser-focused on the mission. If we didn't protect wolfdogs, who would?

Mayhem texted, and I sent back a thumbs-up emoji.

"He's ready," I told Pissy Pants, who couldn't stop glaring at me from the driver's seat. "You're gonna be cool about this, right?"

He dipped his bill, but I didn't trust the good boy act for a second.

"I'll come around to get you."

Cold stare.

"Remember our truce." I got out and hustled around the front bumper. Opening the driver's door went well, but when I reached in to grab him, Poe screeched and dove—talons out—straight at my face, and I batted him away. Poe spiraled backward, rolling across the hood as Mr. Mayhem gasped from the doorway behind me.

Expression angry and mean, he soldiered closer, and I thrust out my hands.

"Wait—please. I can explain. This is not what it looks like."

"Silence, Cat. I'll deal with you in a moment." He cradled Poe in his arms, and Pissy Pants laid it on thick with his whimpering and shit. "Aw, bud, I'm sorry she hurt you."

"I did like hell!" Flames burned all my insides to ash. "That little bastard tried to attack me, and I—"

"Silence." He rotated—painfully slow—rage radiating off him and halting me mid-sentence. In his arms, I swear that freak o' nature winked at me.

With my lips folded around my teeth, I tossed the sad, puppy dog eyes.

Cold and firm, he said, "Follow."

And so, I did, my head hung, sulking up the private stairwell. What would possess me to trust that little bastard? That'd teach me.

Mr. Mayhem held open the door to the suite, and I slogged inside, my moccasins dragging across the carpet. Why'd Pissy Pants have to come? He ruined everything.

Once Poe climbed to his father's shoulder, my mentor told me to sit in an upholstered chair in the living room, where he towered over me. "Now's the time to speak your truth, Cautious Cat."

"Well, we made a pact in the car. A truce." Knee bouncing, I pointed straight at Poe. "And he agreed."

"Is that true, bud?"

A dip of the bill confirmed my story so far.

With a little more confidence that things might go my way, I continued. "So, when you texted, I thought he'd be cool. But then I opened the driver's door, and he lunged straight at my face, talons out like he wanted to slice my—"

The raised hand silenced me.

"Did you lunge at Cat's face?"

Poe rocked his head in an emphatic no.

My balled fist slammed the armrest. "He's lying!"

"Now is not the time to zing unfounded allegations."

"But it's true!"

Mr. Mayhem dragged over the matching chair and sat facing me, tapping praying hands to his lips. The longer he stayed silent, the more my knee hammered the seat cushion. "Is it possible—and please let me finish before blurting out your initial reaction—is it possible that Poe honored your truce and was flying to perch on your shoulder? Hence why he extended his talons."

A continual dip of the bill from Poe.

Crap. Did I imagine an attack because of past experiences? For several seconds, I replayed the scene over and over again in my mind.

"If that's true, then—wow, I totally misread the moment."

"Let me explain something to you, if I may. Agreeing to a truce, for however long of a period, rubs against every fiber of his natural-bred instinct for self-protection. That instinct, along with his adaptability, is why crows inhabit all fifty states. Yet Poe was willing to set aside your shaded past and give you the benefit of the doubt—a magnanimous gesture on his part, I might add—for the benefit of the mission. I need the same from you, Cat, or this mentorship will never work."

Those words cut me in places I didn't even know existed. "I'm sorry. It'll never happen again." I waved praying hands at him. "Please don't give up on me."

"I appreciate your taking responsibility. I really do. However, I am not the one who deserves an apology. Am I?"

Shit. Poe would rub this moment in my face for the rest of our lives, but what else could I do? I couldn't say no. So, I pinned back my shoulders, my spine straightening, and glanced at Pissy Pants, his head bobbing in victory. "If I misread the incident outside, I'm sorry, Poe. I never meant to hurt you, and I hope you're alright."

Nothing in return. Absolutely zero reaction from the little bastard.

"Other than a bruised ego, he's fine, Cat. Crows may not look it at first blush, but they are quite durable." He fluffed Poe's chest feathers. "Aren't you, buddy?"

"Did he accept my apology?" I cocked my head. "I can't tell."

"Ooh, well, even you must admit, the odds were not in your favor from the start. Too much has transpired between you, I'm afraid. Nonetheless, I appreciate the fact that you took responsibility for your actions. Now we can move forward."

"Why do I get the feelin' he's gonna try to get even?"

Mr. Mayhem smirked. "If he does, then we'll deal with it. Poe has long known where the line is, and he will not cross it in my presence."

"What's that mean, exactly? As long as you're around, he won't attack me, but if you leave us alone again, I'm fair game?"

Grinning, he glimpsed his gold watch. "Let's put a pin in this conversation for now and get to work."

I leaped out of my chair—aka the hot seat. "I left the PC in the Caddy. Can I have the keys?"

Exhaling, Mr. Mayhem reached into his leather blazer. Within seconds, he dangled a keyring off one finger. "Quickly, please, Cat."

The second I stepped into the hall outside the suite, I almost collided with some rich bitch, dripping in diamonds. "Sorry." I flashed a quick smile. "Didn't see ya there."

The lady screamed louder than a five-alarm fire and fainted—passed out cold on the rich hardwood floor.

Uh-oh. Not good.

Before I could figure out what to do, hands came from nowhere, and dragged me into the suite. The door slammed behind us.

"Stay put," Mr. Mayhem said, his tone firm and harsh. "Regardless of what you hear, do not leave this room. Understood?"

"Yep. Got it."

When he slipped out the door, I rose on my tippy toes to peer through the wide-angled peephole.

"Ma'am?" He squatted to render aid, and the lady roused. "Are you all right?"

She still seemed out of it. "What happened?"

"Martha!" A silver fox dressed to the nines shouldered Mr. Mayhem out of the way, and I cringed. "Honey, did you fall?"

Before allowing his wife even a second to respond, the impatient asshole whipped out the latest iPhone—evident by the size and shape of multiple cameras on the back—and punched digit after digit. "Try not to move, Martha. I'm notifying the front desk." He raised the cell to his ear. "Pip Hawthorne calling. My wife fell in the hall outside our suite. Send the manager immediately. Obviously, the staff added too much wax to the flooring, and I will hold the hotel accountable for such an egregious error in judgment."

What a douche.

Without so much as a goodbye, Pip Hawthorne disconnected the call, stuffing the phone into the inner pocket of his navy double-breasted suit coat, complete with a blue paisley pocket square and matching vest. The suit alone must cost more than my entire house.

Who names their son Pip?

Martha tried to sit upright, but her husband wouldn't let her. Probably trying to get their room comped, even though this incident had nothing to do with the hotel. The lady freaked out when she saw me. Okay, so, maybe I shouldn't've smiled at her, but I'm sure it wasn't only my teeth that scared the crap out of her. The rich bitch probably thought an entire tribe raided the hotel, searching for money or drugs or something equally racist.

Shicheii once quoted a beloved elder, Chief Dan George. "If you talk to the animals, they will talk to you, and you will know each other. If you do not talk to them, you will not know them, and what you do not know, you will fear. What one fears, one destroys."

The same held true for humans. Judging someone by the shade of their skin or, in my case, the blessed symbols of my ancestors painted on my face and body, would be like hating animals because of an aversion to fur or feathers.

"There's a... a... killer in the hotel," Martha told her husband as two hotel employees raced to her side. "Warpainted savages running loose."

Warpainted savages? Hope Mr. Mayhem slices her throat.

"Oh, my word." Pip's gaze shot to the manager, marked by the embroidered name and title on her shirt pocket. "Is this the type of clientele you allow here?"

"No, sir."

Out of the Hawthorne couple's sightline, Mr. Mayhem gestured to the manager by tilting an imaginary cup to his lips—*she's delusional from alcohol*—and the manager nodded in agreement.

"A woman with blood-red teeth attacked me."

"She attacked you, Martha?" Pip Hawthorne whirled back to the manager. "Call the police."

"If I may make a suggestion..." Mr. Mayhem stepped into the conversation. "Without a detailed description of the perpetrator, the police may cause more harm than good. Perhaps an upgraded suite with better security would help ease your mind." He turned to the manager. "Jessika—beautiful name, if I may be so bold—could the hotel accommodate Mister and Missus Hawthorne? Under the circumstances and all."

"Yes. Yes, we could. Absolutely."

"In the meantime," Mr. Mayhem said, regarding the filthy rich couple, "I'll keep my eyes peeled for anyone matching the description you gave, Missus Hawthorne. My private security firm employs several off-duty officers. If I find your attacker, rest assured that my men will handle it. Free of charge, of course."

"Really? Oh, that would be wonderful. Thank you, Mister...?"

"Daniels."

Un-freakin'-believable. Why did he insist on using my name? Did we marry again or was I his daughter this time?

Poe flew by my cheek, startling the piss out of me, my moccasins shuffling backward to get out of his way. Hovering in place with his talons clawed onto the door, ebony wings flapped in a steady flutter, his beady dark stare aimed through the peephole. Kind of impressive, actually, but I sure as hell wasn't telling him that.

"My pleasure, Missus Hawthorne. I'm pleased you weren't seriously injured."

"Other than my pride, I'm fine, thank you."

"Understandable." Quick tip of the fedora. "Till we meet again." He slipped into our suite, urging me and Poe away from the door.

Before he jumped down my throat for causing a ruckus, I said, "Thanks. That was way too close. Sorry I screwed up."

"Mistakes happen, Cat. Have you had a chance to look at the menu?"

Why wasn't he pissed? "Uh... not yet." I stalled. "Hey, um, can you get the PC for me? I still need it."

"As you wish. Figure out what you want for dinner while I'm gone." He swiveled toward the door, then stopped. "Poe," he said over his shoulder, "no shenanigans while I'm gone, please."

When I glanced over at Pissy Pants, his eyes thinned, and I stuck out my tongue.

Hopefully, he wouldn't make me regret that move.

Chapter 10
*"The old Lakota was wise. He knew that a man's
heart, away from nature, becomes hard. He knew that
lack of respect for growing, living things soon led
to lack of respect for humans, too.
So he kept his children close to nature's softening influence."*
—Luther Standing Bear

8:00 p.m.

Mayhem drove back to Old Cherry Mountain Road. Once he pulled curbside, he fired off a quick text to Shawnee.

Order whatever you'd like. Please order me the filet mignon, the house salad, and a fruit cup. Extra mashed potatoes and gravy on the side for Poe.

Text bubbles emerged.

Aren't you in the parking lot?

Perhaps he should fill her in on his plans.

Wolves howl more frequently at sunrise and sunset. If I hear them, I can narrow in on their location.

Text bubbles emerged, then disappeared, emerged, then disappeared, as though she kept rewording her response.

Wish you waited for me, but whatever. Good luck.

His thumbs worked the keypad.

Please tell room service to leave dinner outside the door. We cannot risk another run-in.

Yep. Got it.

Thank you, Cat. Tell Poe you're ordering food. It'll help relax him.

Hope you're right. ◈

Cruising slowly, Mayhem pressed the window button on the armrest, the glass gliding into the doorframe as he winded along the country road framed by the Natural World's most-cherished sentinels—tall pines, oaks, maple, and ash trees, the leaves exhaling oxygen into the mild New Hampshire air. Kimi loved this area. On weekends, they traded the city for the White Mountains, a well-needed escape from the hustle and bustle of daily life. Buying the brownstone in Boston had its benefits when he worked full time for the Smithsonian and during his past foray with the criminally insane years ago. His heart, however, sang in the wilderness.

A long, steady bay snapped his attention to the forest. He parked, crossed the road. Under the thick canopy of leaves another Wolf joined in, two glorious voices singing in harmony. More and more wolves joined in as Father Sun dipped His head behind the horizon, the area darkening around him.

Strangely, he couldn't detect the signature mashup of barks and howls used by dogs. Only the crystal-clear pitch of wolves. Judging by the vocalization's tone and strength, the holding pen should be another mile or two deeper into the woods.

Mayhem sped his pace, slaloming around trees and hopping streams, until he reached an area where long, steady bays vibrated the earth. Such a glorious song, the cry of nature rejoicing at life. Even in captivity, wolves appreciated all of Mother Earth's blessings.

Armed guards patrolled the perimeter outside a chain-link enclosure. Mid-stride, Mayhem stopped and ducked behind a wide ash tree sided with brush and saplings. Through gnarled branches, he counted four men, rifles resting on their shoulders.

Mayhem prowled closer. With his cell, he snapped photos from various angles of the compound and carnage of the Natural World's most important predators.

Without wolves, ecosystems neared collapse. To ensnare these beautiful animals, chain them against their will, and force them to breed with dogs offended him on such a deep, personal level. Never would any of his People disrespect the Wolf. Hunting for sustenance and survival was one thing. Mistreatment of animals rubbed against everything he stood for, all he'd ever known. Breaking the soul of a Wolf for the monetary value of their sperm was not only uncouth but disgraceful.

The wolves' torture must end, even if it meant the slow slaughter of their captors. Before he lost his patience with these beasts—the men, not the wolves—he backtracked to the Caddy, jumped behind the wheel, then raced to the hotel.

Killing the engine in the back-parking lot, he took a moment to find his center, to resume a state of *hozho*, and to recite a silent prayer.

Looking behind, I am filled with gratitude. Looking forward, I am filled with vision. Looking upward, I am filled with strength. Looking within, I discover peace.

With the laptop bundled under one arm, he clicked the key fob—*bleep, bleep*—hustled to the stairwell door. When he waved the keycard in front of the sensor, the red light flashed thrice, allowing him entry.

Outside the suite, Shawnee's angry tone carried through the door. "Cut it out! Do it again and it's on, asshole. I mean it, I've had about all I can take."

When Mayhem entered the suite, he followed her shouts to the dining table. A sharp intake of air sucked through his teeth. Mashed potatoes and gravy spotted Shawnee's hair, stomach, and arms. "What... on earth... is going on here?"

She thrust an accusatory finger across the table at Poe. "Ask him!"

"Lower the volume, please. I am asking you, Cat."

"He won't stop flinging food at me. Told ya he'd get even for the misunderstanding outside."

It took all his power not to laugh. "All right, all right, relax. No harm done. At least there's no bloodshed this time."

"No harm done?" She pointed that same stiff finger at her head. "Have you seen my hair? I'll never get all this shit outta it." Now standing, she shook the mashed potatoes off her arms and bare stomach. "Aren't you gonna reprimand him?"

"Try to stay positive. At least he didn't hit the beads."

"Seriously?" She planted a fist on her hip. "That's all you're gonna say?"

Mayhem pinched the bridge of his nose. "Cat, I will deal with Poe in my own time, on my own terms. Right now, I would like to enjoy my meal while it's still hot."

"Well, I gotta jump in the shower now. And *Shicheii's* gonna kill me because it'll ruin all his hard work."

"Not to worry." He lifted the dome off his plate, delicious tangy aromas growling his stomach as he sat at the table, Poe hobbling closer to suck up. "I will explain everything to your grandfather upon our return."

"Good, 'cause it's all Poe's fault."

He sliced off a thin section of filet, the bite dangling from the fork in front of his mouth. "Is it?"

"Yeah, I mean, he started it."

Swallowing, Mayhem cocked an eyebrow. "Did he? By your own admission, the food fight was payback for the incident outside."

"Yeah, but... you don't gotta tell *Shicheii* that part."

"Oh, I see." He passed Poe a bite. "You only want me to share half the story. The half that makes you look good."

"Fine." Pouting, she sat back down. "I won't shower."

After swallowing a forkful of garden salad, Mayhem slapped his phone on the table. "I found the wolves."

"Seriously?" She reached for the phone, and Poe batted her hand. "What *is* your frickin' problem?"

"Little mister"—he grimaced—"that is enough. The free-for-all ends now. Am I clear?"

Poe hopped up to Dad's shoulder, nuzzling his neck with a feathery cheek.

"Cat, you should be able to get GPS coordinates from the photo's metadata. Correct?"

"Absolutely." She slid the phone off the table. "It's locked." Mayhem leaned forward, and she scanned his retina. "Thanks."

"If I may make a suggestion..." Waiting for her to acknowledge him with eye contact, he popped a cube of melon in his mouth. "To avoid the face paint, I could wash your hair after dinner if it'll make you feel better."

Appalled by the suggestion, Poe jerked away from Dad's face.

"You'd do that for me?"

"It's the least I can do"—he glared at Poe—"under the circumstances and all. Wouldn't be the first time."

"Um, I was unconscious then. But thanks for reminding me of one of the most embarrassing moments of my life."

Inside, he snickered. "In the meantime, if you could work at the table, I would appreciate it. No sense in soiling the rest of the suite."

"Sure. Where's the PC?"

Mayhem retrieved the laptop from the chair beside him. "A satellite image of the compound would be ideal."

"No problem, but you know it won't be in real time, right?"

"I am cognizant of that, thank you." To even out the house dressing he tossed the salad. "A satellite image should still give us boundary lines, which'll help us form the best plan of attack."

With two fingers, she enlarged the first photo. "Those bastards chained the wolfdogs to the fence? They can barely move." Tears clouded her eyes. "Oh, my God."

"It's worse than that, I'm afraid."

Her jaw slacked. "Whaddaya mean?"

"They're full-blooded Eastern Gray Wolves."

"What?" A splayed hand covered the beads over her heart. "But I thought they were driven out of New England."

"Over the last decade, there've been sightings here and there. Wolves traverse great distances in search of prey. It was only a matter of time before they crossed the border of Canada into New Hampshire and Maine."

"And what, these scumbags waited for them to cross?"

"Apparently."

"Shit." Head hung, she raked her fingers across her scalp, mashed potatoes cemented in her bangs, gravy hardened on her left eyebrow. A moment later, she straightened. "Wait. If these are full-blooded wolves, where are the wolfdogs?"

"Good question."

While Shawnee worked, Mayhem swallowed the last bite of salad, the house vinaigrette lingering on his palate. Beside him, Poe gorged on the remaining fruit cup and slices of filet. The mashed potatoes he'd forfeited when he chose to weaponize them as a projectile, a decision Poe wasn't pleased to hear. Regardless, Mayhem could not allow the petulant behavior to continue, and withholding one of his favorite foods was an easy way to get his point across.

"Got it." Shawnee spun the laptop around. "Satellite image of the compound, but it's dated last year."

"Is it possible to obtain more up-to-date images?"

"If one of the scumbags shared their location with us, we could use Live View on Google Maps, but the chances of that happening are slim to none."

"Not necessarily." A sly grin. "I can be quite persuasive if motivated to do so. We only need one poacher to cooperate?"

"Yeah, but he's gotta be on the compound for Location Sharing to work."

"All right, then. Our mission is clear—separate the weakest from the pack." With the cloth napkin, he dabbed his lips. "Okie doke. Let's get you squared away, then we'll head back to the compound."

"How're you gonna separate him?"

"I'm not. You are."

Poe tossed his head back and cackled. Little rascal.

Chapter 11

9:15 p.m.

After Mr. Mayhem washed my hair with the shower wand—talk about awkward—we drove to the compound. A few miles deep into the woods, he motioned for me to scale a tree, so I climbed up to a high limb. In the distance, staging lights cornered the pen. Wolves trapped inside with thick chains around their necks, their massive paws stomping through their own feces.

Not sure what Mr. Mayhem had planned for these assholes, but I wouldn't object to chaining them in their own shit.

I flashed two fingers at my eyes, then at the compound. Poe flew up the tree to confirm. God forbid he took my word for anything.

Mr. Mayhem motioned by counting off fingers.

Count the number of men. Got it.

For a while I stared, my heart breaking more and more. Two men patrolled the East and North, two for South and West. Turning my gaze to my partner-in-crime, I flashed a four, and he gestured for me to join him on ground-level.

Poe fluttered down to his shoulder perch.

The moment I swung my leg around the trunk, something bolted through my peripheral. What the hell was that? Not a human, not exactly an animal either. The thing moved so fast, I never caught an outline or shape. I flashed a finger for him to wait, then climbed higher to peer through the canopy of leaves. Whatever it was left the area. Where were all the other forest dwellers? The woods seemed oddly devoid of wildlife. Did the presence of wolves scare off other night predators?

Once I hopped down to the ground, Mr. Mayhem jabbed his chin. "Problem?"

"Thought I saw something. Guess not." I shrugged it off. The darkness had a strange way of skewing one's perception, according to Bo Adams, the best cat burglar in the business and my mentor/father figure when we lived on the city streets back in the day. "Anyway, they've got it pretty well covered. Doubt any of 'em will leave their post."

"All right, then. Let's head home. For now, we'll have to work from the satellite images. No fifth man, no boss?"

"Not that I could see, no."

"Interesting."

Through the thick wooded terrain we trekked, with Poe surfing his father's shoulder. Once we reached the road, headlights approached, and Mr. Mayhem's stiff arm stopped me. A newer model BMW cruised by, but instead of continuing down the road, the driver pulled in behind the Caddy. The interior light blazed on as he searched for something in the middle console, engine idling, smoke billowing out the tailpipe.

"Stay put." Mr. Mayhem set Poe on a nearby branch then stepped into the road. Over to the car he strode. "May I help you, friend?"

The driver's window zipped down. "Is that your Cadillac?"

"It is."

"Why is parked on private property?"

"The public road is private property?"

"No, dipshit. The land you just—"

Mid-sentence, Mr. Mayhem stopped him by grabbing his throat, dragging the dude partway through the opened window, the blade of the hunting knife leveled under his chin. "What did you call me?"

Arms spread wide, the guy's hips balanced on the window frame, half inside Daddy's beamer, half out. "Nothin', man. I didn't mean anything by it."

"I see. Are you in the habit of spewing hate to every stranger you meet on the street, or are you simply racist *and* ignorant?"

"Yeah. I mean, no, but—"

Mr. Mayhem dragged the dude's legs through the window. When his work boots hit the pavement, my mentor held him close to his chest, the blade still leveled to his throat. "Name, please?"

"Braiden Windsor."

He waved the hunting knife at me and Poe, standing in the shadows, the thick forest shielding us from sight. "Is that your property, Mister Windsor?"

"No."

"No? Then why so protective of land that does not belong to you?"

"It's my uncle's land. Look, man. I'm sorry I overreacted. I don't want any trouble."

"Nor do I, Braiden." Sheathing the knife, he released the dude, who'd probably pissed his khakis by now. "Thank you for the apology."

"Sure, man." His hands groped for the door handle behind him. "I mean, I've got no beef with you."

"Be on your way now, Mister Windsor." He stood his ground as Braiden scrambled to escape into the beamer. The window zipped closed as he pulled around the Caddy. As soon as cherry-red taillights trailed into the distance, Mr. Mayhem called for Poe. "Cat, you may come out now, as well."

"Whoa." I crossed the street. "Dude's lucky. I thought for sure he'd meet his maker tonight."

Over the roof, his head listed to one side as though he couldn't understand my remark. "Why, pray tell, would you leap to that conclusion? Honestly, Cat, if name calling was an unforgiveable sin, then you wouldn't be standing here."

Leap to a conclusion? He pulled a knife, right? Dumbfounded and silent, I flipped through memory cards, settling in the passenger seat as Poe hopped up to the middle console.

"On the ride home," his deep, raspy voice regained my attention, "if you could run a search for our friend Braiden, last name Windsor, I would greatly appreciate it. Apparently, his uncle owns the property and, quite possibly, the compound as well."

I didn't dare mention I'd overheard the conversation. "Do we know the uncle's first name?"

"We do not. However, try the last name and property address as a starting point."

"Alright." I twisted to reach into the backseat, but Pissy Pants stood his ground, refusing to move out of my way. "Poe"—I faked a cough into a closed fist—"could you please scoot over for a sec so I can grab the PC?" *Let's see the little bastard say no with his father right here.*

With one side-glance from Mr. Mayhem, Poe hopped down to his father's thigh.

"Thanks." *Punk.* I snatched the laptop. With the PC on my lap, I brought up property records for the State of New Hampshire. "What county is this?"

"Coos. Fun fact. Coös, with the accent on the second O, is derived from the Abenaki word meaning 'people among the pines.' Also spelled phonetically as cowass, cohoss, or coo-ash." He pronounced the different variations. "The county names identified the inhabitants of the region. Those living in the area customarily known as Coo-ashe-aukes or 'dwellers in the pine tree place.' That is, of course, prior to the colonists driving the clan off their ancestral land."

Those words gut punched me. "The more I learn, the more ashamed I am of that side of me."

"Don't be. You are who you are. Your father was an honorable man, a good man. To deny that part of you would mean denying his existence. Your mother wouldn't want that, Cat. Would she?"

"No." But still. My white ancestors tortured, enslaved, and slaughtered Native Americans. How could I not be ashamed of their actions?

"Your grandfather and I teach you about the past to educate you." Blue lights of the dash cascaded over his face, gray translucent eyes sparkling. "It's part of our heritage, but certainly not the only part. Half-truths tell one side of your story, not your full story."

"No, I know." Picking at my half-bitten nails, my back molars ground together. "It just sucks."

"We are who we are, but we're also who we become. What we stand for, what we fight for, who we love, the good we do, and yes, even the bad."

"I know. I just wish things didn't go down that way."

"We cannot change the past, but we can ensure it never happens again."

That drew my full attention, my heart speeding to a fast *pitter-patter, pitter-patter, pitter-patter.* "For Maggie and Jude?"

"And their children. And their children's children."

"I get it now." I really did. "We're not fighting for ourselves. We're fighting for a better tomorrow."

"Precisely." With a quick wink, he tapped the computer screen. "Now get to work."

My fingers raced across the keyboard. "Searching property records for Windsor." Pages of properties appeared on the screen. "Huh. I found a few Windsors, but none with land on Old Cherry Mountain Road. Could it be under a different name?"

"An uncle could indeed be young Braiden's mother's brother, thereby giving him a different surname. Bring up a property map of

Old Cherry Mountain Road. That should give us the lot number. We'll have to search from there instead."

Why didn't I think of that? "Good idea." I punched key after key but couldn't find it. "Still in Coos County, right?"

"You may need to drop down to the town records for property maps. Try Carroll—spelled with two Rs and two Ls—instead of Bretton Woods."

On the keys my fingers stalled. "Why would I do that?"

"Bretton Woods is in the Town of Carroll."

"Bretton Woods isn't a town?"

"Not exactly. It is a village within the Town of Carroll. Coos County has one city, nineteen towns, and twenty-three unincorporated places, nineteen of which are unpopulated. Villages like Bretton Woods reside within towns."

Sounded all kinds of fucked up to me, but whatever. I ran a search for Carroll. "Uh, problem."

"What is it, Cat?"

"I'm not great with finding my way around in maps."

Mr. Mayhem chuckled. "Bookmark it, please, and I'll take a look once we arrive home."

Twenty minutes later, we pulled down the long, dirt driveway. *Shicheii* sat on the porch, gigantic flames raging in the yard, much larger than the usual Sacred Fire that burned day and night to protect us. I lowered to the chair beside him, but he didn't acknowledge me, like deep thoughts consumed him.

When Mr. Mayhem climbed the stairs—Poe sound asleep, cradled in one arm—he took one look at *Shicheii* and said, "It's more important than ever, Jacy Lee."

"Then let me help her."

My gaze shifted between them.

"I'm sorry, but you cannot. We've been over this."

"Cheveyo, she is not ready."

He flung a hand at me. "She's as ready as she'll ever be."

"Not in the dark, she's not."

"Um," I said. "What're we talkin' about?"

"Is that why the fire is so massive?" Gray eyes thinned. "Do whatever you feel is necessary, but this is happening tonight. Time is of the essence. We found the wolves, and the armed guards will not go easy on her because she's your granddaughter."

"Fine." *Shicheii* grabbed my hand. "Come, child." He dragged me into the cabin, and I had no clue why. "Sit." Clearly pissed at his lifelong friend, he practically shoved me into the kitchen chair. On the table laid his face and body paints.

"*Shicheii*, what's goin' on?"

A wet cloth washed all the paint off my face and arms, leaving only the image of Spirit Crow on the back of one hand, the golden eagle on the other. When he fumbled to unhook my mother's beads, I laid my hand over his.

"Talk to me, *Shicheii*. Please... Why are you so upset?"

My grandfather waited for Mr. Mayhem to climb the stairs with Poe. From the top tread, he said, "The hunt starts when the moon is high." Seconds later, his bedroom door clicked shut.

"What hunt? What's happening?"

Shicheii ducked to peer out the window at the moon. "We have little time."

"Time for what?"

My face he cupped in warm hands. "Remember how much I love you, Mourning Dove."

"*Shicheii*, you're scaring me. Please tell me what's happening."

"Mister Mayhem will walk down those stairs, not Cheveyo, and I need you to prepare for that."

What the fuck did that mean? "Okay."

"It's not okay. You, my sweet child, are his prey, and he will never stop hunting you. Never."

It finally dawned on me. "Yeah, but he won't kill me or nothin'. It's just a training exercise."

Shicheii rocked an emphatic no. "It is not just a training exercise. Cheveyo would be remiss in his duties if he didn't discover your weaknesses, or how you'll react in hand-to-hand combat. I know how much you admire him, child, but Cheveyo will not be in the woods with you. The Mister Mayhem persona will, and he is your enemy tonight, along with every other creature out there."

Fuck. And now, my grandfather pissed him off.

With a fresh canvas from which to work, my grandfather painted. "With this paint, I will transform."

I repeated, "With this paint, I will transform."

"A rebirth, with new responsibilities, new obligations, new relationships."

Again, I echoed his words.

As he finger-swiped a wide band of black from in front of one ear, across my eyes to the opposite ear and covered my forehead to the scalp line, he sang a blessing in Athabaskan. Some words I recognized, some I didn't, but it didn't matter. Energy oozed from his touch, sheer power surging within me.

The lower half of my face he painted white, with streaks of white on my forehead that he crossed out with a blue thunderbolt. From the center of each eye, he swiped two fingers of red straight down, then curved out around my mouth, with four single red lines from my bottom lip down and under my chin.

In the hand-mirror, a total bad ass stared back at me.

One deep line of blue he drew from the bridge of my nose to my chin. Down my arms, he zigzagged our family's symbols and touched up my Spirit Animals on each hand. His thumb dipped into the yellow, and my breath halted as he pressed it between my eyes—a warning from my grandfather to Mr. Mayhem that I didn't totally understand. Felt like something along the lines of, "She's ready to die in battle, but if she does, I'll hunt you down."

Shicheii brushed out my hair. Smoothed back my bangs and around my face into one long braid, resting on the back length.

"Come, child." He grabbed my hand and led me out to the porch, scuttling down the stairs. Stashed around the side of the cabin, he'd hidden his bow and quiver full of arrows. "Remember what I taught you?"

"Yeah, but my aim sucks, *Shicheii*. I'm not ready."

"Cheveyo thinks you are, so you are. I need you to believe that, Mourning Dove." Quick glimpse of the moon. "We're running out of time. This weapon will save your life. Use it."

"Will Mister Mayhem have weapons?"

"I'll try to talk him out of it, but he won't need a weapon. If he finds you, he'll ambush you—up close and personal."

Gulp.

"Keep him at a distance with the bow, child. You cannot hesitate before releasing the next arrow."

"What if I hit him?"

My grandfather grinned, then caught himself. "You won't hit him."

"Then why gimme this, *Shicheii*?"

"Because you need some sort of protection. Mister Mayhem will not be the only predator out there. Black bear, coyote, mountain lion, moose, even a frightened buck could gain the advantage if you are unarmed. When hiding low to the ground, be mindful of porcupine, raccoon, fisher cat, bobcat—mostly nonlethal to humans, but you certainly wouldn't want to scuffle with one. If you corner any animal, they will fight you, and you will need to defend yourself."

Nerves sizzled beneath my skin as *Shicheii* checked the moon again. "We ran out of time earlier today, but briefly, if you must fight a mountain lion, there are a few ways to win. First, if you can get behind the animal"—he demonstrated on me—"wrap your right arm around its neck like this, with its head in the curve of your elbow. Latch on to your left bicep with your right hand, your left hand on the back of the cougar's neck, and lock it in. Hold on as tightly as you can and don't let go until you've neutralized the threat."

Shicheii spun me around and snapped a thick leather wristband around my left wrist, tying it down with sinew for added protection. From what, I had no idea, my mind flooded with adrenaline.

"During the scuffle, if you end up on the bottom"—without warning, he pulled me to the ground and rolled me on top of him—"manage the distance by hugging the animal's neck in a backward chokehold. Slide your left arm under the cougar's chin like this and anchor with your right hand, fingers gripped to your wristband. Extend both arms to create distance, but do not let go of that wristband. This will neutralize the bite and put the mountain lion to sleep." He rolled me back to my feet. "Now, and this is important, if the animal maintains a bite on the descent to the ground, the distant chokehold will not work. But don't panic."

Don't panic with its teeth sinking into my flesh? Sure, no problem. Not.

"Slip out of your halter," he said like it's perfectly natural to whip off my top while a mountain lion is gnawing on my arm, "wrap the buckskin around the cougar's neck twice, using your knee to hold the material in place while you pull. The animal should fall unconscious within six to ten seconds, and that's when you'll make your escape. Questions?"

What the fuck had I gotten myself into? "Will those same moves work on a black bear?"

"No." Another glimpse of the moon, rising higher by the second. "The best defense is to stand tall and face the bear. Never, ever run away. If you act like prey, you will become prey. Instead, make yourself appear larger by spreading your arms, waving your arms, acting as humanly as possible. Most bears avoid fighting humans. Yelling also works—black bears dislike startling noises—but keep in mind, you will give away your location. If the bear huffs or stomps the ground, it's getting ready to attack. Use your bow and arrows, firing one right after another."

Oh, man, this hunt sounded more and more terrifying by the second. "I really wish we had time to practice these moves, *Shicheii*."

"I may not be with you in body, my love, but I will be there in spirit." He stroked the crown of my head. "Stay grounded by achieving and maintaining *hozho*. Shall we pray before you go?"

"Absolutely. I need all the help I can get."

"O Great Spirit, whose voice I hear in the winds, I come to you as one of your many children."

Staring up at the sky, I echoed his words.

"I need your strength and your wisdom. Make me strong, not to be superior to my brothers and sisters, but to fight my greatest enemy—myself."

After repeating the prayer, I embraced my grandfather—a hug to last a lifetime in case I died out there—then pulled out of his arms. "I'm ready."

A sad smile toyed with his lips. "Yes, you are, Mourning Dove."

"Love you." I jogged into the forest with only the moon to guide me. With my grandfather's bow in hand and a stiff leather quiver slung on my back, I traveled deep into thick wooded terrain.

Please don't let me run into a feral predator. Or worse, a feral Mayhem.

Chapter 12
*"And while I stood there, I saw more than I can tell
and I understood more than I saw,
for I was seeing in a sacred manner the shapes of all
things in the spirit, and the shape of all shapes as they
must live together like one being."*
—Black Elk, Oglala Lakota

11:00 p.m.

In the master suite's full-length mirror, Mayhem added the finishing touches to his face paint—a shockingly red handprint covering his mouth and chin with four straight fingers extended across one cheek, a stiff thumb on the other. He tied crow feathers into the length of his hair, quills pointed at the sky, the ends masked by sinew, and crossed two eagle feathers with one from Spirit Crow, fastened at the crown behind an upright roach.

On his bare chest and arms, he painted one side black, one side red, yellow thumbprints dotting his collarbones. Another handprint in black grabbed the red shoulder and the half-red/half-black thunderbolt across his stomach represented Thunderbird for power and speed. In white on his black forearm, he drew the Sun and Earth symbols for harmony, balance of spirit, and the Natural World. Holes from the birdshot pellets dotted the side of his neck, down the red arm, and across his back, adding texture to help him blend into the environment.

When Mayhem strode down the stairs with Poe perched on one shoulder, his bill and plumage streaked with red, Jacy Lee was leaning against the kitchen island, arms crossed on his chest.

"You should blend well with the muted shades of striped charcoal on your face," he said, avoiding the subject he truly wished to broach.

Mayhem slung his quiver on his back. "That's the idea."

"The handprint across the mouth is a bit much."

"Why? I earned it."

"That you did, Cheveyo. No one can take that away from you." After Mayhem grabbed his bow from the corner of the living room, he reached for the doorhandle.

Jacy Lee stopped him with, "We both know you don't need weapons to defeat her."

Without turning around, he huffed out a breath. "You are not helping your granddaughter by ambushing me on my way out the door. Now, if there's nothing else..."

"Please don't hurt her, Cheveyo. *Please...*" he begged. "She's the only family I have left."

A strike to the gut caved his stomach, but he did not respond. Nor could he face his lifelong friend. Instead, he strode out to the porch then down the stairs. To his faithful companion, he hushed, "Stay close."

Poe leaped off his shoulder, flying inches above Dad as he sprinted past the enhanced Sacred Fire, the smoke releasing birchwood and oak into the mild summer air. Partway into the forest, he extended his forearm. Once his taloned soldier landed, Mayhem closed his eyes. Motionless, all his senses absorbed the environment—attuned to every anomaly that did not belong. Great Horned Owls hooted and barked. Brown bats snaked around trees, leathery wings flapping with vigilance. Paws struck the earth, prey animals scuttling through flora.

Mind-mapping a visual sketch of the landscape, he opened his eyes. Poe pointed one foot toward the South end of the property, and Mayhem acknowledged with a quick dip of the chin. Bow in hand, he hugged the shadows. Scaled a tree to observe from a higher vantage point. Up high, he squatted, his moccasins planing the limb of a proud oak, thick branches obscuring his body from view.

Unlike last time, the feisty feline did not reveal her presence right away. Brava, Cat.

Back on the forest floor, the faint whisper of baby powder rode a gentle breeze. By not using all-natural hygiene products, Shawnee's scent acted as a beacon to her precise location. As he crept closer, Poe clawed into his bare shoulder. Mayhem stopped, raised the bow. One hand reached over his shoulder, retrieving an arrow from the quiver.

When he drew back the bowstring, Shawnee vanished.

He had to hand it to Jacy Lee. The addition of red, black, and white face paint distorted the outline of a human face and helped her blend into the forest. To Shawnee's credit, she'd learned to utilize all her enhancements for better concealment.

The moment Mayhem scaled a nearby tree, an arrow struck the trunk beneath him. Bold move on her part. Too bad she lacked the skill to follow through. Nonetheless, her confidence pleased him.

Because Shawnee was a novice, the arrival of an arrow alluded to her close proximity. The forest floor did not reveal her hiding spot right away. Once he skimmed the treetops, however, there she squatted, her back braced to the trunk, the canopy above her casting shadows in the moonlight. Before she realized he'd found her, he climbed down. Mid-sprint in her direction, he raised the bow—drew back the razor-tipped arrow—vision deadlocked on his prey.

Fired.

See you soon, Cautious Cat.

Chapter 13

11:45 p.m.

An arrow whizzed by my head, missed slashing open my cheek by an inch or two, anchoring my hair to the tree. The razor-like tip was so embedded in bark I couldn't pull it out. To escape, I ripped the strands from my scalp before Mr. Mayhem ambushed me. Fleeing the area, I swerved around trees, hopping dead timber, guided only by the moon. The instinctual need to survive propelled me up the hillside, my hands and feet groping for traction, loose stones tumbling down the rocky terrain.

At the peak, I stopped, the familiar view flattening a hand over my heart. Did I blow *Shicheii's* dry painting into the wind here after Spirit Crow's ceremonial? Pretty sure, yeah. Why'd Mr. Mayhem led me here that day? Did this area hold some special significance for him?

With an Apache warrior hot on my trail, I didn't have time to mull over all the angles, so I slid down the other side of the hill, ultimately landing in a thorny brush patch, burrs velcroed to the ends of my hair and buckskin pants.

An arrow clipped the side of my abs, and I slapped a hand over the wound, blood leaking through my fingers. I whirled around but couldn't find Mr. Mayhem in the trickles of moonlight. Ducked low, I backed out of the brush, my feet clomping through thick overgrowth.

Behind me, a presence loomed. Without turning around, I couldn't distinguish human from animal. Didn't matter. Someone viewed me as prey. To avoid an attack, I sprinted across a well-worn animal trail, my moccasins cushioned by matted vegetation. Once

I got far enough away, I stopped, breath trapped somewhere in my chest. I chanced a peek over my shoulder.

Nothing but darkness. Thank God.

With a deep exhale, I faced front. A sharp intake of air sucked through my teeth as I froze, eyes agape. An enormous mountain lion stood ten feet away, one massive paw suspended mid-step, an icy stare deadlocked on me. All of *Shicheii's* instructions jumbled together. Did he say to wave my arms for mountain lions or black bear? Wait. This morning in the pond Mr. Mayhem told me not to move.

"Nice kitty." I froze, my moccasins rooted to the soil. Those words didn't soothe him one bit. In fact, I think I pissed him off. Snarling, the cougar lunged, claws and teeth strobe-lighting before my eyes as we tumbled across the animal trail. Flat on my back, I tried to block another attack, both hands wedged under his chin to create distance, but my strength waned, elbows buckling under such a powerful animal.

Sharp claws slashed into my flesh, my arms and upper chest riddled with pain. The attack was so violent, so sudden and frenzied, panic thrashed at my ears. I grabbed the cougar's throat in my left hand, threw punches with my right. Nothing worked. Sharp fangs lowered closer and closer to my face, rancid hot breath inches from my nose, saliva dripping down my chin. Memories of my life flashed before my eyes. And I knew, deep in my gut, I'd die out here, my mangled body stuffed in a tree like Underwood.

I love you, Shicheii.

When I couldn't hold him back another second, a red arm slid under the cougar's neck and yanked him off me. Piercing gray eyes shown through the creepiest face paint as Mr. Mayhem held the mountain lion in a chokehold. High on adrenaline, I scrambled to my feet. Swiped the bow off the ground and took off in the opposite direction, my arms and upper chest bathed in warm blood. My blood.

Within seconds, arrows whizzed through my peripheral. First the right, then left. The speed and consistency blasted cool air across both cheeks, and I braced for at least one razor-sharp tip to sever my spinal column. Didn't matter. If I stopped, I'd have to fight Mr. Mayhem, too.

Once I veered into heavily wooded terrain, I banged a quick right, hit the ground, and rolled under a pine tree, piling up leaf litter to hide behind. Still and silent, my breath shallowed. The forest relaxed into its normal rhythm, its pulse hastened only by moccasins padding around the conifer.

Please don't let him find me.

Unbreakable hands gripped my ankles, dragging me into the open. I flipped over and kicked, but he ducked out of the way. All his weight bared down on me, his legs straddling my hips, my arms pinned above my head.

Leaning closer, he cocked his head—an intense stare into my soul—and whispered, "Now what will she do?"

I struggled to break free, but he was too strong. An animalistic roar bellowed from somewhere deep inside me, and he startled for a hot second. Long enough for me to wiggle one arm free. I latched onto his throat, and he backhanded my forearm like swishing dandelion dust away from his face. Somehow, he flipped me over, my bare stomach pressed against sticky pine needles. The red arm slipped around my neck, his rock-solid grip squeezing the life out of me.

Foggy images emerged—crow wings, silky hair, a red handprint—but the quick flashes faded fast as I surrendered to the darkness.

Tuesday, 2 a.m.

In my head, my grandfather called for me.

Mourning Dove, time to wake, child.

"*Shicheii?*"

Mr. Mayhem's deep, gravelly voice said, "No."

When I dragged open my eyelids, I lay across his lap, with Poe standing dead-center on my chest—talons clawed around one of my mom's wooden beads—head cocked, beady eyes evaluating my chances of survival.

Above us, the canopy of leaves disoriented me. "Where am I?"

"High off the ground. Do not move until you've regained clarity."

"You didn't kill me?"

Through the face paint his brow furrowed. "Why would I kill you, Cat?"

"But *Shicheii* said—"

"If you did not fear for your life, the training exercise would lose its authenticity. And you would not have fought as hard as you did."

Confusion squinted my eyes. "*Shicheii* lied to me?"

"Never have we lied to you. In all fairness, however, we may have misled you."

My fingers felt my side for blood. "But you cut me."

"Had you not swerved, that arrow would never have nipped you. I'm much more concerned about the injuries from the cougar. Hence why I ended the exercise."

"Did ya have to choke me out? I'm pretty sure if you said something like—oh, I dunno—'Are you okay?' I woulda gotten the hint."

"Not necessarily. The massive surge of adrenaline skewed all rational thought. Had I asked about your wellbeing, you may have thought I was trying to trick you, and rightfully so. Knocking you out was the only way I could protect you." He slid one hand under the back of my head, and Poe flew up to the branch above me. "Do you still feel lightheaded?"

"Not really," I lied. "I think I can sit up."

"Go slow." Once he helped me rise, he slid to the side so I wouldn't be sitting on his lap. "If you're steady enough, we really should head back. Your grandfather's expecting us. He wants to treat your wounds."

"Whaddaya mean? *Shicheii* knows about the mountain lion? Was he here?"

Instead of answering my questions, he climbed down the tree.

Guess that's my cue to follow. And so, I did. As soon as my moccasins struck the soil, I swiveled left, right, and behind me, scanning the forest floor. "Oh, no—I lost *Shicheii's* bow and quiver."

Rather than panic, Mr. Mayhem hooked an arm for me to follow. Around the back of a nearby tree, two bows and two quivers hung from a branch, and he slung all four on his back. Good thing, too, because deep muscle pain seared my bloody arms, and I could barely lift them, never mind carry anything.

"Cat?" He stopped me. "You seem to be struggling. Can you walk?"

"I dunno. Everything hurts. Not sure how much farther I can go."

"Not to worry, Mourning Dove. I've got you." Mr. Mayhem swept me into his arms, and I laid my head on his shoulder, with no fight left inside me. "Rest. You've endured more than most tonight."

It's true. I didn't even have enough energy to glare at Poe when he landed on his father's shoulder. As he carried me, I said, "Did I pass the exercise?"

"Shh..." Through the forest he strode, my legs dangling over one arm. "Don't worry about that now."

"But... did I?"

"We'll discuss your performance later. Now, quiet please. In case it slipped your mind, we are not alone in these woods."

Slipped my mind? Fat chance of that. My body ached all over, my breath laboring more and more, and I gulped the mild summer air.

For the rest of the walk back, we traveled in silence.

Flames bathed the treetops in a fiery glow as he carried me into the yard. *Shicheii* stood at the door of a sweat lodge, tossing corn pollen into the Sacred Fire.

As Mr. Mayhem approached, my grandfather whirled around, his forehead rutted with concern. "Fear not, Jacy Lee. She's weak but alert."

"Thank you for protecting her, Cheveyo. I should never have doubted you, nor ambushed you earlier. Please accept my sincerest apologies."

"Already forgotten, my friend." Mr. Mayhem ducked under the doorway, lowered me onto the tribal blanket inside, then reached for my protection jewelry. "I'll keep these safe for you."

"Thanks." After unhooking my turquoise armband, Apache Tears, and leather wristband, he un-strapped my mom's beads. "Can I ask you somethin'?"

He sat back on folded legs. "Of course."

"Why did *Shicheii* build the sweat lodge? He foresaw what was gonna happen out there, huh? That's why he looked so scared before I left."

Grinning through the face paint—still creepy as hell, by the way—he offered a single nod. "I realize this is a lot to take in. Our job, however, is not to question your grandfather's abilities but to trust his connection to the Holy Ones. Every move he makes has purpose, every thought focused on how to benefit us."

Did he answer my question? "So, he did know about the mountain lion?"

"If he did, he put his trust in you to handle it. Now, let's do the same for him."

"Yeah, you're right."

"Please save any other questions for later. We must maintain a clear and opened mind during the sweat for the healing to take place." He passed me a towel before rising. "Halter can stay, but you may overheat in pants. I'll give you some privacy."

"Wait—"

Long, windswept hair dangled when he gazed down at me. "Yes, Cat?"

"I thought clothes could melt to your skin."

"The halter top is buckskin, nature's material. You'll be fine. Unless you prefer a more natural experience?"

"Uh, nope, I'm good."

Chuckling, he ducked under the doorway and lowered the blankets over the opening.

With the towel kinda sorta draped over my lap, I slid off my moccasin boots and dropped trou, praying to all that's holy that no one would enter till I knotted the towel around my waist. Not that they could see much anyway. Pitch blackness blanketed the inside with the door shut and no lava rocks burning in the pit yet. Still, I missed my robe, but *Shicheii* couldn't work on my injuries with it on. And I sure as hell wasn't going topless.

A few minutes later, my grandfather poked his head inside. "Are you ready to begin, Mourning Dove?"

"Yes, *Shicheii*, but I don't think I can get up to pray with you."

"Rest easy, child. You only job is to heal." His head disappeared for a hot second. "We're ready, Cheveyo."

Outside the door, Mr. Mayhem said, "Okie doke. I'll carry in the Grandfathers."

"Thank you." *Shicheii* entered, circled the inner perimeter of the sweat lodge, then prayed at the altar before kneeling in front of me. "Lay back, my love. The body requires rest to heal."

And so, I did. The minute the back of my head cradled into the blanket, my eyelids rolled closed. A warm washcloth cleaned my face, upper chest, and arms, and I let go, surrendering to my grandfather's medicinal, spiritual power. Because of his gentle touch, I wasn't sure how long he washed debris out of each wound, or what herbal remedies he used.

In Athabaskan, *Shicheii* sang to the Holy Ones while Mr. Mayhem thrummed the ox-skin drum, the steady beat pulsing through me, my two protectors praying their hearts out, blessings raining down on me, healing me from the inside out.

A cool blast of air struck the top of my head, but I kept my eyes closed. Moments later, another blast of coolness, then a thud—Mr. Mayhem adding seven more Grandfathers to the pit, one by one, while *Shicheii* blessed each lava rock with traditional medicine of sage, Piñon needles, and cedar, the herbal blend wafting through the air.

When Mr. Mayhem lowered the door for the last time, sweltering heat filled the lodge. Water sizzled—*Shicheii* splashing the Grandfathers to create a healing steam—and my skin tingled all over from its indescribable power.

Next, he brewed a concoction then passed me the bowl. "Drink this, child."

"What is it?"

"Healing medicine. It cures. Inhale it, drink it—it makes you well."

I pressed the rim to my lips and sipped. A familiar warm liquid coated my tongue, but I couldn't identify it. Not quite as delicious as *Shicheii's* wild tea, but with a much stronger punch. The last time I drank a similar medicine it knocked me out. Didn't matter. I sucked down every drop.

Within seconds, their two silhouettes blurred, my mind light and airy. Spirit Crow emerged through the darkness. Encircled by a piercing white halo, her wings fluttered in slow motion. When I reached for her—my arm limp, heavy—the lodge whirled for a few moments, my ears ringing, and then... blackness.

Hours later, Spirit Crow held a strip of crispy bacon under my nose, and I roused on the couch in the living room, my entire body cocooned in the tribal blanket, with only my face exposed. Without a word, I opened my mouth, and she gently dropped bacon on my tongue.

"Thank you," my hoarse voice choked out.

Spirit Crow hopped down to the coffee table. She returned with a plastic spoonful of cheesy eggs, and I reopened my mouth. As I chewed, she nuzzled her feathery cheek against mine.

When I swallowed, I kissed the side of her face. "I love you more."

"Doubtful," Mr. Mayhem said from the kitchen table. "Her unconditional love knows no limits."

Spirit Crow continued to hop down to the plate on the coffee table, then back up, her delicate feet standing on my chest while she fed me like the tenderest of mothers. No matter how many times I tried to convince her I could manage, she remained steadfast in her routine. When she returned with a buttery English muffin clamped in her bill, she held the end while I bit into the other side.

"You're amazing." I giggled. "Cheyenne's lucky to have a mom like you."

"Your mother and grandmother were the same way, Mourning Dove." My grandfather's loving tone warmed my insides, but the back of the couch blocked my view of him. "They both loved doting on you. Remember?"

"Not really, no. I only get flashes of my early childhood. Can you help me remember, *Shicheii*?"

"I'd be honored to, my sweet child."

Spirit Crow leaned in with the English muffin again, and I bit in, cheeking the bite to speak. "Did I call my grandmother *Nokomis* like Jude?"

"No, honey. They raised Cheyenne in Chippewa tradition to honor her beautiful mother, and Cheyenne did the same for Jude. The Diné calls one's maternal grandmother *Shimásání*."

"*Shicheii* and *Shimásání*. Love that."

He and Mr. Mayhem both chuckled, forks scraping against their plates. "Cheveyo, since Mourning Dove broached the subject of grandmothers, perhaps you'd like to share the Chippewa Legend of the Dreamcatcher? Might be good for her to learn about other cultures, and I'm sure Spirit Crow would enjoy hearing the story again."

"All right, then." Mr. Mayhem half-sat on the back of the couch, his damp hair pulled back in a low braid. "A spider was quietly spinning his web beside the sleeping space of Nokomis, the Grandmother. Each day, Nokomis watched the spider at work, quietly spinning away. One day, as she was watching him, her grandson came in. 'Nokomis,' he shouted, glancing at the spider. He stomped over, picked up a shoe, then went to hit the spider. 'No, Keegwa,' the old lady whispered. 'Don't hurt him.' The little boy asked, 'Nokomis, why do you protect the spider?'"

Listening intently, Spirit Crow climbed up to perch on his shoulder.

"The old lady smiled but did not answer. When the boy left, the spider went to the old woman and thanked her for saving his life. He said to her, 'For many days, you have watched me spin and weave my web. You have admired my work. In return for saving my life, I will give you a gift.' He smiled his special spider smile and moved away, spinning as he went. Soon, the moon glistened on a magical silvery web gently swaying in the window. 'See how I spin?' he said. 'See and learn, for each web will ensnare bad dreams. Only pleasant dreams will pass through the small hole. This is my gift to you. Use it so you will only remember good dreams. The bad dreams will become hopelessly entangled in the web.'"

He kissed Spirit Crow's cheek. "When she and I tucked little ones in bed, we'd say, 'Sleep well, sweet child. Don't worry your head. Your Dream Catcher is humming above your bed. Listen so softly, I know you can hear the tone of beyond close to your ear. Love is alive and living inside you, beyond all your troubles, where good dreams are true.'"

Spirit Crow fluttered back down to me, and my chest heaved, the precious life they lost laid out before me, tears trickling out the sides of my eyes. "That may be the most beautiful story I've ever heard."

Visibly overcome, Mr. Mayhem flashed a sad smile before strolling back into the kitchen.

From the table, my grandfather said, "How are you feeling, my love?"

"Stronger." I opened my mouth for more food, and Spirit Crow dropped a cube of cantaloupe on my tongue. "Don't you wanna eat?" I said to her. "You're still healing, too."

"Mourning Dove's right." *Shicheii* bustled over and extended his arm for Spirit Crow, but rather than climb aboard, she laid another bacon strip in my mouth. "Come, child. I fixed you a plate next to Poe. You cannot heal by skipping meals."

"I'm okay," I reassured her. "Seriously, I feel much better."

With one last stare into my eyes, into my soul, she rubbed her feathery cheek against mine before stepping on her human perch.

"Hey, *Shicheii*, before you go, can you loosen the blanket so I can get out of this cocoon thingy?"

As he strolled around the couch, he explained, "Swaddling helps reduce pain, stress, anxiety, and stiff muscles while improving sleep, relaxation, and weightlessness."

"Wow." *Mind. Blown.* "Is that why you guys always wrap me up like a mummy?"

Dimples dotted both cheeks as he freed me. "I wouldn't say we *always* swaddle you, but yes, it's done for your benefit. Do you need help to sit up?"

"I think I'm good. Thank you." Holding the wrapped blanket to my chest, my arms and upper chest coated in *Shicheii's* special medicine of coconut oil, ground cranberries, and whatever else he added in the spiritual moments of prayer and song, I swung my legs to the floor. Apparently, the slice from the arrow wasn't deep enough to worry him, because it didn't feel like he added medicine to the wound. But the skin sealed closed, so maybe he did.

Last weekend, when he treated Mr. Mayhem's birdshot wounds, my grandfather explained how cranberries were super high in vitamin C and acidity, reduced inflammation, and warded off bacteria. Combined with coconut oil, which reduced pain, itching, redness, and swelling, the two formed a strong protective barrier between the affected area and outside contaminants.

Although Mr. Mayhem's injuries hadn't totally healed yet, the pellet wounds looked much less raw and open, yellowish-purple bruising still noticeable around each hole. If he could carry on after being shot, I sure as hell couldn't milk my claw marks for long. The stinging wasn't nearly as bad, nor was the deep tissue and muscle pain. I still had trouble wrapping my mind around *Shicheii's* healing power, but no one could deny its existence. My grandfather possessed skills that soared beyond all rational comprehension. And man, could he cook.

After shoveling in the rest of my breakfast, I rose to my bare feet. With a quick peek under my blanket, my gaze shot into the kitchen. "What am I wearing?"

At the sink, my grandfather dunked dirty plates into soapy water, Poe standing on the edge to ensure he didn't toss out any edible scraps. "It's a traditional cotton skirt. Do you like it?"

"That's not the point, *Shicheii*. Why am I wearing it?"

"If I may interject a moment..." Mr. Mayhem cleared the rest of the table. "Your grandfather had difficulty swaddling you with the towel in place. So, he slipped a cotton skirt around your waist before removing it. At no time were you exposed."

"Oh." I lowered the blanket. "Thanks, *Shicheii*."

"My pleasure, honey. We all know how bashful you are."

"I'm not bashful. I just don't think it's appropriate to be naked in front of my family."

"Understood." *Shicheii*'s nose crinkled, his gaze traveling to his lifelong friend. "Adorable, isn't she?"

"When she wants to be, she is." Mr. Mayhem passed me the PC. "Since you're feeling better, could you please pull up the property map of Old Cherry Mountain Road?"

"Cheveyo, no work today. Please. She needs rest."

"It's fine, *Shicheii*. If he can work after getting shot, I can't let a mountain lion attack stop me." My fingers raced across the keyboard. "I bookmarked it, so gimme... one... sec... Here it is."

When I showed my mentor the screen, he leaned in. "Looks like one person owns all the land around the compound. Interesting." He pointed at the map. "See that lot number? Use it to run a search in Carroll's property records. That should give us the landowner's name."

And so, I did. "Oh, my God." My widened gaze shot to Mr. Mayhem. "Killzme Corp. holds the deed. Does that mean Worthington owns the land?"

Killzme Freight was the name on the shipping container where he and I found live eagles, ravens, falcons, and various other majestic animals caged and ready for transport to God knows where.

"Not necessarily. Misters Worthington, Rothschild, and Underwood definitely had their filthy hands in it, but I bet Killzme Corporation is a shell company for the entire subsection of the organization. Perhaps for the primary organization, as well."

"Then what's our next move?"

"Well, shell companies remain intentionally vague about their shareholders, who receive anonymity from prosecution in exchange for funding day-to-day operations." He paused, probably mulling over next steps. "Let's circle back to that. We still need a live feed of the compound, as it's the safest option to see what we are dealing with. Thus, I shall work on segregating one poacher to share his location with us. Monitor the laptop. I'll text once I retrieve his phone. If you could please dig into the Killzme Corporation while you're waiting, your research may benefit us as well."

"Whaddaya mean, like, you want me to stay here?" I jolted to my bare feet. "If you're goin' back to the compound, so am I."

"No, Mourning Dove." My grandfather's firm tone prevented me from leaving. "You need rest."

"You have been through a lot, Cat."

"*Shicheii*, please... I have to see this through. What if I promised to stay in the car?"

"Her computer skills on site would be helpful, Jacy Lee."

Both of us faced my grandfather, waiting for his decision. *Shicheii* dried his wet hands on the dishcloth then strode over to me. To evaluate my health, he framed my face in his palms. "You won't leave the vehicle?"

Shit. That's a direct question. I couldn't lie. "Not unless he needs my help."

"Cheveyo never *needs* help with these types of things. He may find it easier to work with you, but need? No."

Mr. Mayhem must've read the room—my pout and impending sulk—because he said, "*Au contraire*, old friend. Your granddaughter comes in handy from time to time."

"Gee, thanks. Glad I"—I flashed air quotes—"come in handy."

Slight head shake. "Cat, once again, you have missed the point. I am on your side."

"Oh." I stared at the floor. "My bad."

"Actually, Jacy Lee, she cannot promise to remain in the Caddy. It's important for her to acclimate to the wolves' environment. Only then will she feel comfortable enough to transverse within it. Her training cannot cease because of injury. Need I remind you lives are at stake?"

"Mourning Dove?" With one finger, *Shicheii* raised my chin. "Do you promise to listen to your body?"

"Yes."

After a pause that lasted ten years, his soulful dark eyes stared deep into mine. "And if you need to rest, you'll do so?"

"Yes, *Shicheii*."

"All right, then." He turned back to his lifelong friend. "You will keep me informed?"

"I will."

"Honey, I'd like to apply another coat to your wounds before you go." Over his shoulder, he said, "You could also benefit from another layer of medicine, Cheveyo."

"As you wish, my friend."

Not pleased with our decision to leave, *Shicheii* bustled into the kitchen to whip up more medicine.

To get Mr. Mayhem's attention, I jutted my chin. "Since he's gonna be awhile, I'll jump in the shower."

"Ah, ah, ah. Aren't you forgetting something?"

"I don't think so. Am I?"

"Your morning run to strengthen endurance."

Seriously? "But I was just attacked by a mountain lion."

The shoulders half-shrugged. "And?"

"And?" *What did I have to do to get a day off? Die?* I could barely comprehend his reaction. In hindsight, he didn't slow down after getting shot. But still... some concern would've been nice. "What if he finds me and kills me?"

Mr. Mayhem crossed his arms. "Do you plan to avoid all wooded landscapes from here on out?"

"Obviously, I'm not sayin' that."

"Then I don't see the problem. Would you like me to accompany you this morning?"

Hell yeah. "Could ya?"

Heavy sigh. "As you wish." His gaze traveled down to my bare feet. "I put your moccasins and protection jewelry in your room. I'll meet you on the porch in five."

This time, I better ace the test or he might wonder why he's taking the time to mentor me. Maybe, just maybe, with deep claw marks scarring my upper chest and arms—my weeping angel tattoo sliced in half—he'd let me skip the mouthful of water.

Hey, a girl could dream.

Chapter 14
*"When you arise in the morning, give thanks
for the food and for the joy of living.
If you see no reason for giving thanks,
the fault lies only in yourself."*
—Chief Tecumseh

10:40 a.m.

When Shawnee strode onto the deck in her bloodstained buckskin pants and halter, she wore the Apache Tears and stuck out her arm to show off the turquoise armband. "For protection from the mountain lion." Her fingers brushed across the gemstone-and-bone choker. "To remind me who I'm running for."

He smiled inside. "Are you frightened?"

"Maybe a little."

"Sit with me, please." He settled on the top stair, and Shawnee sat beside him. "Changing Woman gave the Apache—One Walks Around You Clan—Cougar as their symbol of protection and healing. Ceremonies and songs tell of the animal's medicinal powers. One Walks Around You Clan sent Cougar to guard Turquoise Girl on Mount Taylor in the South. So, you see? You needn't fear the cougar. Its eyes see evil in the darkness. They're guardians of our People, not foes."

Forehead rutted, she scratched her cheek. "Then why'd he attack me?"

"Because that specific animal read you as a threat. Did you show him respect, or did you panic?"

Her gaze fell to her lap. "Panicked, probably."

"Then you've answered your own question." Mayhem patted her knee. "Let's go." He swiped the water bottle off the railing and strode into the yard, with Shawnee following close behind. "Ready?"

When she opened her mouth, he passed her the bottle, allowing her to choose the amount of water she'd hold. Instead of going easy on herself, she squirted a large mouthful. Quite a bit more than he would've given her.

After gently stroking her Apache Tears, the heartbreaking history whirling through his mind, he sprinted for the wood line. Halfway to the hill, he glanced back. Shawnee struggled with the over-production of mucus. In her defense, nose-breathing wasn't an easy skill to master.

When he was a young boy, he trained for war, even though the war ended decades before. He and the other boys ran up hillsides with mouthfuls of water to learn how to breathe through the nose—endurance strengthening needed for raids. They also engaged in rough wrestling games and mock battles. Relatives taught the geography, attributes, and sanctity of their surroundings. The morning began with a cold dunk in the river, even if they had to break the ice barrier to penetrate the water.

Once a young man felt ready, he began the novice warrior complex of his first four raids, permeated with religious beliefs and rituals. Only after succeeding at this first raid did he receive a war shaman. The war shaman gave him a drinking tube, a scratcher, and a special war cap which, unlike mature warriors, did not bestow spiritual power. Nonetheless, the apprentice warrior remained sacred and identified with their cultural hero, Child of the Water.

Thus, even though Shawnee believed he was hard on her, she had it easy compared to his training.

At the peak of the hill, he stopped, waiting for her to struggle to the top. "Did you swallow the water?"

In front of him, her head wagged from side to side.

"Do you want to?"

Another no.

"Good." He took off down the hill, and Shawnee raced after him.

Partway down, she lost her footing and sailed through the air, water spraying from her mouth as her chest slammed the earth, sliding down the hillside on her bare stomach.

Mayhem cringed. She may not have mastered stealth, but the girl had grit, spunk, and could take a beating.

As he hustled over to assist her, she raised a shaky hand. "I'm okay." She crawled to her feet. "Spit my water out, dammit."

The grin he forced down. "I noticed that."

"Means I failed again, right?"

"You did not complete the exercise. Correct." To raise her spirits, he said, "However, don't be afraid to fail. Failure is how we learn, how we grow, how we overcome. Do you know how many times I failed this exercise?"

She dusted off her pants and stomach. "None, probably."

"Hardly. I failed every single day for two straight weeks."

"Yeah, but you were just a kid."

"I'll tell you a little secret. It's easier for a child whose entire world is steeped in the warrior lifestyle. You've only recently discovered our culture, our way of life, and you're still learning where you fit. You will fail repeatedly and that, dearest Cat, is precisely how it should be."

"Thanks." She mumbled, "Still sucks, though."

Grinning, Mayhem climbed up the hillside, with Shawnee by his side.

Out of the blue, she grabbed his arm. "Remember when *Shicheii* had the vision about the man with the heart of ice?"

"I do."

"What made you think it was Rothschild?"

"Mister Rothschild was the one obsessed with my wife. Why do you ask?"

"I was just thinkin'. Maybe *Shicheii* saw Worthington. He's the one with his hands in everything."

"Unlikely." He gestured toward the path leading to the cabin. "At the time of his vision, Mister Worthington was already deceased."

"True." Veering with him through the trees, she hesitated. "What if we haven't found the ice man yet? Is that possible?"

"Hm. I hadn't considered that."

"*Shicheii* said this guy was the biggest threat to the Natural World, right?"

"He did. However, he also said he was a threat to Spirit Crow, and shortly thereafter, Mister Rothschild abducted her."

"I get that, but what if *Shicheii* envisioned a different guy?" A flat hand halted his response. "All I'm sayin' is, Rothschild's dead, so he's not a threat anymore. Yet the Natural World is still in grave danger. What if the crow hunt and the wolves are only two small jigsaw pieces of a much larger puzzle? We need to chop off the head of the snake—the head honcho who controls this organization. I think he's the man with the heart of ice, not Rothschild."

Interesting theory. The head of the organization could indeed be the one Jacy Lee saw in his vision—a man driven by greed, with no moral compass or appreciation of Mother Earth's delicate balance. Finding him was the biggest obstacle. He could live anywhere, even in a different country. Without more to go on, the man with a heart as cold and hard as ice might as well be a ghost.

Rather than share all his reservations, he steered her back on point. "Though I am not opposed to chopping off the head of the snake, as you say, we first need to free the Eastern Gray Wolves and stop the breeding of wolfdogs."

"Agreed."

"Impressive reasoning, however. Let me sit with it awhile."

"Think I should mention it to *Shicheii*?"

"Not yet. We don't want to influence his visions. He'll let us know if the man with the iced heart remains a threat." Regardless of Jacy Lee's future findings, Mr. Rothschild still targeted Spirit Crow. Thus, Mayhem had no choice but to end his life.

Once he and Shawnee reached the yard, Jacy Lee hustled over. Above his head, Spirit Crow and Poe engaged in aerial dance, each wingbeat in perfect harmony with one another. The outstanding display stole Mayhem's breath, his heart pattering faster and faster, his gaze transfixed on his beloveds.

Jacy Lee slung his arm around his granddaughter. "Are you all right, child?"

"How'd you—?" His warm smile stopped her cold. "Yeah, I'm good, but I spit out the water."

"Let me see if I can help." When he stopped, they stopped. "You're aware of the five common senses—touch, taste, smell, hearing, and sight—but our bodies have four other senses, as well. Close your eyes, Mourning Dove."

When Shawnee did as instructed, Jacy Lee spun her around several times. The moment she reopened her eyes, he told her to walk a straight line. Her feet were a sloppy mess.

"You're experiencing an overload of your vestibular sense. Receptors for your sense of balance alert you to the direction your body is moving in relation to gravity. By learning to be more aware of your vestibular sense, you'll gain greater control over your balance."

"You're blowing my mind right now, *Shicheii*."

He and Mayhem both chuckled.

"Close your eyes again and tell me where your right arm is."

"Huh?"

"Don't question an elder," Mayhem scolded. "Close your eyes."

And so, she did.

Jacy Lee said, "Where is your left leg?"

Shawnee patted her thigh. "Right here."

"Correct. You used your proprioception, or the sense of where your body is in space, to find your left leg. Now, if you had a neurological impairment like a stroke, visually you may need to check where your limbs are, so you don't get your fingers closed in a door."

"Wow."

"The third sense is called thermoception, your sense of temperature. Your body has receptors to help you sense hot and cold. While we link thermoception to our sense of touch, it is distinctive with its own set of receptors. Many of these receptors lay within your skin, but we also have receptors in our body that regulate body temperature. In fact, some people report losing their sense of cold after a lightning strike."

"Really? Wow." She gazed at her grandfather like he held all the answers to life's mysteries—beautiful to witness such admiration. "What's the fourth sense, *Shicheii*?"

"Pain. At first glance, it may seem to be an extension of touch, but your sense of pain is much more complex. Pain receptions run throughout your body, not only in your skin, but throughout your system as well. We have three different types of pain receptors. Mechanical receptors alert you to pain inflicted physically. Temperature pain receptors alert you to extreme heat and cold. Your own body's chemicals trigger chemical receptors. For example, when inflammation occurs, you may feel achy."

"That's exactly what I felt when the mountain lion attacked me. I could barely lift my arms, they hurt so much."

"I'm not surprised. Your nociception was on overload. If you had been cognizant of what was happening within your body, there were ways you could have controlled it."

She whirled toward Mayhem. "Is that how you handled being shot like it was no big deal?"

In return, he nodded. "Yes."

"Cheveyo has perfected the control over his entire body for many, many years. He's a finely tuned instrument, and a lot to live up to. However, neither he nor I expect you to learn any type of control overnight. I'm simply making you aware of these underutilized senses to help you navigate your vessel."

"Wow. I don't know what to say, except... wow. I had no idea."

Jacy Lee's gentle palm swept over the crown of her head. "Of course, you didn't. Why would you?"

Again, she regarded Mayhem. "Will you teach me how to gain control like you?"

"Baby steps, Cat."

"No, I know, but it'll be part of my training, right?"

"Tell you what." A smirk threatened to arch his lips. "Once you master balance, we'll discuss perfecting the other three senses."

"Ha, ha. Everyone's a comedian."

"Cheveyo makes a valid point, child. It's best to concentrate on one sense at a time." He locked her in a bear hug, pulled her away, then kissed her forehead. "Go take your shower. I'll fix you a nice cup of tea for when you get out."

"Love you, *Shicheii*."

After returning the sentiment, he waited for her to stroll into the cabin.

Mayhem sidled up next to Jacy Lee. "What's on your mind, old friend?"

"Has she mentioned Levaughn to you at all? I don't think she's returning his calls."

The question rocked him back on his heels. "That's her business, not ours. Perhaps this is her way of ending the relationship."

"With the silent treatment? That's not very nice. Would you mind...?"

Mayhem jerked away from him. "Meddling in her personal affairs? Jacy Lee, that is not my place. If you're so concerned about it, why don't you broach the subject with her?"

"You are the one who told me to loosen the reins a bit, and I am trying to honor your wishes."

"I meant, with her training, not her personal relationship." He released a loud exhale. "Why would you ask this of me?"

"Please, Cheveyo? She listens to you."

Begging was a low blow. Jacy Lee knew he could never refuse. "What do you hope to achieve with this line of questioning?"

"I simply want her to have a full and happy life."

"What if she does want to end the relationship with Detective Samuels? Will you honor her wishes and not intervene?"

"Of course."

Mayhem eyed him with reservation. "Then what? Will you push her to find another mate—one who *you* believe will make her happy?"

"We all need love, Cheveyo."

"I don't disagree, however, I barely survived Cheyenne's search for the ideal mate. Remember how stressed out I was? No one seemed good enough for my daughter."

"And yet, somehow, she found the perfect husband."

"Perfect?" He scoffed. "Hardly. He's passable at best. Did you see him at my wife's memorial?"

Jacy Lee mulled it over for a bit. "Now that you mention it, no."

"Correct." Cheyenne's sorry excuse for a husband claimed he had to work. The man owned his own business. However, he'd promised Kimi long ago he would never meddle in their daughter's marriage—a vow that wasn't easy to honor once the man skipped his mother-in-law's memorial. "Now, I understand the concern for your granddaughter, but I, dearest friend, want no part of reliving that experience with another emotional female who cannot see the forest for the trees where men are concerned."

"All I'm asking is for you to mention Levaughn. If she ends the relationship, I will leave you out of finding her a mate."

"Thank you." Mayhem strolled toward the cabin.

Halfway there, Jacy Lee hooked his arm. "You'll mention it, won't you?"

He exhaled loud enough to make his point. "Fine. But that is where my job ends. She and I have already established clear boundary lines, and I will not cross them for you."

"I appreciate you, Cheveyo. She's lucky to have you in her life. We both are." He slung his arm around Mayhem's shoulders. "How does a nice cup of tea sound?"

Mayhem chuckled. "Like bribery."

Chapter 15

1 p.m.

Entering the forest on Old Cherry Mountain Road, Poe soared several yards ahead as Mr. Mayhem told me to study the landscape, drawing attention to various plants and herbs growing wild. By learning how the ecosystem worked—something all wildlife inherently knew—it gave me a greater appreciation of the forest and all its inhabitants. Well, almost all its inhabitants. Poe and I still had a few things to iron out before I even considered lovin' on the little bastard.

After an hour or so, Mr. Mayhem and I'd traveled miles through thick woodlands. "Where are the wolves?"

"Can you not hear them?"

"No."

His hand covered my eyes. "By blocking out sight, your other senses should enhance."

Sure enough, the distant songs of wolves carried on a gentle wind.

"Did you locate them?"

I pointed toward the faint but steady bays. "They're not close."

"A Wolf's low pitch and long duration can be heard up to six miles away in the forest and up to ten miles in open terrain. Listen to their song." His hand lowered. "They're calling to their pack, their family."

Chest caving, my heart wept, the back of my throat thick with devastation. "Oh my God, that's heartbreaking."

"Isn't it, though?"

"Where's their tribe?"

The word "tribe" made him smile, but the moment faded fast. "Wolves are wary of humans, and for good reason. Nonetheless, if pack members hear their cries for help, they will come to investigate. They may even bring food like they do for their elders and injured, if armed men weren't standing guard. A Wolf pack is comprised of closely related family members. Think of how you would feel if someone captured your grandfather."

Fury rallied within me, the notion almost too heavy to bear. "I'd never stop hunting the bastards till I brought *Shicheii* home safe."

"Nor would I, Cat." With a quick one-armed squeeze, he jostled me. "Nor would I."

"So, maybe they're hanging around, waiting for an opportunity?"

"It's possible."

"Then let's go." I thrust a hand in the direction of the wolves. "Let's free 'em."

Mr. Mayhem's head listed to one side. "And how do you purpose we do that?"

"I dunno." My voice rose with intensity. "We can't let this continue."

"I don't disagree. That is why we are here, after all. Short of a bloody battle—with casualties on both sides, I might add—we must be intentional in our approach. And that, dearest Cat, begins with the basics. Learning to blend into this environment. Learning stealth and patience. Learning when and where and how to wage war."

"Okay." I shook out my arms, legs, and rolled my neck. "Lay it on me, then."

Poe flew back to his father's shoulder, and Mr. Mayhem thumbed his bill. "Would you mind demonstrating how to blend into the landscape?" Pissy Pants didn't budge. "Close your eyes, please, Cat."

And so, I did. The breeze of the first wingbeat swept strands of hair across my face. Air sweetened with pine, all my senses amplified the forest. A scuffle to my right. Something tiny, like a chipmunk. The faint piercing cries of wolves. Distant, muffled male voices. A slight kiss of tangerine—Mr. Mayhem's shampoo, soap, or deodorant, maybe—a gentle breeze whispering across my cheek. The only being I couldn't detect was Poe.

After a few minutes, he told me to reopen my eyes and locate his taloned soldier.

Tree after tree, limb after limb, I skimmed the area but couldn't find Mr. Personality anywhere. "Do I gotta stay in one spot?"

His hand swept in a semi-circle. "The forest is yours to investigate."

With my head in a continual scan at the treetops, I strolled through the woods with my mentor right behind me, watching my every move, evaluating my technique. That technique got me nowhere, so I stopped, narrowing in on one tree at a time.

A flash caught in my peripheral, and I twirled toward the movement. But again, I couldn't find the source. "Did you see that?"

"See what, Cat?"

"Somethin' just ran past us. Not sure what it is, but it's ridiculously fast. You didn't see it?"

When Mr. Mayhem stared at me like I belonged in a straitjacket, I dropped the subject and got back to work, searching every branch of a bushy conifer, individual limbs of several oak and maple trees, and the curve of birch where the soil drank the most water.

"It's surprising how well black feathers blend." I blew back my bangs. "Either that or he's mastered camouflage."

"Excellent observations. Both are true. Hence why your grandfather insisted that you train with him."

My confident shoulders waned. "I get it now." One last gander at the surrounding trees proved worthless. At this rate, I'd never find the little bastard, who probably relished every second of making me look an idiot in front of his father. "Can you gimme a hint?"

"Would a prey animal give the predator a hint?"

Ugh. Why was he always right? "Fine. Don't help me."

"Why are you merely focusing on the treetops?"

"Um, 'cause he's a bird."

Thick fingers massaged his temple. "And your point is?"

Duh. "Birds live in trees."

"And your point is?"

"Trees are the most logical place to look for him." Body heat rising, my skin tingled all over. "Why would he choose the most logical place to hide?" I dropped to my knees, crawling through pine needles and last year's decomposing leaves, searching through bushes and behind boulders.

The slight arch to my mentor's lips showed I was on the right track. "Now you're thinking like a predator."

Again, I scanned the trees. Only now, my gaze crawled up the trunk from beneath the branches—much clearer view without a thick canopy of leaves. In all, I located two Cardinals, about eight chipmunks, six squirrels with bushy, beautiful tails swishing as they communicated with one another—*Shicheii* taught me that—Blue Jays, Nuthatches, and various other small birds like Tufted Titmouses. Tufted Titmice?

Once I found my groove, I cruised across the forest floor. The second my knee dipped into a hole, I backed away. Angry bees swarmed my head. I swatted to keep them away, but their numbers grew, buzzing strengthening in pitch and volume, the little bastards stinging my legs, arms, stomach... no place was off-limits. Lightning-fast, Mr. Mayhem wrangled my flailing arms, gripped my hand, and sprinted in the opposite direction, my shoulder joint nearing dislocation.

"Stop swatting them," he hollered over his shoulder. "You'll only enhance their anger."

"Ow! Ow! They're stinging the shit outta me!"

By the time he slowed miles later, most of the swarm had dispersed. A few stragglers hung around, but for the most part, the full-blown attack ceased. Stinging pain excoriated my legs, arms, and bare stomach. A few bees even stung my mouth, my lips swelling fatter by the second.

Piercing gray eyes flashed wide, a frantic gaze tracing me from scalp to foot. "Ooh, they viciously attacked. Okie doke." He tugged me across the road, valeted me into the Caddy. Before closing the passenger door, he slapped down the visor. "Start removing the stingers."

Between the cougar attack and the bees, I couldn't catch a friggin' break. What's next, a moose stomping me to death?

While I assessed the damage in the rearview mirror, Mr. Mayhem slid into the driver's seat with Poe, who took one look at me and crow-laughed—in my face. Little bastard's lucky his father was here, or I might be tempted to slap him off the middle console.

Trying to ignore Mr. Personality—tossing his head back, really laying it on thick—I plucked stinger after stinger from my swollen lips, chest, and arms. "Since when do bees live underground?"

He banged a U-turn. "You were not aware of their burrowing capabilities?"

"Um, no. Obviously." My puffy lips twisted into a sarcastic smirk. When I glanced in the mirror again, I flashed my red teeth, then slapped the visor back into place. "Not for nothin', but before I met you, I could hold my own. Maybe not the most beautiful chick in the world, but not homely, either." I flung a finger at my face. "Now look at me. I'm a friggin' walking nightmare."

Pedal to the metal, Mr. Mayhem stayed focused on the road. "Oh, it's not that bad."

"Not that bad? I can't even feel my lips anymore."

One hand riding the steering wheel, he banged a left on to Hotel Drive, following the road up the steep incline. Parked near the private stairwell, he scooped Poe off the console, and darted around to my door, holding it open for me.

"Now that your adrenaline has quelled a bit, how do you feel?"

"It hurts. A lot."

"Understandable." His hand reached to help me out. "Any trouble breathing? Dizziness? Throat swelling at all?"

"I don't think so."

"Excellent." Into the stairwell, he helped me walk, my legs achy and painful. "I don't mean to rush you, Cat, but the quicker we make it upstairs, the faster we can remove the stingers from your legs. We need to stop the venom from flooding your system."

"Venom?" Now he had my full attention. "Without the bees attached?"

As he assisted me up the stairs, Poe perched on his shoulder, stealing quick glimpses of me every so often. "The stingers continue to release venom on their own. Hence why it's imperative to remove them as quickly as possible."

Groaning, I slowed, nausea stirring my stomach acids. "I don't feel so hot. Can we stop for a sec?"

"No. Time is of the essence." He swept me into his arms and hustled up the remaining treads, down the hall, then into the suite, where he carried me into the bathroom, finally setting me down in the oversized whirlpool tub. "Here." He passed me a towel, then turned his back.

"What's this for?"

"I cannot remove the stingers through your pants."

"Oh, so, basically, you need me to strip." I slid my leggings over my knees. "Great." Sarcasm laced my tone. "It's not like I have any pride left, anyway."

Ignoring me, his complete focus was on his cell. "Jacy Lee, I'm placing you on speakerphone."

"What's wrong, Cheveyo?"

Out of the bathroom, he strolled. "Do not panic. I'm merely calling to see if you included Saltbush or Broom Snakewood in the first-aid kit you put together for us."

"Both are in the same glass tube. Blue cap."

"Okie doke. Thank you."

"Cheveyo," *Shicheii* called out, as if he thought his lifelong friend was disconnecting the call. "How badly was she stung?"

"Would you like to speak with her?"

"I would. Thank you."

A knock on the bathroom door. "Are you decent, Cat?"

"Depends on your definition of decent."

Quick chuckle, and he strolled inside, his finger covering the mouthpiece, his voice low and whisperous. "Let's not worry your grandfather too much."

Once he set the phone on the rim of the tub, I added a spike of cheer to my tone. "I'm okay, *Shicheii*."

"What happened, child?"

"I, ah, kneed a hive by accident."

"You didn't swat at the bees, did you?"

"Um, well, only a couple times."

My grandfather gasped. "Did they swarm you?"

"I got her out of there fairly quick, Jacy Lee." Mr. Mayhem withdrew a credit card from his wallet and gestured for me to stand. "Removing the stingers now."

"Thank you, Cheveyo. It sounds like it could have been much worse. You're lucky, honey."

Lucky? Gee, I didn't feel lucky, standing half-naked in a bathtub while Mr. Mayhem scraped my legs with a credit card.

"Once you remove the stingers, Cheveyo, please have her chew the Saltbush. There's also a tea I'd like you to give her. Brown package with the bee drawn on the front. Is she nauseous?"

"A little," I said, minimizing how easily I could shower Mr. Mayhem with vomit.

"All right, child. Remind Cheveyo to make the tea."

"Okay. Love you."

"I love you, too, Mourning Dove. Keep me informed on her progress, Cheveyo."

"Will do."

"All right, then. *Yá'át'ééh*."

A dial tone hummed, and I tapped End.

"This isn't awkward at all," I lied, tucking the towel between my legs, holding it in place with one hand, the other hand flat on the wall so I didn't topple over while he removed the stingers from my upper thighs. "They really nailed my legs."

Silent, Mr. Mayhem focused on the task at hand.

"Why didn't they sting you?"

"Bees will only attack if they feel threatened. Perhaps we should run through a few safety tips for the future."

"Great. Lay it on me."

"Are you sure you feel up to it?"

"It's better than standing here in silence."

"All right, then." *Scratch, scratch, scratch,* the credit card scraping my skin. "If a colony of bees view you as a predator, they first send out a few guard bees to warn you with a headbutt."

"Whaddaya mean, like, a quick sting?"

"No." Squinted eyes gazed up at me. "A headbutt. Are you unfamiliar with the term? The stingers are in the backend."

"Oh. Right. Duh."

"Should you feel a headbutt," he continued, covering the awkward silence between us, "leave immediately. The entire hive is gearing up for a full-scale attack, driven by a pheromone released by the guards. If you are unable to leave right away for whatever reason, hold your breath. A bee's primary sense is smell. They navigate the world through odor. If you take that sense away by holding your breath, you're effectively blinding them to your presence. Now, if the entire hive swarms at once, it's much too late. However, it will work if only a few bees hover nearby."

"Wow. Coo—"

"Never flail your arms or swat at them." Cutting me off mid-stream, he slid the credit card down my inner thigh, scraping out stingers as I tried to look anywhere but at him, my gaze roaming around the bathroom. "By doing so, you're communicating to the bee that you are a predator, ready and willing to attack the hive. When bees feel threatened, they send an alarm scent to call their hive-mates to the scene of the crime. Their natural response is to rise together and defend their queen."

In retrospect, I could easily see where I went wrong.

"If they sting you, pull the stingers out right away, like you did in the Caddy. I'm scraping out the rest because it's quicker, and time really is of the essence. If your grandfather was in the woods with us, he'd have stripped you right there, and rightfully so. Every second counts. I tried to preserve your dignity without risking your life." He hesitated, the credit card hovering a couple centimeters away from my mohawk'd puddy-tat hidden by the towel. "To be perfectly honest with you, that may have been a mistake. The nausea and weakness concern me."

After plucking out the last stinger, Mr. Mayhem hustled into the other room, returned within seconds, and passed me a glass tube. "Chew on the stems but do not swallow the resin."

And so, I did. "Now what?"

He held out a flat hand. "Spit it out and chew the next one."

Mr. Mayhem painted the saliva covered resin over each wound, coating my body in *Shicheii's* medicine. "Use the last mouthful for your lips, to help reduce the swelling. I'll go make the tea."

"What do I do?"

"Stand there and dry, please. I don't want you stepping on a stinger. When I return, I'll lift you out."

Moments later, he hustled into the bathroom with a mug for me. "Hold it steady." Without warning, he scooped me out of the tub and carried me into the bedroom, where he laid me down on the mattress, propping up my back with pillows. "Drink it all."

Seated on the edge of the mattress, he waited for me to gulp down the scalding liquid, burning the shit out of my tongue and throat, *Shicheii's* medicine heating me from the inside out. Poe flew through the doorway and landed by my feet.

Mr. Mayhem stroked the crown of his head. "She'll be all right, bud."

"Yeah. I'm sure he's all broken up over this."

Laughing his ass off—seriously, whatever I said amused him to no end—joyful tears teemed his eyes. "Oh, Cat, at least you haven't lost your sense of humor. It's a good sign." He took the mug from my hands and rose. "Rest a while." From the foot of the bed, he snatched a blanket and shook out the folds, soft cotton covering me, tucking the bottom hem under my feet.

"How do my lips look? Any better?"

Sucking air through clenched teeth, he hesitated. "Give the medicine time to work. The important thing to remember is this—you survived not one but two brutal attacks in a short period. I cannot teach that special type of grit of mental acuity and action, the inherent instinctual drive to survive. True warriors are born with an inbred fight response rather than merely flight. And you, dearest Cat, have many of the same attributes."

A warmness fluttered through my system. "I do?"

"Indeed, you do." Grinning, he nodded. "How are you feeling?"

"Tired."

"Okie doke. Poe and I will get out of your hair so you can rest." He glance down at Pissy Pants, who'd gotten awfully comfortable at the foot of my bed. "Ready for a little fun?"

"Wait. What? You're leaving?"

"We still need a live feed of the compound, do we not?"

"Well, yeah, but—"

Poe springboarded to his father's shoulder.

"Lives are stake, Cat. I thought you and I were on the same page."

"We are." *Just once, I'd love to out-think him.* "Okay, fine. Whatever. Good luck."

"Luck has nothing to do with it." He winked. "See you soon." He strode out the door, then leaned back through the doorway. "If you get hungry, order room service."

"Why? Are you guys gonna be gone long?"

"Not necessarily."

"Alright, then maybe I'll wait."

"Don't go hungry on our account. Your body needs fuel to heal." His hand tapped the doorframe. "Oh, and one other thing. Please don't leave the suite unless it's absolutely necessary. We cannot risk another run-in with Mister or Missus Hawthorne."

"Got it."

"Remember, I'm just a phone call away."

I hated the fact that they left me here, but my body betrayed me and all I could do was lie there. Why'd I have to knee a hive? Fulfilling my destiny was a lot harder than I expected. What's next, a bear mauling? Man, that'd suck.

Chapter 16
"When you are in doubt, be still and wait.
When doubt no longer exists for you, then go forward with courage.
So long as mist envelopes you, be still.
Be still until the sunlight pours through and dispels the mists,
as it surely will. Then act with courage."
—Ponca Chief White Eagle

6:25 p.m.

Accompanied by his loyal crow companion, Mayhem parked the Caddy, crossed Old Cherry Mountain Road, then began the long trek to the compound that held the Innocent Ones—majestic Eastern Gray Wolves—guarded by despicable white men in fatigues who viewed them as dollar signs. To treat one of Mother Earth's most precious inhabitants with blatant disregard was not merely disgraceful. It violated the Natural Law.

Unlike the white man, who believed all Indigenous People were alike, tribes had vastly different views about many things. Even so, almost every Native American culture believed one thing above all. Every creature—animal, plant, rock, tree, mountain, even water—had a soul. Thus, all of nature must be respected and honored.

As a young boy, Mayhem took a stroll with his grandmother. Near a stream, he spotted a palm-sized stone on the bank. Without thinking, he picked it up and tossed it into the water. Immediately, his grandmother said, "Why did you do that? How long did it take that rock to escape the water? And you put it right back in. Why did you toss the rock in the water, Cheveyo? It wasn't bothering you."

Stunned by her reaction, he held his tongue.

"The truth is," she continued, "you had no reason for your actions. None. Do you realize that?"

On that day, he learned a valuable lesson about intentions. She was not angry because of some silly superstition. The scold stemmed from an inherent respect for nature. All of nature—from inanimate objects to breathing beings—deserved respect simply because they existed before humankind and would thrive long afterward. Nature's dependable cycles continued for eternity.

Regardless of technological advancements and social issues, humans are not a separate entity from nature. Humans are but one link in its chain—all connected as one—an intricate part of a living whole.

Why was this simple truth so difficult to comprehend?

Once he reached the area near the compound, Poe stiffened on his shoulder then leaped into the air. The wolves whipped into a frenzy, their voices spiraling through the trees. Mayhem stopped, his sight narrowed on Poe, who circled wide before vanishing into the forest. A true master of his environment.

The moment he returned, he flew straight to Dad, stunning black wings riding the thermals. As he neared, Mayhem extended his arm. Poe landed, chest heaving with adrenaline.

"Problem?"

A dip of the bill confirmed.

"Is someone threatening the wolves?"

Poe bill-tapped his ankle band once.

"One Wolf is in trouble?"

Another dip of the bill.

"Show me."

Rather than fly toward the compound, Poe banged a sharp right then soared up a hillside. Why would they bring a lone Wolf here? Did the animal escape?

Mayhem jogged up the incline. At the top, he flattened against the earth as an armed guard dragged a muzzled Wolf by a thick chain, the animal digging in, fighting him every step of the way. Around the side of a large boulder, he watched. Waited. The fatigues-clad man stopped. The Wolf barked and spat. A low, guttural growl rumbled his larynx, his teeth no doubt bared behind the muzzle.

Mayhem crept over the crest then down the other side. When the poacher withdrew a pistol from his shoulder holster, Mayhem lunged, tackling the armed guard and knocking the gun out of his hand. Wrestling the poacher beneath him, he knelt on his chest, the hunting blade pressed under his chin.

The Wolf did not flee.

"Good boy."

To help soothe the Wolf, Poe cooed.

"One moment, please, and I shall free you from that contraption."

The poacher struggled to break loose. "Who the fuck are you?"

At the colorful language, he winced. "A better question may be, who are you?"

"None of your fuckin' business." The poacher tried to buck Mayhem off. "When my men get here, you're a dead man."

Mayhem glanced left and right. "Then I shall look forward to their company. In the meantime, let's chat, Mister...?"

"Smith."

Little doubt existed that he lied, yet in the grand scheme of things, his surname mattered not. Regardless of the poacher's truthfulness, he would not survive this encounter.

Nonetheless, Mayhem played along. "All right, Mister Smith. Take a good, hard look at the beautiful animal you planned to kill in cold blood. Do you see how malnourished he is?"

The guy refused to look at the Wolf.

"I gave you an instruction, Mister Smith. And I expect you to follow it." His vice-gripped fingers forced the man's head to the side. "Look him in the eye and tell me what you see."

"Nothing. He's a stupid animal."

Through his nose he inhaled a cleansing breath, petting the beast within. "Where might your phone be, Mister Smith?"

"None of your fuckin' business. That's where."

Mayhem slapped a hand over his mouth and leaned in, their noses almost touching. The poacher might as well be dead inside. No zest for life, no spark of a soul, an empty shell of a man. With a quick slash, he severed the poacher's throat, ducking out of the way of the arched blood from his carotid and jugular.

When he rose, the Wolf cowered. "What did those monsters do to you, handsome?" Mayhem dug into the poacher's pockets for his cell, unlocked the screen with his lifeless fingerprint, and enabled Location Sharing before setting the phone on the boulder.

"One moment, please," he told the Wolf, then carved into the poacher's side, reached in, and ripped out his liver.

In front of the Wolf, he knelt, gazing into the animal's soulful eyes. "When I remove the muzzle and chain, feel free to indulge on this." He dropped the bloody liver at the animal's paws. "I am not on the menu. Are we clear?"

The Wolf remained motionless, and Mayhem took it as a good sign. To ensure a smooth transition, Poe fluttered down to Dad's shoulder. The symbiotic relationship between crows, ravens, and wolves dated back hundreds of years. Wolves trusted crows, and vice versa.

Almost immediately, Poe's presence soothed the lone Wolf, and he lowered his belly to the dirt, with the human liver between both paws. The body language showed trust. Mayhem removed the chain from around his neck, the fur worn down, skin raw and open. Next, he unbuckled the muzzle and tossed it aside.

"Poe and I shall return to free the rest of your family," he promised. "In the meantime, please steer clear of the compound."

The Wolf tore into the raw meat like he hadn't eaten in weeks.

With slow, controlled movements, Mayhem rose and swept a hand toward the dead man. "Once you finish the liver, please drag the rest of your meal into the woods. Poe and I shall see you soon, handsome."

Poe hopped over to the Wolf, ready to start playing with a tug of his tail.

"Don't you dare, little mister."

Poe shot him a glare, as if to say, "Why not?"

"Please let him eat in peace. You two can play upon our return." Satisfied with that response, he flew to Dad's shoulder. "Thank you."

As he trekked back up the hillside with his loyal companion, two or three men hollered in the distance. Rather than getting involved in the discord, he gave them a wide berth. Jacy Lee might not approve of leaving human remains out in the open, but what choice did he have? Without sustenance, the Wolf wouldn't survive another day or two. Which might be why the poacher planned to end his life. In their view, he was no longer useful.

Shame on them.

Halfway to the Caddy, all his tiny neck hairs rose at once. Someone was following him. The question was, who?

Chapter 17

8 p.m.

I woke from my nap and crawled out of bed. Whatever *Shicheii* put in the tea worked. Not that I felt like running a marathon or anything. After all, my body still needed time to heal from the cougar attack, too. My lips didn't seem as puffy, either. Far from perfect but improving.

Man, was I starving, though. Mr. Mayhem left a long time ago. Too long. What if the poachers ambushed him? Or worse, shot him on sight. Pacing back and forth in the suite, I couldn't settle, every nerve in my body screaming for me to do something, anything. If the poachers captured Mr. Mayhem and were holding him hostage, he'd have no way to get in touch with me.

Except for Poe.

I hustled out to the balcony. Father Sun dropped behind the horizon, the dark sky diamondized with stars.

Should I call *Shicheii*? Before I sent him into panic-mode, I bustled back inside, scanning the living room for my cell, swiped the iPhone off the table, and banged out a text.

R U OK?

Not sure how long I stared at the screen, waiting, but text bubbles never emerged. *Think, Shawnee, think.* What would Mr. Mayhem do? Rifling through my overnight bag, I grabbed jeans, T-shirt, and a black hoodie. Gotta be comfortable to kick some poacher ass.

Out the door I flew, hustled down the private stairwell, and a vision of the room key flashed through my mind two seconds after the door clicked shut. Balls. Just my luck.

Maybe it was all the trauma I'd experienced lately, or the lack of water, but my shin muscles tightened while I speed-walked down the steep incline. The moment I veered on to Hotel Drive, I checked my phone.

Still no text. Something must be wrong. Mr. Mayhem would never ignore me.

I would've pinged his phone back in the room, but if my texts weren't going through, there wasn't much point. Besides, the only place he could be was Old Cherry Mountain Road. With one route there and back, he consistently drove the same road to the hotel. Roughly five minutes by car, probably thirty on foot. In the dark, maybe longer.

Didn't matter. Instinct screamed for me to hurry.

The moment I headed down Old Cherry Mountain Road, headlights spiraled through my legs from behind, and I whirled around.

A pickup truck pulled alongside me. The passenger window lowered, revealing two guys in camouflage jackets and knit hats. "Hey, good looking," said the passenger, his voice high and squeaky. "What're you doing out here all by onesie?"

Without a word, I flashed my pearly reds, and both men jeered back.

The window zipped closed, and the truck peeled out, taillights trailing in the distance.

Whaddaya know, the teeth worked in my favor for once. Maybe I should leave 'em like this. 'Course, I'd probably never get laid again.

Alanis Morissette belted out *Isn't it Ironic*, and almost stopped my heart. I fumbled to answer the call before she sang it again. "Mister M?"

"What would possess you to leave the comfort of the hotel?" Controlled anger laced his tone. "If you were hungry, all you had to do was pick up the phone. Honestly, Cat, I don't know what has gotten into you."

"Are you done?"

Silence.

"Remember when you said you were just a phone call away?"

"I do."

"Well, I texted, and you didn't text me back. So, I figured something must be wrong."

His tone evened out. "Where are you now, Cat?"

"On Old Cherry Mountain Road."

"At the compound?" His voice spiked, and I pulled the phone away from my ear. "What on earth are you doing there?"

"Lookin' for you! I thought they grabbed you. I thought you were hurt. I thought—I don't know what I thought, but I knew I had to come here in case you needed me."

A long pause of silence fell between us.

"I don't mean to frighten you, Cat, but you need to hightail it out of there now. Right now. Not five minutes from now. Leave this instant. Do not hug the wood line. Run straight down the middle of the road."

"What?" My heart froze mid-beat. "Why?"

"No time for questions. Run, Cat, run." A car door slammed shut. "Poe and I are heading your way. Do not slow or stop until I reach you. Understood?"

"Am I in danger?"

"Yes."

A dial tone flatlined.

What the hell? My gaze shot left, right, and behind me, my head in a constant swivel as I booked it into the middle of the road. From the corner of my eye, someone—or something—whizzed past me. Whatever—or whoever—it was moved too fast for me to determine human from animal. All I knew for sure was that I wasn't alone. Far from it. I increased my pace, arms pumping to raise my momentum, gaze bouncing from tree to tree, stump to stump, and through the few bare patches in between. My heart pumped faster than copter blades, my adrenaline maxed out, so much so I thought for sure my chest would explode.

The waning moon barely illuminated Old Cherry Mountain Road, my sneakers pounding the pavement—*slap, slap, slap*—ricocheting off the trees. The cool night air whipped my face, my eyes struggling to adjust to the darkness. Several yards ahead, a deer leaped across the road and into the forest.

Slap, slap, slap, slap, slap.

The same deer—seemed like it, anyway—reversed direction and crossed in front of me, lunging for the woods from which it came, as if fleeing an apex predator. For a moment, I slowed, not willing to go head-to-head with another mountain lion, nor a Wolf, coyote, or bear. Once I passed the trail, I sprinted, charging for the next bend in the road.

Slap, slap, slap, slap, slap.

An eerie, haunting siren filled the air, the heart-stopping cry shooting through my core, rattling my ribcage. What the fuck was that? Not quite human, not quite animal. More like a mixture a both, but how could that be true?

Slap, slap, slap, slap, slap.

My mind played tricks on me. Did *Shicheii's* tea include a hallucinogenic? No. Why would Mr. Mayhem tell me I was in danger if I wasn't? He must've meant the apex predators stalking the forest, and he's right. With no weapons to defend myself, I became easy prey.

Slap, slap, slap, slap, slap.

Wolves, cougars, coyotes, and bears were all pursuit predators. The mere act of me running could trigger one or all of the aforementioned animals to give chase, tackle, and then attack.

O Great Spirit, please don't let me die out here.

Slap, slap, slap, slap, slap.

Two cylindrical spheres of light cascaded through the treetops as a vehicle turned on to Old Cherry Mountain Road, and I waved my arms over my head. If it wasn't Mr. Mayhem, I'd look like a complete lunatic, but I didn't care. I needed the safety of a vehicle. Any vehicle.

The headlights blinded me. What if it's the cops? Leaving room for the car to pass, I bolted to the side of the road and kept running.

"Cautious Cat—"

I whirled around. "Mister M?"

The Caddy reversed down the road. Once it pulled alongside me, I jogged around the back bumper, hopped in the passenger seat, then slammed the door, my breath labored from adrenaline overload.

"Are you all right?"

Poe cocked his head from the middle console.

"Yeah, I'm good. You?"

"Always." He backed into the sandy shoulder, slid the shifter into Drive. "I've been working alone for a long time."

"I know, but now you've got me."

He offered me a sad smile. "If I worried you, I apologize."

"Don't ignore me again, okay?"

"Ignore you? What on earth would give you that impression?"

"Y'mean, you didn't get my text?" I tapped the icon on my phone then flashed him the screen. "See? I asked if you were okay."

A slight grin when he glanced at my phone.

"What?" I studied the text message.

R U OK? What's funny about that?

But then, text bubbles emerged—*pulsed... pulsed... pulsed*—and my gaze shot to Mr. Mayhem, who looked awfully pleased with himself for some reason. When I refocused on the screen, a return text appeared.

I miss you. <3

And my gaze shot back to Mr. Mayhem. "Did you, um, text me back?"

Expressionless, he turned on to Hotel Drive. "Cat, I have already apologized for my delay. Now, we have more pressing matters to discuss, I'm afraid."

"No, I know, but—" Squinted eyes crinkled my nose. "We do?"

"Location Sharing is enabled."

"Shut the front door." I play-slapped his bicep. "How'd you get one of the poachers alone?"

Another text popped up.

I love you, Shawn. I've loved you from the moment we met.

"Err"—I flashed him the screen—"can we talk about this first?"

"Quickly, then we need to get back to work."

"Alright." How could I put this? "I consider you family. You know that, right?"

"I do."

"I'd kill for you, I really would."

"Thank you. I would do the same."

Poe's head swiveled between us.

"It's not that the thought has never crossed my mind. I'd have to be dead not to notice what amazing shape you're in with all those rippling muscles—"

His throat cleared. "Cat—"

"Lemme finish. Please. And you must know you're, um, really good lookin'. I mean, again, I'd have to be dead not to notice."

"Cat—"

Poe released an eardrum-rattling caw.

"Thank you, buddy. The direction of this conversation was beginning to make me uncomfortable, as well." Stroking the crown of Poe's head, he drove up the steep incline.

Speechless, I searched for the right words as he pulled around back to our private stairwell.

Parked, he killed the engine. "May I see your phone, please?"

I passed him the cell, and he scrolled through the messages. Once he reached the I-love-you's, he smirked. "If you are under the impression that I sent these messages, I can assure you, I did no such thing." He passed the phone back to me. "In the future, if you could please double check the sender's name and/or number, I would greatly appreciate it."

"Whaddaya...?" My gaze raised to the top of the screen. "Oh, my God. I texted Levaughn."

"You did indeed, and he—not I—responded."

My forehead fell into a cupped hand. I just made a complete idiot of myself. Did I really just admit I'd thought about—? Good God. Someone shoot me. Please. One little bullet to the brain is all I ask.

The driver's door swung open by his hand. "Poe, perhaps you and I should give Cat some privacy to return Detective Samuel's call."

When Mr. Mayhem extended his forearm, Pissy Pants refused to step on his perch. Instead, he cocked his head, staring at me like I'd lost my mind, or evaluating my intentions to see if I was a homewrecker or not. One thing became obvious. He'd never forget what I said. Never. That bird had a memory like an elephant, and he'd tucked all the sordid details into the ol' memory bank, probably took mental snapshots of my face while saying it to show Spirit Crow, too. Fuck.

The crazy part was I never got to finish my spiel. If I had, they'd both know that, although I admired Mr. Mayhem and couldn't deny his good looks, I would never cross that line. Not ever. He and I were buds—family—nowhere near lovers. Besides, I wasn't desperate enough to date a guy with a daughter my age. C'mon, gimme a little credit. Lest we not forget, he tried to murder me more than once. Sure, we'd moved past that time in our lives, but that didn't erase it from our history.

"Little mister," he warned with a shake of the forearm.

"It's cool. I'm not calling him back, anyway."

"No?"

"I can't deal with him right now." I climbed out of the passenger seat, turned, then spoke over the roof. "I know I need to at some point, but not tonight."

"I hope I'm not overstepping boundaries by saying your grandfather is more than a little concerned about your relationship."

"What'd he say?"

With Poe on his perch, he shut the driver's door. "He wants what all parents want for their children, for them to live a full and happy life."

"Full, meaning what, exactly? That only a man can complete me?"

"Honestly, this conversation is better suited for your grandfather. Wouldn't you agree?"

"Probably."

At the private stairwell, he waved the keycard in front of the sensor. "Go easy on him, Cat. Jacy Lee is very traditional, however, not closed-minded to matters of the heart. His fondness for Detective Samuels proves that."

"Why, 'cause he's black?"

"Honestly, Cat, where is this coming from?" He held open the door for me. "Might I remind you, your mother married outside her race. And both your grandparents adored him. We all championed their union."

"You're right. I'm sorry." Could I sink any lower? "Guess I'm a little sensitive when it comes to Levaughn."

"Then perhaps you should respond to his text messages. You can only expect a man to wait in the wings for so long."

He's not wrong. "Fine." I withdrew my phone and texted back.

Love you, too. We'll talk when I get home. I know it's not fair to you, but I need to concentrate on my family for now. Don't hate me.

Almost immediately, he texted back.

I could never hate you, babe. Do what you gotta do. Just don't shut me out.

My thumbs worked the keypad.

I won't. Talk soon.

By the time we reached the suite, I'd slipped my phone into my back pocket. "Thanks. I probably shoulda texted him days ago." He held open the door for me to stroll into the suite. "Hey, about what I said earlier..."

"Already forgotten, Cat."

"Cool."

Even though I didn't buy it for a second—who could forget something like that?—I played along, and settled in the loveseat with the PC. First, I brought up Live View on Google Maps. A satellite image of the compound filled the screen, and I narrowed in, the Wolf pen and guards clearing more and more. But now, only three men patrolled the grounds.

My head popped up from the screen, and I spun the PC around. "One of the guards is—"

Where'd he go? Though Mr. Mayhem wasn't here, his freakishly human crow stood on the coffee table, glaring at me with murder on his mind. I half-expected his foot to tap while waiting for me to explain my intentions for his father.

"Look." Drops of saliva hitched down my dry throat. "What you overheard was all a big misunderstanding. Stupid, really." I raised my right hand. "As God is my witness, I would never—*ever*—betray your mother. I love Spirit Crow."

With one robotically slow step toward me, the eyes thinned even more, like he longed to rip my throat out.

Gulp. "You and I have had our differences, and maybe the thing in the parking lot was all my fault. I'll give you that. But even you gotta admit how silly this is, right?"

No reaction.

"Poe, please. For all our sakes, can't you cut me a break this one time and not rat me out?"

No reaction.

My knee bobbed up and down. "Spirit Crow's still healing. Why would you wanna upset her over a stupid misunderstanding? Did I say things I probably shouldn't've said? Sure. That's on me, too. But you're blowing this way outta proportion. Nothing's changed between me and your dad. Nothing."

No reaction.

"Okay, fine. What's it gonna cost for your silence? Want me to order mashed potatoes and gravy?"

One slow nod.

"That it?"

His head rocked a no.

"Fruit cup?"

Another dip of the bill.

"That it?"

Another no.

"How 'bought I grab a menu?"

Another slow nod.

"Then you'll be cool, right? The awkward conversation in the Caddy will stay between us?"

Poe raised a leg, tapping his gold ankle band.

"Want some new bling?"

The bill dipped, rose.

"Then you'll be cool?"

Another yes.

"Okay, fine. Deal. Not sure where to buy that type of thing, but whatever. I might need a little time to find it."

He wagged a no.

"Twenty-four hours. Can you gimme that?"

One quick bounce of the wings.

"Fine." I gritted my teeth. "We'll go tonight."

Fuckin' freakshow.

Chapter 18
"Live your life that the fear of death can never enter your heart.
Trouble no one about their religion,
respect others in their view
and demand that they respect yours."
—Chief Tecumseh

9:25 p.m.

Into the suite, Mayhem rolled a cart with silver domes over the entrees. A symbiotic energy passed between Shawnee and Poe, as though they'd come to some sort of mutual understanding.

Shawnee scuttled over to the cart. "What'd you get me?"

He lifted the dome off her plate. "Because you enjoyed the porkchop at Thorn Hill, I ordered you Berkshire Pork, with rich braise, sweet and sour red cabbage, and a natural reduction of pears and apples. If that doesn't appeal to you, I also ordered the plant-based Surf and Turf, coffee-barbecue-rubbed tempeh, plant-based scallops, with roasted summer squash and zucchini."

"No mashed potatoes and gravy?"

"Ooh." He lifted the dome off the third plate. "For Poe, yes."

"Okay, cool. I told him he could have mine if you didn't order him any."

"You did?" *Wonders never cease.* "My, my, it's refreshing to see you two working together for a change. Thank you, Cat."

As she carried her plate to the table, she said, "Hey, um, where'd you get Poe's gold ankle band?"

"In Boston. My wife custom-ordered it for him."

At the table, Shawnee settled in the chair. "From a jewelry store or...?"

"Yes." Suspicious, he narrowed focus on her. "Why do you ask?"

"No reason." Refusing eye contact, she cut into the pork. "Looks good."

"The pork?"

"Well, I mean, this looks good, too, but I meant his ankle band."

How sweet. "Thank you. I'm sure he appreciates the compliment." In front of Poe, he set down the plate of mashed potatoes. "Don't you, handsome?"

Rather than acknowledge Shawnee, Poe dug in, slurping up the gravy.

When Mayhem finally sat, he steepled his hands. "How'd you make out with the satellite images?"

"Good. Live feed is up. Want me to get the PC?"

"No, no. Enjoy your meal. I'll take a look after we eat."

"Hey, um, mind if I borrow the Caddy later? Need to run an errand real quick."

Mayhem glimpsed his watch. At this hour? "I can take you wherever you need to go."

"Why?" Her forearms slapped down on the table. "Don't you trust me?"

Unwilling to skate on this slippery slope, he agreed. "Don't smile at anyone. Also, please steer clear of Old Cherry Mountain Road until we discuss the area more fully. There's been a development you should be aware of."

Head down, she sliced the pork and cabbage into bite-sized pieces. "What kind of development?"

Rather than get into a drawn-out *tête-à-tête* that might ruin her appetite, he sidestepped the question. "It can wait, as long as you promise not to go anywhere near there."

"Fine, I promise."

"If you crash the Caddy or soil the pigskin, you and I will have a problem. Are you cognizant of that?"

Visibly, she gulped. "Yep. Got it."

"Super." He laid the keyring on the table. "How's the Berkshire Pork? It smells divine."

"Amazing."

He winked. "Stick with me, kid."

During the meal, he and Shawnee engaged in pleasant chitchat. However, something still felt off. Nothing he could quite pinpoint, but she and Poe hadn't had this much eye contact since they met. The atmosphere reminded him of when Cheyenne was in high school, sneaking out after dark to meet a secret boyfriend. But after the awkward conversation in the car earlier, he didn't dare ask for clarification.

Time alone sounded nice. He hadn't had a moment to himself since he drove up last week. Not that he didn't enjoy Shawnee and Jacy Lee's company—quite the opposite, in fact—but a human soul required silent contemplation, as well.

As for the lack of discord between Poe and Shawnee, time had a funny way of revealing the truth. Till then, he played along.

What are you up to, Cautious Cat?

Chapter 19

10:30 p.m.

For over an hour, Mr. Mayhem and I stared at the live feed of the compound, but he still hadn't told me why my life was in danger or why I should steer clear of Old Cherry Mountain Road. I hadn't pushed the issue, either, figuring he probably didn't want me walking alone in the dark with all the apex predators in the area. Not that I could blame him. Most people didn't get attacked by a mountain lion and an entire hive of bees in a twenty-four-hour period.

Lucky me.

Beady-eyed glares from Poe grew more and more persistent. If he kept this up much longer, no way wouldn't his father figure it out. After all, we were supposed to act like buds now. Yeah, right. Fat chance of that ever happening. If our past didn't have enough reasons for him to hate me, the misunderstanding in the car pretty much sealed my fate.

I wrung my hands. "Mind if I hit the road now?"

"Are you sure you wouldn't prefer that I drive you? You have been through a lot lately."

"No. It's cool. I won't be long." Halfway to the door, Poe shrilled, and stopped me cold. "What now?"

He flew straight at me, and I ducked out of the way.

"I'll take you out, bud." Mr. Mayhem bustled toward the door, extending a forearm for Poe. But instead of landing on his father, he fluttered down to my shoulder. "Oh, my." Gray eyes shifted between the two of us.

I froze. "What's happening right now?"

"I believe he would like to accompany you on your errand."

I pulled my face away from Poe. "Seriously?"

A dip of the bill confirmed.

"Would you mind terribly, Cat?"

"Fine." Gritted teeth ached my jaw. "He can come."

"Best behavior, young man." Big smile at me. "Thank you. It warms my heart to see you two mending past regressions."

I flashed my pearly reds. "Yeah. Me, too." Not even close to the truth.

Out the door and down the stairwell I trekked with Poe's talons dug into my shoulder. In the parking lot, he flew to a thicket of trees.

I flung up my hands. "Whaddaya doin'? We gotta go."

When he turned his back, I figured the mashed potatoes beckoned a potty break.

"Oh. My bad." I pressed the key fob. *Bleep, bleep.* "I'll leave the passenger door open for ya." Within a few seconds, he soared into the Caddy, landing on the middle console. "Let's just get this over with already." I raced around the front bumper to shut the door then jumped behind the wheel. Threw it in Drive, coasted down the hill—all the while a little voice inside my head screamed this was a bad idea.

What could I do? If Poe told Spirit Crow, she'd never trust me again. I'd caused enough trouble in her marriage. If Kimi hadn't protected me, she'd still be living as a wife and mother instead of stuck inside the body of a crow. How she didn't hate me already, I had no idea. And I couldn't stroll into a jewelry store during business hours with blood-red teeth. Look what happened with Mrs. Hawthorne. If Pissy Pants could wait a couple days, I'd order bling online. But no. God forbid he made this easy.

Downtown, a jewelry store in a red barn seemed like an easy mark. After hitting an ATM, I parked a couple streets over and rummaged through the trunk for the duffel bag I used at

Worthington's place. When I slammed the lid, Poe appeared in the back windshield, screeching at decibels that could crack glass.

I whipped open the driver's door. "Shut the hell up."

He flew past me and landed on the hood.

"Oh, no." My head rocked on its own. "No way. You're not coming with me. I work alone, pal."

He shrilled again, and I shushed him.

"Fine." I stomped one foot. "But if you try to get me busted, I'll wring your scrawny neck."

Black wings flapping, he flew a few feet ahead of me as I hopped two fences, sprinted through three backyards, then emerged on a desolate back road behind the red barn. As I neared, a clearer picture of the obstacles appeared. Surrounding this barn on three sides was a frickin' moat.

I stood at the water's edge, reviewing my limited options, when Poe soared across and landed on the roof. He stomped closer to the gutters and spread his wings, as if to say, "What's the problem?"

My upper lip curled, twitched. "I hate you with every fiber of my being. You know that, right?"

One floor below Poe sat an opened window. Interesting. Waving my hand, I called him back. When he landed on my forearm, I pointed across the moat. "See that window? You can fit through there, right?"

He rocked his head from side to side.

"Of course, you can. You might have to squeeze a little, but you can get inside."

Another no.

"Work with me here. You're the one who wants new bling."

He whipped his face away from me.

"Fine—" My back molars ground together. "Go wait for me."

The moment he leaped into the air, I snapped on black latex gloves from the duffle bag, stripped down to my bra and thong, and clenched three folded hundred-dollar bills between my puffy lips. Into the water I inched. The temperature wasn't too bad.

There better not be anything that bites in here, or I'll kill the little bastard.

Across the moat, I paddled, scanning the barn's exterior, searching for security cameras. One lone spotlight brightened the backdoor. Still didn't mean there wasn't an alarm, but it didn't matter with an opened window. As long as I didn't break into any other doors or windows, the alarm shouldn't squeal. Keyword "shouldn't."

What if the owners lived on the premises? Man, that'd suck.

Even though we only had a couple days left of June, my body still numbed from the neck down. Gotta admit, though, the cool water soothed all my injuries, the long claw marks down my arms and upper chest—areas not covered by Mom's wooden beads—and stinger holes from angry bees. The latex somewhat protected the scabs on my hands from Mr. Personality's little hissy fit last weekend.

Once I made it to shore, I shook my head like a dog, water spraying in all directions. A towel would've been a dream about now, but I'd rarely been that lucky in life. The second floor seemed much higher up close. Gesturing to Poe, I pointed two fingers at my eyes, then swept them in a semicircle around the property, and he marched to the peak to play lookout while I wrestled with how to scale the siding.

At the East corner, I dug my fingertips around the lip of the corner planks. Good thing they used genuine wood—the barn several decades old—or this would suck even more. Still wasn't easy, but at least my fingers and toes could grip the wood. Foot by foot, I climbed higher and higher. Once I reached the second floor, I swung one leg to the roof and dragged my body up to the gritty, rough shingles, scraping the shit out of my bare skin.

On the roof, I hunched low and darted to the opened window. Lying flat on my stomach, I slid my legs over the edge, feet dangling, toes feeling around for the wooden frame, then clung to the drainpipe, my hands sliding down to the sill. Crouching, I peered through the glass like a raccoon in search of an easy meal.

No contact points or wiring showed they hadn't alarmed the second floor. Perfect. With my gloved fingers under the frame, I glided the window up the tracks. Snickering, I poked my head through the opening. Security lights bathed the interior in a warm, golden smolder. A cool catwalk encircled the second floor. I backed out to tell Poe, but he didn't give me a chance before swooping inside.

In and out of exposed roof trusses, he soared, ebony wings slaloming around thick wooden beams, a soft coo rattling his gullet. Since I had no idea if the security lights came with motion detectors, I pointed at the lower level, and he dove, flapping above the jewelry counters, admiring all the shiny stuff.

Someone enjoyed this trip a little too much.

When he didn't set off the alarm, I climbed down the wooden ladder. Over to a glass cabinet, I padded, the cool hardwood wetted by my bare feet. Filled with jewelry for kids, Christening bracelets gave the impression they might fit, so I bustled around the counter, my gaze in a continual scan for keys.

No such luck. God forbid, I strolled down Easy Street for once. But that didn't discount the fact that I needed some way to pick the lock. All my tools—and clothes, by the way—were in the duffel bag on the bank of the moat. If the cops came, they'd find a half-naked cat burglar, soaking wet, with lips the size of inflatable rafts.

Built-in drawers spanned the wall behind me. I dug through the top drawer. Nothing but price tags and markers. Second one down held paperwork and spare rolls of register tape. The third also offered no love. In total, I dug through six before finding a box of paperclips.

Not ideal, but I rolled with it.

Squatted at the level of the lock, I inserted one end of the paperclip into the top, the other into the bottom. A few jostles dropped the pins into place. Snickering, I slid apart the glass doors.

Atop the glass cabinet, I laid three bracelets—one silver fishbone chain, one a tricolored gold braid, and one 14-carat gold-plated links—each the size of a newborn's wrist.

To Poe, I whispered, "Pick one."

Dark and beady eyes inspected the jewelry. And, of course, the little bastard chose the most expensive. Friggin' diva. The bowed head prompted me to slip the tricolored gold braid around his neck. I slapped three hundred bucks on the counter. "C'mon. We gotta boogie."

I bolted for the ladder, my arms pumping, sprinting across the catwalk. Wet footprints marked my escape, but there wasn't much I could about it. The moment I cleared the window, Poe shot into the sky. I cringed. Imagine if the chain slipped off into the moat? Maybe a necklace wasn't the best idea. Ah, well, too late now.

By the time I reached the Caddy—clothes drenched from my wet skin—my body pleaded for rest. Poe strutted across the roof, head held high and proud, new bling shimmering in the moonlight.

"We're even now, right?"

A dip of the bill confirmed.

"Great." I swung open the driver's door. "Get in."

All happy and shit, Poe settled on the middle console.

"You're welcome, by the way." I wrapped the tribal blanket around my waist, slipped behind the wheel, and made it back to the hotel in record time.

In the parking lot, I reached for the necklace, and he hopped into the passenger seat. "Look. Just gimme it for a little while so your dad doesn't see it."

Poe looked at me like I'd asked for the key to his chastity belt before diving into the backseat.

I grabbed clumps of hair, almost tearing the strands from my scalp. "Be reasonable. How are we gonna explain it?"

The machine gun blast he released almost popped my eardrums, and I whipped open the driver's door. Mr. Mayhem jumped back, the door missing him by inches.

"Oh, hey." I smiled like everything was cool. Normal, even. "What are you doin' out here?"

"Why, pray tell, are you all wet?"

"Me?" My voice pitched. "Oh... um... well..."

When Poe flew out the door, Mr. Mayhem's eyebrows V'd, squinting at his chest as he pranced across the roof, showing off his new bling.

Fuck. "I can explain."

Without taking his gaze off Poe—who acted like a damn runway model, prancing back and forth—he said, "I'm listening, Cat."

"Right. So, I... err... bought it for him as a peace offering. Y'know, to mend fences since we'll be working together."

"You bought Poe a necklace," he said as a statement, not a question.

"Yep."

"After eleven p.m."

Shit, shit, shit. "Yep."

"And you paid for the necklace?"

"Yeah. Cost me three hundred bucks."

His focus stayed with Poe—really hamming it up for his dad. "Cat?"

"Yeah?"

"If you bought the necklace, you can produce a receipt. Correct?"

Fuck. "Not exactly."

"Be honest with me." Finally, he faced me. "Did you steal the necklace?"

"No, sir. I swear I didn't. Ask him if you don't believe me."

"Perhaps I should rephrase." Praying hands tapped his lips. "Was the store open when you allegedly paid for the jewelry?"

I picked at my cuticles. "No, but I swear I didn't steal it."

"And the reason you couldn't wait for the store to reopen is...?"

"Because Pissy Pants over there"—I jutted a thumb over my shoulder—"wouldn't even gimme twenty-four hours. If anyone should be in trouble, it's him. Unless you condone blackmail?"

He rocked back. "Blackmail?"

"Yep. Your precious little angel threatened to tell Spirit Crow what I said about you if I didn't get him mashed potatoes, fruit, and new bling."

He whirled around. "Is this true, young man?"

Lost in a dream world, probably envisioning himself on a stage with crowds of raving fans, Poe sauntered down the windshield to the hood. Paused, spun, then strutted back up to the roof. The slick move worked to capture his father's full attention. Mr. Mayhem might've even cracked a smile as his beloved companion modeled his new bling for an imaginary audience.

"Cautious Cat?" he said, polishing off the hard edge to his tone. "Next time, come to me prior to engaging in illegal activities with my vehicle."

"Right. Sorry. Will do."

"Thank you. Time to go, handsome." He extended a forearm, and Poe stepped aboard. To the private stairwell he strode, where he held open the door for me. "I told your grandfather not to expect us back this evening. There's been a development, I'm afraid."

"What kind of development?"

"I'd rather show you."

I pushed for more information, but he kept telling me to wait until I checked the footage from the live feed. Why all the secrecy?

Back in the suite, I changed into sweatpants and a dry T-shirt. When I strolled out of the bedroom, Mr. Mayhem asked me to sit beside him on the loveseat, where he rewound the footage from satellite images. Not of the compound, though. The recording showed thick wooden terrain surrounding the wolves.

Staring at the screen, I rubbed the back of my neck. "I don't get it. What am I lookin' for?"

"Keep watching."

Burning red eyes peered through the darkness—the same eyes I saw out my bedroom window.

"Oh, my God." My hand rose to parted lips. "I didn't dream it."

"I don't think we should jump to conclusions."

"Those are the same eyes." I jolted to my bare feet. "We gotta tell *Shicheii*. All alone, he's in real danger. C'mon, we gotta get back there." I swung left and right, scouring the floor. "Where the hell are my sneakers? Was I wearing sneakers?"

"Cat."

I whirled around. "Why are you just sitting there? We woke the beast! Oh, my God." I slapped my mouth. "Is that why you told me to run on Old Cherry Mountain Road? How long have you known about this?"

"Cat."

I flung up my hands, slapping my thighs on the way down. "Why aren't you freakin' out? *Shicheii* could die!"

Mr. Mayhem rose. "Cat," he said in a soothing tone, "breathe."

"C'mon, we've gotta get back to Jackson. Oh, my God. If anything happens to *Shicheii*, I don't know how I'll—"

Heavy forearms weighed down my shoulders, his minty breath striking my nose. "Breathe, Cat. You are not thinking clearly."

"Yes, I am. I'm the only one who is. Why'd you call and tell him we wouldn't be back? For chrissakes, he can't go mano-a-mano with a Wen—"

He slapped a hand over my mouth.

My eyes flashed wide.

"I apologize. However, we may never speak its name aloud. Understood?"

When I nodded, he lowered his hand.

"Thank you. Now, please sit so you and I can discuss this rationally."

Silent, I lowered to the loveseat.

"Thank you. Would you care for a glass of wine before we get started? Might help calm your nerves."

"Wine? No. But I'd kill for a Peppermintini or two."

"All right, then. I know the perfect place." His gaze traced me up and down. "However, you will need to change into something more suitable for a five-star establishment."

"What about Missus Hawthorne?"

"It's called the Cave for a reason. Nice and dark. As long as you don't smile at anyone up-close, you should be fine."

"You wanna discuss the details in public so I don't freak out again, huh?"

Silent, he smirked.

"Nicely played."

He tipped the fedora.

In the bedroom, I rummaged through my suitcase. Whatever he had to tell me couldn't compare to the quick flash of burning red eyes on Old Cherry Mountain Road. No wonder he sounded so frightened on the phone earlier. That thing could've killed me. Still could, if he planned to fight it.

A cold, hard shudder ran through me. Good God, how do you battle an ancient supernatural beast?

Chapter 20

"The Red Nation shall rise again, and it shall be a blessing for a sick world.
A world filled with broken promises, selfishness, and separations.
A world longing for light again."
—Crazy Horse, Oglala Sioux Chief

11:40 p.m.

Mayhem led Shawnee through a tunnel of stone—the entrance to the Cave bar within the hotel—the roofed entryway created from long boulders angled to a point, with periodic lights weaved through the rock sidewalls. Padded stools at a rich oak bar stood beneath a curved brick ceiling inlaid into wooded frames. Ambianced with candles in glass holders, the Cave offered privacy to guests. Unlike the restaurants and rooftop lounge, this bar wasn't open to the public.

By the shoulders, he aimed Shawnee toward tables with upholstered chairs in the corner. "Why don't you secure us a table while I order our cocktails."

"Alright."

When she turned halfway, he hooked her arm. "Please don't smile at anyone."

"I know." With a biting tone, she yanked her arm away, mumbling, "Always gotta bring up the teeth."

The attitude wasn't necessary, but he allowed her some leeway due to her injuries. "Thank you, Cat."

"Yeah, yeah."

A forty-something bartender approached Mayhem and slapped down a bar napkin. "Welcome to the Cave, sir."

173

"Thank you, Ryan." The brass nameplate pinned to the bartender's black collared shirt revealed his name. "I'll have a Moscow Mule, please, and a Peppermintini for the lady."

"You got it."

The exquisite décor commanded his attention. Behind the bar stood an archway of brick—a tunneled window into the game room, with pool tables and dartboards. Glasses hung from a wooden beam, curved stained glass nestled beneath the ornate ceiling of brick. Stone walls surrounded the Cave, accented with more brick and rich hardwoods.

"One Moscow Mule. One Peppermintini." The bartender set the drinks on the oak bar. "Would you like the drinks charged to your room, sir?"

"Yes, please." He showed the keycard for Ryan to jot down the suite number. "For you, my good man." From two fingers he extended a folded fifty-dollar bill.

"Thank you, sir."

"My pleasure. Could I trouble you for one small favor?"

"Sure. Name it."

Without going into specifics about this request, he said, "In ten minutes, could you please send over a second Peppermintini?"

"Absolutely."

"Thank you, Ryan." Over to the table he strode, cocktails in hand. Seated across from Shawnee in an upholstered chair, he slid the Peppermintini in front of her. "Beautiful lounge."

"Thanks." As usual, she sniffed the cocktail before sipping from the rim, her tongue sweeping crushed peppermint off her upper lip. "So good."

"Glad you're enjoying it." Mayhem raised the signature copper mug, sampled the Moscow Mule, mint leaves tickling his nose. "I don't mean to frighten you, Cat. However, I'd be remiss if I neglected to mention key facts related to the beast that shall remain nameless."

He stole another sip, vodka, ginger beer, and lime juice enlivening his tastebuds. "The beast appears gaunt to the point of emaciation, its desiccated skin pulled taut over its bones, pushing against its skin. Its complexion is the ash gray of death, its eyes sunken deep into its sockets. What lips it once had are now tattered and flecked with blood and its body unclean, suffering from suppurations of the flesh, emitting a strange and eerie odor of decay and decomposition, of death and corruption. Hence why your grandfather thought Misters Worthington, Underwood, and—"

"I know all this."

"Oh, I'm sorry. Did the middle of my sentence interrupt the beginning of yours?"

Laughing, the candlelight illuminated her blood-red teeth, and he winced.

Once her mouth clamped closed, he continued. "The English translation of its Algonquian name is 'evil that devours.' Its breath reeks of burnt flesh. As a compulsive maneater, it's always hungry, always on the hunt for food, and by 'food' I mean the sweet fat of children, the soft skin of women, the course muscles of men, especially warriors and hunters, and the brittle bones of the elderly."

Her jaw dropped open. "That describes all of us. No wonder Maggie freaked out. She knew kids were at the top of its menu?"

"Apparently."

She shot back the Peppermintini, and belched. "Might need another to get through this conversation."

A strawberry-blonde server—delightful young woman named Audrey—replaced the empty martini glass with a fresh cocktail.

"Wow." Shawnee rocked back in the chair. "Unbelievable service. I literally just swallowed the last drop."

Without a word, Audrey smiled at Mayhem, and he slipped a crisp fifty on her tray. "Thank you, sir. May I get you another Moscow Mule?"

"No, thank you, Audrey. We're all set for now."

"Give a holler if you change your mind."

"Will do, Audrey. Thank you." He waited for the server to get far enough away before continuing, his voice low and whisperous. "Unlike the film industry's ridiculous portrayal, this beast is not horned, nor antlered. It stands about twelve feet tall, with long, bony limbs, a pale-greenish skin tone, and visible bones. Its maw filled with crooked yellowed fanglike teeth, its hands and feet end in razor-like talons, its tongue a disgusting dark blue. Humanoid, it's a hideous, abhorrent beast. Its sheer size is so massive, the human mind cannot fully comprehend it."

Shawnee gulped down one-third of her cocktail. "I'm sure I'll regret asking this, but—" Again, she belched. "You wanna fight this thing, huh?"

"Do I want to? Absolutely not. But we cannot allow it to roam free, not with innocent lives at stake. Hikers frequent those trails."

"Great." Sarcasm laced her tone. "And your plan is what, exactly?"

"Here's the intriguing part." He rested his chin on woven fingers. "Although this beast is a dire threat to mankind, it has a deep affection for wildlife. The beast willingly shares food with bears, wolves, crows, ravens, and eagles."

"Really? Wow. Is that why it's hanging around the compound?"

"I believe so, yes. In fact, the mistreatment of wolves for monetary gain may have woken it from its dormancy." Lowering his clasped hands, he leaned forward. "Some say the evil spirit that transformed a cannibal into this beast thrives on gluttony, greed, and selfishness."

Like an umpire calling foul, her arms waved. "Are you saying our carelessness didn't wake this thing? The poachers did it?"

"It's possible. No," he relented. "More than possible. It's probable."

For several seconds, she held his gaze. "That's why you weren't worried about *Shicheii*?"

"He's safe. If I thought for one moment that his life was in danger, I'd drive straight home. Never would I knowingly put your grandfather in danger. You should know that by now."

"No, I know." Her stiff shoulders slumped. "I shouldn't've freaked out in the room. But those eyes scared the crap outta me. They're the same ones I saw out my bedroom window."

"I'm glad you brought that up." Because of the private nature of this conversation, Mayhem scanned the other patrons to ensure no one dared to eavesdrop. "For a while I've mulled over the details you shared with me that morning. Did you, by chance, smell anything when you saw the eyes?"

"Yeah. The stench of death. Why?"

"There *was* an olfactory component. Interesting. Is it possible—and please, let me finish before you respond—is it possible that perhaps, you had a vision? Might explain why it felt so lucid."

"Whaddaya mean, like, *Shicheii's* visions?"

"Less focused than what he experiences, perhaps, but similar. After all, you are his granddaughter. Let me ask you this. Has he told you much about his parents, your maternal great-grandparents?"

"No. Why?"

"Both were very spiritual. Powerful people, your great-grandparents."

"You're blowing my mind right now." For a brief moment, her forehead fell into a cupped hand. "Did you know them?"

Rather than answer the question, he grinned. "When this is over, ask your grandfather about his folks. In the meantime, start thinking about how Poe and the Wolf I saved earlier can help us free the others."

"Wait, wait, wait." She teed her hands. "Back up. You saved a Wolf? When? Where was I?"

"Napping in the suite, I presume." He left it at that. Leaning back in the upholstered chair, he sipped his cocktail. "So, what do you think of the Cave?"

"It's friggin' sick."

"Quite unique, isn't it?" In the hopes of settling her busy mind, he brought her attention to the décor. If left to her own devices, she had a tendency to make quick decisions, often resulting in negativity, suspicion, and wariness. And that could prove disastrous. To emerge victorious, this new fight demanded the utmost preparedness, with every step timed to perfection.

Many battled the Wendigo. Very few survived to tell the tale.

Chapter 21

Wednesday, *10:03 a.m.*

After my conversation with Mr. Mayhem last night, I didn't sleep much, my mind buzzing with images of the supernatural beast. How do you fight something like that? At least skinwalkers fluctuated between human and otherworldly creature. Maybe if my mentor filled me in, I'd relax more, but he remained vague on the details of how he planned to free the wolves with this thing hanging around the compound. I figured he wanted time to prepare me—calm my busy brain, as he would say—before he told my grandfather. He also mentioned it'd be a rough training day, because if I didn't fully invest, we might all lose this battle.

Took me a while to wrap my head around the news, but somehow, his plan worked. Not only had I accepted the upcoming war, but my constitution strengthened. Whatever else he threw at me, I'd catch. Poe couldn't wait to return. And honestly, I'd had just about enough of him prancing around the suite like God's gift to females.

You'd think a three-hundred-dollar chain would buy me a few brownie points. Oh, hell no. In his eyes, I bought his silence, not his friendship.

Back at the cabin in Jackson, the second Mr. Mayhem opened the driver's door, Poe springboarded from the center console, dove through the opening and into the air, wings flapping straight to the roosting conifer. *Ca-caw, caw, caw* trailing through the yard.

Over the roof, Mr. Mayhem smirked. "You do realize you created a monster."

"Don't remind me. His head barely fit through the door as it is."

Chuckling, he headed up the stairs.

"You two look happy." *Shicheii* met us on the porch with Spirit Crow perched on his shoulder.

"*Yá'át'ééh*, my friend." He shook my grandfather's hand then extended his forearm. Spirit Crow stepped aboard. "Good morning, my love."

In return, she cooed.

When I parted my lips to greet *Shicheii*, Poe soared through the yard, yacking with three of his cronies as they flew to the porch. Across the table, Poe struck several poses like he was auditioning for the cover of Audubon Magazine. Spirit Crow tossed Mr. Mayhem a hard glare, and he flashed his palms.

"I had nothing to do with it, darling."

"Guilty as charged, Your Honor." My neck turtled in my shoulders. "Had I known it'd go straight to his head, I probably woulda bought something a little less flashy."

"What a thoughtful gift, Mourning Dove." *Shicheii* rocked me in his arms. "I'm so proud of you."

If he only knew.

To closer inspect the jewelry, Spirit Crow fluttered down to the table. Shit. She wasn't stupid. No way wouldn't she figure out it cost me some dough. When her and Poe's gazes locked for an eternity of minutes, my breath stalled. It'd be just like Poe to rat me out to save his own ass.

Mr. Mayhem must've reached the same conclusion because he tried to divert her attention with a few gentle caresses of her back. "You must admit, darling, Poe earned every strand of that braid."

"Hello?" Closed fists flew to my hips. "I'm standing right here."

The porch erupted in laughter, obliterating the awkwardness, and Spirit Crow leaped to my shoulder, her feathery cheek nuzzling against mine. God, I loved this family.

"Jacy Lee," a somberness edged his tone, "there's been a development at the compound."

"Hold that thought a moment, Cheveyo." My grandfather bustled inside, returning moments later with a serving tray of three mugs and the honey pot. "I made a fresh batch of wild tea this morning." He set down the tray, passed us each a mug, and sat in his usual chair at the head of the table by the screen door.

At the opposite end of the table, Mr. Mayhem sat, sliding the honey pot in front of me. "Ladies first."

"Being female has its advantages around you two." I swished the dipper, drizzling nature's sweet nectar into my mug. "Do all Native men treat women like this?"

"The Diné view women as sacred," *Shicheii* said as I passed him the honey pot. "Traditionally, both sexes have important distinctive, complementary roles to ensure the survival of all our People."

Mr. Mayhem chimed in. "To answer your question, no. It's unreasonable to conclude all Native men would treat women in the same way. The ones who choose not to respect the opposite sex disregard tradition. In Apache society, women often accompanied warriors on raids, took up arms to defend our People, counseled men in battle strategy, engaged in peace negotiations, and served as shamans for spiritual questions. Because of their prominent role, we instilled Apache tradition in Cheyenne."

In an instant, my busy brain froze. "But I thought you guys raised her Chippewa."

"Normally, I would defer to my wife to explain. Alas, these are not ordinary times. Isn't that right, darling?" He blew Spirit Crow a kiss, and I tilted my head to ensure the airborne smooch hit its target. "Our daughter's Chippewa roots run deep, but she's also part Apache. Thus, we combined the traditions of both cultures much in the same way my parents did for me. Though, unlike Cheyenne, I have more Apache blood than Chippewa."

"Huh." Learned a new tidbit about my mentor. "I wondered about that."

Quick wink. "All you had to do was ask, Cat."

Yeah, right. I asked for his real surname, and he refused to answer. Granted, my timing sucked, but still. He revealed what he wanted, where he wanted, when he wanted, and nothing I did or said could ever change that.

"Now that your inquisitive mind has sufficiently been quelled," he said, jarring me from my thoughts, "would you mind gathering the laptop from the Caddy? We need to show your grandfather the footage."

"I'm on it."

As I leaped off the top stair, I said a silent prayer for *Shicheii*. The news of a Wendigo near the compound probably wouldn't go over well, but we had no choice. A key ingredient of battling supernatural forces included a spiritual leader like a Medicine Man. Without his help, we didn't stand a chance.

In less than a minute—okay, okay, maybe two or three—I settled in my chair with the PC, brought up the footage, and spun the screen to face my grandfather. "Ready?" Without waiting for a response, I pressed PLAY.

After a few seconds, his posture turned rigid, and he pushed the screen away. "Cheveyo, I warned you of the dangers—"

"Please let me explain. The arousal of its dormancy may have nothing to do with us. Legend says it thrives on greed, gluttony, and selfishness. Correct?"

"Correct."

Firm, intense eye contact lingered between them. "Poaching and animal trafficking is the epitome of greed and selfishness, is it not?"

"It is. An argument could be made those activities are gluttonous as well."

"Precisely. And do you not also agree the beast that shall remain nameless has a fondness for wildlife?"

"I would. It even shares food with bears, eagles, ravens, crows, and—" A gasp escaped *Shicheii's* lips. "Wolves."

"Precisely. So, my question to you is this. Could the mistreatment of wolves for monetary gain wake the beast?"

For a long while, my grandfather didn't respond. Instead, he stared at the heavens, as if searching for answers while sipping his tea. "It could, Cheveyo. Mother Earth is out of balance, the Natural World no longer harmonious. An unstable environment combined with the greed, gluttony, and selfishness of man could indeed drive evil supernatural forces to manifest." He laid his hand over mine. "If I asked you to let Cheveyo and I handle this, would you agree?"

"Sorry, *Shicheii*, but no. Please don't ask me to stay behind. If my destiny is to help the Innocent Ones, I need to fight this war right alongside you."

"She has a point, Jacy Lee."

"She does." He palmed my cheek. "All right, sweet child. I have faith in you." His hand dropped as he regarded his lifelong friend. "Cheveyo, where does she stand in her training?"

"The footage has accelerated our timeline."

"Good. Now, if you'll excuse me, I need to pray for ways to move forward."

As he strode into the yard, tears pooled in my eyes. "He looks... so... broken."

"Broken? Hardly. What you're witnessing is incredible strength, determination, and focus." To get my attention, my sight still glued to my grandfather, Mr. Mayhem tapped the table in front of me. "Let's go. You and I have work to do."

"Where are we goin'?"

Rather than answer my question, he rose. "Have you grown accustomed to blood-red teeth?"

Shit. I slapped my forehead.

"While you freshen up, you may want to change into more appropriate clothing for training."

"Sweatpants won't work?" As he held open the screen door for me, Poe, Spirit Crow, and the others took flight, black and white wings flapping in synchronicity toward *Shicheii*. "My buckskins have dried blood all over them."

"Your grandfather scrubbed out the bloodstains. Before we left, they were hanging in the upstairs bathroom. He may have put them on your bed by now."

"Okay, cool. Thanks."

"Training begins in ten minutes."

"Got it."

Past the granite island, I bustled down the hall to my room. Before I forgot to brush my teeth again, I headed straight into the bathroom. In the mirror, I barely recognized the reflection as mine. The scratches on my cheek from Poe's hissy fit during his—quote, unquote—*abduction* last weekend didn't seem all that bad compared to my venom-infused lips, greenthread-stained teeth, and blood-scabbed claw marks across my upper chest and arms. Violent and angry bees stung too many spots to count, inflamed bumps dotting my skin from head to toe.

Electric toothbrush in hand, I turned my back, unwilling to dwell on my haggard appearance while a maneater stalked the woods around the compound. Hikers favored those trails. Would a Wendigo hide from the public? Most stories told of the beast targeting those who ventured off on their own. In some cases, it even tricked victims into separating from their friends, family, or group.

What if it attacked an innocent bystander? Hang on. What if it slaughtered the poachers? Might solve our problem. I scrawled a mental note to ask Mr. Mayhem about it later. For now, I roamed into my room to get dressed. No buckskin halter and pants on the bed, in the closet, or in any drawer of my bureau.

Down the hall I trekked and zipped up the stairs. Rather than knock on Mr. Mayhem's door, I veered into *Shicheii's* bedroom since the bathroom connected both rooms. I swung open the door and there stood Mr. Mayhem—naked as the day he was born—a hand towel covering his manhood.

"Oh." I slapped a hand over my eyes. "Sorry."

"Is there some reason you barged into my bathroom without knocking?"

With my bare feet rooted to the floor, I couldn't move, couldn't leave. "Err... yeah. Sorry. Thought you were in your room."

"And you're still standing here because...?"

"Oh... err... my buckskins?"

"Are on the hanger outside the door. You walked right past them."

Frozen in place, I tried to act natural. "Cool, cool, alright. Thanks."

"Cat—"

"Yeah?"

"Run along now."

"Right." I spun, headed into *Shicheii's* room, closing the door behind me. A click confirmed he'd locked it. "Sorry," I called through the wood.

When I turned to grab my clothes, Poe was standing at the foot of my grandfather's bed. Bill slightly parted, his beady-eyed glare drilled into me.

"I can understand how that probably looked pretty bad, but I swear, it's not what you think. I came for my—" I grabbed the hanger. "These. See? You misread the room." As I inched sideways, his hard stare never left me. I booked it down the stairs, my bare feet slapping the open treads. When I swung off the railing and banged a right down the hall, the screen door opened behind me.

"Mourning Dove?"

Stopped mid-stride, I didn't dare turn around. "Yeah?"

"Is Cheveyo upstairs?"

"Umm... I think so." I wiggled my buckskins in the air. "Just ran up to get these." When I rotated, Spirit Crow was on his shoulder. "Oh, hi." My voice pitched so high it cracked. "I gotta get dressed. Can't be late for training." I darted down the hall, calling over my head, "Thanks for washing out the bloodstains, *Shicheii.*"

When I hit my room, I slammed the door. Fuck. Not cool, Shawnee, not cool. Get your head in the game.

In the bathroom, I sprayed down my head with ice water, snapping my focus into place. Changed into my warrior gear—buckskin pants and halter, knee-high moccasins, turquoise armband for protection, and Apache Tears choker—and strode out the door, down the hall, through the kitchen, past Poe and Spirit Crow wolfing down a fruit bowl, then out to the porch.

In the yard, Mr. Mayhem waited clad in knee-high moccasins and buckskin pants sporting fringe down the outer seam. Shirtless, his loose hair hung halfway down his back.

Without a word, I jogged over, and with as little eye-contact as possible, accepted the water bottle he offered.

"Are you ready?" As though nothing transpired between us upstairs, he acted like the incident never took place.

Works for me. "Yep. Ready."

"Different route today."

"Okay."

"I am what I am," he said, and I repeated the line. "In having faith in the beauty within me, I develop trust. In softness, I have strength. In silence, I walk the higher realms. In peace, I understand myself and the world. In conflict, I stay calm, cool, collected. In detachment, I am free."

While I reiterated those words, he leaned closer.

Mr. Mayhem continued the same prayer as before, ending with, "I am what I am—eternal, immortal, universal, and infinite."

"I am what I am," I echoed, "eternal, immortal, universal, and infinite."

With a single nod from him, I squirted the water into my mouth. He took off like a flash of light, long hair blowing behind him. Arms pumping, I jetted after him, but he was so fast I lost sight of him among the trees in the forest. Mucus overpowered all my senses, snot pouring out my nose as I stopped, my lungs pleading for air.

A stick hit my head, and I glanced up. From the top of a tall oak, he waved.

How the hell did he get up there so fast?

"Join me, please," he hollered down.

Climb up there with a mouthful of water? Even though nothing about this seemed like a good idea, I shot a thumbs-up, wrapped my arms around the trunk, steadied my right foot on the bark, following through with my left. This wouldn't be so bad if I could breathe through my mouth. After all, I climbed shit all the time as a cat burglar. But I didn't have the luxury of mouth-breathing today.

Hand over hand, I inched higher and higher. The combination of mucus and elevation lightened my head, and I swayed, my arms locked around the trunk while I stopped, regrouped. A fall from this height could do some serious damage. I blinked. Blinked again and again. Tried to master my breathing.

Once I somewhat regained control, I climbed higher. Mr. Mayhem's opened hand shook at me. The second I latched on, he yanked me up to the limb, almost dislocating my shoulder in the process.

"Did you swallow the water?"

I wagged my head no.

"Do you want to?"

Dear God, yes. But I wasn't about to admit it. So, instead, I rocked another no.

"Why not?"

I swept my fingertips across the Apache Tears choker.

"Correct. Your suffering honors all those who came before us. Your suffering, however, cannot compare to theirs. Remember them when you want to quit. Remember their families."

Chin slightly dipped, I nodded in agreement.

"Enough rest. See that branch over there?"

My eyes flashed wide. The one in the next tree? He's out of his frickin' mind. Or maybe, this was payback for the bathroom fiasco.

"Do you see the branch, Cat?"

As much as I hated to do it, I confirmed with a nod.

"Good. Go there now, please."

And my eyeballs almost rolled out the sockets.

"Would you like me to demonstrate?"

This time, I exaggerated the nod. In other words, hell yeah.

"Notice how I position my body." When he rose, he gripped the branches above his head then ran full force to the end of the limb and right over to the next tree like it was the most natural thing in the world, like he'd done this a gazillion times before.

I couldn't believe how easy he made it look. In hindsight, maybe that's why I rose with such confidence. With my hands latched to the same branches, I inched farther out on the limb.

"Faster, Cat." His fingers snapped. "Stealth is quick, not slow. Back up and start again."

And so, I did. The second time, I moved faster. Still not as fast as him, but quicker than before. Halfway across, he stopped me.

"Faster." More snapping. "Back up and start again."

In my head, I called him every name in the book, but I still backed all the way to the trunk. This time, I said screw it, blocked out all distractions, and stayed focused on my mentor. Sprinting across the limb, pure instinct drove me off the end of one branch and on to the other.

"Brava." He clapped—loud and slow. "I knew you could do it. Ready to continue?"

With renewed confidence, I chased him from one tree to another. Once I hit the fourth tree, it dawned on me I was still holding a mouthful of water, nose-breathing a lot easier now for some reason.

When he finally stopped, his arm hooked the trunk of a Hemlock, and I mimicked the stance on the other side. "Did you spit out the water?"

With a half-smile, I wagged a no.

"It's easier now, isn't it?"

I rocked a yes.

"Do you know why?"

I shook my head from side to side.

"Because you weren't cognizant of the water during the exercise. Hence why I brought you up here. Your full focus had to remain on the mission and not on losing the ability to breathe through your mouth."

Wow. Cool. On its own, my head rocked up and down, his theory resonating with me.

"Do you need a minute before we climb down?"

I wagged a no. Strangely, I really didn't a need a break.

"Excellent."

Descending the tree was a lot harder than climbing it in the first place. Once I reached about the ten-foot mark, I jumped down to the forest floor, knees bending, absorbing the impact.

"Now that you've grown accustomed to nose-breathing, let's move on to the next exercise. I presume you haven't swallowed the water?"

I rocked another no.

"Perfect. All right, then. To trail an animal—or human—we need to first find their tracks. Stay mindful of your surroundings at all times while you search for prints in the soil, or a predator could sneak up on you while you're staring at the ground. Make sense?"

I nodded yes.

"Super. Let me know when you find a fresh track."

I pointed two fingers at my chest, then at the forest floor.

"Yes, you. Fear not, Cat. I'll stay right beside you. However, you cannot rely on me to check your surroundings. You must stay cognizant of the environment, as well."

After acknowledgment, I first skimmed left, right, and behind me. The last thing I needed was another run-in with a mountain lion. When the coast was clear, so to speak, I lowered to my knees, crawling across soil and pine needles, searching for animal prints while praying to all that's holy that I wouldn't disturb another hive.

Imagine? Man, that'd suck.

"It's an interesting technique," he said, "but not at all useful. If a predator charges you, how will you defend yourself from the ground? Kneeling—or in your case, crawling like a toddler—puts you at a disadvantage. Did you learn nothing from the cougar or the bees?"

Rising, I shot him a glower. Why bring up the attacks? Was he trying to scare me? Or had he planned a face-to-face meeting between me and the mountain lion?

Chapter 22

11:30 a.m.

Focused on the exercise, I searched the soil for prints, but almost everywhere had some sort of mark and/or depression.

After several mindboggling minutes, he snapped a branch off a nearby tree and de-limbed it. "Here. Let me help you." One end of the straight shaft he aimed at the soil, the other end angled upward at my face. "Follow the tracking stick straight down. Do you see the hoofprint?"

I'd stared at the print a few times but hadn't recognized it as a hoofprint till he pointed it out. To answer his question, I nodded yes.

"White-tail deer. We know this by the size of the cloven hoof. As you can see, white-tail deer prints resemble a split heart, roughly two-and-a-half to three inches in length. Moose also have a cloven hoof, but their tracks are much larger, about four-and-a-half to six inches. See how the tips of the white-tail deer print curve inward to a point? A moose print has a larger separation between the toes."

Unsheathing his knife confused me. But then he lifted the end of the tracking stick, slashing evenly spaced gouges up the shaft. "The notches are twelve inches apart."

Ah, okay. It's a ruler. Duh.

"Now, measure the distance between the heel of this track and the heel of the next. This is how you'll learn and get familiar with this specific deer's stride. By recognizing the stride, you'll ensure you're still trailing the same animal if obstacles cause you to lose sight of the tracks."

Without the ability to speak, I could only nod.

His hand swept toward the hoofprints. "Whenever you're ready, you may begin."

The stride measured about eighteen inches between steps. With the end of the stick, I drew a one and an eight.

"Correct." The grin faded fast. "Have you ever trailed an animal before?"

Even though it was a ridiculous question, I wagged my head no. Where would I have supposedly done this? I grew up in the city, for chrissakes. And he knew it! Living on the streets didn't allow for sleep-away camp or outings in the wilderness. My only objective was learning how to survive.

"All right, then. We have a lot to get through today, so I'd prefer not to spend too much time on this. Briefly, it's important to mark each track with a mental anchor. By recalling the location of the last good track, you can return to that point if the animal trail disappears. Understood?"

I nodded yes.

"Kick tracking or scuffing is the act of following your own tracks. Learning how to follow your own footprints is a vital skill that'll help you learn how to trail animals. All we do is make a scuff mark in the soil every so often. The key is to create just enough of a disturbance for you to recognize the trail as yours, but not enough of a disturbance for others to recognize it as a marker. Make sense?"

Kinda sorta. If I had questions later, I could always ask *Shicheii*, so I agreed.

"There's a trick to trailing an animal through the forest. Hooved animals break pine needles as they tromp through wooded terrain. Lighter animals do not."

From the ground he swiped a few pine needles. "When pine needles break, they bruise." His pinky finger waved across the end. "See where the morning dew darkened the split end?" After dropping the needles, his hands brushed together. "While trailing an animal, look for freshly broken pine needles, bruises, shading, and areas where a pile has been disturbed."

From behind me, he scooted my body over to the left. "Keep the trail between you and the Sun. The light casts shadows in the tracks, thus making the trail easier to follow. Never stare straight down." His arm came across my shoulder. "Look ahead at the trail of tracks. Also, remain mindful of other animal signs like scat and/or droppings, scratches in tree bark, chewed vegetation, fur snagged on branches or in bark, gnawed bone, discarded feathers, tree rubbings, nut shells, burrows, dens, nests, and well-worn animal trails."

With so much information being thrown at me, I could barely absorb it all.

"That about covers it. Questions?"

I pointed at my puffed cheeks. How could I ask questions with a mouthful of water?

"Right. Lost my head for a moment. All right, then." Grinning, he enjoyed my silence a little too much. "Whenever you're ready, please begin."

For over an hour, I followed that damn animal through mud and muck, down to the water's edge, then back up the steep incline. Most of which sucked on various levels. Topping the list was Mr. Mayhem's refusal to allow me to spit out the damn water. Why, I had no idea. After all this time, hadn't I proven I could nose-breathe?

Just when doubt crept in, and I'd resigned to the fact that I may never find this animal, I caught a glimpse of tan fur between two conifers. In the distance, a well-nourished buck stared over his shoulder at me, as if posing for a wildlife photographer. What a special moment—one unlike anything I'd ever experienced. For at that moment, the silky threads of life's web connected me to that animal, to Mr. Mayhem, to the Blue Jays chattering above our heads, to the squirrels chasing each other around trees, and to every other being out here, our souls entwining as one, my destiny clearer and more focused than ever before.

A branch snapped to my right. Instead of panicking, I rotated, and there stood the mountain lion. But unlike the last time we met, he didn't snarl. Or lunge. Instead, his gaze lingered on me for a moment, then he turned and prowled away, a long muscular tail vanishing into a thicket of trees.

When I pivoted back to my mentor, he slung an arm around my neck. "Nicely done, Cat. Now, you may spit out the water."

And so, I did. "That's what you were waiting for?"

"Yes."

"Why?"

Brief smile. "Come on, let's head back." He headed down the trail, and I hustled to catch up.

"You're not gonna tell me?"

"Do you know why the cougar did not view you as a threat this time?"

"Because I'm not."

"Yes, but you weren't a threat to him before, either. Why was the encounter different today?"

"I was silenced."

"And?"

"Centered."

"And?

"Connected."

"To?"

"Everything and everyone. I still feel it, actually."

The smile grew wider.

"It's incredible. I thought I knew what *hozho* was before, but this feels more deep-rooted, more meaningful, more harmonious and balanced." An eruption of emotion heaved my chest. "This is the secret to life, isn't it?"

A gentle palm swept over the crown of my head. "What do you think?"

"Definitely is. I wish I could share it."

"With whom?"

I sloughed off a shrug. "Anyone who needs it."

"May you never lose your beautiful spirit, Mourning Dove."

The utterance of my traditional name from his lips made me even more emotional, happy tears streaming down my face as we veered down the trail that led to the cabin, our legs moving in unison. Spirit Crow soared around the bend. The sudden disruption of polar-white plumage caught me off-guard, her angelicness knifing my chest, forcing me to cry even harder. She fluttered down to my shoulder, then craned her neck to her soulmate.

"Release of adrenaline and fear," he said as if answering a concern delivered telepathically, "combined with the intake of oxygen post-depletion, and a major breakthrough, darling. She has reached, and thus far is maintaining, *hozho*."

Rattle, rattle, rattle. Coo...

Strands of my hair slipped through her bill, gentle twisting motions from the scalp down, preening, nurturing me like the most-attentive mother, purring in my ear, my heart overflowing with love.

And then, Poe's alarm call ricocheted through the trees.

Oh, my God. My breath halted. Something was wrong.

Chapter 23
"You already possess everything necessary to become great."
—Crow Wisdom

1:30 p.m.

Mayhem led Shawnee and Spirit Crow out of the forest. In the yard, Jacy Lee performed a ceremonial dance. Gray hair down and loose, he wore a ceremonial mask with a turquoise strap from ear to ear and from one corner of the face to the other. A band of yellow, red, and blue rectangles ran across the lower portion of the mask. Special beads and silver bracelets adorned the brightly colored Dancer Regalia. Fox hung behind him. A bustle attached to a backboard—called a crow belt—displayed eagle and hawk feathers on his lower back. More eagle feathers adorned the magnificent roach atop his head, each one earned over many years.

Shawnee latched on to Mayhem's forearm. "What's happening right now?"

"Not here." Taking hold of her hand, he jogged to the porch, swung open the door, then escorted her into the cabin. "Your grandfather is praying to *Tonenili*, God of Water. He's responsible for rain, sleet, snow, and causes thunder and lightning."

Head slightly tilted, her face scrunched in confusion. "He's doin' a rain dance?"

The white man had a knack for minimizing spiritual ceremonials by stereotyping with simple names. However, now was not the time to broach that conversation. "In short, yes."

"Okay, but why?"

"To cleanse Mother Earth of evil spirits."

She gasped.

"You and I need to help him. Unfortunately, we don't have the luxury of time to teach you the dance, so you'll have to learn the steps through observation. First, however—" His gaze traced her up and down. "Your grandfather is better suited for these types of things."

"Whaddaya mean?" Her tone hardened. "What things?"

"All your skin must remain covered. Females can only show their bare feet." When his gaze sidled to Spirit Crow, she leaped off Shawnee's shoulder, circled once to draw his full attention, and flew up the stairs. "Apparently, she wants you to follow her for some reason."

As Shawnee darted up the stairs, he hustled to the window. When he couldn't spot Poe on the porch or in the surrounding trees—the entire local murder mysteriously absent—he proceeded up the stairs to his bedroom, where he found Shawnee standing in front of the opened closet. "Are there no boundaries in this house?"

Rather than respond, she stepped aside to reveal Spirit Crow, leafing through the hangers.

"My mistake, Cat." He hustled closer. "Darling, we really don't have time for—"

Spirit Crow lifted the shoulder of her Dancer Regalia, flooding his mind with memories of how she moved so elegantly when she danced, so breathtakingly beautiful, his heart aching to relive those moments.

Pulling the garments from the closet, his voice quavered. "I thought I had given this to our daughter." The Regalia still held Kimi's scent, the faint sweetness of honeysuckle slashing open his heart.

"I appreciate the generous offer"—Shawnee backed away—"but I don't think I should wear it."

"Cat, she would not have offered if she opposed the idea."

"Alright, but how do you feel about it?"

Conflicted, the right words escaped him, tears blooming in his eyes. Hiding his face, he grabbed his Regalia from the closet. "You can change in here. I shall... err... meet you downstairs."

On his way out the door, Shawnee's voice stopped him mid-stride. "Are you alright?"

"I will be."

Down the stairs he trod. Halfway between the kitchen and bathroom, Poe's cry speared through his core, and he jogged out to the porch, the railing lined with crows. More alert calls from Poe raised the light hairs of his forearms. All-terrain vehicles roared nearby, and all the crows came into focus, Father Sky shadowed by taloned soldiers.

He sprinted into the cabin and up the stairs. "Cat!"

"Be out in a minute," she called through the door.

"Don't change your clothes. We need to go—now."

"What is it?" The door swung open. "What happened?"

"No time to explain." He grabbed her hand, dragging her behind him down the stairs, through the living room, then out to the porch, where he spun her around, slapping a hand over her eyes. "Listen."

Jacy Lee's traditional yelps echoed through the yard, his unparalleled faith on display, praying and dancing for the Holy Ones. In the background, multiple all-terrain vehicles growled closer.

When Mayhem reached into the cabin for his bow and quiver, Spirit Crow screeched, soaring straight at him. "Sorry, darling." He slammed the door shut, and she clawed at the screen, shrilling.

"Fuck. I mean... fuck." The danger finally dawned on Shawnee, and she slid a chair in front of the screen door, ensuring Spirit Crow couldn't escape. "Whaddawe do?"

"First, breathe. The colorful language is not helpful. Second, we cannot allow them to breach the cabin grounds. Or disturb your grandfather."

"Alright." Deeply, she inhaled, exhaled. "So, whaddawe do?"

"Cut them off." He slid his hand down Shawnee's arm. Laced his fingers with hers and gave her a gentle squeeze, staring straight into her eyes. "Remember your training. And find your center."

With no further instruction, he released her. Slung the quiver on his back and leaped the side railing of the porch. Behind the cabin, he charged through thickets of trees, batting branches out of the way, Shawnee right on his heels.

Deep into the forest he bounded, zigzagging around trees, hopping logs, racing up hillsides, stealing quick glimpses of the sky to pinpoint the enemy's location. Dozens of black wings dipped, circled, and dived, the wind stirring forty angry cries, Mother Earth vibrating through the soles of his moccasins.

Up ahead, engines revved, male voices howling with anticipation. Mayhem stopped short, and Shawnee slammed off his back.

When he craned his neck, glancing over his shoulder, she mouthed, "Sorry."

He flashed four fingers.

Palms up, she shrugged, mouthed, "Four men?"

By the back of the neck, he brought her closer, his voice a low whisper. "Four engines."

"How many men, y'think?"

"Between four and twelve. Manageable."

"Manageable?" Her head snapped backward, emerald eyes flashed wide. "What if they're armed?"

"Release the frightened kitten inside you, please. I need the warrior who ran through the treetops with me, the warrior who trailed a magnificent buck through this very terrain, the warrior who came face-to-face with a cougar and did not flinch. She is logical. She is intelligent. She is invincible, unstoppable."

Back straightening, her shoulders squared, chin held high and proud. "What's our next move?"

He patted the trunk of an Eastern Hemlock. "At the peak, you should have an unobstructed view of all four vehicles. From there, you can direct me. I'll teach you Plains Sign Language when we have more time. For now, we'll abbreviate." Four closed fingers he raised at chest-level, with the thumb braced across the palm. "For North." He aimed them down. "For South." Pointed the straight and spaceless fingers to the left. "West." To the right. "East. All gestured in front of your chest."

"Got it."

"Once you show me direction, show me how many yards away by spreading your fingers, also at chest-level." He rested the back of his wrist against his forehead. "Fingers raised above your scalp show feet instead of yards."

"Got it."

The roar of the engines grew closer with each passing moment. "What direction are you facing?"

"East."

"Perfect."

Bent at the waist, he wove his hands into a stirrup. The heel of her moccasin slipped into his palm, her foot pushing off to scale the tree. Halfway up, he slapped the trunk to draw her attention. She glanced down, cherry-streaked dark hair dangling below an ivory complexion. Two fingers he aimed at his chest, spinning them toward the area where he'd lie in wait. She shot him a thumbs-up before he took off, zigzagging around flora, leaping streams and broken timber, zipping up an incline, ultimately crouching behind a grove of Eastern Red Cedar.

All-terrain vehicles advanced closer, more persistent in their pursuit. Sliding an arrow from the quiver on his back, he glimpsed Shawnee's tree. The bushy canopy of leaves shook, but she did not emerge. Moments later, she descended partway down the trunk.

Where on earth was she headed?

Chapter 24

2:00 p.m.

How did my partner-in-crime expect to spot my pale fingers from fifty to one-hundred yards away? Not to mention the elevation. Unless he had amazing vision like an eagle, the sign language would never work.

With an ear cocked toward the ATVs, I climbed partway down the trunk. Zipped far enough out on a lower limb to snap off a bundle of branches from the black cherry tree next to me. Clenching the split ends between my teeth, I scaled higher into the hickory's canopy of leaves. I popped two un-ripened cherries into my mouth. As I chewed, an explosion of sourness squinted my eyes.

After spitting out the mush, I rubbed my hands together, my fingers and palms dyed red. *Brilliant idea, if I do say so myself.*

Below me, two all-terrain vehicles trained through a well-worn animal trail, heading straight for Mr. Mayhem. Since he never showed me the signal for more than one ATV in line with another, I improvised by signing East for the direction they were heading. Bunny ears held at my wrist to show the number of four-wheelers. At chest-level, I raised my left forefinger. The fingers of my right hand formed one zero, then another. Last step, I pressed the backs of two splayed hands to my forehead and flashed two tens.

He shot me a thumbs-up.

He understood all that? Huh. Guess sign language did work.

With a red hand shading my eyes, I searched for the other two ATVs. Both engines rumbled, but thick canopies of leaves obscured my view. The crows split into two groups, one mobbing the vehicles heading straight for Mr. Mayhem, the second trailing the other two four-wheelers—those men much farther behind the first group. If I guessed wrong, Mr. Mayhem could get seriously injured. Or die. So, I dipped lower and climbed farther out on the limb.

Hello, assholes.

Snickering, I breached the tree canopy, but I couldn't find my hunting partner anywhere. He blended into the landscape so well, the eye passed right over him. Super impressive. And so, I scanned in a grid pattern near the lead ATV. A razor-tipped arrow sailed across the driver's neck, slashing open his throat, blood waterfalling down his chest, crimsoning the white T-shirt peering between the folds of unbuttoned camouflage. The dude on the back didn't have a clue—still hooping and howling—until his ride smashed headlong into a tree and cannoned him over the hood, arms and legs flailing as he tumbled down the hillside.

Quicker than a lightning bolt, Mr. Mayhem leaped down from a tree, landing a few feet from the scumbag. Sunlight kissed the blade of his hunting knife when he severed the poacher's throat. Then, like a mirage, he vanished. The second ATV pulled beside the wreck, and I held my breath, anticipating a bloodbath.

Eagle-eyed, I waited—mind racing—my heart thundering out my chest. But nothing happened. The second I abandoned the search, Mr. Mayhem caught in my peripheral, staring straight at me.

Aw, shit. He expected detailed instructions.

The other two all-terrain vehicles barreled down separate trails, both circling wide, heading for the cabin. And *Shicheii*. At chest-level, I flashed two fingers. Paused. Then one to show the first ATV, signing East plus North—northeast—fifty yards, ten feet. For the second rig, I flashed two fingers, then West plus North—northwest—sixty yards, fifteen feet. In return, he motioned for me to join him. I dipped below the canopy, climbing down the trunk a lot faster than I intended, my forearms scraped, littered with friction burns.

As soon as my moccasins hit the soil, I hauled ass, zigging and zagging around trees, hopping logs and forest debris. The ATV that escaped the accident scene stopped me cold. Upside-down, the tires whirled, the engine still roaring. Two dead men lay beside it, throats severed almost to the point of decapitation, fatigues crimsoning, their bodies releasing vital fluids. Blood gurgling in the mouth of a third man slacked my jaw, my eyes pinned wide-open. Sprawled atop the overturned rig, the poacher's hands groped his neck wound, mouth moving to form words, desperately trying to communicate.

A firm hand gripped my shoulder, spinning me around, and I cocked a fist, ready to ram my knuckles down someone's throat.

For a moment, Mr. Mayhem smirked. "We need to split up. Time is not on our side." He passed me the bow and quiver. "Do not hesitate to shoot. If they get past you, they will murder your grandfather."

A firebolt electrified my heart. "What? Why?"

"Retribution for killing their men, exposing their operation, or both."

Aw, man, not good. "This isn't about protecting Spirit Crow?"

"Not entirely, no. Though she will also become a casualty of war if they breach the cabin. Head northwest. After I take care of the other men, I'll catch up with you. If I am delayed, head straight to the cabin. Go." Sharpness edged his tone. "Now."

I sprinted through the woods, my moccasins barely touching the forest floor. An engine's growl loudened with every step. The poachers couldn't be far. One problem. Unlike my mentor, I was nowhere near an expert marksman. My aim improved through training, but I also missed the bullseye more times than I cared to admit. The easiest way to stop trophy hunters hellbent on human prey might involve crashing their vehicle. So, I ducked behind a wide ash tree, withdrew an arrow from the quiver, loaded the bow, heart jackhammering in my chest, ribs rattling against the surge of adrenaline.

Breathe, Shawnee, breathe. I closed my eyes, inhaled for one... two... three... exhaled for one... two... three... In seconds, my heartbeat slowed, my pulse evening out.

The poachers' hoops and howls grew louder and more persistent. After a quick ten-count, I stepped into the open, released the bowstring. The arrow sailed past the tire.

Missed. Fuck.

I shot again and again, some arrows aimed high, some low. Then ducked behind the tree.

"Sonofabitch," one poacher yelled as though I'd hit him. "Get her!"

Gunfire rang my eardrums, bullets flying, chipping off bark. Bits of wood scattered everywhere.

Before they got too close, I piled leaf litter from the ash tree to a maple. Hopped behind the makeshift barrier. Crouched low, I blocked out every other living creature, my full concentration on the ATV. Bowstring drawn, I waited for the men to move into my target area. The second they were in range, I fired.

Nailed the driver in the chest.

The vehicle swerved. One front tire rolled up the side of a boulder. The four-wheeler flipped, all three poachers ended up trapped underneath. Disoriented from the crash, no one shot back. Gunfire ceased.

While dragging another arrow from the quiver, I jetted closer. Now within feet of the trapped poachers, I fired, the razor-tipped arrow lodging in the passenger's jaw. But it didn't kill him. Or silence him.

"You crazy bitch! When I get out of here, I'm coming for you."

"Whatever you say, pal." Squatting beside him, I surveyed the interior. The dude in the back folded in the crash, ankles dangling above his head, literally in the position of kissing his ass goodbye. Did I hit him? No arrow in his body, but he wasn't breathing. Not that I could tell, anyway.

"Looks like you're all by your onesie now." I faked a pout. "Here, lemme help you."

"You touch me, and I'll—"

"You'll what? Pretend I'm a defenseless animal and shoot me? You fuckin' cowards make me sick." A twig snapped behind me, and I glanced over my shoulder.

Feet away, the mountain lion stopped mid-stride, one massive paw hovering above the soil.

"Hello, Karma. Hungry?" Smiling, I swept a hand at the dude spouting empty threats. "Help yourself. The one with the arrow looks extra juicy."

Nice and slow, I backed away. The poacher was screaming, swearing, begging me to shoot the cougar. Yeah, right. He had a better shot of seeing Elvis rise from the grave.

Deeper into the forest, I trekked, the poacher's cries coiling through the trees. And then... Karma silenced him forever. Score one for the good guys. Granted, I had blood on my hands now, but it didn't bother me as much as I thought it would. Those scumbags made a living off the slaughter of animals—the brutal, heartless destruction of Mother Earth's Innocent Ones.

Did their actions grant me a license to kill? Maybe, maybe not. But I sure as hell wasn't about to let them murder me or my family. Besides, even the law allowed for self-defense and killing in defense of others.

All at once, the angry caws, male voices, and roar of engines quieted. Why? Did Mr. Mayhem already wipe out the last of the poachers, or were they too far away? The question only lingered until I strode around the bend.

Up ahead on the trail, a crow dragged one wing across the dirt path, a long crooked line indenting the soil behind him.

"Hey—" I jogged closer. "Are you alright?"

When the crow turned, a tricolored-gold braid shimmered on his chest feathers.

"Poe?" I knelt to one knee. "Are you okay? Stupid question. Of course, you're not alright. Is the wing broken?"

Head cocked, he probably wondered why I acted so concerned. Poe and I'd had our differences, but it killed me to watch him struggle like this.

"It's not safe for you down here." I extended my forearm, my hands stained red to the wrists. "Hop on, and I'll carry you home. I'm heading back to the cabin, anyway."

Without hesitation or protest, he stepped aboard. Huh. Maybe he finally realized I wasn't the enemy. Either that, or he couldn't resist the smell of black cherry. Hard to tell which.

A gunshot rang out, and his whole body stiffened, sharp claws digging into my bare skin.

"Don't hate me for this."

With one hand pressing him to my chest, I bolted for the cabin, feet clomping through leaf litter and flora. If anything happened to *Shicheii*, I'd never recover. Not ever. His death would break me in so many ways, and on so many levels, life wouldn't be worth living.

Chapter 25
*"Each of us is put here in this time and this place
to decide the future of humankind.
Did you think you were put here for something less?*
—Chief Arvol Looking Horse

2:30 p.m.

The all-terrain vehicle zipped past Mayhem as he reached the trail. He ran faster, pushed harder, chasing the ATV. The poacher in back leveled his shotgun, and Mayhem veered off-trail, slapping branches out of his way. Each time he ventured into view, a gunshot rang out. He needed a new plan. Another three hundred feet and they'd breach the cabin grounds.

That he could never allow.

With the hunting knife clenched between his teeth, he scaled the nearest tree. Near the top, he rose, gripping the branches above his head. Sprinted—at full speed—from one tree to another, covering a lot more land faster than if he followed animal trails.

The ATV accelerated, too. Only one-hundred-fifty feet stood between his lifelong friend—family—and poachers hellbent on revenge.

Hand over hand, branches slid through his palms as he raced across tree limbs. In the distance, Jacy Lee danced and prayed, seemingly unaware of the danger.

Time stalled.

Once Mayhem passed the vehicle, positioning himself between his family and the poachers, he climbed lower, lying in wait for the men to roll closer. Gauging their speed, he pounced, landing on top of the burly man in the back, whose throat he severed before tossing him onto the trail. With the butt of his newly acquired shotgun, he struck the passenger in the face then shoved him off the vehicle. Mayhem leaped toward the driver, but the poacher dove off the ATV on his own.

The driver's shotgun laid on the floorboards. Only one of the two escapees had a weapon now. Still not an ideal situation, with two poachers alive, on foot, and within walking distance of the cabin. Jacy Lee's life hung in limbo.

After stopping the ATV, he cut the wires and wiring harness, disabling the vehicle so the men couldn't circle back and flee. But that took precious time—time he couldn't afford to waste. So, he scaled a nearby oak for a better vantage point.

The unarmed poacher unsheathed a blade from his belt as he stalked down the trail, leading into the yard. Jacy Lee's praise and worship directed him to his precise location.

As Mayhem hastened into the next tree, a loud crack split the sky. Glorious rain showered down from the Holy Ones, soaking him. The limb under his feet grew too slick to continue.

Halfway down the trunk, Shawnee bellowed like a lioness, charging full force at the poacher with a crow pressed to her chest.

Oh, my. "Cat," he called out, but she couldn't hear him over the rain. "Cat!"

The massive murder all emerged at once, ebony wings narrowing in on Shawnee and the poacher. Mayhem jumped to the ground and took off, arms pumping, careening down the trail, rain slapping his face and bare chest. When he caught up to Shawnee, he drew an arrow from the quiver on her back and slapped a hand on her shoulder, slowing her down enough to swipe the bow.

He stopped.

Aimed.

Fired.

The arrow sliced through the rain, the razor tip slashing open the poacher's cheek, blood leaking down the side of his face. "C'mon." The stranger egged on Mayhem, a splayed hand thumping his chest. "Fight me like a man."

Dropping the bow, Mayhem lunged, flames excoriating his insides, and tackled the poacher. Vice-gripped the poacher's throat in one hand, the other punching him over and over, the bones of his nose breaking under his fist, blood splattering all over his face. Again, and again, he hammered the intruder, breaking both cheekbones, both jaws, right eye socket, then the left.

Roaring into the poacher's shattered face, he leaned in, adrenaline heaving his chest. "I... will... rip... you... apart!" Again, he pummeled him, his mind focused solely on the source of his rage. When he unsheathed the hunting knife from his hip, he cocked an arm across his chest, ready to end this once and for all.

"Cheveyo!"

Poised for the kill, his gaze shot through the trees to Jacy Lee. The other poacher pressed a sawed-off shotgun to his elder's temple, one arm braced around his neck. Upper cheek twitching, he rose, grabbed a fistful of poacher hair, then dragged the battered man down the trail. In the yard, he let go.

Crows soared in from all directions, mobbing the enemy in their midst, stomping on his head, the shotgun wobbling up and down the side of Jacy Lee's face.

Soldiering closer, Mayhem wolf whistled. Poe alerted the murder, stopping the chaos before the gun fired by accident.

"Your man is alive," Mayhem said, tone firm and harsh. "He won't stay that way for long unless you release your hostage this instant." He spread his arms. "Fight me. I'm the one responsible for killing your men."

"Fine." He shoved Jacy Lee to the ground. "Killing an old man does nothing for me, anyway."

The sight of his family tossed aside like garbage unchained the beast within, and he closed the gap between them.

The barrel of the shotgun raised to Mayhem's chest. "Slow your roll, buddy."

Feet away from the armed man, he sniggered, rain pouring, water curtains billowing between them. "Oh, how I love titillating moments like this. What will his next move be, I wonder?"

"Get your hands up."

"Surrender?" Mayhem snickered. "To whom, you?"

"I'm the one with the shotgun, so, yeah."

"Hm. Let me mull over your enticing proposition for a moment." He tapped a stiff finger to his lips. "Surrender or what, exactly?"

"I'll kill you."

"I doubt you'd succeed, but you could give it the ol' college try, I suppose. Let's call that option one. Would you care to hear option two?"

"I would." Bow raised, razor-tipped arrow locked and loaded in cherry-red hands, Shawnee stepped from the wooded perimeter behind the poacher, quickening her pace to join in the fun. Now well within the armed man's peripheral, her top knuckles whitened on the bowstring. "You okay, *Shicheii*?"

"I'm fine, honey." Off to the side, Jacy Lee stood motionless—conflicted—seemingly unsure whether to render aid to the bludgeoned man behind Mayhem or stay put. "Cheveyo?"

"Hold that thought, my friend. Now, where was I?"

Shawnee said, "Option two."

"Right. Option two is thus. If you answer a few questions, we will spare your life." He jutted a thumb over his shoulder. "You may even take your friend with you. How does that sound?"

"Like bullshit." He jiggled the shotgun. "As long as I have this, I'm the one in control, not you."

"Jacy Lee," he said, "please return to the safety of the cabin."

"But Cheveyo—"

Shawnee chimed in. "Please go, *Shicheii*. I don't want you to see what comes next."

"All right, child."

Shielding their spiritual leader from harm, Mayhem waited for him to leave. Then, with a wolf whistle, he ordered the murder to converge, crows dipping and diving, mobbing the poacher from all directions with military precision and accuracy. A finely tuned army of winged soldiers cloaked in black feathers. Once they knocked the poacher off-balance, Mayhem gripped the slick barrel of the shotgun, ducking before buck shot pellets sprayed from the muzzle.

When he straightened, he slammed the poacher in the face with the butt of the gun. A loud pop echoed through the downpour, raindrops pelting his scalp, shoulders, and chest, blessed waves of water whitewashing his sins.

Stumbling backward, blood poured through the poacher's fingers cupped over his shattered nose. Shawnee fired. The arrow slashed open the enemy's neck and missed striking multiple crows by mere inches.

"Cat," he admonished, rain rolling down his face.

"What?" Her bare wet shoulder lifted. "Wasn't that the plan?"

"Did you not hear my proposal? I said I wanted to question him."

"You were serious about that?"

With an exaggerated exhale, he flung his hands in the air. "Of course. A dead man cannot provide intel on the organization." Peeling her fingers off the bow, mounting frustration hardened his tone. "A man—or woman—is only as good as his or her word. I thought you were cognizant of that."

"I am, but..." Her finger pointed at the gurgling poacher, bleeding out in the dirt. "That bastard planned to kill *Shicheii*." Tears mixing with raindrops, her chest heaved. "Do you know what that would do to me? I can't lose him." She cried harder. "He's the only family I have left."

"You also have me, Cat." He pulled her into his chest. "Please don't cry." He tightened his embrace, and she bawled even harder, blubbering all over his wet shoulder, her entire body shuddering. "I shouldn't have raised my voice." After a few moments, he stroked the back of her head, her wet hair, and patted her back, but she still didn't let go. "Mourning Dove?"

Lips quivering, her gaze raised.

"Never be ashamed of protecting your family. You did the right thing." He framed her face in his palms, pressed his lips to her forehead. "Are you all right?"

Chin dimpling, she nodded yes.

Squawking to break them apart, Poe fluttered down to Dad's shoulder.

"Poe?" She jerked out of his arms. "If you're here, then—?" She sprinted into the forest, branches swaying from her escape. A few moments later, she re-emerged with an injured crow perched on her forearm, a tricolored gold necklace dangling on her chest.

Eyebrows arched, his gaze roamed to Poe. "Is that who I think it is?"

Poe nuzzled his feathery cheek against his.

"Oh, my."

In front of him, Shawnee stopped, a finger flung at the crow on her arm. "Who is this?"

Rattle, rattle, rattle. Coo... coo...

"May I?" Grinning, he pressed his forearm against Shawnee's, extending a new perch for the lady who'd captured Poe's heart. "Nice to see you again, Lenore."

"Lenore?" Shawnee echoed in disbelief.

"Let's get you inside, darling." He strolled to the cabin with Poe on his shoulder, rattling and cooing at his lady friend, renewed love blooming before his eyes.

Jogging alongside him, Shawnee said, "Am I missing somethin'?"

He chuckled. If she only knew.

Chapter 26

4 p.m.

How did Mr. Mayhem know the injured crow? Did he name all the members of the local murder? And why the hell was she wearing Poe's necklace? That thing cost me three-hundred bucks.

My grandfather met us on the porch, passing us each a towel so we didn't drip all over the wide-pine floors inside. "Lenore?"

Shicheii knew her, too? Right, right. He lived here for several months before we reunited. Is that when they met?

"So nice to see you again, child." He extended his wrist for her. "Let me take a look at that wing."

While Mr. Mayhem held the door, I followed my grandfather into the cabin. Still towel-drying my hair, I stopped short. Uh-oh.

Feathers erect, Spirit Crow stood on the kitchen island—spittin' mad—glowering at her soulmate for entrapping her inside before he left.

Out the corner of my mouth I hushed, "She's pissed."

"I am painfully aware of that, thank you."

When he smiled at her—dangerous move—I jabbed him with my elbow, rocking an emphatic no.

"Ahem." Towel-drying his hair, he took his life in his hands by approaching her. "Sweetheart, I understand why you're upset, but I had no choice. Your past actions at Thorn Hill spoke volumes about how much you will risk. And I cannot—will not—condone reckless behavior. I lost you once. I cannot do it again. If that angers you, then so be it. As far as your safety is concerned, I have no regrets."

Bold move on his part. Might not be the smartest play ever, but ya gotta give him kudos for giving it a shot.

After a few grueling seconds, Spirit Crow's feathers relaxed, angelic-white plumage settling back into place. Even her eyes softened.

Wow. He actually pulled it off. I felt like slapping him a high-five, but it probably wasn't appropriate now. Maybe later.

The back of his fingers stroked her cheek—knuckles split and bloody from beating one poacher to death—his chin jabbed at Lenore, gray eyes twinkling with delight.

At the counter by the sink, *Shicheii* felt the wing for broken bones. Poe acted like a nervous wreck, pacing back and forth like an expectant father.

"Oh, my God," slipped out my mouth, and Pissy Pants' beady-eyed glare snapped toward me. "Sorry." I swiped my comment away. "My total bad." Sidled up next to Mr. Mayhem and Spirit Crow, my back turned to Poe, I mouthed, "Is he in love?"

Two slow nods of confirmation.

Mr. Mayhem whispered, "Please tell me you are not responsible for breaking her wing."

"Me?" Splayed red fingers spanned my chest. "Why would you think—? God, no. I found her on the trail, dragging her wing. If I hadn't picked her up, Karma woulda gotten her."

"Whom?"

"Karma." I half-shrugged. "My ol' mountain lion pal."

"Karma," he said, glib.

"Seemed fitting at the time."

He sniggered. "Did you, uh..." Gray eyes side-shifted to *Shicheii*, his voice a low whisper. "Feed Karma?"

"In a manner of speaking, yeah."

"Karma," he repeated, a grin lifting the corners of his lips. "Has a nice ring to it."

"Doesn't it, though."

"Okie doke." A subtle hint to change the subject before *Shicheii* overheard us. "I would love a cup of Jacy Lee's wild tea. Anyone else?"

Thought he'd never ask. "Yep. Great idea."

"Tea sounds nice, Cheveyo. Thank you." Focusing on Lenore, *Shicheii* said, "The good news is, I don't feel any fractures. You dislocated your shoulder joint, child." From below the sink, he snapped a dishtowel off the handle of the bottom cabinet, twirling the material into a whiplike roll. "While I pop it back in place, bite down on this."

Ca-caw, caw, caw, caw!

"Poe," Mr. Mayhem scolded. "If you cannot stay out of Jacy Lee's way, verbally or physically, perhaps you should wait on the porch."

Tossing his father the stink eye, the pacing continued, Poe stomping back and forth across the counter, unwilling or unable to watch *Shicheii* inflect pain on his dream girl.

At the stove, Mr. Mayhem stirred the wild tea, blended herbs wafting from the saucepan.

I was practically drooling. "Man, that smells good."

A loud pop coiled through the kitchen, and I cringed. Other than a muffled yelp, Lenore handled it like a champ. A lot better than Poe, who fainted on the spot. Seriously. Sprawled on the counter, he was out cold. If *Shicheii* hadn't caught him in one hand as he rolled off the edge, he would've needed a full body cast.

Didn't look so tough now, did he? Just sayin'.

4:30 *p.m.*
Thirty minutes later, I leaned back in my usual chair at the outside table with *Shicheii* and Mr. Mayhem. Spirit Crow nested in front of her soulmate, watching Poe swoon all over Lenore. Even after the fainting episode, he showed no embarrassment, probably hoping she missed it. She didn't. Lenore saw the whole thing, but

why shatter his disillusionment? For once, torturing me wasn't his main objective.

Between sips of tea, honey tickling my tastebuds, I said, "The necklace looks beautiful on you, Lenore."

She strolled over to me—hips wiggling like Spirit Crow, tail feathers swishing—climbed up my arm, and nuzzled her head in the crook of my neck. Apparently, Poe hadn't sent her the memo about me yet. Strangely, he didn't seem upset, either. Maybe saving the love of his life earned me a few brownie points.

"So, anyone wanna clue me in on how these two know each other?"

"Later." Mr. Mayhem's hands clasped around his mug, his split knuckles stretching taut. "We have more important matters to discuss, I'm afraid."

The pelting of rain eased up. Through a light sprinkling mist, moaning and groaning murmured in the distance.

Swiveling in my chair, I gaped at the dude Mr. Mayhem beat to a pulp as he rolled onto his side. "He's alive?"

Chair legs scraped against the deck boards, and *Shicheii* rose.

"Jacy Lee, please don't."

My grandfather thrust a hand at the poacher. "That man needs medical attention."

"I don't disagree. However, he can wait until we finish our tea."

"I'm surprised at you, Cheveyo. You are not a heartless man."

"Might I remind you"—he flung a pointed finger at the dude writhing in pain—"that so-called man was coming here to kill you."

I laid my hand on my grandfather's forearm. "He's right, *Shicheii*. Let him suffer awhile."

"Mourning Dove," he said, voice full of appalment. "I will do no such thing. Honestly, I'm surprised at you, child. This is not how your mother raised you."

Before I could respond, Mr. Mayhem answered for me. "I respectfully disagree, old friend. Your daughter put family above all else, including her personal safety. Look at the lengths she went to protect her daughter." Mr. Mayhem jutted a thumb at me. "How can you fault Cat for doing the same for her grandfather?"

"Nonetheless, we cannot let that man lay there and suffer."

"Fine." Mr. Mayhem rose from the table. "I presume this is your line in the sand?"

"It is."

A breath huffed out his mouth. "Then at least let me bring him here so you don't have to schlep back and forth."

My grandfather sat back down. "Thank you, Cheveyo."

I rose partway. "Need help?"

"No, thank you, Cat. One of us should enjoy our tea while it's hot."

Into the yard, Mr. Mayhem soldiered. The moment the poacher saw him approach, he recoiled, screaming behind an apparent busted jaw, squirming in the mud-like soil to escape. Over his shoulder, Mr. Mayhem glanced back, and I took it as my cue to keep my grandfather occupied so he didn't watch how he treated the scumbag who wouldn't hesitate to put a bullet between our eyes. But try convincing my grandfather of that. *Shicheii* didn't have a mean bone in his body. Maybe it's because of his upbringing.

My and Mr. Mayhem's conversation at the Cave bar flitted through my mind. Perfect way to distract him. "Hey, *Shicheii*?"

"Yes, my sweet?"

"Can you tell me about my great-grandparents?" I left out the part about my mentor telling me to ask, or the limited details he'd shared. "You never talk about them."

"My parents?"

"Yeah. Were they kind like you?"

"Kinder." A smile erased all traces of concern for the injured poacher, dimples dotting both cheeks. "They would have loved you, Mourning Dove. My father was a powerful Medicine Man. Very spiritual. He taught my mother, and together they cared for all the People on the reservation, regardless of clan affiliation. Back then, there was a group of men who'd gotten involved with the Witchery Ways, and my parents battled them more than once—and won."

"*Yenaldlooshi*?" To avoid upsetting him, I purposefully used the Diné word for skinwalker. "What happened?"

Out the corner of my eye, I checked on my mentor, who dragged the bloody poacher across the yard by his hair, arms and legs flailing but helpless to fight back. When the dude's screams grew louder and more persistent, Mr. Mayhem stopped, knelt, and slapped a hand over the scumbag's mouth. Whatever he said worked, because the animal killer didn't dare utter a peep while Mr. Mayhem dragged him closer.

Ten or fifteen feet from the porch, he manhandled the poacher to his feet, slung the dude's arm around his neck, and walked him the rest of the way. Letting him drop at the foot of the stairs, he brushed his palms together.

My eyes widened. Up close, the full damage of what he'd done came into focus. Even more injuries than I thought, Mr. Mayhem broke every bone of the scumbag's face. Seriously, he could model for Picasso. Now the split knuckles made sense. No wonder Mr. Mayhem earned multiple handprints. My mentor was the last guy anyone should mess with. At the same time, he might be the most humble, gentle, and caring man I'd ever met, aside from *Shicheii*.

"He's all yours, my friend." He tromped up the stairs. "May I finish my tea in peace now?"

"Thank you for doing right by him, Cheveyo. I appreciate it."

I suppressed a snicker. *Doubt he'd say that if he saw how the poacher got here.*

My grandfather refocused on me. "Would you mind if we continued our chat later?"

"Not at all, *Shicheii*. Do your thing."

His warm hand palmed my cheek. "I love you."

"Love you, too. Whaddaya need, anything?"

He turned to his lifelong friend. "Is it possible to bring him inside?"

"No, Jacy Lee. It is not possible. This is our home, our sanctuary. And he—whether you choose to believe it or not—is our enemy."

"All right, Cheveyo." *Shicheii* flashed his palms. "I don't want to upset you."

"Then leave him where he is."

My grandfather bustled down the stairs then knelt next to the battered scumbag. After examining the dude's injuries, *Shicheii* glanced back in disbelief. "You fractured all of his facial bones."

"Correct."

"This man needs major reconstructive surgery."

Unfazed, Mr. Mayhem sipped his tea. "And your point is?"

"We need to call an ambulance."

"We will do no such thing." He set down the mug. "I'll tell you what. If he answers my questions, your granddaughter and I will drop him off at the hospital."

"Be reasonable, Cheveyo. The man cannot speak with a shattered jaw."

"His filthy hands still work." Crossing his arms, Mr. Mayhem leaned back in his chair. "That's the deal. Take it or leave it."

"At least let me manage his pain. Mourning Dove, my bag is inside the door."

When I pushed off the table to rise, Mr. Mayhem clamped a hand on my forearm, but his gaze never strayed from my grandfather. "Cat, do not touch that bag until he tells us what we need to know."

Torn between what to do, I froze. "*Shicheii*, I love you, but I'm in training. Even you said never to disobey my mentor."

He held Mr. Mayhem's gaze.

"Cat, there's a notepad and pen on the coffee table. Would you mind retrieving it, please?"

"I'm on it." I hustled into the cabin, grabbed the pen and paper. After hurrying back out to the porch, I stalled, unsure who to give it to.

"Would you like to help him, or shall I?" Mr. Mayhem wasn't talking to me.

"Mourning Dove, bring it here, please."

I passed my grandfather the notepad and pen. *Shicheii* raised the dude's back and sat behind him, his arms aligned with the poacher's. He positioned the notepad on the dude's leg and stuck the pen in his hand.

Mr. Mayhem sat on the top stair, elbows resting on parted knees. "First question. Who sent you here?"

The guy wrote,

Fuck you!

"This is the type of man you want to bring into our home?" Again, he wasn't talking to me. "Do you need me to repeat the question, Mister...?"

Fuck. Off.

"I'd hoped we could accomplish this with some civility, but you have made it perfectly clear that is no longer an option. Okie doke." He hopped to the ground and grabbed the guy's free hand. "Every time you refuse to answer my question, I will chop off one finger."

"Cheveyo!"

At my grandfather he flashed his palm. "Who sent you?" Holding the dude's hand against the dirt, he unsheathed the hunting knife.

The poacher didn't dare write one word.

"Are his eardrums damaged, Jacy Lee?"

Shicheii checked. "They don't appear to be, no."

"Thank you." The blade lowered to the pinky finger. "Who sent you?"

Despite the danger, the poacher refused to scribble a name.

"Wait—" To spare my grandfather trauma, I scrambled down the stairs. "Look, pal. I wouldn't test him if I were you. He'll do it. Just give us a name, and we'll take you to the hospital. What's the big deal?"

The guy wrote,

John

An exaggerated exhale. "Last name?"

Doe

Fed up with this guy's bullshit, my mentor hacked off the pinky finger, the poacher screaming behind a broken jaw.

My grandfather gasped. "Cheveyo!"

The scene got twice as chaotic when Poe flew down the stairs, clasped the severed finger in his talons, flew back to Lenore, then mic dropped the friggin' thing like he'd recovered the winning football at the Super Bowl. Spirit Crow expressed her displeasure by picking up the finger, flying off the porch, dropping the disembodied finger in the Sacred Fire.

Guess doctors won't be sewing that back on. Poor bastard.

"I will ask you one last time. Should you choose not to answer my question, you will lose more than a finger. Am I clear?"

The pen didn't move.

Clearly uncomfortable, *Shicheii's* widened eyes shifted between his lifelong friend and the notepad as though watching a nail-biting tennis match.

"Silence will not save you. Do you understand the terms and consequences I have put forth?"

Yes

"Thank you. Pain is a marvelous motivator, wouldn't you agree?" He didn't wait for a response. "Now, who sent you?"

Pip

Mr. Mayhem and I both sprang back. In stereo, we said, "Hawthorne?"

Yes

"Pip Hawthorne is part of the network?" He flashed a flat hand. "Let me rephrase. Does Mister Hawthorne sign your paychecks?"

Yes

"Does Mister Hawthorne have partners?"

Yes

"Do you know the names of these partners?"

Some

"Do the names Chip Worthington and Curran Rothschild ring a bell?"

Yes

"Does Mister Hawthorne answer to a boss-like figure, someone higher in the organization?"

Yes

"Do you know his or her name?"

Above my paygrade

"I see. Does Mister Hawthorne live locally?"

No

"Do you know when he plans to leave the area?"

After hunt

"What are they hunting?"

Wolf

My jaw dropped. Those trophy hunting bastards planned to release their prisoners—critically endangered Eastern Gray Wolves—so rich people could kill them to hang the corpses on their walls? Un-fuckin'-believable. Did they also breed the wolves with domestic dogs? Or were two different cells operating here? Or maybe the armed guards squeezed every drop of semen out of the wolves before they freed them for slaughter. Hard to say for sure at this point.

"When is this"—Mr. Mayhem's Adam's apple rose and fell—"Wolf hunt?"

Saturday

"This Saturday? As in, three days from now?"

Yes

"At the compound where they're holding the wolves?"

Yes

"Does Mister Hawthorne know who we are? More simply put, did he give you a name and/or photograph?"

Address

"No names?"

No

"And your mission was to…?"

Silence you

"By any means necessary?"

Yes

"Any other orders?"

Capture

"Capture whom?"

Her

Mr. Mayhem's sorrowful gaze met mine. "Why do they want her?"

?

"You don't know why they want her?"

Sex

"Pardon?" Gray eyes thinned and darkening, his bare chest heaved in slow motion as if trying to tame his inner beast. "Jacy Lee—"

Without a word, my grandfather scrambled out from behind the poacher, tears streaming down his cheeks. He grabbed me, holding me so tightly I could barely breathe. Over his shoulder, I stared at Mr. Mayhem, who rose, pacing like a caged tiger.

When he stopped, he faced me. "Do you recall the question I asked you on the deck at Thorn Hill?"

Blood or answers? "Yeah."

"The choice is yours, Cat."

Wrapped in my grandfather's arms, his love all-consuming and powerful, I could only respond one way. "Answers."

"That a girl." He winked. "Never allow scum like this to sacrifice your humanity." He squatted next to the poacher. "Well, Mister... Doe... it looks like you'll be staying with us for a while."

Hospital!

"Not yet, I'm afraid." He slipped the pen out of the poacher's hand. "However, if you continue to cooperate and behave yourself, I will allow my friend to manage your pain. And on Saturday, I will personally drive you to the hospital." He strode to the Caddy. After reaching inside, the trunk rose.

I patted my grandfather's arm for him to let go. "*Shicheii*, I gotta go help him."

"Sorry, honey." Releasing me, he palmed my cheek. "Are you all right? Do you want to talk about it?"

"No. I really don't."

"I'm here if you change your mind."

"I know. Thanks, *Shicheii*." I hustled to the Caddy, where Mr. Mayhem was rummaging through the trunk. "We're not really gonna let that scumbag stay in the cabin, right?"

"Good Lord, no." He passed me a loop of rope.

The blood in my veins chilled. "Are we tying him to a tree like Underwood?"

"With Karma roaming around? It's a tempting proposition, isn't it?" Second wink. "Alas, I'm afraid your grandfather will never go for that."

"Then... where?"

"Out back in the shed."

"The shed?" My heart thudded. "What if *Shicheii* frees him when we head back to the hotel? We are goin' back for Hawthorne, right?"

"We are, yes. Don't worry about your grandfather. He would never risk your safety."

"But holding a man prisoner rubs against everything he stands for. Should I have chosen blood?"

"No." Leaning against the Caddy, his hands clasped near his waist. "Remember when we discussed giving away your power, allowing others to control your emotions?"

"Yeah."

"By choosing answers instead of blood, you retained your power, your control. The simple answer was blood, but you chose the tougher alternative. Why?"

"I dunno." I sloughed off a shrug. "Seemed like the right thing to do."

"Why did it feel right?"

"Because—I dunno—when we were defending our family, we had no choice but to fight fire with fire. Once the immediate threat passed, killing him didn't seem necessary anymore."

"Even after what he said about you?"

"Especially then."

"Why?"

"Because if he dies, that'd be it."

"Meaning?"

"We wouldn't know what's coming next."

"Precisely. Now you have the tools to answer your original question. Did you make the right decision?"

"I did."

"You certainly did." He slung an arm around my neck. "Nicely done, Cat."

A chorus of angels sang from my heart. "Thanks."

The arm dropped. "Well, we should probably deal with Mister... Doe."

"You know that's a fake name, right?"

Fingers pinched the bridge of his nose. "Cat, what am I going to do with you?"

"What? I'm just sayin'." As we strolled back to the porch, I flashed my beet-red hands. "By the way, will soap take this off?"

"Have you never spilled fruit juice before?"

"Well, yeah."

"We're you able to scrub the stain out?"

"No, but—"

"Precisely." He chuckled. "Think of it as a good thing. They match your teeth."

"Ha, ha. Everyone's a comedian."

Fuck. At this rate, my sex life is basically over.

Chapter 27
"It is not necessary for eagles to be crows."
—Sitting Bull

Thursday night, 8 p.m.

Most of the day consisted of squabbling back and forth with Jacy Lee about holding the poacher hostage. Mayhem's lifelong friend's innate compassion for every being within the Natural World, including men who tried to end their lives less than thirty-six hours earlier, drove him to vocalize his displeasure. And nothing Mayhem said could change his mind.

In the Caddy, he and Shawnee headed North to the suite at Omni Mount Washington Resort. Yet even this drive offered no escape from family disputes. In retrospect, perhaps he shouldn't have asked Jacy Lee to refrain from whitening her teeth right away. However, it taught her a vital lesson in self-care.

Now, tonight's mission required them to blend into the fabric of society without drawing unnecessary attention. Thus, Jacy Lee showed her the teeth-whitening home remedy of three-parts mustard oil to one-part salt. After a few applications, her teeth regained their natural sheen. Not completely, but white enough that few, if any, could notice any anomalies. Banana peel removed the stains on her hands, brightening the skin.

For the entire car ride, however, she refused to let sleeping dogs lie. "I specifically asked you if *Shicheii* could whip something up for my teeth, and you said no."

"Did I?" Focused on the road, his foot pressed the gas pedal. "My apologies. I must have misheard you."

"Misheard me? Yeah, right."

"Cautious Cat, we've been rehashing this for over an hour when we should be planning next steps. Your hands and teeth look great, so if you wouldn't mind…"

"Fine." The sharpness in her tone revealed anger. "Just don't pull the I've-never-lied-to-you card again, 'cause we both know that's not true."

"I beg your pardon." He glanced her up and down. "You asked if there was an herbal remedy, and I told you it was a rite of passage, something we all had to learn growing up."

"Withholding the truth is the same as lying."

"Is it? Because if memory serves—and please, correct me if I'm mistaken—I believe you indicated the opposite was true when it came to telling your grandfather about your past, as well as other more recent events that he may find, for lack of a better word, offensive."

Vitriol filled the glower she tossed.

Around the back of the Omni Mount Washington Resort, he parked. "Have we put the matter to rest?"

"Yeah." The visor she slapped into place. "You made your point."

"Excellent. Thank you." He exited the vehicle. Over the roof, he offered two viable options for how to proceed. "We could either leave the PC here and search for Mister Hawthorne on foot or swing by the suite first and tap into the hotel's surveillance. Do you have a preference?"

"Whaddawe do when we find him?"

As usual, she jumped over the most crucial step of the plan. "Let's concentrate on locating him first, then we'll discuss next steps. So, your preference is…?"

"Let's see if we can spot him on foot. If we can't, we've always got option two."

"Good idea." Dressed in a black pinstriped suit, he met her at the foot of the Caddy. "It'd look less conspicuous if we used the main entrance." He traced her up and down—black fitted skirt, Cheyenne's Ferragamo heels, and a vibrant red blouse, accenting the chunky streaks in her raven hair. "You look stunning tonight."

She beamed, her skin almost as radiant as her smile. "Thanks."

As they strolled around the corner of the building, he wove his fingers with hers and led her to the grand double-door entryway, sided by flower gardens, the blooms releasing a sweet floral into the warm summer breeze.

Through the lobby he and Shawnee strode. Yellow-and-white striped wallpaper lined cathedral-high walls with painted accents. Tall ivory columns framed a walkway between overstuffed sofas, upholstered chairs, and tables on either side. The ceiling—dotted with chandeliers—glowed, the lights illuminating the tasteful but elegant décor.

Visibly uncomfortable in this environment, Shawnee's grip tightened around his.

"Relax." Alas, she found no comfort in his words. He pulled her closer, hushed, "Cease the self-sabotage. You have as much right to be here as any other guest."

A slight smile emerged but did not linger.

"Would a Peppermintini help?"

"I think so."

"You think, or you know?"

That brought a genuine smile. "Definitely would."

"All right, then. Outside deck or inside lounge?"

"Deck. But if he's not out there, can we still stay for a drink?"

"Of course." He stopped at the elevators. "May I ask why?"

"I need time to adjust. This place is... just so... so..."

"Elegant?"

"Over the top." Unsettled in her stance, she twirled left and right. "Aren't we goin' out to the deck?"

"The Observatory Bar is on the roof."

"How do you know that?" Her hand firmed on her hip. "Lemme guess. You guys stayed here before."

Holding the elevator door from closing as she strolled into the car, he grinned. "Once or twice." He and Kimi much preferred the coziness of Thorn Hill, but he withheld that private nugget. Inside the elevator, he thumbed the button for the rooftop.

They rode up in silence, Shawnee fidgeting the entire time.

When the doors parted, stunning teakwood pavers lined an L-shaped deck that offered a magnificent view of the nearby Presidential Mountains. A veranda-covered bar sat in the center, high-backed stools around three sides, with tables and sleek, ivory-padded wicker chairs around the perimeter.

The outside lounge bustled with guests, occupying most of the seats. Thus far, no sign of Mister or Missus Hawthorne.

"Over here." She tugged him toward a table off to the side.

Out of the way of patrons encircling the bar, Shawnee chose an ideal spot.

He gripped the lapel of his suit coat. "Is it too cool for you up here?"

"I'm good." She swiped his question away. "Nothing a little booze can't handle."

"All right, Cat. If you change your mind, I'd be happy to loan you my jacket." He patted the back of the chair. After she slid into the seat, he motioned to the server—a delightful young man named Reed, according to the brass nameplate pinned to his breast pocket. "Thank you for your promptness, Reed." He sat beside Shawnee. "We appreciate the quick service. The lady would like a Peppermintini, please."

"Sure." He scribbled the order on his notepad. "And for you, sir?"

"Do you have a wine list?"

Shawnee said, "No Moscow Mule?"

"Oh, all right." He lifted his shoulders to Reed. "She's fond of the copper mug."

Bright white teeth smiled back at him, the enamel clearly enhanced by dental treatments. "They are pretty cool."

"I suppose." He chuckled. "Thank you, Reed." Once he left, Mayhem hushed, "He's a nice looking fellow, isn't he?"

One might think he'd suggested an arranged marriage by how her upper lip snarled. "Seriously? His name is Reed."

"And your point is?"

"He's wearing boat shoes."

Befuddlement squinted his eyes. "And your point is?"

"One plus one equals entitled rich boy."

"You formed that opinion from his name, which he had no control over, and his choice of footwear?"

"Yeah." She scratched her cheek. "Betcha a hundred bucks I'm right, too."

"A wager?" A little thrill zipped up his spine, and he peeled off a hundred-dollar bill, slapping it down on the table. "Challenge accepted."

When the server returned with the cocktails, Shawnee twirled her finger around a strand of hair, flirting with him. "So, Reed, what kind of boat do you own?"

"How did you know I—?"

"The shoes."

"Oh. Right. Boston Whaler. My dad bought it for my graduation present."

"Sweet." Two fingers slid the hundred-dollar bill off the table. "Isn't that nice, hon? His father sounds like a generous man."

"He does indeed, darling. What does your father do, Reed?"

"He owns the resort."

His eyebrows rose. "This resort?"

"Yeah, among others. I manage the bar a couple nights per week, but we're short-handed tonight."

"I see." Entitled rich boy did indeed seem likely. It's impressive how quickly Shawnee pegged him. "Well, Reed, we won't keep you. Thank you for humoring our inquisitiveness."

"No problem. When you're ready for another round, give me a holler."

"Will do, Reed. Thank you."

The moment he left, Shawnee flipped her hair over one shoulder. "See? If there's one thing the streets taught me, it's how to make quick judgments about men. Safer that way."

"I suppose it is." A sad smile toyed with his lips, his mind journeying back in time. "I owe you an apology, Cat."

"For what?"

A thickness formed in his throat, his Adam's apple rising and falling. "For sentencing you to a life on the streets."

She sloughed off a shrug. "Hey, I don't blame you for not risking your daughter's life. You were protecting your family."

"Nonetheless, if I were to live those years over again, I might make different choices."

"No, you wouldn't. You did the right thing. Bo was very good to me. I loved him almost as much as my dad."

"Bo was a good man." Though he appreciated her trying to lessen his burden, she still endured more than any young child should. Sadly, neither he nor Kimi had a safe alternative without endangering their daughter's life. Red Buffalo—Shawnee's biological half-brother, Kajika Lee, who immersed himself in the Witchery Ways—would never have stopped hunting his family, nor would the Gray Wolf, head of the *Yenaldlooshi* group and Kajika's birth father.

"Yeah, he was." Her fingers picked crushed peppermint off the rim of her glass. "Can I tell you somethin'?"

"Of course."

Still staring at her cocktail, she refused eye contact. "One time, these three gangbangers jumped me in an alley."

"I remember," he said, the scene as vivid today as it was then.

After an argument with Bo Adams—a highly skilled cat burglar, who filled the father role post the brutal slaying of her parents—Shawnee stormed off and straight into gangland territory. When she veered into an alleyway, three heartless punks jumped her, robbed her, and attempted to sexually violate her. Had Mayhem reacted sooner, her injuries might not've resulted in unconsciousness, her petite frame marred by blood, rib fractures, and bruising, broken blood vessels turning the whites of her eyes bright red, both eyelids nearly swollen shut.

If only he'd arrived sooner...

Leaning forward, she rubbed her eyebrow. "You're the one who beat the crap outta those punks?"

Every patron and employee on the rooftop faded into the background, his sole focus on her while he confessed to his role that night.

"How'd I get back to the tunnel?"

"I carried you."

"I don't even know what to say." After chugging half of her Peppermintini, her tongue dragged across her upper lip. "Bo took the credit, y'know."

"I know," he said, his voice barely above a whisper. "The cover story was safer than the truth."

"You really have been there my whole life."

"Most. Not all."

"Why'd you stop lookin' out for me?"

"Once you reached adulthood, you had to live your own life, make your own mistakes, find your own path without my meddling." Tears rose in his chest, and he swallowed, the past hitting him harder than expected. "It wasn't easy for any of us to let you go after Bo died, but you needed to learn how to fly solo."

"How'd you know I'd be safe?"

"Any time your half-brother left the reservation, your grandfather called on me to track his movements."

Seemingly satisfied with that answer, she leaned back in the chair, legs crossed, sipping her Peppermintini, brilliant emerald eyes admiring the mountains. "What a view, huh?"

With so many lives at stake, Mayhem snapped his attention back to the mission, his gaze in a continual scan from one end of the bar to the other. The moment he raised the copper mug, mint leaves peeking out from the rim, the elevator doors parted.

"Cat?"

She leaned forward. "Yeah?"

"Follow my lead. It's showtime."

Chapter 28

8:40 p.m.

All casual-like, I surveyed the rooftop, then startled when a man's voice shot over my head.

"Mister Daniels, how nice to see you again." Pip Hawthorne approached our table in a black tuxedo. "Have you made any progress with finding my wife's attacker?"

The rich prick didn't even bother to acknowledge me.

"Have you met my wife?" Mr. Mayhem's hand swayed toward me. "Darling, this is Mister Hawthorne, the client I told you about."

"Oh." I stuck out a limp wrist like rich people did in the movies. "Nice to meet you, Mister Hawthorne."

He barely touched my fingers, never mind shake my hand. "Pleasure is all mine, Missus Daniels."

"Now that we've gotten the pleasantries out of the way, I do have a progress report for you. Where is your lovely wife this evening?"

"In the spa. I'm meeting with business associates."

"I see. Okie doke. Then let's stroll to the bar." Mr. Mayhem patted the top of my hand. "Would you like another Peppermintini, dear?"

"Sure, hon." Two could play this game. "Another cocktail sounds nice. Thank you."

"The pleasure is all mine." He slung an arm around the asshole's back, nudging him away from the table. "Shall we, Mister Hawthorne?"

Nothing I hated more than the male ego bullshit. Why couldn't they talk in front of me? Just because Pip treated his wife like a second-class citizen didn't mean my faux husband had to do the same. Arms folded, my knee bounced on my other leg, my foot swirling my heel as I stared at the two of them, chatting at the bar. I couldn't make out what they said, but Pip Hawthorne acted pleased with his alleged progress.

With Mr. Mayhem's class and refinement, he morphed into a chameleon who could fit in anywhere, regardless of the situation or environment. How he carried on a conversation with the prick who sent killers to the cabin, never mind what they planned to do with me, I had no idea. But to look at the two of them standing there, laughing and shit, you'd think they'd known each other for years. It's an ingenious skill, actually. Get up close and personal with the target, then strike when they least expected it.

Pip Hawthorne said he was here with business associates. What business? Poaching? Animal trafficking? Possibly a legal enterprise? Did his wife know how her husband made his money? Or didn't she care as long as the never-ending river of gold and diamonds didn't run dry?

Women like that disgusted me. Too many were willing to look the other way as long as it didn't affect their bottom line—the luncheons, the jewelry, the country club memberships. Some also allowed cheating, if their husbands acted discreet enough. They even pumped out two-point-five kids to keep up appearances. In my opinion, they were nothing but glorified sex workers—no offense to sex workers—who drove nicer cars, lived in better homes, and mingled among the upper echelon, all the while praying for their meal ticket's death.

How many Native women played a similar game? Doubt it was many. Sure, all races had some bad seeds. But Caucasians had a shitload. Just sayin'. Here too we forfeited a beautiful, spiritual union before God in pursuit of the almighty dollar. How much money did it take to buy a woman's self-respect?

And some wondered why I preferred animals to humans.

I gulped down the last of my Peppermintini, my insides screaming, raging, my foot swirling faster and faster, my knee propelling my leg up and down.

Mr. Mayhem set two fresh cocktails on the table. "That went better than expected." Smiling at me, he slid into his chair, but it'd be a cold day in hell before I let him get away with treating *me* like a second-class citizen.

"Why couldn't you two talk here?"

Eyebrows arched, he held my gaze for an eternity of minutes. Then, with the slightest of grins, his chin rested on a closed fist. "If you felt slighted, I apologize. Disgraceful though it may be, their circle operates in a world where women are not involved in business conversations. I hope by now you'd know I'd never deliberately disrespect any woman, especially you."

"Right." All at once my knee stalled. "I do. Sorry."

"You have nothing to apologize for, Cat. Commanding respect and vocalizing unfairness are both admirable traits."

"Thanks." Mentally, I kicked myself for projecting my bullshit onto him. "So, what'd you tell him?"

"I simply assured him that my men were on the case, following leads as we spoke. A better question may be, what did I learn?"

"Alright, I'll bite. What'd you learn?"

"The associates he referred to are in town until Sunday."

"The day after the hunt?" Clawing back my hair, strands slipped through my fingers. "That can't be a coincidence."

"No, it cannot. Let me ask you this." His hands steepled. "Can you read any man as quickly as you pegged Reed?"

My shoulders rose, dropped. "Yeah. Why?"

"Regardless of age?"

"Pretty much, yeah."

"Regardless of race?"

"Mm." I waved a splayed hand from side to side. "Mezza, mezza. White men are a lot easier to read."

"Fair enough. Noted. Mister Hawthorne is meeting his associates at the Cave. Let's give them time to acclimate, grow nice and chatty, then we'll make our way down there."

"Whaddaya hope to find out? We already know Hawthorne gave the order." It finally dawned on me. "Ohhh. You want the name of his boss—to chop off the head of the snake."

He winked. "Precisely."

"What's my job?"

"To read and categorize each poacher by job level. Once we build the pyramid, we'll burn it to the ground."

Three Peppermintinis later, all my stiff muscles relaxed, the schnapps warming my insides as the elevator descended. One floor down, the doors parted for Ken and Barbie wannabes to stroll in. They stood at the back wall behind us. Neither acknowledged our presence, the couple groping each other, making out like they were alone, kissing and sucking noises echoing through the car.

Talk about awkward. I pushed the main floor button four or five times, praying for the elevator to hurry up and land so we could escape before the foreplay morphed into full-on sex acts.

Staring straight ahead at the closed doors, Mr. Mayhem remained stoic, unemotional.

It took about ten years for the elevator to stop. Even longer for the doors to open. The second they parted, I jumped out. Not that Ken and Barbie noticed, the two overdosing on hormones and booze.

In the lobby, Mr. Mayhem didn't hold my hand like he usually did when we ventured through hotels as pretend husband and wife. Maybe the oversexed couple made him uncomfortable, too, not that he'd ever show it.

To lighten the mood, I bumped his elbow with mine. "Some people's kids, eh?"

Chuckling, he laced his fingers with mine. "Never a dull moment with you, Cat."

"Thanks." *Was that a compliment?* "I think."

Through the tunnel of stone—the entrance to the Cave bar—we strolled, our path framed in rock, periodic lights twinkling in the crevices. At the end, Mr. Mayhem held open the door while I moseyed to the rich oak bar topped with a curved brick ceiling, inlaid into wooded frames.

Wicked cool.

A dude about forty approached me and slapped down a bar napkin. "What can I getcha?"

"I'll have a Peppermintini and my husband—"

Mr. Mayhem snuck up behind me, stopping me cold. "Please continue."

"Um, he'll have a Moscow Mule." I jabbed my chin at him. "Right?"

"Actually, I'd prefer a Corpse Reviver II, please," he told the bartender, and the dude actually understood that nonsense.

On its own my face scrunched. "A what?"

"Corpse. Reviver."

"No, I got that part, but..." I leaned closer, lowering my voice. "Shouldn't we be keeping a low profile?"

And he laughed—hard—his eyes pooling with joyful tears. "Oh, Cat, you amuse me."

What's so funny?

Continuing to laugh at my expense, he only shut up once the bartender returned. "One Peppermintini and one Corpse Reviver II. Anything else I can getcha?"

"Actually." I cast a side-glance at Mr. Mayhem to ensure I had his full attention. "I'll have a shot, too. How 'bout a slippery nipple?"

Eyebrows arched in surprise, that silenced him, a slight smirk rising on his lips. "Thanks, Ryan." He wasn't the only one who could read nameplates.

"Sure. No problem."

Holding my gaze, Mr. Mayhem cocked his head like a confused dog, trying to figure me out. In return, I swayed a defiant shoulder and faced the bar.

Once the bartender set down the slippery nipple, I shot it back. Flipping my hair over one shoulder, I snapped up my Peppermintini then strutted toward the tables. I'd planned to pay with the c-note I won, but after laughing at me, I stuck him with the tab.

In the corner, I sat with my back to the rock wall, one leg crossed over the other. Two tables away, Hawthorne sipped Scotch with four other fat cats in tuxedos. Thankfully, good ol' Pip wasn't facing me, or I might have to move. From my vantage point, I had the perfect view of the back of his silver-haired cantaloupe doubling as a head.

Silent, Mr. Mayhem slid into the chair beside me. After decades of marriage to Kimi, he knew better than to ask if he'd pissed me off. Instead, he went with, "To answer your question, Corpse Revivor cocktails date back to the mid-eighteen-hundreds, when they first appeared as a hair-of-the-dog hangover cure, popularized by the 1930 book, *The Savoy Cocktail*, that listed two of the four Corpse Reviver recipes. The second of which took off in popularity due to its light and refreshing nature. It's quite tasty." He slid the glass toward me. "Would you like to try it?"

"Depends." I resisted the urge to sniff his cocktail. "What's in it?"

"Dry gin with a strong juniper flavor, freshly squeezed lemon juice, Triple Sec, Lillet Blanc—an aromatized white wine with herbal notes and just the right touch of sweetness—and a slight accent of Absinthe sprayed on the glass, offering a subtle but delightful licorice finish."

Sorry I asked. That's a lot more info than I needed. "No, thanks. I'll pass."

"All right, then." Sipping his cocktail, he glanced over my head at the rock wall. With a slight grin, his gaze lowered to mine. "The tuxedos are an interesting choice, aren't they?"

"Funny, I was thinkin' the same thing."

"Have you reached any conclusions?"

"Not yet." Preoccupied by the petty crap at the bar, I hadn't studied them for more than a few minutes. Maybe the Apache Tears really did mess with my emotions. Pretty sure Mr. Mayhem said that might happen till my system acclimated to the powerful gemstones. "What type of events require a tux?"

"Wedding, opera, banquet, gala, even some upscale grand openings. An art exhibit, for example. One might wear a tuxedo to any number of black-tie affairs."

"Okay, but they're flyin' stag, so we can probably scratch off a wedding or opera."

After a sip of his cocktail, he agreed.

"What type of banquet requires black-tie?" Jaw slacked, my eyes widened. "What about a fundraiser?"

"Possibly. Or a silent auction."

I rubbed the back of my neck. "Would you wear a tux to an auction?"

"A silent auction is an elegant and glamorous affair, often followed by, or combined with, a gala."

"Alright, but wouldn't you bring your wife to something like that?"

"I would, yes. My wife and I went everywhere together before ALS stole her mobility." A frown tugged at his lips, his gaze rising over my head again. "For those men—and I use the term loosely—it would depend, I suppose."

"On what?"

"On what—or who—they planned to auction off."

"Oh, my God." The slippery nipple churned my stomach acids. "Am I supposed to be standing on the auction block tonight?"

"That I don't know, Cat. If the uncertainty frightens you, we can walk away right now, return to Massachusetts, and never look back. Say the word, and the mission ends tonight."

"Hell no." My fist slammed the tabletop. "What about the wolves? If we don't help 'em, those trophy hunting bastards will kill 'em all. We can't stop now. Don't you think we've reached the point of no return?" I leaned forward so he couldn't ignore me. "In case you forgot, this is my destiny we're talkin' about, and it'll be a cold day in hell before I allow some rich pricks in fancy suits scare me off. I mean, seriously? For once in my life, I have a purpose. How could you even suggest something like that? If you were here alone, nothing would stop you. Why would it be any different for me?"

"There's the passion I was searching for." Pleased with himself, his gray, almost translucent, eyes twinkled in the candlelight. "I had to make sure we were still on the same page."

"We are, so stop testing me. I will never—*ever*—quit. They'll have to kill me first." I sucked down half my cocktail, my tongue sweeping crushed peppermint off my lips. "By the way, only three outta five wear wedding bands and the other two don't have tan lines on their ring fingers." Meaning, they didn't remove the bands to pick up chicks.

"Excellent observations, Cat." Another glance above my head. "Have you noticed anything else?"

"Whaddaya keep lookin' at?" I twisted around. The smooth stones reflected the entire table of tuxedo-clad scum like a mirror. "Wow, you're good."

"You are too kind, Cat." His hand patted the top of mine. "Thank you. How is the pyramid coming along?"

"Not great. The tuxes are throwing me off. Might need a closer interaction."

One of the single guys rose from the table. Perfect timing.

"Gimme two secs. Be right back." Before the dude squeezed around the other fat cats, I hustled to the narrow hall outside the bathrooms. Leaning against the wall in front of the ladies' room door, I waited for the bastard to round the corner—straight into my web of lies and innuendos. Minutes crawled by, and still no sign of him.

Geez, I'm growing old here. How long does it take to walk twenty feet?

Mr. Mayhem careened around the corner. "We need to leave. Now."

"Why? Did Hawthorne say something to you? Does he know we're not who we say we are?"

"I'm afraid your questions will have to wait." He grabbed my hand, dragging me out of the Cave, my feet wobbling in the heels.

What the hell happened?

Chapter 29
"Behold, the Spring has come.
The earth has received the embraces of the Sun and
we shall soon see the results...
Every seed is awakened, and all animal life.
It is through this mysterious power that we, too, have our being,
and we therefore yield to our neighbors, even to our animal neighbors,
the same right as ourselves, to inhabit this vast land."
—Sitting Bull

11:03 p.m.

As Mayhem led Shawnee through the lobby, she squawked and complained that he never told her anything, but he did not have time to waste. If they didn't leave now, Mayhem might lose the trail. Silent auctions were notoriously cloaked in secrecy, attendants often notified at the last minute to ensure no outsiders unearthed the address.

In the parking lot, Shawnee ground in her feet. "Wait—"

Releasing her hand, Mayhem stopped.

"Thanks." She whipped off her heels, apparently preferring to continue barefooted. "I can barely walk in these things, never mind run in 'em."

"May we continue now? Time is of the essence."

The shoulders shrugged. "Waitin' on you, partner."

"Thank you." He hustled around the side of the building, then flattened against the wall, blending into the shadows.

Without instruction, Shawnee mimicked his motions, whispering, "Who are we waiting for?"

"All will be revealed soon."

Moments later, two men from Mr. Hawthorne's group exited the hotel, tuxedo-clad legs striding across the lot. They hopped into the backseat of a black Escalade with tinted windows.

The driver, he did not expect. Now, the men could flee a lot faster.

"Run, Cat, run." He pushed off the wall, sprinted for the Caddy. Clicked the key fob from twenty feet away, Shawnee's arms pumping to keep up with him. At the passenger door, he swung open the door, then slid across the hood. Into the driver's seat, he slipped, slapping the engine button, slamming the shifter into reverse. With an arm slung around the passenger seat, he gunned it—backward—brakes squealing as he spun the wheel.

Once he hit Hotel Drive, the black Escalade's taillights faded into the darkness of the road.

"Step on it." She slapped the dash. "We can't lose 'em."

Foot pinned to the floorboards, the Caddy lurched into high gear. "Stating the obvious is not helpful."

"There they are!" Her finger pointed straight ahead. "They're taking a right."

"I assure you, my eyesight is just fine, thank you."

"Geez, you don't gotta get all pissy about it. Just tryin' to help."

With a heavy sigh, he relented. "You're right, Cat. My apologies." He banged a right, one hand spinning the wheel, straightening the tires. "Now, if you wouldn't mind sitting back in your seat, I would greatly appreciate it."

"Where do you think they're goin'?"

"That's the question, isn't it?"

Up ahead, the black Escalade pulled to the side of the road, the right directional blinking on and off, on and off, on and off. No one exited the vehicle.

"Shoot," he said.

"What's wrong?"

"The driver's well-trained. Cautious of other vehicles. We'll have to pass them and circle back on foot. The trees should offer concealment."

"Are you being serious right now?" By two fingers she raised Cheyenne's Ferragamo heels. "You expect me to run through heavily wooded terrain in these?"

For now, he ignored her, cruised past the Escalade, and banged an immediate right down a side street. However, Shawnee raised a valid point. She wouldn't get far in stilettos. While killing the headlights, he veered to the side of the road, and adjusted the rearview mirror. Following his gaze, Shawnee twisted to peer out the back windshield.

Neither spoke, both eagle-eyed on the main drag.

Several minutes ticked by. And still, no sight of the Escalade.

"Think they made us?"

"They may have." He shifted into Drive and banged a U-turn. At the end of the side street, he glanced left. The black Escalade idled in the same spot, smoke billowing out its tailpipe.

The back of her hand tapped his bicep. "Do you see what I see?"

"I do."

"What do we do about it?"

Mayhem slung an arm around her seat, backing down the road, spinning the wheel, reversing to the left side of the street, where he shifted into Park and killed the engine. Questions hammered him from the passenger seat.

"What're you doin'? Why're are we parking here? How're we supposed to find 'em if we don't cruise past the Escalade again?" She slapped the dash. "Why aren't you answering me?"

"I'm waiting for you to take a breath."

Silent, her lips smoothed into a straight line.

"Thank you. Now, since the Escalade has not moved, the silent auction must be close. Do you agree with that statement?"

The head nodded. "Yeah."

"Thank you for the verbal response. Now, because these individuals are involved in a covert operation, the building will most likely be unmarked and/or hidden in some way. Do you agree with that assessment?"

"Yeah. Makes sense."

"Excellent. With that understanding, what is the most logical next step?"

"Find the building."

"Correct. How?"

"On foot."

"Precisely. Now, your footwear does indeed pose a problem in wooded terrain. However, if we split up and you stayed on the asphalt, we could cover more ground. Are you comfortable with strolling down the street alone?"

"Seriously? I lived on the streets for most of my childhood. Why wouldn't I be comfortable?"

"I meant, are you comfortable traversing alone after what we learned about their intentions for you. It might be dangerous."

"Yeah. So? Danger goes with the gig. Look, I don't care what they said. Don't start shielding me like I'm some fragile egg that you need to protect. Hate that shit. I am a warrior in training, dammit—the same girl you hunted like prey two days ago, the same girl who fought a friggin' cougar, and ran through the treetops."

"Indeed, you are." *It's beautiful to watch her lean into her power.* "I would have preferred cleaner language, but you made your point." The smirk he forced down. "Call my cell, please. The open line between us will not only ensure your safety but pinpoint your location, as well. Any questions before we proceed?"

"A big one, yeah. What about the beast that shall remain nameless?"

With a slight shake of the head, he said, "I don't follow."

"You'll be alone. In the woods. After dark."

He grinned. "Are you worried about my safety?"

"Maybe." One shoulder half-shrugged. "We have no way of knowing if it travels beyond the Old Cherry Mountain Road area."

"Fear not, Cautious Cat. I didn't get this far in life by acting reckless." He tapped the screen of the iPhone in her hands. "Place the call, please."

Moments later, his cell rang. "Thank you. Are you clear on where you're headed?"

"Yep."

"Please stay cognizant of your surroundings." He peeled off his suitcoat, passed it to her, and set the fedora on her head. "To help mask your identity."

"Gotcha."

"See you soon, Cat." Out the door he fled, hustling into the wood line. Jacy Lee might not approve of his decision to split up, but what choice did he have? Finding the location of the silent auction was an opportunity they couldn't afford to miss. As long as Shawnee stuck to the plan, she should be fine.

O Great Spirit, please watch over her as she traverses the darkened streets alone.

Chapter 30

11:33 p.m.

Down the side street I strode, wearing Mr. Mayhem's suitcoat and hat, my iPhone clutched to my ear. I'd be lying if I said this excursion didn't give me pause, but I had to push past the nerves. *Shicheii* said he'd witnessed me fulfilling my destiny in a vision, a lifepath filled with perilous traps, and danger around every bend. This new road wouldn't be easy, but everything about it felt right. Even tonight, every molecule in my body cheered me on, shoving me out of my comfort zone and into the badass warrior I was always meant to become.

At the corner, I crossed the street, the area dark and broody like a trophy hunter's soul.

With any luck, the Escalade driver hadn't noticed me yet. In case he did—or she, but I doubt those sexist pigs hired women—I played it cool, mouthing words into the mic, pretending to chat on the phone. Mr. Mayhem's breath echoed over the line as though he was running through the forest, hopping whatever, swerving around trees and leaf litter. Or climbing. Wouldn't put it past him to scale a sturdy maple, oak, or ash for an aerial view. Up high, he could also keep tabs on me.

Even though he claimed he wouldn't worry about my safety, he'd protected me all my life. Well, half my life. Guess he stopped once I reached seventeen or eighteen. Nonetheless, at the Observatory Bar on the rooftop, he indicated that watching over me wasn't an easy habit to break. Except for, y'know, the times he tried to kill me. Back then, he said if he wanted me dead, I would be, and I never doubted that statement.

What about the night I stumbled into the wrong house at the wrong time? Didn't he recognize me? Granted, many years had passed between us. But my eyes hadn't changed. If they're truly windows to the soul, how couldn't he connect the dots? Or maybe he did. Maybe by hunting me, threatening my very existence, he was testing my survival skills.

Could that be why he trapped me in the underground bunker back then?

"Cautious Cat." His firm and harsh tone echoed over the open line.

"Yeah?"

"Concentrate on your job and not on our past history."

I stared at the screen. "How'd you—?" No sense in asking how he knew the things he did. He'd never tell me, anyway. "*Ahem.* The Escalade is still in the same spot. I'm movin' in."

"Under no circumstances should you approach that vehicle." Over the line, his voice boomed, and I pulled the phone away from my ear, decreasing the vibration from rattling my eardrum. "Are you not searching for the venue?"

I tsked my tongue. "No, I am."

"All right, Cat. My mistake." His tone normalized. "Once you pass the Escalade, head southwest. What direction are you facing now?"

"Err... One sec." I broke a thin branch off the nearest tree, then split it in half. With two twelve-inch pieces, I held them up to the sky, the back stick lower than the front. Once I pinpointed the Central Fire—also called Polaris or North Star—at the end of Little Bear's tail, also known as the Little Dipper, I froze, studying the navigational star's rhythm, its pulse. Once it rose upward, I had my answer. "East."

If the star traveled downward, I'd be facing West. Left movement indicated North, right for South. Cool little trick *Shicheii* taught me, though at the time, we lay flat on our stomachs with the two sticks jammed into Mother Earth, ensuring an ideal angle from which to view starlight. Over time, I mastered navigation from the ground, then practiced while standing, for times when lying flat wasn't an option. Like tonight.

"Good job," he said. "If someone follows you—"

"I'll lead 'em in the opposite direction."

"Perfect. Remember to keep this line open."

"Yep. I know."

About twenty feet ahead on the opposite side of the street, the Escalade idled out front of a ranch-style home, smoke billowing out its chimney. Couldn't tell from here if someone was in the passenger seat, but I also couldn't stare, or it'd look too obvious.

"What if the silent auction's in the basement of the ranch?"

"It isn't."

"Worth a look, though, no?"

"Cat, I am staring at the venue as we speak. Hence why I directed you to me."

I yanked the phone away from my ear, staring at it like green slime seeped out the mic. "You found the silent auction?"

"I did."

"And you're just telling me this now?"

"Concentrate on your surroundings, please. We do not have time for a flurry of questions."

"Okay, okay, fine. Just threw me is all." I whispered, "Passing the Escalade now."

The driver wore a black suit coat, white shirt, and chauffer hat. On the window frame, a muscular arm rested, a lit cigarette smoldering between two meaty fingers. As far as I could tell, he was alone, the passenger seat empty.

My heels *tap, tap, tapped,* echoing in the stillness as I crossed behind the Escalade.

Mr. Mayhem said, "Talk to me about mundane things."

"Aw, I love that movie. Did you and Reed go to the theater or stream it at home?" I paused, pretending to listen. "Uh-ha. Stop it. Then what happened?" Fake laughter. "No way."

A few feet from the sidewalk, a man stepped from the passenger side of the Escalade, and startled the shit out of me. "Hang up the phone."

At a dead stop, I glanced over my right shoulder, left shoulder, then laid splayed fingers on my chest. "You talkin' to me?"

"Put the phone away now, bitch."

"Bitch?" I acted offended. "You can fuck right off, pal. How 'bout that?" Before he could make a move, I slid off one heel, then the other, bundling them in my arms, the phone still clenched in my hand, and took off down the hill instead of veering on to the side street.

Heavy footfalls clambered behind me.

But I couldn't tell if he was gaining on me without a glance back, and that wasn't about to happen anytime soon. It'd slow me down too much. While jetting down the hill, I said, "Problem," into the phone, my fearful breath laboring.

A man's meaty hand clamped down on my shoulder, and I spun, slamming the heel into the side of the stranger's face. Shit. Missed. I was aiming for his neck. When I ripped out the heel, blood poured down his cheek, and he slapped his massive mitt over the hole. That was my cue to get the hell out of there.

Behind me, he hollered something, but I couldn't make out what he said over the roaring engine behind me. *Shit!* I careened into a neighboring yard, hopped one fence, then another. Raced through two backyards, then a third. Now closer to where Mr. Mayhem told me to go, I couldn't step into the open without the chauffer and his goon spotting me. I also couldn't find my partner-in-crime.

Crouched behind a rhododendron bush at the side of a Colonial-style home, I waited for the black Escalade to pass. But instead, the SUV putted down the side street uber-slow, the dude I stabbed hanging out the passenger window with his hand pressed to the cheek wound.

Into the phone, I whispered, "Where are you?"

"Look up."

When I reclined my head, a bundle of branches waved at me. Across from my hiding spot, Mr. Mayhem crouched in a tall oak tree, his entire body cloaked in darkness. The slivered moon offered a feeble attempt at brightening the area, a golden smolder misting the treetops.

Maybe that's a good thing. I backtracked, stuffed a stiletto into each coat pocket, clenched my iPhone between my teeth, and climbed an ash tree, my bare feet clutching to thick, edgy bark. Once I ascended into the canopy of leaves, my heartbeat slowed to a quick *pitter patter, pitter patter, pitter patter.*

Below me, the Escalade rolled across the asphalt. Once it reached the end of the road, I pressed the phone to my ear. "Whew. That was way too close."

Silence.

"Mister M?"

Silence.

"Mister M?"

The phone hadn't disconnected, so why wasn't he answering me? "Mister M?"

Inches from my hiding spot, he popped up through the leaves, scaring the living shit out of me.

With a hand clutched over my heart, I mouth-breathed. "Are you tryin' to send me into cardiac arrest?"

"You may disconnect the call now, Cat."

"Oh. Right." I tapped END. "What if they saw you cross the street?"

"Impossible."

"No. It's not." Heat barreling through my system, my chest tightened. "The dude I stabbed was hanging out the window like a frickin' bloodhound."

"True. However, like most do in these types of situations, he neglected to search one critical direction."

"Above."

With a slight nod, he grinned. "Precisely."

"They're probably on their way to the ER. I nailed the dude who chased me pretty good."

"Your aim needs work." A coy smile lurked but never emerged. "Unless, of course, you meant to strike his cheek."

"So, you were watchin' me?"

"I may have checked in once or twice. The point is, both sentinels can now recognize us by sight. At the gala, we'll need to steer clear of them."

"Gala?" I chewed my bottom lip. "What gala?"

"Come. I'll show you."

At the base of the tree, I passed him the fedora, sloughed off the suit coat, combed my fingers through my hair, and straightened my skirt. "One sec." Hopping on one foot, I slid on one stiletto before he stopped me by passing me a bandana. "What's this for?"

"Blood and remnants of flesh."

"Right. Thanks." After wiping down the bloody heel, I smoothed out my red blouse while he tucked the soiled bandana into a Ziploc baggie. "Okay, I'm ready."

"Stunning as ever, Cat. Let's proceed. The gala is one street over."

"Is Hawthorne there?"

"He is."

"But he knows who we are. Whaddawe do about that?"

"The gala is a public event."

"Wait. What?" All rational thought froze, my mind buzzing with nothingness. "Why couldn't we drive there?"

"Had we known we were looking for a fundraising gala and not a silent auction, we could have."

"I don't get it." Ghostly wings fluttered my stomach. "Why'd that guy try to jump me, then?"

"You didn't recognize him?"

Recognize him? "No. Why? Should I?"

Rather than answer me, he pulled his shirt collar aside, revealing the buckshot wounds running up the side of his neck.

"Stop it." All the saliva in my mouth dried to dust, my hand rising to parted lips. "He's the guy who shot you?"

"One in the same."

"Fuck." The hard glare halted my breath. "Slipped out. Sorry." My borrowed stilettos *tap, tap, tapped* across the asphalt, our stride in perfect tempo. "So, they know you killed their men?"

"Apparently."

"No wonder he looked pissed."

The stakes were even higher now. If we weren't super careful, this mission might be our last.

Chapter 31

"The love of possessions is a disease with them.
They take tithes from the poor and weak to support the rich who rule.
They claim this mother of ours, the Earth, for their own
and fence the neighbors away.
If America had been twice the size it is, there
still would not have been enough."

—Sitting Bull

Friday, 12:20 a.m.

Thankfully, he and Shawnee weren't the only couple in regular evening attire instead of black-tie tuxedos and full-length gowns. The gala doubled as a fundraiser event, meant to raise money for conservation.

Ironic, to say the least.

Shawnee fidgeted more than usual. One day, perhaps she'd learn to relax in upscale environments. Not tonight, apparently. When he squeezed her hand to offer encouragement, a few stiff muscles relaxed in her forearm. Not a lot, but better.

Entering the banquet room, she clung to his arm. "I can't believe the tickets cost five-hundred bucks apiece. Whaddaya bet that dough's goin' straight into Killzme's pockets."

"Not here." A cocktail waitress strolled by with a tray of champagne-filled flutes, and Mayhem stopped her. "May we?"

"Help yourself, sir."

"Splendid." No nametag on her ruffled tuxedo shirt. He lifted two flutes off the tray, passing one to Shawnee. "Thank you kindly."

The server continued from one group to another while he and Shawnee strolled around the perimeter, the mix of various colognes, body spray, and perfumes flaring his nostril. Couples waltzed across the dance floor, musicians playing live on stage. In the far corner, a muscular man in a dark suit guarded a mysterious door. Mayhem steered Shawnee to an empty table off to the side. As always, he pulled out the chair for her. Seated across from her, he had an ideal view of the suspicious exit.

Shawnee leaned forward, her voice low and whisperous. "I think I'm underdressed."

"Focus on how you hold yourself and less on what clothes you're wearing. Real beauty comes from within. Thus, a confident, proud woman can make any evening ensemble work for her."

Her shoulders drew back, and she sat taller and more confident. "Like this?"

He winked. "Precisely."

Mr. Hawthorne snuck up behind him and rested a hand on Mayhem's upper back. "Had I known you were interested in conservation, I'd have offered you a formal invitation to the gala." The animal trafficker shook his hand. "Nice to see you, Mister Daniels."

"Pleasure is all mine, Mister Hawthorne."

"Hope you brought your checkbook." He focused on Shawnee. "Gorgeous as ever, Missus Daniels."

"So kind of you to say, Mister Hawthorne." Tittering like a schoolgirl, she offered him her hand, and he kissed the top of her fingers. "Thank you."

"Save me a dance."

Eyes wide, her gaze shot to Mayhem.

"Of course, she will. My wife loves to dance."

Under the table, Shawnee kicked his shin.

"Looking forward to it. Well, I better return to my party. Just wanted to say hello."

"We're so glad you did, Mister Hawthorne." He tipped the fedora. "I'll be in touch."

On the other side of the dance floor, their target briefly stopped to whisper in the stage manager's ear before continuing to his table. The same four men from the Cave bar sat around him—the organizers of this event.

Shawnee rose. "Want somethin' stronger from the bar?" At the neckline her fingers slipped under her blouse and withdrew a folded hundred-dollar bill—his hundred—from her brassiere. "My treat."

"Allow me." He rose partway off the chair. "Relax. I'll get the cocktails."

"Nah, I'm good. Sit. I wanna check the place out, anyway."

"Please be careful." A woman fetching drinks for the man rubbed against every fiber of his nature. Some might misconstrue chivalry as sexist. When in fact, quite the opposite was true. Chivalry stemmed from an innate respect for the opposite sex.

"I will. What're you in the mood for?"

"Surprise me."

"How? I know nothing about the fancy stuff you drink at these places."

"True." The chuckle he suppressed. "In that case, let's keep things simple. I'll have a Moscow Mule, please."

"Okay, cool."

When she turned, he grabbed hold of her hand, urging her closer as he dug in his pocket for his bill fold. "Save your money." He peeled off a crisp hundred. "Please leave the change for the bartender. They survive on tips."

"Sure, no problem."

Shawnee snaked around tables and cut across the edge of the dancefloor, rather than around it. The woman never met a rule she didn't break. After a brief exchange with two tuxedo-clad gentlemen at the bar, the men stepped back, providing space for her to approach the bartender. While she waited for the cocktails, she leaned against the bar and swiveled back. The thumbs-up signal made him chuckle.

Ahh, never a dull moment. If only Kimi could watch her in action. She'd get a kick out of Cat's antics.

The music stopped when Mr. Hawthorne took the stage. Front and center, he addressed the crowd at the mic. "I hope you're all having a wonderful time. Thank you for supporting such a worthy cause. The night's still young, so keep those checkbooks handy." Obvious fake laughter echoed through the speakers as Shawnee paid for the drinks. "We'll hear another inspirational story soon. In the meantime, eat, drink, and enjoy."

Covering the mic, Mr. Hawthorne asked the musicians a question. What he said remained unclear, yet the band leader nodded in the affirmative. Then he hustled over to the stage manager, shielding his mouth as he spoke. Moments later, both men glanced at Shawnee, leaving the bar with a martini glass in one hand, the traditional copper mug in the other.

A sharp tingle in his chest stalled his heart, gaze shifting between Mr. Hawthorne and his pretend wife, now cutting across the dancefloor on her return trip to the table.

Back at the mic, Mr. Hawthorne signaled to the stage manager, and a spotlight encircled Shawnee, stopping her mid-stride. Frozen, her brilliant emerald gaze shot to Mayhem.

"Ladies and gentlemen, Missus Daniels has graciously agreed to dance the tango with her husband."

Oh, my.

The audience cheered.

All at once, Shawnee's rosy cheeks drained to white, her eyes widening even more, her body board stiff.

Somehow, he had to stop this before she blew their cover. When he stood, the spotlight bathed him in brightness.

Into the mic, Mr. Hawthorne announced, "Hope you don't mind us putting you on the spot, Mister Daniels. It's for a good cause."

"That it is, Mister Hawthorne. That it is." Rather than respond to the speaker, he addressed the audience. "The waltz may be a more appropriate dance for this setting. Wouldn't you agree?"

Mr. Hawthorne egged on the crowd. "Tango, tango, tango."

Until soon, the entire gala joined in. "Tango, tango, tango."

"All right, all right." To quiet the audience, he waved both hands downward. "Tango it is." For a brief moment, he thanked the Great Spirit for Kimi's absence tonight. Suffice it to say, she would not be pleased with her husband tangoing with another woman. It's such a sensual, passionate dance. "I hope you'll all join us on the dancefloor."

Everyone cheered.

Mr. Hawthorne whirled back to the band. "Hit it."

Shawnee practically ran to their table, liquor splashing over the rims of both glasses. "I probably should've mentioned this sooner, but... I can't dance."

He jerked back. "At all?"

"No." She gulped down half her Peppermintini. "Never had a reason to learn."

"Have you ever seen the tango?"

Fear shone in her eyes. "Only in *Scent of a Woman*, with Al Pacino."

"Then it's time for a crash course." Face to face, he rested his hands on her shoulders. "The most important part of the tango is for our bodies to move as one. At times, that changes, but I'll signal to you beforehand. Pay attention. The dance only allows non-verbal communication."

Reclining her head, she polished off her cocktail. "Can't we just leave?"

"Not without blowing our cover. Keep a positive, centered mindset that says, we are the only two people on that dancefloor, the only two people in this ballroom. No one else matters."

A mousy voice squeaked out, "Okay."

"Do you recall how Pacino's dance partner held her arms?"

"Kinda, yeah. Nadine made me watch the movie, like, ten times."

"Good. Exaggerate all your movements. If I spin you, end with extended arms." He dragged her over to the dancefloor, ringed with couples. A generous area in the center reserved for Mr. and Mrs. Daniels. Before stepping into the ring, he rattled off a few basics. "Start with three steps backward, knees bent throughout. First your right foot, then left. When you land on your right foot for the second time, point the toes of your left toward the ceiling—brief pause—and slide the left foot out to the side, dragging the right knee to your left without closing the feet. Ready?"

"Not even a little, no."

"Keep your chin high and proud. Trust that you can do this, Cat. And don't fight me when I lead." Into the center ring, he sauntered, with Shawnee braced to his side. Facing her, he held his arms in a frame, and she matched the pose.

The band played "La Cumparsita," the traditional tango anthem, and he stepped forward, pressing his thigh into hers, leading her backward. Couples danced around the outer edges, showcasing the center as Mayhem stopped, rocking back, a hand planted in the base of Shawnee's spine, rolling her with him. Off center, he cradled her, moving forward, slow steps around her, leading her to do the same. Then he twisted, his heart aimed at hers, staring into her eyes. When he crossed his right foot over his left, the other dancers spread out, blending them into the crowd.

Without the spotlight on her, she relaxed a bit, her body more pliable and loose now. Or the Peppermintini kicked in. Difficult to determine which. Regardless, he and Shawnee moved as one, tangoing across the dancefloor, dipping and spinning, side-stepping and gliding.

When he dramatically released her to the swingout position, panic flashed in her eyes, and he closed the gap between them, grasping her, holding her close as he dipped, the side of her nose touching his, the brim of his fedora resting against her forehead. Holding the position added drama to the dance, but every muscle in her body tensed.

Mayhem swung her to his right, closed into a tighter pivot hold. Stepping between her feet, he rocked her back on his thigh. Dipped her once more from the side, then released. This time, she strutted like a real dancer. He extended his arms, and she jumped into a swan position. Lifting her above his head, he spun as she held the pose.

When the music stopped, he rolled her into cradling arms, and the audience went wild. Even the other dancers cheered. He had to admit, it was quite the finish. For someone who never danced before, she had no problem with the tango.

Hand-in-hand, he led her back to the table before the crowd wanted an encore performance.

A wide smile brightened her face. "That was awesome."

"You're a natural."

"Thanks. I had a good teacher. Whew." Her fingers pulled blouse away from her chest, billowing the material in and out. "I'm parched."

On the other side of the dance floor, Mr. Hawthorne's table sat empty. "Clever, clever boy."

"Who?"

"Mister Hawthorne used us as a cover to sneak down to the silent auction."

"Think he knows who we are?"

"He may."

"Not good. Whaddawe do now?"

"We need to know what—or whom—they're auctioning off. Come." He rose, extending his hand. "We'll have more control from the outside."

"What does that mean?"

Perhaps it's best if he let her learn the plan as it unfolded. If he forewarned her, she may object.

Chapter 32

1 a.m.

As usual, my so-called partner left me in the dark. Instead, he dragged me around the outside of the building, where guards patrolled the grounds. Hidden in the tree line, he and I waited for an opening, but each time one muscle-bound sentinel rounded the back corner another one appeared from the front. With four guys, they had this building locked down tight.

In between guard shifts, Mr. Mayhem hushed, "Do you recall your performance at the shipyard?"

"Y'mean, when I almost got arrested for DUI? Um, yeah."

"We need an encore, only on foot."

"What, like, approach one of these guys like I'm drunk and lost?"

"And vulnerable, yes. You only need to capture his attention for a moment—long enough for me to move in."

"And then what?"

"Cat"—he sighed—"if you could please concentrate on your role, and only your role, I shall concentrate on mine."

"Okay, okay, fine." I flashed my hands in surrender. "Clearly, I touched a nerve."

"Thank you. Now, whenever you're ready, please move in."

And so, I waited for the first goon to round the back corner. When he did, I hustled across the grass, then slowed, my feet sloppy, wobbling in my heels. As the next guard soldiered around from the front of the building, I accidentally on purpose fell into his arms.

"Oh, sorry." I rubbed his pecs. "Wow. You're a big boy, aren't 'cha?" I batted my lashes, really laying it on thick as I caressed his massive arms. "You must be really strong with all these muscles, so many muscles."

Up close, his ridiculous dark eyebrows looked penciled on. They really popped against his ruddy complexion.

"You haven't seen my most impressive muscle of all." A shit eatin' grin crossed his ruby red, flaky lips—*bogus*. "What're you doing later?"

I blew in his ear, whispering, "What's wrong with now, lover?"

Without warning, the dude's head wrenched backward, a blade slicing his throat, blood smacking me in the face, neck, and chest.

"What. The. Fuck!" Hands splayed, I stepped back, gaze running down the front of me. "You coulda warned me."

"Cat, please grab his ankles." Cool and calm, Mr. Mayhem dragged him toward the wood line, the dude gurgling on his own blood. "We don't have time for a drawn-out *tête-à-tête* this time."

Hidden by a thicket of trees, he handed me a fresh bandana, and I wiped the blood off my face the best I could without a mirror, a metallic sweetness churning my stomach acids. But then, a male voice emanated from the guard's waistband, and I lifted his jacket.

"Shit. He's got a radio."

Mr. Mayhem gestured for me to pass it to him. And so, I unclipped the handheld from the dude's belt.

The male voice said, "Bravo, is the West side clear?"

Mr. Mayhem squeezed the button. "Clear."

"Alpha's back so he'll take over. Move to the South end."

"Roger that." My partner-in-crime added more gravel to his voice to match the dying man's.

I whispered, "Who do you think Alpha is?"

His chin jabbed at a sinewy armed dude rounding the side yard from the front of the building, stark-white gauze taped to one cheek.

Uh-oh. The drunk girl ruse wouldn't work now. Palms up, my neck turtled in my shoulders, motioning that I no idea what to do. Rather than panic, Mr. Mayhem raised the volume of the radio. Static crackled over the line, drawing the attention of the guy I stabbed, coaxing him closer.

"Bravo?" he said, his tone drenched in befuddlement. "What're you doing, taking a leak?"

Before I knew what was happening, Mr. Mayhem shoved me into the open, with smeared blood all over me, the bandana still in my hand.

"You!" He grabbed me, and I froze. "What the fuck did you do to Bravo?" He reached for his radio, and Mr. Mayhem pounced, snapping the guy's neck in one swift movement. After catching the big lug in his arms, he dragged him deeper into the woods.

"Um, thanks?"

"You're welcome, Cat."

He laced his fingers with mine and took off, racing toward the building, jerking my arm. When he slid across the grass to the basement window, I smashed headfirst into the concrete. Dizzy, I stumbled backward, spiked heels sinking into the grass, twisting my ankle, my legs crumbling beneath me.

Mr. Mayhem glanced back. "Ooh, my apologies. I thought you'd slide with me."

"Maybe if you warned me first, I woulda. Thanks for that, by the way. My night wouldn't be complete without a raging migraine." I felt my forehead for a fracture. "Nice. I'm growing an egg. Perfect. Maybe you can—oh, I dunno—rip out all my hair next. Or set me on fire. That'd be fun, huh?"

"Cautious Cat," he said, his tone serious with a hint of aggravation.

A balled fist I flung to my hip. "What now?"

"Are you done?"

"Just sayin'. Geez..."

At the basement window, he snapped photos of the silent auction with his phone. "We need to identify these men."

It wasn't till then that I witnessed what these bastards were doing. Cages lined the back and sides of a wooden stage, all marked with a metal number tag. The auctioneer held up an imprisoned golden eagle, stuffed inside a cage that could barely hold an upright pigeon, its wings flattened to its sides, its head rolled forward, black-tipped golden bill resting on its chest—a juvenile who didn't have enough life experience to escape the poacher's trap. Spirit broken, this incredible animal was now an empty shell of its former self, like it'd given up all hope of survival.

Heart aching, a fury raged within me. Any injuries I sustained couldn't compare to the hell endured by these endangered species. What about their families? Had they witnessed the capture and torture of their mothers, fathers, grandparents, siblings, and/or lifelong mates?

Elders of all species—including humans, by the way—held knowledge that benefited their kin. Like us, the ancient knowledge they passed down through generation after generation. Without elders, the entire tribe suffered. So, although these scumbags might reason away their actions with misnomers—they only capture a few birds and mammals, what's the big deal?—the harsh reality was poaching and animal trafficking crippled countless future generations, like the majestic juvenile eagle being auctioned off.

Even if I could set that argument aside, which I couldn't, what gave these scumbags the right to entrap the voiceless? Who the fuck did they think they were? Animals were not put on this planet for exploitation. Mother Earth's Innocent Ones played a vital role in the Natural World by balancing and maintaining life-sustaining ecosystems. That, in turn, enabled us to thrive. For that reason alone, why wouldn't we protect them? Why wouldn't we respect them? Why wouldn't we treat them as equals?

Other cages held two adult golden eagles, three bald eagles, three peregrine falcons, four loons, and two common nighthawks. On the floor behind the auctioneer, four Canada lynxes didn't even have enough room in their prisons to lie down, their bodies braced upright by thick, iron bars.

Tears washed my face as Mr. Mayhem grabbed my hand, urging me to stand and get the hell out of there before the next guard shift. I'd barely made it to the tree line before the radio crackled to life.

"Alpha, stay on your toes. Bravo is MIA."

1 *:45 a.m.*
Forty-five minutes later, we were in the Caddy, heading home to the cabin. Neither of us spoke for most of the drive. After washing my face, chest, and hands with wet wipes in the mirror, I slapped up the visor. Flashcards of what I'd witnessed spiraled through my mind, memories of the heart-wrenching scene rattling my nerves. Antsy and pissed off, I couldn't relax, couldn't settle, my knee bobbing with excess energy.

I glanced over at Mr. Mayhem. Blue lights of the dash cascaded over his face, sadness and pain evident in his blank stare at the dark road ahead.

"Are you okay?" I asked.

"Are you?"

"Not really, no."

"Nor am I, Cat. Nor am I." He turned into the driveway, framed in tall pines, ash, and maple trees, the log cabin cloaked in nature, hidden from the main drag.

Four Sacred Fires blazed in the yard, warming the night air, orange sparks spiraling into the darkness of night. The crackling fires represented the four seasons, the four human needs—physical, mental, emotional, spiritual—the four kingdoms of animal, mineral, plant, and human, and the four Sacred Medicines of sweetgrass, tobacco, cedar, and sage.

"What's our next move?"

"You should get some rest." He shut me down. "It's been a long day."

"What about you? Aren't you goin' to bed?"

"Not yet. With your grandfather asleep, now is the perfect time for Mister Doe and I to get better acquainted."

"Wanna have a quick tea first?"

Grinning, he slid the shifter into Park. "Tea sounds nice. Are you certain you wouldn't rather turn in for the night?"

"After what we witnessed back there? Doubt I'll be sleeping for a while."

The top half of his body twisted toward me. "Blood or answers? The choice is yours, Cat."

"Answers. We need to know who those guys are."

"Agreed."

"Ask me again if he refuses to cooperate." I exaggerated a wink, and he snickered.

Up the stairs I trod, Cheyenne's heels clutched to my chest. Mr. Mayhem swung open the screen door for me. The living room glowed from an abundance of jarred candles, flames dancing in melted wax, vanilla, blueberry, and cedar wafting in the air. He pressed a stiff finger to his lips—*don't wake your grandfather*—and I shot him a thumbs-up.

In the kitchen, Mr. Mayhem poured the refrigerated wild tea into a saucepan, and I grabbed two mugs from the cabinet. After carrying the honey pot out to the porch, I darted back inside, holding the screen door from slapping the frame as it closed.

While he stood at the stove, stirring the tea, I padded down the hall to my bedroom, where I stripped down to my bra and thong then stuffed my bloody clothes into the hamper. Never even considered closing the door till Mr. Mayhem appeared.

With a widened gaze, he bowed his head, a flat hand shielding his eyes. "My apologies, Cat. I... err... came to tell you..."

Never saw him tongue-tied before. Kinda funny, actually.

Before this encounter grew even more awkward, I slipped my arms into the plush terrycloth robe from The Inn at Thorn Hill Restaurant and Spa. "What'd you come to tell me?" The subtle hint meant I'd covered my nakedness, but he didn't take the bait.

Instead, he swiveled to leave. "It'll keep."

"It's all good." I latched on to his forearm. "I put my robe on."

When the hand lowered from his eyes, a blush skipped across his cheekbones. "Again, my apologies. I would never intentionally intrude on your privacy. The tea's ready. I'll meet you on the porch."

Right then, Poe landed on his father's shoulder, tricolored bling sparkling against black chest feathers. Tracing me up and down with a beady-eyed stare, his bill parted as though he'd caught us in the throes of passion. In slow motion, his ankles—knees?—bent, ready to take off and tattle, filling his mother's head with lies about the homewrecker who forced her husband to cheat.

The moment Poe's weight shifted, his father scooped him off his shoulder, cradling him in his arms like a spoiled brat. "Rest easy, bud. You have misread this encounter. I simply came to tell Cat the tea was ready. Nothing more, nothing less."

Rattle, rattle, rattle. Poe's love language.

"Now, if you'll excuse us, Cat, we shall meet you on the porch."

"I'll be right behind ya."

"Splendid." He thumbed Poe's bill. "Since you'll be joining us, would you like a fruit cup? Jacy Lee left cubed melon in the refrigerator."

Coo... rattle, rattle... coo...

My mouth watered. "I could go for some cantaloupe."

Pissy Pants shot me a glower that even I could translate. *How dare you even suggest sharing. First, my dad, then my food? Who do you think you are, bitch?*

Flashing my palms, I backed away. "Okay, alright. Forget I mentioned it."

Chuckling, Mr. Mayhem strode down the hall. When I poked my head through the doorway, Poe's head rotated like a possessed marionette and he tossed me the stink eye. Man, that bird harbored some deep resentment. Not even a three-hundred-dollar necklace could repair the damage I'd done.

As much as I hated to admit it, he wasn't wrong. But it'd be a cold day in hell before I cowed down to that frickin' diva. In the bathroom, I shampooed my hair with the shower wand, blood circling the drain. After a quick towel dry, I combed the spiky side angles toward my face and shuffled my bangs into place.

Down the hall I hustled, past the kitchen island then through the living room. On the porch, the night air prickled my wet scalp, but I rolled with it and sat in my designated chair backed by the log wall.

"I took the liberty of adding honey to your tea." He slid me a mug. "If you'd like more, help yourself."

From the rim, I sipped, warm nectar and herbs waltzing across my tongue. "It's perfect. Thanks."

"My pleasure." He set the fedora on the railing and reclined in his chair, legs extended, ankles crossed. "Beautiful night, isn't it?"

"With the four Sacred Fires burning, it is."

Poe sauntered from one end of the table to the other, spun on his heels, and pranced back to his dad, chest out, showing off his bling like a runway model.

I jabbed a chin at Pissy Pants. "What's with him? Thought he gave the necklace to Lenore."

"*Au contraire.* He loaned Lenore the necklace for two reasons. One, so he wouldn't lose the jewelry during the battle. And two, for a good luck charm to help with pain. Once your grandfather popped her shoulder back into place, she must have returned it."

"But I thought he L-O-V-E'd her."

"Oh, he does. Always has. Whether the feeling is mutual remains unclear." Leaning forward, his hands clasped around the mug on the table. "You see, Cat. In the bird world, females wield great power. If Poe fails to complete certain tasks better and faster than the other males wooing Lenore, a gold necklace won't make a difference. She must choose the strongest partner to ensure the survival of future offspring."

"Think he's up for the challenge?"

"Look at that gorgeous specimen." An opened hand swept to Poe, who glared at me for prying into his personal life. Or daydreaming about the night he kills me once and for all. "How could she not choose him?"

"I could think of a few reasons," I mumbled into my mug.

Eyes thinned straight at me, Poe soldiered to his bowl of cubed cantaloupe and honey dew melon, seedless black cherries sprinkled over the top. The slurping that followed he exaggerated, rubbing it in my face, fruit juices leaking out the sides of his bill, really laying it on thick. Little bastard.

Again, Mr. Mayhem reclined in his chair, totally clueless about the power struggle between me and his loyal companion. Either that, or he didn't give a shit. Hard to tell which.

"Hey, um." I lifted my bangs. "Does this look as bad as it feels? Forgot to check in the bathroom mirror."

Tossing his head back, Poe let out a cackle, and my fingers balled into a fist.

"I'll take that as a yes?"

"Oh, it's not that bad." He swiped away my remark, a smirk lingering behind his straight face. "The swelling should recede fairly quickly. Has your headache improved?"

"Kinda. I dunno." I flimflammed. "It's a little better, I guess."

"Drink your tea. It'll help open your blood vessels."

"Huh? No clue what that means."

"Most headaches occur in the nerves, blood vessels, and muscles that span the head and neck. Sometimes the muscles or blood vessels swell, tighten, or go through other changes that stimulate the surrounding nerves or put them under pressure. These nerves send a rush of pain messages to the brain, resulting in a headache."

"Oh, really?" The added sarcasm was intentional. "Do those same principles apply when someone slams your head into a concrete wall? I could be spitballin' here, but I'm pretty sure that's what caused my headache."

His lips smoothed. "As I mentioned at the time, I thought you'd slide with me. Do you require an additional apology?"

"No. Just sayin'."

Poe's head bounced between us, ever-changing expressions from love to hate, love to hate, and I resisted the urge to slap the smug look off his face. In front of him, two lonely cubes of cantaloupe floated in fruit juices.

"If you're not gonna finish that—"

One claw slid the bowl out of my reach. To smear it in my face even more, he stabbed both cubes with his bill, clawed them off his face, and bit in, squirting juices everywhere, chewing in slow motion, eyelids partly closed to show the deliciousness.

"Y'know, Poe, I could just go to the fridge and get my own."

Mr. Mayhem cleared his throat. "Please refrain from watching him eat, Cat. He doesn't like it."

"You're callin' me out?" I flung a hand at Pissy Pants. "What about him? He's the one making a federal case outta every single bite."

"All right, all right." His hand patted the top of mine before he rose to clear the table. "If you're still game, let's question Mister Doe before our window closes for the night. But again, if you'd rather sit this one out, say the word and I shall handle it alone."

"Nope. I'm good."

"Okie doke." After loading *Shicheii's* serving tray with our mugs and the honey pot, his gaze traced me up and down. "Is that what you plan to wear?"

My shoulders bumped up and down. "Yeah. Why? I gotta dress up to question a hostage in a shed?"

"Of course not. However, I know how fond you are of that robe."

"No clue what that means. Is something gonna happen to it if I keep it on?"

"Not necessarily. Though, should the interrogation escalate, I would hate for you to stain the material."

"Me stain it? Or you?"

"Either. White's a difficult color to maintain."

"Fine." I huffed out a breath. "I'll go change."

"Good idea. Better safe than sorry." He passed me the serving tray, then swung open the door. "Would you mind leaving the mugs on the counter by the sink?"

"Why, you're not comin' in?"

"Poe and I will meet you out back."

"Alright, I guess. Thought we were doing this together, but whatever." I strolled through the living room, left the tray on the counter, then continued to my room. This time, I closed the door before I disrobed.

Digging through the chest of drawers, I had no idea what to wear. Dark colors? Probably best. Too damn tired to fuss about it, I slipped into charcoal sweatpants, a black T-shirt, and my red Converse high-tops.

Good enough.

When I whipped open the door, *Shicheii* was standing there with a fist raised, ready to knock.

Uh-oh.

Chapter 33

2:25 a.m.

Dressed in a red and ivory robe—silhouettes of bear, moose, and pine trees printed across each wide stripe, framed by charcoal and hunter green braids—long gray hair flowed down my grandfather's chest, loose strands almost reaching his belt.

"Oh, hey, *Shicheii*." His all-consuming presence melted my spine, and I dove into his chest, resting my cheek against his heart. "What're you doin' up?"

One hand stroked my damp hair. "I heard you mulling about and came to check on you." He lifted my chin, my face framed in warm palms. "Are you going somewhere, Mourning Dove?"

To avoid the question, I said, "Love the robe. It's so soft."

"Thank you, honey. Cheveyo bought it for me last Christmas. It's made from one-hundred-percent recycled microfiber. I could ask him where he found it, if you'd like one."

"Cool. Yeah. We can be twins."

Giggling, dimples indented both cheeks. "Speaking of Cheveyo, where is he? Did he not return with you?"

Shit. What could I say? I couldn't lie. But if I told him the truth, he might try to stop the interrogation.

"He's around here somewhere." I checked both ends of the hall, pretending to look for him. "We just had tea on the porch."

"How nice." Big smile. "Are you two heading to bed soon? It's late."

"Yep. I'm gonna just... err... wash the mugs."

Now that I said it, I had to do it. Otherwise, I'd be lying to elder, to my only living relative, to the person I loved most in this world.

And that wasn't an option. Never would I disrespect *Shicheii*. Never. Some of my choices he might not agree with—like feeding a poacher to Karma—but blatantly spitting untruths seemed much worse.

"The dishes will keep, sweet child." His warm gaze filled me with love. "I'll take care of them in the morning. Your body requires rest to fully heal."

"I promise I won't stay up too long."

"All right, then." He kissed the egg on my forehead, then lifted my bangs. "What happened here?"

"Oh, that?" My voice pitched. "Nothing. I bumped into a wall." Wasn't a lie, though I left out the part about how it happened. And thankfully, he didn't ask. After another embrace in his loving arms, I walked him down the hall, into the kitchen, and over to the stairs. "Night-night, *Shicheii*. Love you."

"I love you, too, honey."

Up the open staircase, he climbed, bare feet ascending higher and higher. Once his bedroom door clicked shut, I bolted outside, leaped off the porch, and jogged to the shed out back. When I whipped opened the door, Mr. Mayhem was standing in front of the hostage with the poacher's shoeless foot in one gloved hand, the hunting knife in the other. Sprawled on his back in the dirt, the scumbag groaned through a shattered jaw, practically screaming—a spotlight aimed into his swollen eyes.

On the shelf behind Mr. Mayhem, Poe stood, cawing this eerie shrill that raised all my neck hairs at once. Friggin' psycho.

"Before we proceed," Mr. Mayhem said to the poacher, "allow me to enlighten you. The long connective tissue spanning the sole of the foot is called the fascia. The fascia connects to the paratenon and Achilles tendons, which run up the back of your leg."

An icy tongue licked the vertebrae of my spine as I shut the door behind me. In the past, Mr. Mayhem had me in a similar position with an interchangeable speech.

The tip of the razor-sharp blade pierced the arch of his bare foot, and I winced. "Should you force me to sever the fascia, Mister Doe, unbearable pain will instantly flood your system. Compared to your existing injuries, this new pain will far exceed anything you've ever experienced. Unless, of course, you've been set on fire in the past."

More muffled screaming.

"Are you willing to answer my questions now?"

The poacher's swollen face rocked up and down.

"Excellent." With the foot braced in one hand, he clenched the hunting knife between his teeth, dug in his pocket, then passed me his iPhone. "Please show Mister Doe the photographs." Adjusting the metal shade suspended from the ceiling, he aimed the light bulb at the poacher's chest. "You may need to enlarge the images to show individual faces, Cat. His eyes are quite swollen."

"It's locked." Meaning, the phone.

Mr. Mayhem leaned forward and widened his eyes, allowing me to scan his retina. I tapped the Photos icon and scrolled back a few frames. Squatted beside the poacher, I showed him a blown-up image of the auctioneer. With a glance up at my mentor, I waited for him to repeat the question that, apparently, the hostage refused to answer before I arrived. Hence how he wound up in this predicament.

"Do you recognize the man in the photo, Mister Doe?"

The dude nodded yes.

"Cat, would you mind sitting behind our guest to brace him in an upright position?"

Hell yeah, I minded. Why'd I always get the shit jobs? Maybe he'd listen to reason. "I'd rather not. He reeks of piss and blood, not to mention the B.O."

"Though I agree—he is a bit pungent—Mister Doe needs to be able to write his responses. Please, Cat."

"Fine."

Balls. I yanked the poacher upright by his bloody shirt. Behind him, I sat in the dirt with the scumbag between my legs, his back leaning against my chest. No wonder Mr. Mayhem didn't want me to wear my robe. After passing the hostage a pen and the notepad, I flashed the photo again.

"Thank you, Cat. Now, Mister Doe, please share the name of the man in the photograph."

Marvin

"And Marvin's surname is...?"

Tottenham

"Thank you. I appreciate your willingness to cooperate. What is Mister Tottenham's role within the organization?"

Auctioneer

"I am cognizant of that, thank you. Perhaps I should rephrase. Does Mister Tottenham hold a prominent position within the organization? In other words, does he control one of the cells operating in New Hampshire?"

No

"I see. Thank you. Moving on. Cat, please scroll to the next photo."

I showed the poacher a tuxedo-clad asshole in the front row.

"Do you recognize that man, Mister Doe?"

Yes

"I need a name, please."

Bo

Gloved fingers pinched the bridge of his nose. "Please include the surname in your responses."

Witherspoon

"Thank you. Does Mister Witherspoon hold a prominent position within the organization?"

Yes

"And what is that position?"

Boss

"Higher than Mister Hawthorne?"

Yes

Both eyebrows arched in surprise. "Does Mister Witherspoon operate outside the State of New Hampshire?"

Yes

"Interesting. What territory does he control?"

Northern Alaska

"Alaska?"

Yes

"My apologies. That was rhetorical. Is Mister Witherspoon responsible for organizing polar bear hunts in northern Alaska?"

More

"Meaning, more trophy hunts or more responsibilities? For clarity sake, let's break that down a bit. Does Mister Witherspoon organize trophy hunts for other large game?"

Yes

"All of the Big Five?"

Yes

"What's the Big Five?" Man, this dude stank. My nostrils screamed for me to let him go, but I couldn't. Not yet.

"In Alaska, the most coveted species are bears—grizzly, black bear, Kodiak, and polar—moose, caribou, Dall sheep, and wolves. Hunters call this group the Big Five." His focus returned to the hostage in my lap. "Does Mister Witherspoon organize other trophy hunts? And if so, please note the animal."

Beluga Whale, Orca, Sea Lion

"Stellar Sea Lion?"

Yes

"All endangered. Why am I not surprised?" A hard breath huffed out his mouth. "Thank you for the clarification. Please continue."

Northern Sea Otter, Blue Whale, North Pacific Whale

"North Pacific Whale," he repeated as if trying to wrap his mind around this information, "are one of the rarest whale species in the world."

Big $$$

A thick vein popped in Mr. Mayhem's forehead. Silent, his gaze roamed around the shed, probably trying to resist killing this scumbag on the spot. For once, Poe stayed silent, intently focused on the conversation as though he understood the stakes.

"What else, Mister Doe?"

Arctic Fox

When Mr. Mayhem glimpsed the name of the animal scribbled on the notepad, the forehead vein swelled even more. "Let's move on, shall we?" His Adam's apple rose and fell. "Cat, please show Mister Doe the next photo."

Southerland

"Pardon?"

My name, Chauncey Southerland

"Thank you, Mister Southerland. I appreciate your candor."

I flashed the next photo, a close-up of the rich prick beside Bo Witherspoon, who, by the way, also accompanied Hawthorne to the Cave bar.

"What is the full name of this man?"

Hugo Gordon-Lennox

"And what is Mister Gordon-Lennox's role within the organization?"

Transport

"Transport? Interesting. Do you know the business name he operates under?"

Killzme Corp.

Heartbeat derailed, my gaze shot to Mr. Mayhem. "Un-fuckin-believable."

He winced. "Language, please."

"Seriously? You're gettin' ready to rip open a guy's foot, but I can't swear?" I batted my comment away. "Whatever. I thought Worthington and Rothschild owned Killzme Corp."

"Most shell companies have multiple shareholders. Please show Mister Southerland the next photo."

With two fingers, I enlarged the face of the guy standing off to the side with Hawthorne. The poacher's hand trembled, the pen tip juddering on the notepad, but he didn't write anything, his back trembling against my chest.

"The name, Mister Southerland."

?

"Your body has betrayed you, Mister Southerland. Tell us his name, please."

?

Tightened fingers stretched the black leather knuckles on the handle of the hunting knife. "One way or another, you will give us the name of this man. Whether you choose the easy road or the hard is up to you."

The hostage drove the pen deep into my thigh, and I screamed out in pain.

"Motherfucker!"

Right then, Mr. Mayhem slashed open Southerland's sole from toe to heel, blood spraying in all directions, guttural muffled cries coiling through the shed, Poe cawing in ecstasy. But instead of surrendering, he ripped out the pen and stabbed me again, white-hot pain radiating up and down my leg as I squirmed out from behind him. The second I cleared the hostage, Mr. Mayhem dove on top of him, severing his throat from ear to ear, the flesh gaped wide-open.

Blood.

Everywhere.

On the walls, on the ceiling, on the lawn mower, snowblower, rakes, and shovels, the entire shed bathed in crimson.

Without a word, my mentor degloved and scooped me off the floor, careened out the shed, then raced into the cabin, my legs dangling over one arm. Through the kitchen he sprinted, down the hall, and into my en suite bathroom, where he stood me in the bathtub and yanked my sweatpants to my ankles.

Thank God I wore underwear, even if it was a thong.

After knotting a towel around my waist, he lifted me again then set me down with the gentleness of snuggling a newborn into a bassinette, my back resting against an inflatable pillow suction-cupped to one end of the tub. Warm water poured from the spout, and he fled the bathroom. By the time the water reached my waist, he returned, adding some sort of powder to the water, swirling it around with his hand.

Until finally, he acknowledged me. "How do you feel, Cat?"

Other than dying from embarrassment? "It's not the best time I've ever had. My leg hurts. Bad."

"Understandable. I need to clean the stab wounds."

"Okay." Feeling like a failure, I bowed my head. "Sorry I let you down. I shoulda known he'd—"

"Hey, hey, hey. You have nothing to apologize for, Cat. That sorry excuse of a man attacked you." With one hand under my thigh, he washed the puncture holes with a soapy washcloth. "I should have put him down sooner."

"It's not your fault, either." The man carried enough baggage without me adding to the list. "Look at all the info. we got. If you offed him right away, we woulda never learned any of that crap."

Intently focused on cleaning ink out of my thigh, he stayed quiet.

"Hey, do you think the last photo we showed him could be the ice man *Shicheii* saw in his vision?" To cheer him up, I added, "The head honcho? The big enchilada? The snake whose head we'll chop?"

A slow grin arched his lips. "Perhaps."

"Text me the photo when we're done here, and I'll see if I can run it through facial recognition software."

"I'll send it to you in the morning, Cat." He lowered my leg into the water, slung my arm around his neck, and lifted me out. As he carried me into the bedroom, he stared straight ahead. "I am cognizant that my swift action was not a comfortable situation for either of us. However, with the deepness of the stab wounds, your well-being took precedent over awkwardness."

On the edge of the mattress, he lowered me, bracing my foot against his thigh to keep my leg raised. And I tucked the soaking wet towel between my legs, so we didn't end this night with a gap shot.

"They look better already." Meaning, the stab wounds. "Has the pain decreased?"

"Somewhat, yeah. Thanks."

Beside me on the bed sat a first-aid kit, from which he withdrew an antiseptic tube, gauze pads, and hospital tape. "The wounds may need a stitch or two."

"Err... please don't sew my leg—again." Been there, done that, got the scars to prove it. "Got any of those butterfly thingies?"

"Actually, I do." He snatched the package from the kit. "Good idea." After he doused each stab wound with antiseptic, he tugged my skin, sealing the holes with butterfly stitches. "Your grandfather may choose a more traditional medicine, but at least we'll avoid infection until then."

"I was hoping not to tell him. Why, do you think I should?"

"Not necessarily. If you'd rather avoid an uncomfortable conversation, I'll respect your wishes."

"Okay, cool. Yeah, let's not mention it, then. What about Southerland, though? *Shicheii's* gonna notice all the blood in the shed."

"No, he won't. Once I'm done here, I'll head out and hose it down."

"I can help. You shouldn't have to do it alone."

"Though I appreciate the offer, Cat, you've been through enough for one night. In the morning, however, we'll need to dispose of the body."

I droned, "Can't wait." Not.

Chapter 34

"Walk tall as the trees. Live strong as the mountains.
Be gentle as the spring winds.
Keep the warmth of the summer sun in your heart,
and the Great Spirit will always be with you."
—Native American Proverb

4 a.m.

With Mr. Southerland cocooned in plastic in the trunk, the shed hosed down, and the dishes washed, Mayhem lounged on the porch, smoking a Dunhill International Red, enjoying the peacefulness of predawn.

Fifteen minutes later, Jacy Lee strolled out with the serving tray. "Good morning, Cheveyo. Did you sleep well?"

"I did not, I'm afraid."

"Anything I can do to help?"

"No, thank you, dear friend." With a brief smile, he lifted a mug from the tray. "This is all the medicine I require."

Jacy Lee rose partway off his chair. "I should see if our guest would like a cup."

"Unnecessary." Mayhem massaged his stiff neck. "Mister Southerland is no longer in the shed."

"No?"

"No."

"Did you take him to the hospital?"

"Jacy Lee, he is no longer our guest. Thus, not our concern. All right?"

"Thank you, Cheveyo. I knew you would do right by him." With dimples dotting each cheek, he leaned back in his chair, reveling in the early morning hour. "Beautiful, isn't it?"

"That it is, my friend. That it is." Mayhem glanced through the living room window. "You'll be pleased to know, your granddaughter contacted Detective Samuels."

"Did she?"

"She did. Seemed like it went well, too."

Jacy Lee's smile grew wider. "How nice."

"My obligation is over now. Correct?"

"Is Levaughn heading up to see her?"

"Not that I'm aware of, no."

"Hm."

"Jacy Lee, we have more pressing matters to focus on. Do we not?"

"We do. I was simply wondering if—"

The screen door swung open, stopping his elder mid-sentence. Thank goodness Shawnee arrived when she did, or Jacy Lee might be tempted to ask for another favor.

"Cool. You made tea." Dressed in another of her "broken in" T-shirts and equally ratty sweatpants hiked to her knees—apparently the woman owned plenty of those, as well—Shawnee sat in her usual chair. "What were you wondering about, *Shicheii*?"

"Nothing, my love." He patted the top of her hand. "You look tired, child."

"To be honest, I am." She regarded Mayhem. "Remember when you told me to think about how Poe and the Wolf could help us?"

"I do."

"Well, I thought of a plan."

A flutter tingled his core. "Did you?"

"Yep. Kinda brilliant, too, if I do say so myself."

Clearly, she longed for more recognition. "Brava, Cat. Now, please share your revelation."

"Actually"—Jacy Lee rose—"will it keep till after morning prayer?"

Medicine Men required mindfulness and peace to glorify the Holy Ones. If Mayhem wasn't so exhausted, he might've suggested the same.

"Absolutely."

"Wonderful. Thank you. Cheveyo, would you mind playing the flute this morning?"

"I'd be honored." He rose, as well. "Meet you in the yard in five?"

"Perfect. Thank you."

"Pleasure is mine, old friend." He swung open the screen door, holding it open for Shawnee, but she did not take the hint. "Cat," he prompted.

"Oh. Right." She sucked down the rest of her tea. "Want me to clean the table, *Shicheii*?"

"No, thank you, honey. I'll take care of it."

Into the cabin Shawnee lumbered with a slight limp to her gait.

Mayhem sidled up beside her, hushed, "Is the leg bothering you?"

"Wicked."

"Perhaps I should take a quick peek at the wounds. We'll need to hurry." Gaze shifting from the stairs to the back bedroom, he hesitated.

"It'll be quicker if we use my room." She hooked an arm. "C'mon."

In the hall, her limp worsened. Not a good sign. Once he and Shawnee reached her bedroom, she stretched the hem of her T-shirt over her lady bits and lowered the sweatpants, revealing the two stab wounds.

"Sit." He patted the mattress. When she obeyed, he braced her foot on his thigh. Deep purple bruising encircled the outer edges of each puncture. "Hm."

"What's 'Hm' mean?"

He peeled off the butterfly stitches. Inflamed redness rimmed the stab wounds.

Behind him, Jacy Lee gasped, and his stomach dropped to his ankles. Speechless, he didn't dare turn around.

Shawnee's neck craned around the side of Mayhem's legs. "This isn't what it looks like, *Shicheii*."

"Cheveyo, may I have a word in the hall, please?"

Rather than respond, he grabbed Shawnee's ankle and stepped to the side, flashing the stab wounds at Jacy Lee.

"Ooh." When he shuffled closer, Mayhem laid Shawnee's foot in his opened palm. "What happened to you, child?"

Silent, her gaze shifted between he and Jacy Lee.

Standing behind them, Mayhem's jaw pulsed. "Mister Southerland, our former guest, attacked her."

In slow motion, Jacy Lee craned his neck, staring over his shoulder at Mayhem. "Is that why he no longer occupies the shed?"

"It is."

"I'm at a loss for why you didn't wake me, Cheveyo."

"Don't blame Mister M. I told him not to."

He spun back to his granddaughter. "Why?"

"Because I didn't want to worry you, *Shicheii*."

"Aw, honey." A gentle palm swept down the side of her face. "You can always come to me."

"I know, but I'd already woken you once. Please don't be mad. We were tryin' to let you rest 'cause we love you so much."

Impressive move, Cat. Jacy Lee could never get upset over a kind gesture. It simply wasn't in his nature.

"I apologize, Cheveyo. The harshness in my tone was uncalled for and unnecessary. Please forgive me?"

"Of course." To change the subject, he leaned over Shawnee's leg. "I'm afraid my attempt at rendering first-aid looks less than adequate."

"Nonsense. You did fine. The wounds look nice and clean. What did he stab her with?"

"A pen."

"All right. Ink is non-toxic these days. That's the good news. The bad news is by closing the wounds, infection becomes more likely. It's best to leave puncture wounds open so they can breathe. Hence why I did not close your birdshot wounds. Did I?"

"No, you did not."

"I presume you didn't soak the wounds, correct?"

"Ooh, I did." The throb of his heartbeat stilled. "At the time, the ink concerned me."

"See, this is why you should have woken me, Cheveyo." The hard edge returned to his tone. "Deep punctures should stay dry." Big sigh. "We'll need to regenerate the tissue now. Could you please fetch the honey for me?"

"Of course." Mayhem hustled out to the porch, where he raised the serving tray from the table. Honey pot in hand, he left the dirty mugs on the granite island and hurried back into the bedroom.

"Thank you, Cheveyo." He coated the stab wounds with nectar. "Honey safely inhibits the growth of bacteria and comprises a wide range of active compounds, including flavonoids, phenolic acid, organic acids, amino acids, enzymes, antifungal properties, and vitamins that improve wound healing and fight infection. The low water activity of honey helps transport oxygen and nutrients from the deep tissue into the wound areas. Also, its low pH increases tissue oxygenation while free radicals, which lead to tissue damage, are removed by flavonoids and aromatic acids."

Jacy Lee blew on the puncture wounds. "How does that feel, child?"

"Better."

"In the future, you two will come to me first before attempting to treat any wounds, regardless of severity. Have I made myself clear?"

"You have, Jacy Lee."

"Crystal," Shawnee said, her chin dropping to her chest. "Sorry, *Shicheii*. Won't happen again."

Jacy Lee wrapped gauze around his granddaughter's thigh, tucking the end into the fold. "I would prefer it if you stayed off this leg for a day or two."

"But *Shicheii*, the hunt's tomorrow."

He whirled back to Mayhem. "The hunt?"

"I'd planned to tell you over breakfast. Mister Southerland informed us of their plans for the Eastern Gray Wolves."

Before Mayhem could fully explain, Shawnee chimed in again. "*Shicheii*, they're releasing the wolves to hunt them."

Visibly hurt by the news, his stomach caved, eyelids sliding closed. Once he recovered from the initial shock, he straightened. "Morning prayer is more important than ever. I know you don't want to hear this, Cheveyo, but we may need Spirit Crow's help up North."

"Why?" A lightning rod speared his heart. "Why must we involve her? Poe's on board. She, however, still needs time to heal."

"I am aware of that, Cheveyo. The beast that shall remain nameless should already be in a weakened state from the purifying rain. Agreed?"

Let's hope that's true. "Agreed."

"Thus, our angelic Spirit Crow will be irresistible. It will feel compelled to follow her."

"Might I remind you, this group captured her once already?" Mounting frustration intensified his tone. "She barely survived the encounter. What if the beast feels threatened by her pure spirit? We are discussing a demonic creature, are we not?" Chest tightening, his heart fisted. "I don't like it. Too many variables. Please don't ask me to risk her safety. There must be another way."

Jacy Lee rested a soothing hand on Mayhem's shoulder. "Believe me, Cheveyo, I know how much you've sacrificed for our People. Nonetheless, Spirit Crow's presence is the most effective way to lure the beast away from the compound."

O Great Spirit, please show us an alternate route to follow. If my beloved fails in her mission, our destiny will forever shatter, an eternity devoid of the purest soul, our reunion on the other side no longer possible, an afterlife without her by my side.

Chapter 35

6:33 a.m.

At the kitchen table, no one chitchatted during breakfast—palpable sadness and concern filling a massive storm overhead. The silence amplified Poe's slurping on the island. Fork teeth scraped across plates while I smiled at Spirit Crow, standing in Mr. Mayhem's lap, her delicate talons wrapped around a crunchy strip of bacon. Too cute.

After I helped *Shicheii* do the dishes, he strode upstairs to lie down for a while. Apparently, Mr. Mayhem and I weren't the only ones who didn't sleep last night.

Once my grandfather's door clicked shut, my mentor said we had to leave to dispose of Southerland's body. I'd figured as much. Without protest, I followed him out to the Caddy.

While backing into the driveway to turn around, he kept one hand on the back of my seat. "Care to share your latest revelation?"

"Oh. Right. Yeah." I swiveled to face him, the good leg folded under the bad, taut skin tugging at the puncture wounds. "Last night—early this morning, whatever—I searched the deep web for ways to fight the beast that shall remain nameless."

One hand straightened the steering wheel, the other shifted into Drive. "And?"

"Is it true that once it has enough food... once it, y'know, consumes enough meat"—*gulp*—"it goes dormant again?"

"It is."

"Alright, then maybe we don't have to fight it. All we gotta do is feed it."

"Feed it," he said, glib.

"Y'know. Feed. It. If you catch my drift."

"Feed it," he echoed, as though my meaning finally dawned on him.

"Yeah."

"Interesting idea."

A brownie point flipped my way. "I thought so."

He pulled on to the main drag. "Feed it, she says."

"Yeah. Will it work?"

"It may. Any thoughts on how to get your grandfather to go along with this plan?"

"That's the part I haven't figured out yet. Unless..." I paused, mulling over how to put this.

"Unless...?"

"Unless he was too busy with the wolves to notice what we're doing."

The pause lasted ten years. "They would benefit from medical care."

"Definitely would. Did you see how skinny they are?"

"I did. The entire pack is suffering from malnutrition." He hesitated again, but I didn't know why. "Let me sit with it for a while. Brilliant idea, though."

A warmth flushed my cheeks. "Thanks. I learned from the best."

"You are too kind, Cat." Grinning, he patted my folded knee. "Thank you."

"So, where're stashing the scumbag in the trunk?"

"At the Crow's Nest, of course," he said as if I should've known.

"The Crow's Nest?" Eyes wide, I jolted back in my seat. "They'll be guarding it after leaving Underwood there, no?"

"Most likely, yes."

No clue what that meant. "Then why would we go there? Isn't it too risky?"

Rather than give me a straight answer, he volleyed the question back to me. "You tell me."

"Definitely too risky."

"Are we not at war with the Killzme Corporation? They know who we are, what we look like, and where we live. Do they not?"

"Well, yeah, but—"

"You heard Mister Southerland, correct?" His hand thumped the steering wheel. "All those animals he mentioned are critically endangered."

"I know, but—"

"The stakes could not be clearer."

"I know, but—"

"But what, Cat?" His tone sharpened. "Do you believe your life exceeds theirs?"

I picked at my half-bitten fingernails. "Well, no, but—"

"Do you benefit your environment more than they do?"

"No."

"Do ecosystems thrive because of your presence?"

"No."

"Do ecosystems benefit from their existence?"

"Yes."

"Then who is more important to Mother Earth?"

"They are," I admitted.

"Correct." Idling outside the gates to Jackson Village Cemetery, he focused on me. "If you have any reservations at all, say the word and we'll dispose of Mister Southerland elsewhere." A flash of the palm. "Don't answer right away. I want you to mull it over and form a clear decision."

My gaze bounced from window to window. "Here?"

"Would you prefer that I parked?"

"Kinda would, yeah."

"All right, then." He pulled curbside, killed the engine, reclined the driver's seat, and dragged the fedora over his face. "Take all the time you need."

"Don't fall asleep, though, okay? Waking you isn't high on my favorite things to do."

A muffled chuckle jiggled the hat. "Not to worry, Cat. I am merely resting my eyes."

Uh-huh. If he were only resting his eyes, he wouldn't need to block the morning sunshine with the hat.

A gazillion questions fled through my mind. Did warriors run from a threat or face things head on? The latter, I admitted. Fulfilling my destiny required risk. How could I expect to save the Innocent Ones if I avoided danger? I couldn't. Killzme Corp. had power, money, and would kill to protect their bottom line. Even if we stopped now, they'd never quit hunting us.

Visions of all those animals, all those souls, cried out to me, shredding my heart more and more with each passing moment. If we didn't help them, who would? "Mister M?"

"Yes?"

"I made my decision."

As his seat straightened, he slid the hat back. "And?"

"Let's go to the Crow's Nest."

"May I ask what changed your mind?"

"Because we can't let 'em win. Warriors don't run from a fight."

A slow smile built on his face, gray eyes sparkling in delight. "Precisely. We most certainly do not."

"Besides, we're not fighting for ourselves. We're fighting for all those who came before us. We're fighting for all those who come after us. We're fighting for the voiceless, the Innocent Ones, who can't fight for themselves. We're not fighting for today. We're fighting for a better tomorrow."

For several minutes—felt more like days—he held my gaze, clawing through my soul, as though searching for even a whisper of uncertainty or hesitancy. He wouldn't find either. I stood by every word.

"Anything else you'd like to share before we proceed?"

"As a matter of fact, I would." My back straightened. "Today is good day to die."

"I could not be prouder than I am at this very moment. You're a remarkable human, Mourning Dove. Compassionate, intelligent, empathetic, and beautiful, inside and out."

All these compliments heaved my chest, my lips quivering against the flood of tears, threatening my resolve. "I am?"

"Why are you unaware of your best attributes?"

Tears spilled over the rims of my eyes, and I could only shrug.

"I wish you could see yourself through my eyes."

A squeal escaped my lips—full on bawling now—and he dragged me over the middle console, wrapping me in his powerful arms while I blubbered all over his leather blazer. Once I wrangled my emotions under control, I quieted, but I didn't let go, even when he patted my back.

"Cat?" he said, my name muffled by lips pressed to my scalp.

"Yeah?"

"Mister Southerland is decomposing in the trunk."

"Way to ruin a moment." I settled back in my seat, flipped down the visor, and finger-swiped under each eye, trying not to smear my black eyeliner. What little of it I had left, anyway. "Can I ask you somethin' before we split?"

"Of course."

"What's your real last name?"

A slight snicker. "I'll tell you what. Once you've successfully completed your first three trials—remember, you must complete four before graduating to warrior—I will reveal my surname."

"Promise?"

"My word is my bond."

"Alright." I jutted out my hand, and he shook it. "Deal."

"Now that we've put that matter to rest, let's proceed." He cruised under the wrought-iron archway, following the winding road to the back of the cemetery. Before reaching the Crow's Nest he pulled curbside, sloughed off his leather blazer and fedora, then swung his legs out the door.

At the trunk, he stared deep into my eyes, our bodies inches apart. "O Great Spirit, hear my voice. I believe in your power and your ability to defend me. In the name of all that is good, I ask for your help with this battle, my battle, with those who intend to harm me."

When he paused, I echoed his words.

"O Powerful Indian Spirit, you are the Great Chief, and you know my problems. Help me with your warrior medicine and guide me to safety with your Divine protection. Faithful Indian Spirit, I humbly ask for your protection. With your warrior shield, shield me from the attacks of my enemies."

Once again, I repeated his words.

"With your bow and arrow, protect me from the evil thoughts and actions hurled toward me. With your hatchet, cut the chains and ropes that bind me. With your feathers, brush away the negative energy surrounding me. With your eyes, see that no jealousy and envy penetrate me. With your peace pipe, create harmony where there is discord. Father Black Hawk, have my back and be a watchman on the wall. See that no evil befalls me. Fight the battle to destroy those who will harm me. Take revenge on my behalf and destroy the insurrection of the wicked."

As I said the prayer, our gazes locked, all bystanders irrelevant in this Sacred moment.

"Protect me from all evil, danger, slander, and threat. In peace and protection, walk before me. In honor and courage, walk behind me. In power and resolve, fly above me. In truth and beauty, walk below me. This prayer I ask not just for myself but for all of my relations, past and present, and for those yet to come."

At the end, I added, "In the name of all my relations, I pray."

With a single nod, he waved his foot under the back bumper. The trunk rose on its own. A nauseating cloud of blood, piss, and other human gases enveloped me, jarring me out of my happy place, clarifying the danger and the stakes.

"On second thought, let's see what we're dealing with first." Mr. Mayhem pocketed a few supplies. "We'll return for Mister Southerland afterward."

"Works for me." I shut the trunk. "How do you wanna handle this?"

"I'll show you." Holding my hand, he led me into the woods surrounding the cemetery.

At the foot of a massive oak tree, he bent over, his fingers woven into a stirrup, and I leaped up the trunk, scaling the tree in seconds. Child's play. In the canopy of leaves, Mr. Mayhem pointed at the Crow's Nest, where two men decked out in full camouflage guarded the main entrance, feet spread apart, hands clasped behind their backs. No doubt former military, judging by the stance.

"I just see two," I whispered. "You?"

"Only the two." Sight deadlocked on the sentinels, he stayed quiet, probably plotting our next move. "Okie doke. Let's proceed."

"Where're we goin'?"

"Climb down. We'll continue on foot."

"Continue to where?"

An exaggerated breath huffed out his mouth. "Cat, please begin your descent."

"Fine." Near the base of the tree, the soles of my moccasins hadn't even touched grass yet when he leaped over my head, knees bending on impact. What'd he do, jump from the limb? *Shicheii's* right. Mr. Mayhem's a finely tuned instrument. Almost indestructible.

Ducked low, he sprinted around the perimeter of the cemetery. I stayed right on his heels. Behind the Crow's Nest, he stopped among a thicket of trees.

No guards in the back. That's a plus. "Now what?" I low-talked. "There's twenty feet of grass between here and there, and we got no way of knowing if they're comin' or not. If one dude's gotta take a leak, we're screwed."

"Though I would have preferred a less visual argument, your concern is warranted. A safer alternative involves an approach from above." His gaze flicked down at my thigh. "Your wounds seem to be improving."

"The leg? Yeah, way better. Only hurts when I hit where he stabbed me."

"Then my advice is to not hit those areas." He winked. "Shall we proceed?"

"Waitin' on you, partner."

"All right, then. Follow me, please." He jetted toward a maple that stood ten feet away, closer to the Crow's Nest. In the tree canopy, he waited for me.

Once I popped through thick leaves, he rose, grasped the branches above his head and sprinted—full force—from one tree to another. I followed, but with far less grace, my body demanding I stop. Or slow. Neither was an option.

On a branch above the Crow's Nest, Mr. Mayhem squatted with each hand by his side, fingers curled around the limb by his moccasins. And so, I mimicked the position. When he dropped down, arms stretched above his head, body suspended by the branch, he still had a good fifteen-foot drop. I waited for him to let go, but he didn't.

Instead, he said, "Use me as a ladder to reach the roof."

"Seriously?"

"Do I look like I am in any position to lack truthfulness?"

"Okay, okay, I'm goin'." Not sure if he meant to climb down the front of him or the back, so when I squatted, I hesitated.

"Cautious Cat," he hushed, tone firm and harsh, "please proceed. We are running out of time."

"Right. Sorry." I stepped on one shoulder, then another, turned to face him, and slid down his chest, my toes gripped to his belt, my muff a mere inch from his nose and mouth, and his head swiveled to the side. Talk about awkward.

In hindsight, I could easily see where I went wrong.

When my face passed his, I mouthed, "Sorry 'bout that." Hanging from his ankles, I waited a beat before letting go. By pointing my toes, I rolled the soles of my feet on the asphalt shingles to avoid landing with a heavy thud.

Almost weightless, Mr. Mayhem dropped down beside me in complete silence. And I added soundless to his list of superpowers.

Through hand motions, he told me to stay vigilant and stationary while he checked on the two guards. When he returned, he withdrew a soaked bandana in a Ziploc from his jeans pocket. More gesturing instructed me to follow him to the far end of the rooftop, above the main entrance. While standing above two sinewy armed dudes with buzzcuts, his fingers slipped into black leather gloves. He passed me the baggy, and I crammed it in my back pocket.

"On three," he mouthed. "Ready?"

Flat hands flew straight out in front of me. "Wait," I mouthed. "What do I do?"

"Jump."

"On top of 'em?"

With a single nod, he started the silent count. "One."

When I teed my hands, he dragged me back to the other end of the roof. "What is the problem, Cat?" Minty breath struck my nose, his voice low and whisperous.

"What do I do when I land on my guy?"

"Invite him for lunch. What do you think you should do?"

"Knock him out?"

"Precisely."

"What if he's armed?"

"Improvise." Slight head shake. "Are you unfamiliar with this type of ambush?"

"No. Well, I mean, I've never personally done it, but I've seen you do it a few times."

"Great. Then may we please proceed? With every passing moment, Mister Southerland's remains turn more and more rancid, and I would really like to move things along before the smell permeates."

"Okay, alright, I'm ready."

"Thank you."

Above the main entrance, he counted off with his fingers. "One... two..."

Again, I teed my hands, mouthed, "Jump on three, right?"

With a single nod, he started over. "One... two... and... three."

The moment his moccasins pushed off the roof, I jumped, but unlike his guy who stayed clueless, mine looked up, stepped back, and caught me in his arms like a bride on her wedding day. Totally threw me off my game, and I froze. Which only confused him more, unsure if he should kill me or kiss me.

With the other guard pinned to the ground, Mr. Mayhem sucker-punched him about five times in rapid succession, then glanced over at me and Romeo, still locked in an awkward embrace.

"The bandana, Cat," he hollered in between punches, the bloody dude beneath him helpless to fight back. "Use it now."

Right then, my guy latched on to my throat, fingers squeezing my airway while I struggled to grab the Ziploc from my back pocket before I passed out. A headbutt loosened his grip long enough for me to tear open the baggy. Pinned to the wall, chest to chest, I slapped the chloroform-ladened rag over his nose and mouth. Too close, apparently. Found that out the hard way when his massive frame melted to the soil, and I rolled off him—arms out like wings—my head swimming and light.

"Cat—"

I tried to raise my hand to signal I was fine—groovy, even—but I couldn't, my arm weighted and heavy. Was that chloroform? Is it a drug? *What a beautiful clear sky. Where am I?*

Out of nowhere, Mr. Mayhem's face appeared over mine, translucent gray eyes staring.

"Hey, fancy meeting you here. What's cookin', good lookin'?"

"Oh, my word." He scooped me into his arms then took off faster than a locomotion, headstones and rich green grass whipping past me.

At the Caddy, he tossed me in the backseat, disappeared, and rustled through the trunk, I think, before climbing inside with me. After jerking me upright, he squirted something foul up my nose and clamped a clear mask over my face. Pure oxygen expanded my lungs.

"Do not remove the mask," he said before shutting the door. Behind the wheel, he adjusted the rearview mirror. "Breathe, Cat. Slow, steady, and deep breaths."

When he punched the pedal to the metal, my neck snapped backward, the Caddy sailing toward the Crow's Nest. Once he threw the shifter into Park, the fuzziness in my head had already somewhat cleared. With one eye closed to stop the double vision, I peered through the windshield at the two dudes seated on the ground, bound together and gagged, their heads rolled forward. Out cold, neither budged.

The trunk rose behind me. Seconds later, Mr. Mayhem lugged a plastic-wrapped body on one shoulder by my window. He swung open the door to the Crow's Nest, tossed Southerland inside, then re-engaged the padlock. With a quick pat of the head, he squatted in front of the unconscious sentinels and sliced off their gags and zip ties with the hunting knife, pocketing all the cut pieces. Both men slumped to the ground.

Behind the wheel, he spoke into the rearview mirror. "How do you feel?"

"Better." I pulled the mask away. "I don't need this anymore."

"All right, then. Please turn off the oxygen tank."

And so, I did.

As he cruised through the cemetery, I squirmed over the middle console to slip into the passenger seat.

"Hey, um, was that chloroform?"

"You've watched too many movies, Cat. Chloroform is less than adequate as an anesthetic. I prefer Sevoflurane."

"That a drug?"

"It is. Unlike Chloroform that can take a full five minutes to knock out your opponent and doesn't last more than a few minutes, Sevoflurane is a fast-acting anesthesia that lasts thirty to forty minutes. It's quite effective in a pinch."

"What'd you squirt up my nose?"

"Naloxone."

"Isn't that what they give for drug overdoses?"

"One in the same. You're welcome."

"Thanks." I didn't dare ask why or how he obtained these drugs, because honestly, I'd rather not know. "And the oxygen tank?"

"Belonged to my wife. I'd planned to donate it to the local nursing home, where she would go and read to the patients before ALS stole her mobility."

Shit. Now he couldn't donate it 'cause of me. "Aw, man. I'm sorry."

"You have nothing to apologize for, Cat. Had I known you'd be in such close quarters, I'd have forewarned you of Sevoflurane's potency." A smirk lingered. "Interesting technique, you used back there. Did you two exchange phone numbers?"

"Ha, ha. Everyone's a comedian." Tall pines stood like soldiers out my window, row after row zooming past. "How was I supposed to know he'd catch me? You're just lucky your guy didn't look up."

"*Au contraire.* Luck has nothing to do with it. You hesitated. I, on the other hand, did not. Hence why you gave him time to view your descent."

Bullshit. "I didn't hesitate."

"You waited for me, did you not?"

"Well, yeah, but—"

"Thus, hesitation."

My hand balled into a fist. "It was a split second."

"Correct. And that split second was all he needed. This organization employs highly trained individuals. Any hesitation at all gives them the advantage. Let me ask you this. If I were to ask you to score your performance, how do you think you did?"

"I dunno. I was holding my own for a while there, so maybe a C?"

Incredulous, his head shook ever so slightly. "A C?"

"Yeah. Solid C, maybe C minus, if you wanna be nitpicky."

"Solid C, even though you wound up flat on your back, slipping in and out of consciousness?"

"Absolutely. Because unlike you, I'm not dismissing all the stuff I did right."

"I admire your ability to see the forest for the trees, I really do. However, if you require me to save your life—or your dignity—your score drops dramatically."

"So, like, you sayin' I failed?"

The raised eyebrows told me all I needed to know.

"Fine. I failed." Balls.

"Cat?"

"What?"

"Warriors do not pout." He pulled down the long, dirt driveway, framed in trees. "Perhaps another run will help put things into perspective."

Crap. This warrior shit ain't easy.

Chapter 36
"I have yet to see an animal that hates.
I suppose that is something else we can learn from them."
—April Peerless

8:30 a.m.

As Mayhem exited the Caddy, Jacy Lee hustled out to the porch. "Cheveyo, Mister Southerland deceived you."

Since he'd never question an elder, he accepted this truth. "How so?"

"The hunt doesn't start tomorrow. It begins at dusk, continues through the night, and ends at dawn."

He rocked back on his heels. "Tonight?"

Jacy Lee nodded yes. "The Holy Ones showed me."

He glimpsed the Sun. "That doesn't give us much time to prepare."

At the outside table, Shawnee plopped in her chair. "I should probably skip my run, then, right?"

Before Mayhem could respond, Jacy Lee said, "No, Mourning Dove. Your training is more important than ever."

"But, *Shicheii*, we need time to prepare."

Mayhem towered over her. "You heard your grandfather. Grab the water bottle and get moving. Time is of the essence."

Quailed back with her hands in surrender, she rose. "Okay, alright, I'm goin'." Into the cabin she hustled, returning moments later with the water bottle. "Here." She opened her mouth.

Since she'd had quite the morning already, he gave her a little squirt this time, and her eyes popped wide, her lips folding inward in a coy smile. At the bottom of the stairs, she hooked an arm at him.

"I will not be joining you, I'm afraid. You must endure this exercise alone."

One might think he'd betrayed her by the look she tossed his way.

"Cheveyo's right, child. There's power in solitude."

"Run along now, Cat. When you return, we shall fill you in on our progress." Thank goodness she couldn't speak, or she might be tempted to use foul language. Regardless, this morning was a vital turning point in her training, whether she believed it or not. Once she sprinted across the yard, he sidled up next to Jacy Lee. "Water is a blessing."

"Indeed, it is, Cheveyo." Smiling, he patted Mayhem's shoulder. "Sit. I made tea."

"Tea sounds delightful, my friend. Thank you."

As he waited for Jacy Lee to return, he set the fedora on the railing. After shedding his leather blazer, he leaned back in the chair, ankles crossed out in front of him, fingers woven behind his head. In the distance, Spirit Crow and Poe dove and swooped, an aerial waltz that stole his breath, glorious wings riding the thermals. The dance worked two-fold. Not only did pure joy radiate off every wingbeat, but exercise helped strengthen his beloved's constitution, an important part of the healing process. Lenore landed on the railing next to him.

"Hello, beautiful. How are you feeling?"

Rattle, rattle. Lenore spread her magnificent wings.

"Simply gorgeous, darling." He extended his forearm, and she climbed aboard. "If I may be so bold... Poe may have his moments, but you'll never find a greater love. His birth father, Thoreau, worshipped his mate, Annabelle, and he passed that same loyalty on to Poe. Should you choose him as your mate, he will stand beside you for the rest of your days. In the grand schemes of things, what more can we ask for?"

For a brief moment, Lenore lowered her necessitating membrane, showing she understood. Whether his speech would impact her ultimate decision remained unclear. However, he wouldn't feel right if he didn't try to at least help his loyal and loving companion.

The screen door swung open. Jacy Lee lowered the serving tray to the table, passing Mayhem a hot mug of wild tea—medicine for the upcoming *coup de grâce*.

"Hello, sweet child." His hooked finger fluffed Lenore's chest feathers. "I trust the wing is improving?"

Rattle, rattle, coo…

"After you, dear friend." Mayhem gestured toward the honey pot, his gaze roaming back to Spirit Crow and Poe. "Have the Holy Ones shown you an alternate route in regard to what we discussed earlier?"

"I'm sorry, Cheveyo. No. We must trust them to protect her."

His stomach sank. "Great Horned Owls and Sharp-Shinned Hawks stalk that area, as well."

"I'm aware of that." Honey drizzled into his mug. "You have my word that she will never leave my sight."

That brought some comfort, though he still grappled with using Spirit Crow as bait for an ancient supernatural beast. Sadness and pain warred within him, twisting him up inside. "Should she succeed in this quest, she may decide it's time to depart."

"If she does, she'll wait for you on the other side."

"Thank you, my friend. I needed to hear that today."

"I know." Jacy Lee smiled before sipping his tea. "How do you think Mourning Dove's doing on her run?"

Movement in the treetops caught in his peripheral and his gaze shot to the forest. A slow grin arched his lips. "See for yourself." He pointed at Shawnee standing on the top limb of a one-hundred-and-fifty-foot maple tree, her cherry-streaked raven hair blowing in the gentle breeze.

Following his gaze, Jacy Lee leaned aside to peer around a support beam. "Wow." He waved at her. "She is impressive, isn't she?"

"She is, indeed."

Without turning around, reveling in his granddaughter's abilities, he said, "You've had a positive impact on her life, Cheveyo, and I'm so grateful."

"She's had a positive impact on mine, as well."

Jacy Lee turned back. "I cannot tell you how happy that makes me."

Thirty minutes later, Shawnee sprinted down the driveway. Once she hit the middle of the yard, she folded at the waist, hands cupped on bent knees. When she straightened, she pointed at her puffed cheeks.

"You may release the water," Mayhem said from the porch, and she spat. "How do you feel?"

"Good, but I gotta tell ya somethin'. Where's the PC?"

"Trunk."

She jogged to the Caddy, snatched the PC from the trunk, then leaped up the stairs. "If Southerland lied about the date, how do we know he didn't lie about the hunt location, too?"

Excellent question. "Check the live feed."

"What brought on this revelation, child?" Jacy Lee lifted the tinfoil cap off her mug.

"Ooh, awesome. Thanks, *Shicheii*." She dragged the stirrer through the honey. "This is gonna sound crazy, but I think Karma told me."

"Karma?"

"The mountain lion who attacked her that she later befriended." Mayhem slipped the mug and honey pot from her grasp. "I'll do this while you check the live feed."

Before she flipped open the laptop, Jacy Lee covered her hand with his. "You befriended the cougar?"

"Yeah. We're buds now."

"And you named him Karma because…?"

Mayhem cleared his throat. "Let's circle back to that. If she's right, using our time wisely is more important than ever."

"You're right, Cheveyo. My apologies." He didn't release Shawnee's hand. "Please share your revelation."

Her gaze shot to Mayhem—clearly torn between her grandfather and her mentor—and he granted permission with a single nod, adding a rolling hand for her to make it quick. If she's right, the poachers may have already moved the captive wolves.

"Alright, so, I'm sittin' in a tree, catching my breath for a minute like he taught me, and Karma stops below me, staring up at me. This next part is gonna sound like I'm totally off my rocker, but it is what it is. A soft beam of light connected me to Karma, and I felt this energetic pulse flowing between us, like we were alone out there, tethered together as one, an overwhelming sense of kinship, of family, deep within me. And in that moment, no communication barriers came between us. I could talk to him and him to me." A tear rolled out the corner of her eye, and she swept it away as quickly as it fell. "It was beautiful. Spiritual."

As if reliving the time she spent with the cougar, her gaze hollowed. "Karma showed me an empty enclosure—a mental snapshot—and I swear it's the same one at the compound. Before he left, images of wolves in cages flashed through my mind." She turned to Mayhem. "Like the ones at the silent auction that held the lynxes, with thick iron bars."

With a single nod, he validated her story.

"So, after he left, I sat a while, mulling it over like you always tell me to do. I think he was telling me we're lookin' in the wrong spot. The hunt isn't at the compound." She flipped open the PC, her fingers racing across the keyboard. "Or maybe it's the drugs. I dunno."

"Drugs?" Jacy Lee's voice softened when he asked Mayhem, "Did she dip into the peyote?"

He lifted his shoulders. "Not with me, she didn't."

"Honey"—again, he reached for her, but she stayed vigilant on the task at hand—"peyote is a cactus, not a drug."

Perhaps he should intervene. "You're focused on what I can only assume is a slip-of-the-tongue rather than the miraculous gift she inherited from you."

Tears filled his eyes. Visibly overcome by raw emotion, his head rocked up and down, a hand patting his heart.

"Oh. My. God." Shawnee spun the screen. "Look."

All-terrain vehicles encircled the perimeter of the Wolf pen. Trailers hooked to the back of each single-rider ATV, with fatigues-clad poachers assembling iron-barred cages on top.

"I'm right, aren't I?"

"Certainly appears that way."

"We've gotta get up there before they leave." She shot out of her chair. "Why aren't you moving?"

"Drink your tea, Cat."

Her hand thrust at the PC. "They're moving the wolves. We gotta go."

The hard stare he returned lowered her into the chair. "Thank you. Now, please take a deep breath. A half-cocked weapon is of no use to anyone."

For once, she stayed silent, her knee bouncing with excess energy.

"We have time," he assured her. "Not a lot, but enough to plan how to move forward. They cannot transport live wolves—in cages, no less—during daylight hours without attracting the public's attention."

Her chest deflated. "Makes sense."

"Remember when we discussed how not to allow others to steal your power? This is a prime example. Think of the mission as a game of chess. They've made their move. It is now our turn. Would you rather act with mindfulness or spontaneously react?"

"Mindfulness."

"Then we shall."

"Simple as that?"

"Most things in life are not complicated. Without a balanced, harmonious spirit, humans often cause their own complications. Most of which they can avoid with forethought and planning."

"Listen to Cheveyo, honey. He is your mentor, after all."

"Alright." Mug in hand, Shawnee leaned back in her chair. "I'll chill." Silence enveloped her for several minutes. "What you said makes a ton of sense. I can actually feel the rush of adrenaline weakening."

"Because you have regained control. The mind powers the entire body. Hence why your grandfather and I urge you to master *hozho*. Mindfulness, balance, and harmony are all vital, lifesaving tools."

By switching to a new hunting ground, Mr. Hawthorne upended Mayhem's carefully plotted plan, though he refrained from voicing concern. A new plan would eventually reveal itself. Hopefully, soon. Otherwise, they may not win this battle.

He focused on the live feed. Where would poachers take their prey?

Chapter 37

9:30 a.m.

More relaxed, *Shicheii's* wild tea filled me with warmth and love. "That reminds me." I slapped the table in front of Mr. Mayhem. "I also ran into your grandfather on my run."

"*My* grandfather."

"That's what I said. Your grandfather."

"*My* grandfather."

Did he think I lost my hearing or somethin'? "I know. I said, *your* grandfather."

Shicheii touched my forearm. "Honey, what Cheveyo means is, the Apache highly revere bears. Thus, when Cheveyo called him *my grandfather* or *my uncle*, he showed the animal the utmost respect. His People will never touch a bear, nor their prints and bedding. If the animal crosses their path, they instruct him or her to go deep into the forest where no other entities set foot. Again, out of respect for the bear."

"Oh." Crap. Now I felt like a dick. "Sorry, Mister M. I didn't know."

"Thank you, Cat." Slight grin. "How was the encounter this time around?"

"I didn't freak out, if that's what you're askin'."

Okay, so maybe, I stretched that truth a little. On my run I sprinted up Mr. Mayhem's favorite hillside, cresting the peak as the bear lumbered up the other side. Our locked gazes almost stopped my heart. To get the hell out of his way, I scrambled up the nearest tree. Within three or four seconds, hot breath struck the back of my knees. All my blood sloshed, and I froze. Had someone mentioned their climbing abilities, I might've chosen a better escape route. But no, had to learn that tidbit on my own. Anyway, the bear sniffed me over pretty good—deep grunts and huffs rattling my ribcage—then must've decided I wasn't worth the effort because he just climbed down. But I sure as hell wasn't about to give my mentor the satisfaction of a confession.

Clawing through my subconscious with his piercing stare, Mr. Mayhem popped his eyebrows, a smirk arching his lips. *Crap. He knows.* "Why don't you rest for a few hours before we head out."

"Yeah? That's the best idea I've heard all day." I kissed my grandfather's cheek. "Thanks for the tea, *Shicheii*. Love you."

"Love you more."

With the PC sleeved under one arm, Mr. Mayhem held open the door for me. "Jacy Lee?"

"No thank you, Cheveyo. I'd rather sit awhile and reflect."

"All right, then. Enjoy the peace."

"Sleep well, my loves."

In the kitchen, I jabbed a chin at the laptop. "Want me take that?"

"No, no. You rest. I'll keep an eye on the live feed."

"But you've been up all night. I at least slept a few hours."

"Cat," he teased, grinning, "are you concerned about me?"

"Maybe I am. Or not." Two could play this game. "Hey, um..." I chanced a peek through the window. "What about our plan to, y'know, feed it? Will it follow the wolves?"

"It should."

"So, that's still the plan?"

"Sleep well, Cat." And he strode up the stairs.

Did I miss a wink or some other form of a yes? Aack. Why waste brain cells?

Hours later, I woke to crow feet on the side of my head, my bangs slipping through Spirit Crow's bill, preening me with love. "Oh, hey. I was just dreaming about you."

Rattle, rattle, rattle.

"Love you more." I reached for her, and she climbed onto my wrist. "Is everyone up?"

Her bill lowered, raised.

"Can you tell 'em I'll be right out? I'm naked under here."

With one last feathery cheek rub, she flew out the door. Not sure who opened it. Could've sworn I closed it before showering. The hanger hooked to the top drawer of my dresser solved that mystery. There hung my buckskins, my protection jewelry laid out on top.

Thanks, *Shicheii*.

Decked out in warrior gear, I strutted down the hall. The most heavenly aromas encircled my head. *Shicheii* and Mr. Mayhem were already seated in the kitchen, both dressed in buckskin pants and matching shirts, with knee-high moccasins like mine. On the table sat bowls stuffed with fruit, nuts, and these tortilla-like things, only puffier, rolled with a toothpick to hold the stuffing from falling out.

"What are those, *Shicheii*?" In my chair, I flapped open a napkin. "They smell amazing."

"Thank you, honey."

Mr. Mayhem passed me the platter. "Please refrain from sniffing them, Cat. It'd be disrespectful to do so."

"Alright, then tell me what's in the middle."

"Did you not just say they smelled amazing?"

I dropped the closest one on my plate. "Well, yeah, but..."

Mr. Mayhem held the platter for my grandfather, showing his elder the respect he so richly deserved. While his back was turned, I raised the unfamiliar food to my nose.

"Cat," he warned, "you will fail this exercise if you inhale one molecule of that tortilla."

"So, it is a tortilla."

"It is. The shell is made from corn. Your grandfather worked hard on them."

"Okay, cool." Now we're getting somewhere. "What's inside the wrap?"

Heavy forearms thudded against the table. "Would your grandfather feed you poison?"

"No, but—"

"Then live a little and try it. They're delicious and nutritious."

"Perhaps I should tell her, Cheveyo."

"No." Mr. Mayhem's voice deepened. "She needs to learn how to overcome blatant mistrust."

My grandfather's palms flashed in surrender. "I won't say a word."

"Thank you." His hard stare settled on me. "Cat, we cannot start eating until you do, and we'd like to enjoy our meal while it's hot, so if you wouldn't mind..."

"Okay, okay, fine." I grabbed the puffy tortilla-wrapped-whatever and bit in, spices and an indescribable flavor firing all my tastebuds at once. "Oh, my God. So good."

A wide smile spread across my grandfather's face, his beautiful teeth showcased by a warm chestnut complexion.

I swallowed the first bite. "Now, can you tell me what's in here?"

"You tell us." Mr. Mayhem bit into his sandwich. Raising a closed fist in front of his mouth, his gaze shot to *Shicheii*. "You've outdone yourself, my friend."

"Thank you, Cheveyo."

To determine what was in my mouth—and hating every second of this game—I chewed, trying to segregate the flavors. "Corn, some kinda nut, maybe?"

"Acorn," my mentor said between bites. "What else?"

"Lettuce. Reminds me of a taco, only better." I engulfed three-quarters of the tortilla. "The hamburg's wicked tender, but it doesn't taste like regular hamburg."

Neither of them responded until I overpacked my mouth, my cheeks bloated and full. At that point, Mr. Mayhem said, "Tastier than hamburg, wouldn't you agree?"

"Hm-mm," was about all I could manage. Gulping down half the mouthful, I cheeked the rest. "What kinda meat is it?"

"Mutton." Mr. Mayhem devoured the rest of his sandwich.

No clue what that meant, so I resumed chewing.

"High quality mutton is the tender loin, rib, or rump of sheep."

Gagging, I spit the rest on my plate, wiping down my tongue with the napkin. "You fed me the ass of Mary's little lamb?"

"Let's shelve the crazy, shall we?"

"Crazy?" My stomach flipped and flopped. "Aw, man, I'm gonna be sick."

Mr. Mayhem's hard stare pierced my soul.

"Sorry, *Shicheii*. I mean no disrespect." I just insulted his cooking, a meal that he probably slaved over for hours. Could I sink any lower? "It's delicious, but I'm struggling with the sheep thing."

"It's a traditional dish in our culture. Growing up, your mother loved mutton tacos."

My stomach quieted. "She did?"

"In fact, you ate them all the time when you were little."

"I did?"

"They were your favorite. Whenever you came to visit us, you'd gaze up at your grandmother with those big, innocent green eyes, and say, '*Shimásání*, can I help you make tacos? Pretty please with sugar on top.' And she gave in every time."

Wow. How could I not remember that? "Really?"

"Really."

Mr. Mayhem sliced the last tortilla in half. "Would you like to split the last one with me? Might help bring the memory into focus."

"Okay." I'd do just about anything to recall those early years of my life. "Thanks, by the way."

"For what?"

"I realize now you were trying to help me fill in gaps from my childhood."

"As I've told you, Cat, I will never let you fall."

"I know." He really did have my best interest at heart. "Once I finish this half, will I pass the exercise?"

"Is that why you're eating it?"

"No."

"Then yes."

After lunch, we all piled into the Caddy. My grandfather said he wanted to show me something, so I sat in the backseat with him while Poe and Spirit Crow co-piloted next to Mr. Mayhem.

The breathtaking beauty of Mother Nature whizzed by my window as *Shicheii* flipped open his sketchpad, where he'd drawn a Wolf, a deer, and a coyote. "Wolves play a pivotal role in a healthy ecosystem by managing deer, moose, and elk populations, which in turn, benefits many other plant and animal species. Remember when we talked about the ripple effect?"

Nodding, I said, "I remember."

Last weekend, my grandfather told me to envision all wildlife as tiny individual pebbles tossed into a lake. Everything a species did—what it ate, where it lived, how and where it defecated—rippled the water and radiated outward. Eventually, the ripples merged with every living being in its ecosystem. While every class of animal had an important role to fill, Mother Earth depended on large-bodied mammals to create ecological tidal waves for the enrichment and survival of other species. Every time an apex predator fed, they subtly changed the composition of the world around them, and not merely by keeping prey populations in check.

"When a Wolf hunts," *Shicheii's* sultry voice drew me back to the sketch in his lap, "the prey's carcass redistributes nutrients, providing food for other wildlife species, such as grizzly bears and scavengers. Wolves are called a keystone species—any species that other plants and animals depend on within an ecosystem. If the keystone species is extirpated, as it was in New England, the ecosystem undergoes dramatic changes, and in some cases, may collapse."

"Did it collapse here in New Hampshire?"

"That's a much longer conversation, honey. I will say, the absence of wolves caused the native white-tail deer population to explode."

Isn't that a good thing? I didn't dare ask. Instead, I went with, "How many deer are we talkin' about?"

"One hundred thousand or more. Over the last thirty years, the population has more than tripled. Thus, deer cause one-hundred-twenty to two hundred human deaths per year by jumping out in front of vehicles. A staggering ten thousand personal injuries are caused by deer every year nationwide. Without wolves, New Hampshire Fish and Game are in charge of managing prey species. Who do you think does a better job, a fallible human or one of Mother Earth's top predators?"

From the front seat, Mr. Mayhem spoke into the rearview mirror. "Humans can also be bought. Wolves cannot."

"Cheveyo's right, unfortunately." *Shicheii's* nose crinkled. "The mere presence of wolves improve habitat and increase populations of countless species—from birds of prey to pronghorn and even trout—by influencing the population and behavior of their prey. Because with wolves around, prey animals change their browsing and foraging patterns, as well as how they traverse through the landscape."

On the middle console, Poe turned halfway, glanced me up and down, then faced front. What was his problem?

"In many cases around the United States," *Shicheii's* velvety voice lured me back into the lesson, "the Wolf is one of the few members, if not the only one, of the mammalian biotic community that was present in historic times but is now currently missing from the ecosystem. Although an ecosystem may seem natural without them, wolves were meant to inhabit native territories. When present, the Wolf acts as an apex predator in the food chain, completing predator-prey relationships. The reintroduction of the Gray Wolf would cause changes in plant and animal populations, and help the ecosystem return to its previous, historic state, as our Creator intended."

"Then why don't we do it?"

"Farmers are the main reason. However, what farmers don't realize is wolves benefit livestock by killing only the weak, sick, and old. Not only are those animals easier to kill, but the Wolf takes less risk than, say, taking down a healthy adult moose. In New Hampshire, because of the growing white-tail deer population, vast amounts of vegetation are in decline, and the problem is only worsening. Not to mention, white-tail deer carry parasites, Lyme, and chronic wasting disease, which coyote are also susceptible to, along with rabies, parvo, and canine distemper. And coyotes are one of the main predators of livestock. Wolves would manage the coyote, as well, and that decrease in population would result in fewer diseases passed from wildlife to domestic animals and livestock."

Again, Poe turned enough to glance me up and down with disgust.

"Gee, I wonder what Lenore's doing," I said, and my grandfather gasped. "Bet the guys are fawning all over her."

An ear-splitting shrill vibrated from Poe's gullet, and Mr. Mayhem adjusted the rearview mirror, thinning his eyes at me. "Did you gain pleasure from upsetting him?"

"He tossed me a dirty look—twice." I flung a hand at Pissy Pants. "If he can't take it, he shouldn't dish it out."

I swear that bird winked at me. Friggin' psycho. Hopefully, he wouldn't make me eat those words at the worst possible moment.

Chapter 38

5:30 p.m.

We snuck into the hotel through the private stairwell. After my grandfather had time to acclimate—though to be honest, he seemed more uncomfortable than me in an upscale environment—he and Mr. Mayhem shed their shirts for the face and body painting ceremonial.

In front of my chair at the dining table, *Shicheii* brushed my bangs into a braid that rested on the back of my hair. "With this paint, I will transform."

"With this paint," I repeated, "I will transform."

"A rebirth, with new responsibilities, new obligations, new relationships."

Again, I echoed his words.

Paint equaled spiritual and physical power. The Sacred act of body painting likened to a prayer to the Great Spirit and to nature, unifying strength and spirit, hopes and visions. The ritual was also a prayer for survival in battle, in hunting, for the wellbeing of family members, or the People as a whole. Sometimes painting honored the dead or the brave, gave thanks, or celebrated personal, family, or tribal milestones. Nature imparted a vital power in the paints that transferred to the wearer.

If I hadn't experienced its power myself, I might not believe it.

As he painted a wide band of black from in front of one ear, across my eyes to the opposite ear, he sang a blessing in Athabaskan. Some of it I understood, some I didn't, but it didn't matter. Energy oozed from his touch, palpable power surging within me.

The lower half of my face he painted white, like last time, with streaks of white on my forehead that he crossed out with a blue thunderbolt. From the center of each eye, he swiped two fingers of red straight down, then curved out around my mouth, with four single red lines from my bottom lip down my chin.

In the hand-mirror, my reflection looked sick as hell. Totally bad ass.

One deep line of blue ran from the bridge of my nose to my chin. Down my arms he zigzagged our family's symbols. On the top of one hand, he drew a golden eagle, and on the other, a mountain lion.

"Your new Spirit Animal," he said.

"What about Spirit Crow? She's not one of my totems anymore?"

"You never lose Animal Totems, you gain them. Please stand, honey."

Once I rose, he painted the spitting image of Spirit Crow between my lower ribs, below the bottom band of my halter—bigger and brighter than anything he'd ever blessed me with before. Did it double as some sort of signal to the Wendigo?

His thumb dipped into the yellow, and I held my breath as he transferred the print to between my eyes—a warning from *Shicheii* to anyone, or any creature, who dared to mess with me. That one yellow oval carried the essence of my grandfather—the deltas, loops, and whorls of my family, my blood—the identifying mark made possible by the collective unit of my ancestors. Because fingerprints were the direct result of a baby rubbing the inner womb walls—learned that tidbit at work a couple years ago—and every infant touched the womb differently, no one in the world possessed *Shicheii's* exact thumbprint.

Except me.

That yellow oval doubled as a tether between my grandfather and me, connecting us through space and time if we got separated tonight, a bond that could never, ever break.

Mr. Mayhem strolled out of the bedroom with that same creepy paint he wore when he hunted me like prey. Muted charcoal stripes hid behind a shockingly red handprint over his mouth and chin. Four straight fingers extended across one cheek, a stiff thumb on the other, as if someone had slapped a hand over his face to silence a freakishly impressive warrior.

One side of his bare chest and arms, he'd painted jet black, the other side blood-red, with yellow thumbprints dotting both collarbones. My mind spiraled from the sheer number of them. The night I earned my yellow dot, I almost died. What did Mr. Mayhem endure to earn that many? Decades of service to our People? Almost all of his symbols signified courage and bravery in battle, the handprint one of the most difficult to obtain. And he had two.

The second handprint—black—grabbed the red shoulder. A half red/half black thunderbolt crossed his twelve-pack abs, representing Thunderbird for power and speed. In white on his black forearm, Father Sun and Mother Earth symbolized harmony and balance of spirit and the Natural World. That's what *Shicheii* told me after the cougar attacked me. Birdshot pellet holes running up the side of his neck, down the red arm, and across his back, actually benefited him by adding texture to the paint, thereby blending him into the environment even more.

Not that he needed the help. More than once, Mr. Mayhem vanished right before my eyes.

"Beautiful job, my friend," he told my grandfather. "Might I make one small suggestion?"

"Of course, Cheveyo. We both value your input."

"Thank you. Then please paint her back, as well, to help blend her ivory skin tone with the darkened forest."

"Excellent idea." *Shicheii* hesitated, and I couldn't figure out why. "Do you have an additional suggestion?"

"I do. Thank you. What if you painted her back with various shades of dark and light charcoal similar to my face?"

"Brilliant." By the shoulders, *Shicheii* spun me around. "The blend should work well to camouflage her. Are you sure you wouldn't mind, Cheveyo?"

"Not at all. Many apprentices wear some of their mentor's paint."

When my grandfather's warm hands skated across my back, I glanced to my right. Mr. Mayhem stood in front of an oversized wall mirror, tying crow feathers into the length of his loose hair, quills jutted at the sky.

To lighten the seriousness of this night, I said, "You just wanna be twinsies with me, huh?"

"You are a character." Half-chuckling, he crossed two bald eagle feathers with one from Spirit Crow, fastened at the crown behind a low, upright roach.

Once *Shicheii* completed my back, he gathered his paints and strode into his bedroom, the door clicking shut behind him. It was such an abrupt departure, I wasn't sure what to make of it. So, I sidled up next to my mentor, my back to the mirror, craning my neck to catch a peek of my reflection.

"Here, let me help you." Mr. Mayhem angled the hand-mirror in front of me.

"Totally bad ass."

"Looks good." He smiled. "Would you mind assisting me?"

"Not at all. Whaddaya need?"

He spun to show me his bare back.

"Want me to paint it?"

"If you wouldn't mind. I couldn't stay in that bedroom another second."

No clue what that meant. Since it didn't feel like my business, I let it slide. "I'd be honored, but I've never painted someone before. Do I do half black/half red like the front?"

The long braid he held to one side. "Yes, please."

Studying his chest gave me a starting point of how to cut him in half so he wasn't lopsided. Once I pinpointed dead center, I painted a single line from the nape of his neck straight down the spine. Down one side, I lathered the red, my palms sliding over pellet holes, my fingers dipping into every sculptured muscle. Man, was he ripped. Kinda impressive.

Not in a romantic way. Just stating the facts.

"Hey, is *Shicheii* okay? He left in such a hurry."

"He will be. A Medicine Man requires silent contemplation and prayer to open himself to the Holy Ones. Not an easy task for him here."

"Yeah, I got the feeling this place threw him off balance."

"Not to worry, Cat. With time and solitude, he'll be fine. Do you recall how quiet he was before we battled the *Yenaldlooshi* in Lynn Woods?"

"Yeah. He was quiet then, too." I smeared black down the other side of his back, saving in between the fingertips of the red handprint for last. "Where's Spirit Crow and Poe?"

"Still in the bedroom, I'm afraid. She's trying to convince him to leave the necklace behind. Hence why I left."

"Aw, man. I created a monster."

"It was a beautiful gesture, Cat."

Gesture? Hardly. More like sheer blackmail.

Once I blackened one side of his back, my fingers hovered over the handprint.

As if reading my mind, he said, "Use the tip of your pinky to reach in between the fingertips. Normally, I would apply the handprint last, but the power struggle in that bedroom is quite intense."

"I bet." Chuckling, I ran lines of black between the red fingers. Poe didn't stand a chance against Spirit Crow. "Done."

"One last thing, if you wouldn't mind." He passed me white paint. "Splay your fingers and press a handprint dead center."

"For peace?"

"White is for peace, yes, but the handprint will also keep you and I connected."

"Can I have one?"

"Not until you've earned it, I'm afraid. However, you have earned a different symbol."

"I have?" Excitement spiraled up my spine, but I couldn't show it yet. So, dead center in the middle of his back, I pressed my hand. "Done."

"Thank you, Cat." He turned to face me, dipped his thumb into yellow and transferred his print right below the Apache Tears at the base of my throat. "For your bravery while battling poachers at the cabin."

Tears rose in my chest, but I couldn't let them escape without ruining *Shicheii's* hard work. "Do I get to keep this one?"

"Of course. You've earned it."

"Thanks." I stared at my reflection in the mirror, my gaze narrowing on his thumbprint. "Means a lot, coming from you."

"The pleasure is all mine." He passed me handwipes. "Okie doke. We have work to do. If you could please check the live feed again, that'd be helpful."

"Sure, no problem." I hustled to the upholstered chair, inching my butt cheeks onto the cushiony seat without smudging the body paint on my back. When I flipped open the PC, not much had changed. "Looks like they assembled the cages, but the wolves are still in the enclosure."

"Perfect. Thank you."

"If the hunt starts at dusk, when do you think they'll start moving 'em?"

"The hunting party will assemble at dusk. If Mister Worthington's former behavior is any indication, the poachers will release the wolves after sunset to, quote, make the hunt more interesting and fun, as disgraceful as that sounds."

"Complete and utter scum." I lowered my voice so *Shicheii* wouldn't overhear. "Be ruthless when you catch 'em."

"Once *we* catch them." Grinning, he winked. "After all, this is your first of four trials. Everything you've worked so hard to achieve will be pushed to the breaking point. It's an important night for you, Cat." He shoved the coffee table out of the way then lowered to the floor, cross-legged. "Come. Sit with me." He patted the spot in front of him, and I sat cross-legged, our knees almost touching. "As soon as your grandfather exits the bedroom, we must be fully prepared to hit the road."

"Gotcha." Across from him, I inhaled a deep breath through my nose, exhaled out my mouth.

"I call to those who went before me for guidance to travel this day's path," he said, and I repeated the first line of the prayer. "I ask those who are yet to come what this holds for me. I ask for the Wolf to be at one with the Man and for the Man to walk beside the Wolf."

"I ask those who are yet to come what this holds for me. I ask for the Wolf to be at one with the Woman and for the Woman to walk beside the Wolf."

He gave a slight grin at my alteration to his words. "I offer this prayer to the Spirits above and humbly ask for their Divine help to live my life to the fullest and bring honor to me and my People."

After I echoed the line, I rattled off the warrior's prayer, ending with, "I am what I am—eternal, immortal, universal, and infinite."

"Indeed, you are, Cat. Nicely done."

I must've blushed all over. "Thanks."

His gaze raised above my head, then settled back on me. "It's time."

Shit. No turning back now.

Chapter 39

"Having a soft heart in a cruel world is courage, not weakness."
—Katherine Henson

7:45 p.m.

Father Sun began His descent into the horizon as Mayhem led Shawnee and Jacy Lee through the thick fauna beside Old Cherry Mountain Road. While Spirit Crow rode his shoulder, Poe flew a few yards ahead to ensure safe passage. In silence, he and his clan moved through the forest, blending with the magnificent hunters of the night.

Straight ahead, a piercing chorus sang from the hearts of each Wolf, their undying love and devotion fully displayed. Even under the worst of circumstances, they never wavered, their spirts pure and ligh'Not far from the compound, Mayhem laced his free fingers with Shawnee's, the other hand gripping the bow, and stopped. Jacy Lee passed his bow to her, slung the quiver on her back, then lifted Spirit Crow off Mayhem's shoulder. Without a word, he continued on alone.

As Poe fluttered down to the branch above his head, Mayhem leaned in, staring deep into Shawnee's eyes to assess her mental state. Sensing some reluctance or fear, he leaned in and widened his eyes, her gaze transfixed on his, their souls entwining as one.

Shawnee brushed her fingertips across the Apache Tears.

With a single nod, he confirmed. "Today is a good day to die."

Now in the same headspace, he gestured to Poe, who leaped into the night air, magnificent ebony wings flapping toward the compound. With a quick hand signal to Shawnee, Mayhem raced to the South side of the compound, where he scaled a mighty oak, Shawnee right on his heels. The canopy and waning moon shielded them from sight.

One hundred feet below, men in fatigues dragged muzzled wolves into iron-barred prisons latched to the back of each single-rider ATV. Two wolves per cage, crammed into spaces too small for even one animal. Thick neck chains tossed over the top, confining movement even more.

Shawnee whispered, "Why aren't we stopping this?"

"Without following them, how would we find the hunting grounds?"

"For the record, I hate every second of this."

"As do I, Cat. As do I."

Once the poachers squeezed the last Wolf into his prison—ten wolves in total—the men jumped on the ATVs, revving the engines, the roar of multiple motors coiling through the forest.

Mayhem rose, gripped the branch above his head, and Shawnee mimicked his movements. "Keep your sight locked straight ahead at me. If you hesitate, you will die."

"Got it."

She handled that news rather well. "Would you like me to carry your bow?"

"Could ya?"

"Of course." He slung the bow over the same shoulder that held his. From his quiver he withdrew two leather straps with finger loops that tied at the wrist. When he passed them to his apprentice, she slipped them on like she'd worn them before. Interesting. "Once they leave, we'll leave. And we cannot stop along the way or we'll lose momentum."

"Got it."

"Questions? Now's the time to ask."

"Nope. I'm good."

"You are, aren't you?"

A quick bounce of the shoulders. "I know, it's weird, but yeah. I'm ready."

"All right, then." As soon as the first ATV hit the trail, he sprinted out on the limb, hopped over to the next tree, and kept moving, sliding branches through his black leather gloves. Although he had no visual of Shawnee, he sensed her keeping up as he leaped from limb to limb, tree to tree, engines growling beneath them, wolves howling in unison. The entire forest erupted, unsettled. Absolute bedlam unfolded below.

At one point along the way, a flash of white plumage caught in his peripheral, but he couldn't stop, couldn't take the time to check on her, couldn't help her distract the Wendigo. Instead, he put his faith in Jacy Lee.

Snapping his attention back to his singular mission—each member of his clan had a vital role to play—a part of him slowly wilted. Nevertheless, he pushed through the emotional upheaval. If he hesitated to ponder all the ramifications and angles of how a supernatural beast might harm his beloved, that hesitation could mean the difference between Shawnee's survival or her death. Many years ago, he promised Kimi and Jacy Lee to protect her. And that was precisely what he intended to do.

Her life mattered.

As her mentor, he shouldered the responsibility to help her fulfill her destiny, for the greater good, for all the People, for Mother Earth and Her most precious beings. One day, Shawnee might have to forge ahead on her own. Until then, he and Jacy Lee would sculp her into the most powerful warrior this world had ever seen, spiritually and physically, her destiny written in the stars long ago.

Wind whipped his face as he charged faster, loose strands of hair blowing behind him, Poe riding the thermals up ahead. Below, the ATVs slowed, zigzagging through the trees toward a mountainside, where a group of camouflaged white men surrounded another chain-link enclosure. The telltale chorus of bark-muddled howls vibrated through the treetops.

Oh, my. Could it be?

Poe circled back to warn him, and Mayhem released the branch long enough to wave downward, signaling for Shawnee to slow. A crash at this height could kill them both. When the patter of footfalls decreased the limb's vibration, he slowed to a stop at the trunk of an ash tree, steadied his gate with a hand on thick, edgy bark, his moccasins planed to the limb. Above him, Poe landed on his own branch, gaze bouncing between Dad and the secondary compound.

Shawnee's brilliant emerald eyes widened. "Are they who I think they are?"

"Who do you think they are?"

"Wolfdogs?"

"Then yes."

"We found the wolfdogs." She cheered. "I can't believe it."

"Patience and perseverance will always serve you well. Hence why we could not ambush the poachers at the Wolf compound."

"You knew they'd lead us here?"

"I suspected as much. Think about it. If you were an animal trafficker—and trust me when I say, I realize how difficult that is to envision—wouldn't it be more lucrative to delay the night's festivities at a locale where your guests can admire the animals you breed and sell to the highest bidder? Should the hunters fail in their quest to slaughter wolves, a wolfdog may be an acceptable replacement."

"Wait." For a moment, her head shook, as if unable to grasp this reprehensible act. "Y'mean, they'll buy one to kill it?"

"Sadly, it's an easy way to add a lookalike bust to their trophy wall. Most admirers of said wall could never tell the difference between a Wolf and a wolfdog, and the trophy hunter's ego remains intact."

"Wow. Just when I thought these scumbags couldn't sink any lower, they... I have no words."

"Nor do I, Cat. Animal trafficking is an ugly business." He passed her the bow. "While they finish their cocktails and admire their prey, you and I will lie in wait."

"From up here?"

"No. Ground-level." Before she pummeled him with questions, he swung his leg around the trunk and began his descent. At about the halfway mark, he checked on the hunting party, who taunted the imprisoned wolves. Ten beautiful animals in cages, still latched to the back of all-terrain vehicles.

Have your fun while it lasts, Entitled Ones. Soon, you will be hunted by the most ruthless animal of all. For I am the storm you've feared—I am Mayhem—and I will show no mercy for your unforgiveable sins.

Chapter 40

8:30 p.m.

At the base of the tree, Mr. Mayhem hooked an arm for me to follow. Hunched low, he and I snaked around trees, our moccasins silent, skimming dead leaves and pine needles without so much as a crunch, each footstep intentional and deliberate, rolling the soles of my feet from heel to toe, heel to toe like my mentor taught me.

We crouched behind a wide barrier of tangled branches and brush on the East trail. The trophy hunters' voices weren't as clear from here, as our hiding spot resided a good hundred yards from the secondary compound. Unlike the wolves, the wolfdogs ran loose inside the enclosure, pups of various ages speckled among the pack, every one of them well-fed and groomed.

Guess they had to look good to sell for thousands.

A gunshot rang my eardrums, and my mind snapped to high alert, my complete focus on the trail ahead.

"The moment you spot a hunter," Mr. Mayhem hushed, "draw back the bowstring as you inhale, hold your breath to steady your aim, then exhale as you release the arrow. It'll help you hit your target."

Why didn't he tell me this before? A little practice during training would've been nice. Since now wasn't the time to argue, I rolled with it. "Okay, cool. Got it."

"If you need me, I'll be at the foot of the West trail. Remember our hand-signals in case either of us needs to warn the other." He turned to leave—hesitated—then whirled back around. "One last thing. Should you encounter the beast that shall remain nameless, use the arrowheads in the pocket of your quiver. Aim for its heart. The goal is to shatter it."

Fuck. Running into this thing was a possibility? "What if I miss?"

"Do not take the shot unless you're certain you won't miss. I will do everything in my power not to put you in that situation, but it'd be irresponsible not to warn you."

"Alright," I said, even though nothing about this situation sat well with me. "Got it."

"Good. Stay in contact with me."

I shot him a thumbs-up, and he took off, vanishing into the forest within seconds. How would I stay in contact if I couldn't find him? Pushing negativity aside, I closed my eyes for a hot second, allowing the environment to envelope me. One with nature, one with my family, I reached *hozho*, my heartbeat slow and even, my pulse at a resting rate, my breathing steady and strong. I crouched behind the tangled branches, my entire focus narrowed on the enemy—entitled rich assholes sport-hunting wolves.

No sign of *Shicheii* or Spirit Crow anywhere. Poe, on the other hand, soared around the perimeter of the compound, his gold ankle band shimmering in the moonlight. As much as it pained me to admit, he really was a master of disguise, stealth, and staying below the radar. When he flew toward me, he drew my full attention. Perched on a low-hanging branch, he lifted one foot, opening and closing his talons two times.

I flashed two fingers, and he dipped his bill.

"Thank you," I mouthed.

He leaped into the night sky, flapping in the opposite direction toward his father.

Two hunters headed my way, leaf litter crunching under their boots. I rose, my back pressed to a tree trunk, and waited. Within a minute or two, a flash of red shot through my peripheral. Mr.

Mayhem? A Wolf sprinted past me. I stepped into the open, raised the bow. Took a deep breath in, held it while I pulled back the bowstring.

Once the men hustled closer, I exhaled. The arrow whizzed through the air, clipping the side of one hunter's neck, slicing through his carotid. At the same time, another arrow landed dead center in the other guy's heart. He dropped dead. The guy I shot clawed at his throat with one hand while fumbling with the rifle with the other. I loaded a second arrow when Mr. Mayhem jumped on top of the dude and finished him off with the hunting knife.

Blood splattered everywhere.

When Mr. Mayhem rose, he turned back to assess my mental fitness, crimson dripping down one cheek. Intense translucent gray eyes burrowed into my soul, but I didn't react. Instead, I concentrated on maintaining *hozho*, my breath steady and strong, my heart and mind open and responsive, connected with all living beings—the wolves, the wolfdogs, the owls, the nighthawks, even the prey scurrying for safety, the unconditional love of *Shicheii* and Spirit Crow, the unyielding protectiveness of my mentor, and Poe. For at that moment, I had no foes.

Except one—our collective enemy hellbent on slaughtering Mother Earth's Innocent Ones.

Mr. Mayhem dragged two dead poachers behind a wall of thick shrubbery, shuffled the leaf litter over the blood, masking the kill site. Another Wolf shot through the trees. I scaled the nearest tree for a better vantage point. Below me, three hunters pursued the lone Wolf while another group chased two wolves on the West side.

Mr. Mayhem vanished. I slung the bow on my back, gripped the branches above me. Charged for the next tree, and the next, my sight glued to the pack of wolves, all running in opposite directions. At the trunk, I stopped to regroup and scanned the tree line.

Poe screeched, and my attention snapped forward. Mr. Mayhem stood about fifty yards ahead of me in another tree, with Poe perched on one shoulder. At chest level, I signed six men, three heading East, three heading West. Above my head I flashed ten fingers to show him the distance. With a single nod, he took off, long hair sweeping across his back, leaves trembling in his wake.

I hauled ass for the other three. After gaining on them, I climbed down, zigzagged around trees, looped around to hedge them off. In the distance, wolves sang long, steady bays—a prayer for their pack's survival. Crystal clear voices pierced my heart, and I ran faster, my arms pumping harder.

In between the trophy hunters and the wolves, I stopped, slid an arrow from the quiver, then took aim. The second I spotted camouflage, I fired. Grabbed another arrow. Aimed. Fired. Grabbed another arrow. Aimed. Fired. I didn't stop till I'd shot six times, pelting the poachers with arrows, bullets rocketing into the sky as they fell, the pine-sweetened air tainted by gunpowder.

In seconds, I closed the gap between us. Three men writhed in pain on the ground. I ripped out the arrows, blood smacking me in the face, stomach, and arms, crimson splattered across Mom's beads on my chest. The strange part was, I had no anger. Empowerment resonated through my core. Their selfishness and entitlement brought us to this moment, not mine. If I hadn't ended their lives, God only knew how many species they'd wipe off the planet. Their actions likened to spitting in Mother Earth's face. In my view, they forfeited their right to live when they targeted the voiceless, the most innocent of us all. If that made me a murderer, then so be it. I'd never stop protecting them. Never. Mr. Mayhem and I filled a necessary role.

If we didn't protect the furred, feathered, scaled, and finned, who would? Legally, conservation groups could only do so much. Screw the law. Mr. Mayhem, *Shicheii*, and I answered to a much higher authority.

As I stared at the lifeless hunters by my moccasins, a red arm locked around my neck, my feet swept out from beneath me, and I landed face-up on the ground. Straddling my hips, Mr. Mayhem leaned in real close, his minty breath striking my nose, his hair sweeping across my collarbones, gray eyes burrowing into mine.

In my head his voice resonated. *What are you doing?*

My job. What're you doing?

Don't make me ask you twice, Cat.

"I was just—" I whispered. "Okay, so, maybe I took a minute to think about, y'know, things. And maybe it wasn't the right time, but I was just self-assessing how I'm feeling."

"And your self-assessment revealed…?"

"That I'm totally good. That I know what we're fighting for. That I know what's at stake if we fail."

"Failure is not an option." He rose and extended his hand. When I latched on, he yanked me to my feet. "Another hunting party is leaving the compound. Are you ready?"

"I was born ready." I pinned back my shoulders. "Let's wipe the forest floor with these scumbags."

"Though I admire your spunk and the sentiment behind it, step first with humility. For it is far better to have less thunder in the mouth and more lightning in the hands."

Did he just tell me to shut the fuck up and get back to work? "Got it."

He winked. Turned. Took off like a bullet, disappearing into the darkness. Maybe someday I'd become as impressive. Until then, I concentrated on every step, each body movement, my mind on high alert, absorbing the beauty around me, becoming one with the Natural World, my place within it clear and grounded, my soul rooted to Mother Earth and my People.

While scaling an oak tree on the northern side of the East trail, I stopped briefly to sweep my fingertips across the Apache Tears. Mr. Mayhem was right. This night wasn't about me. It was about all those who came before me and those yet to emerge.

Up in the canopy of leaves, I surveyed the scene below. Shit. Forgot to hide the bodies and cover the blood pool. If the hunting party ran across their dead brethren, we'd lose our only advantage—the art of surprise—our presence no longer a secret. Somehow, I had to fix this. But the camouflaged men stalked closer.

Didn't matter. What choice did I have? So, I scrambled down the trunk and hauled ass, sprinting to the kill site. With a firm grip on the wrists of the first guy, I hauled him off trail. Blood drenched drag marks through dead leaves led straight to him. Shit. Couldn't deal with it now. I raced back for the second poacher, dragged him across the same path, dropped his ankles, then jetted back to the kill site. With poacher number three, I slid my hands under his armpits and was in the middle of dragging his fat ass behind the bush when a male voice pierced the night air.

"Who made a kill?" he said.

Another guy answered, "No one yet."

"Then whose blood is this?"

"Shh... they could still be here."

If they followed that bloody path, I'm screwed. What would Mr. Mayhem do?

In the darkness I searched for a moonlight-kissed leaf. When I found a shiny maple, I waved my head till I spotted my shadow. Backstepped into the bush and gathered gnarled branches in front of me. *Shicheii* told me hiding was not losing if it saved my life. And so, I crouched, my face and body paint blending me into the environment, my gaze transfixed on that maple leaf.

One camouflage-clad hunter stepped into view. I slowed my breathing.

"Over here." He waved his compadres closer. "We're not the only hunters out here."

Pip Hawthorne said, "Spread out and find them. Now."

Hawthorne's legs stood less than two feet from me. Motionless, I didn't dare move, didn't dare breathe. If he squatted to search for signs of life, he might spot me. But I couldn't move, couldn't escape—trapped like easy prey.

Dear God, don't let them find me. O Great Spirit, shield me from harm, protect me, wrap your loving arms around me. In the name of all my relations, I pray.

Chapter 41

"All European tradition, Marxism included, has conspired to defy the natural order of all things. Mother Earth has been abused, the powers have been abused, and this cannot go on forever. No theory can alter that simple fact. Mother Earth will retaliate, the whole environment will retaliate, and the abusers will be eliminated. Things come full circle, back to where they started. That's revolution."
—Russell Means

10 p.m.

Mayhem severed the third poacher's throat in a hunting party of three, the other two dead by his moccasins. Poe rocketed out of a nearby tree, landed on a low branch, tail feathers flickering, chest heaving like something had gone wrong.

"Is Cat in trouble?"

One dip of the bill.

"Show me, please."

Poe flew low, zipping around tree limbs, glancing back at Dad every few minutes. Mayhem stayed right on his tail feathers. When his taloned soldier circled back to perch on his forearm, Mayhem slowed, skimming the landscape for anomalies and reflective surfaces. In the distance, two men in fatigues stalked the woods off-trail. Beyond them, Mr. Pip Hawthorne ordered them to spread out.

At eye-level, he fluffed Poe's chest feathers. "Find Cat."

With a dip of the bill, he confirmed. In flight, magnificent ebony wings soared straight over Mr. Hawthorne's head. Once he landed on a limb, he stretched one leg toward a thick bush—Cat's hiding spot.

Not ideal, but doable.

While keeping track of all three men, he jetted across the forest floor. Ran up the side of a trunk—backflipped—kicking the rifle from one man's grasp, landing on the other man's shoulders before snapping his neck. As the poacher dropped, Mayhem's moccasins hit the soil. The second poacher he sucker-punched, the so-called man stumbling backward, unsteady on his feet. Mayhem moved in, death-gripped his throat in one hand, the leathered fingers of the other tightened around the knife handle.

"Mister Daniels"—the voice came from behind him—"how nice of you to join us."

"No need for pleasantries, Mister Hawthorne." As Mayhem turned, he curled the poacher into his chest, the blade leveled to his throat. "Now is not the time nor the place for idle chitchat." He slashed open the poacher's throat, tossed him to the ground. "Your move, Mister Hawthorne."

"I must admit, I thought my wife had lost her mind when she described warpainted savages, yet here you stand."

He pitched toward him.

Mr. Hawthorne raised the rifle. "Stay back."

"Or what? You'll shoot me?" He sniggered. "Better not miss."

"Get your hands up."

"Surrender? To whom, Mister Hawthorne, you?"

"I am the one holding the rifle, yes."

"Hm. Let me mull over your enticing proposition for a moment." He tapped a stiff finger to his lips. "Surrender or what, exactly?"

"I'll kill you."

"You people are so predictable." He gazed up at Poe. "Haven't we done this once already?"

Ca-caw, caw, caw.

Mayhem sighed. "All right. I shall play my part. Mister Hawthorne, I doubt you'll succeed, but you could give it the ol' college try, I suppose. Let's call that option one. Would you care to hear option two?"

"I would." With the bow raised, razor-tipped arrow locked and loaded, Shawnee stepped out of the bush, quickening her steps to the side of Mr. Hawthorne. "And yeah, I got wicked *déjà vu*."

"Refresh my memory, Cat. How did Mister Hawthorne's men fair the last time we danced this particular number?"

"Not well. They all died."

"They died? Imagine that, Mister Hawthorne." He stepped closer. "Now, would you care to hear option two?"

"No."

"No? All right, then." He nodded to Shawnee. "You may end Mister Hawthorne's life. He's of no use to us."

As predicted, Mr. Hawthorne whirled toward her, and Mayhem pounced, ripping the gun from his delicate hands before it fired. He tossed the weapon to the ground as he muscled him to the soil.

The hunting blade nipped the hostage's throat. "How many others are at the compound?"

"Three, four, not many. Please, Mister Daniels. I have a family."

"So do the wolves." In two hands he raised the knife over his head. With immense force, he plunged the blade into a cold, destructive heart. Tears drained out the sides of Mr. Hawthorne's eyes, lids fluttering closed. When he glanced up, Shawnee's lips parted. "Speak your mind, Cautious Cat."

"That was so... so..."

"Violent? War is ugly."

"No. Awesome."

"Oh." A warmth flushed his cheeks. "You are too kind, Cat. Thank you."

"No, seriously. I have a family, he whined. So do the wolves, you said. It was just so... so... frickin' perfect. And those backflips. Wow. Incredible."

"Well, I'm, uh..." he cleared his throat, this conversation venturing outside his comfort level, "pleased you enjoyed the show."

With the hem of Mr. Hawthorne's jacket, he wiped down the hunting knife. "Let's take care of the men at the compound. Then we need to check on your grandfather."

"Can you teach me that backflip move in our next training session?"

The grin he forced down. "Oh, Cautious Cat." He slung his arm over her shoulders. "What am I going to do with you?"

"Hey." She pulled away. "Watch the paint."

He flashed his palms in surrender. "My mistake." With a silent sigh, he resisted rolling his eyes. Women.

Chapter 42

11 p.m.

As we crested the hill to the compound, the roar of ATVs coiled through the darkness. Mr. Mayhem's pace quickened, and I jogged to catch up.

"What's goin' on? Are they leaving?"

"Our activities haven't gone unnoticed, I'm afraid. We need to hedge them off."

"How?"

Silent, he slung the bow on his back and took off, sprinting at top speed, his moccasins barely touching the forest floor. I chased him, snaking around trees, hopping fallen timber, my arms pumping, my body pushed to the limit. Still, I fell behind. No one could catch him. The man moved like a lightning bolt. The only reason I found him after ten or fifteen straight minutes of running full force was because he stopped to scale a tree. Thirty feet in the air, he peered down at Old Cherry Mountain Road.

The moment I emerged through the canopy of leaves, all the engines quieted, the woods relaxing into its regular rhythm, reanimating its energetic pulse of life, nature's stillness thronged with wildlife. Below at street-level, three men in camouflage protected a slim, dark-haired hunter, ushering him into the back of a limousine.

"Isn't that the same guy from the auction that Southerland refused to ID?"

"It does look like him, doesn't it?"

"Why are we still sitting here?" I latched on to his arm. "Is he the ice man from *Shicheii's* vision?"

"Could very well be."

"Let's go." I thrust my hand at the limo. "We can't let him escape for chrissakes."

"First of all, watch your language. And your tone." He grimaced. "How do you propose we catch a motor vehicle on foot?"

"Fuck." I flashed my palm. "Slipped out. Sorry."

The guards secured the ice man while multiple trophy hunters scrambled into two black Escalades, one in front of the limo, one behind it.

"So, we just let 'em escape?"

Moving as a caravan, all three vehicles sped down Old Cherry Mountain Road. As soon as the last red taillight trailed into the darkness, my mentor focused on me. "Let me explain something to you, Cat. We must pick our battles. You and I chose to save endangered wolves, and we'll succeed in that mission once we free the wolfdogs, as well. Remember when we discussed how to retain our power rather than reacting to outside stimuli?"

My stiff shoulders dropped. "Yes."

"We made our move. They made theirs. Now it's our turn again."

"Okay, so, whaddawe do?"

"First, we need to find your grandfather."

"Oh, my God." Truth be told, I'd been so preoccupied with the poachers, I forgot all about the Wendigo. "What if *Shicheii* and Spirit Crow—?"

"Ah, ah, ah." His head rocked an emphatic no. "Do not allow negativity to enter your headspace. Warriors maintain a positive, hopeful mindset."

"Got it." Easier said than done. Still, I tried my best to push negative thoughts aside while climbing down the trunk. Near the base of the tree, Mr. Mayhem leaped over my head, knees bending to absorb the impact when he landed. Fingers laced with mine, he led me toward Old Cherry Mountain Road, but *Shicheii* and Spirit Crow went in the opposite direction. Didn't they?

Confusion rocked my senses till Mr. Mayhem approached an abandoned ATV, the key still in the ignition. Smart. Why didn't I think of that? He slung a leg over the seat, and I planted a fist on my hip.

"Problem?"

"Why do I gotta ride bitch?"

Chuckling, he started the engine. "Would you prefer to walk?"

"Fine." I straddled the seat and snaked my arms around his waist. "Next time, I'm driving."

Ignoring me, he gunned it, the ATV sailing through the trees, and I tightened my grip. After a few miles—seemed more like days—I fumbled to hang on while I yanked out mouthfuls of hair, spitting off the side, his long strands slapping me in the face, basically blinding me. If someone jumped out, I'd never react in time.

For now, I rolled with it. Whatever shampoo he used smelled great but tasted like shit, a fact I kept to myself. After losing feeling in my ass, I'd had just about enough of this ride.

The ATV slowed to a stop. I couldn't figure out why, still fighting with his hair in my mouth, eyes, up my nose, and embedded in my face paint.

Without a word, he dismounted at the top of a hillside.

When I slid off the seat, my jaw slacked at the scene below. An indescribable beast—bones jutting through its greenish skin—stood on massive razorlike talons on the ends of its legs. The Wendigo towered over my grandfather, roaring with a maw filled with fanglike crooked yellow teeth, burning red eyes flaming in deep, hollow sockets. Spirit Crow flew circles around its head, disorientating the beast as my grandfather blew a powdery potion at its face.

"*Shicheii!*" I lifted one leg to bolt down the hill, but before my foot made contact, Mr. Mayhem literally swept me off my feet, cradling me in his arms, preventing me from helping my only living relative.

"Lemme go!" I struggled to break free, but he refused to loosen his grip. "I need to help *Shicheii* before that thing attacks him!"

"In your current state you're of no use to anyone."

Legs flailing, I swung a fist at his face, and he bobbed out of the way. Eyebrows raised, he released me. But the minute my moccasins hit the earth, he tapped my cheek.

"All right, Cat." Egging on a fight, he beckoned me toward him. "Let's see what you've got."

I swung, but he caught my fist and shoved me backward. Roaring like the beast, I dove, firing undercuts to his abs. But he wouldn't fight back. I leaped to my feet, thumbed my nose, bobbing back and forth. "C'mon, hit me."

And he laughed—in my face.

I swung a right hook, and he swerved out of the way.

With both hands, I thumped my chest. "Fight me, mutherfucker."

Before I knew what was happening, he grabbed my throat in one hand and swept my legs. I fell backward, landing hard on the earth. With a knee on each arm, pinning me down, he loosened his grip and leaned in.

"Did you get it out of your system yet?"

Just as intensely I stared back. "Not. Even. Close."

"What do you need to move pass this?"

"Fight me."

"I am fighting you."

"No. You're blocking, not fighting, and it's pissin' me off."

Behind him, the beast roared even louder.

With a quick glance to the side, he said, "Do you need me to knock you out? Is that what this is? You can't face the fact that your grandfather is in mortal danger?"

Tears clouded my vision. "I can't lose him."

"I would never let that happen."

"Let go of my arms."

When his knees moved, I latched on to his neck, hugging him tight, praying for *Shicheii's* survival. "Don't let him die. Please, I'm beggin' you. Save him."

One hand patted my bare back. "All right, all right, shh... Please don't cry, Cat."

When I let go, he raised me to my feet, interlocked his gloved fingers with mine. We crested the hill.

"Slide," he said, and jerked me forward, sliding down the hill behind a large boulder. From the quiver he withdrew an all-red arrow with a silver tip. "Do not move from this spot."

I nodded yes.

"Promise me."

"I promise I won't move."

"Thank you." To the top of the boulder he climbed, and I scrambled to peer around the side. He pulled back the bowstring then fired. The arrow sailed through the air, striking the beast in the heart, glass exploding from its chest, shards flying in all directions. The Wendigo dropped, the earth rumbling like an earthquake. Mr. Mayhem sprinted down the hill, ripped out the arrow, and stabbed the beast over and over and over in the heart. Beside him, *Shicheii* prayed, singing to the Holy Ones as powder sifted through his fingers into open wounds. Once he finished, he sat back on folded legs.

"*Shicheii*," I called out, climbing atop the boulder, and Mr. Mayhem glanced back, closing the gap between us in seconds. I bobbed my head around him. "*Shicheii*, you okay?"

Gloved palms sided my arms. "I understand this is a difficult moment for you, but you must leave him be."

Tears washed my face. "But I wanna see him. I need to."

"I know you do, Cat. Your grandfather has endured a violent battle with supernatural forces, robbing him of energy, and he needs time to process, reflect, and pray to the Holy Ones."

"Can't I just see how he is?"

"Will you stay calm?"

"Yes. I promise."

"All right, then. Be respectful in your approach. And silent. He may not respond to you. I need you to be aware of that."

Overwhelmed, I could only nod. After walking a couple yards, I glanced back at Mr. Mayhem, seated on the boulder. Why wasn't he coming with me?

Halfway there, Spirit Crow flapped toward me, landing on my shoulder for moral support. "Thanks," I hushed, and she dipped her bill.

Once I reached my grandfather, I lowered to the ground across from him, tears waterfalling down my face. The most important person in my world morphed into an empty, hollow shell, like he'd relinquished every molecule of energy, like he had nothing left inside, his soul wounded on the deepest level. Forever scarred by an ancient supernatural beast, awakened by the sins of entitlement and greed, privileged scum who enslaved and slaughtered the voiceless—the most innocent of us all—for profit.

Lacking the know-how to help him, I slipped my hands into his, chest heaving in desperation. The worst part? *Shicheii* never had to battle this beast. He endured this war to protect strangers he'd never meet, people who'd never learn of his sacrifice, self-absorbed folks who'd probably never give him the time of day. And yet, my grandfather loved each one as brothers and sisters, like family, because in his world we all mattered, regardless of skin tone or religious beliefs. As members of the same species, he believed humans should live as one.

Look what he got for his sacrifice. My grandfather was a shell of his former self—hollowed gaze at the heavens, disheveled gray hair limped across his shoulders.

Hyperventilating, I squeaked out, "I love you, *Shicheii*. Please come back to me. I won't make it without you."

Soon, his gaze settled on me, the warmness returning to his eyes. "Mourning Dove?"

"It's me, *Shicheii*." Back swelling with gratitude, I lost it, wailing like a newborn. "I thought I lost you."

"Come, child." He patted his heart, and I dove into his embrace, blubbering all over his painted chest. "Mourning Dove?"

Enveloped in his arms, I quieted. "Yeah?"

"I saw your mom. She's so proud of you, honey."

A soft squeal escaped my lips, pain squeezing my heart. "Mom was here?"

"Spirit Crow brought her." Warm palms cradled my face. "We both love you so much."

"Can I talk to her, *Shicheii*?" I bawled. "Please..."

From the sidelines, Spirit Crow cooed.

"When you need her most, she'll be there."

"But I need her now. I need her every day."

"My sweet child, look at all you've accomplished on your own. You haven't even scratched the surface of what you're capable of."

Somehow, I lassoed my emotions enough to regain focus. "We saved the wolves."

He kissed my forehead. "You sure did."

"We need help with the wolfdogs, but if you don't feel up to it—"

"My sweet, sweet child"—he swept a gentle hand down my cheek—"fulfilling one's destiny is never easy. It is, however, important. On that note, would you mind assisting me?"

"Not at all." I helped him stand. "Watch out for the glass."

"It's ice, honey, not glass."

A heart made of ice? "Is that the ice man?"

"That is a supernatural beast, not a man. It lost all humanity long ago."

With his arm slung around my neck, we headed up the hillside.

Mr. Mayhem sprinted down to meet us and held *Shicheii* in a similar position, my grandfather braced to his side. "I've got him, Cat. Please collect our bows and quivers."

"I'm on it."

With the mission only half-finished, I didn't have time to process my feelings about Mom, *Shicheii*, Spirit Crow, or how I treated Mr. Mayhem earlier—a man who set aside his life to mentor me. What'd I do to repay his kindness? I attacked him. So not cool. *Why, Shawnee, why?*

On the long trek to the compound, I vowed to do better, try harder, make them all proud of me. But first, we needed to free the imprisoned Innocent Ones.

Chapter 43

1:14 a.m.

Outside the enclosure, wolfdogs barked and howled, some bounding off the sides of the chain-link fence, others pacing back and forth, food and water bowls flipped over. Complete and utter restless mayhem within the walls of their prison.

When I reached for the chain around the door, Mr. Mayhem stepped closer. "Care to fill us in on your plan, Cautious Cat?"

"Whaddaya mean? I'm gonna free 'em."

Ca-caw, caw, caw. Pissy Pants added his two cents from his father's shoulder, which I didn't need.

"Here?" Head listed to one side, his eyebrows V'd. "With a starving Wolf pack nearby?"

"Honey, what Cheveyo means is, we need to ensure their safety post-release."

"Okay." Wolfdogs paced inside the enclosure. "How?"

Mr. Mayhem lowered Poe to the top of the fence. "With forethought and mindfulness."

"Do *you* have a plan?"

"Well, let's talk it out." Spirit Crow landed beside Poe, both cooing at the wolfdogs to soothe them. "Ideally, they should be released elsewhere. Do you agree with that statement?"

I nodded. "Yeah."

"Thus, we'll need a way to transport them."

"What about the ATVs? The poachers never bothered to remove the cages."

"One per cage?"

"Definitely. They weren't built for two, and I'm not about to abuse 'em like those rich pricks did."

"Agreed. One problem solved. What is the next logical step?"

"Figure out how to get 'em into the cages?"

"Correct. See how a little forethought and planning keeps everyone on the same page?"

As much as it pained me to admit, I agreed. I also was well aware that he was letting me take charge for once. Was this an evaluation? Or a final exam to see if I passed my first of four trials?

"I may be able to help with the wolfdogs, Mourning Dove. Unless Cheveyo has an objection?"

"Not at all. You and I are instruments in her toolbox. She should take advantage of her full arsenal."

"Really?" A little thrill zipped up my spine. "I'm the chief?"

"For the time being, yes." A smile emerged through the creepy face paint, trickles of poacher blood still siding one cheek. "Don't let the power go to your head."

"Cool." I rubbed my palms together. "Alright. *Shicheii*, you tell the wolfdogs what we're doin'. Poe and Spirit Crow keep cooing. They seem to like it. Mister M, you're with me." I stalked over to an ATV then swung my leg over the seat. "Let's line 'em up closer to the door."

"As you wish." Behind me, he settled on the next all-terrain vehicle in line.

Over my shoulder, I called out, "We may have to circle around the pen to get close enough."

"I'll stay right behind you, Cat."

"Cool. Let's do this." The engine roared to life. One problem—I'd never driven an ATV before. Meh. How hard could it be? Once I figured out where the accelerator was, I putted along the trail. Banged a sharp right at the corner of the enclosure and got bucked off the side, the ATV rolling on top of me, tires whining above me.

In a split-second, Mr. Mayhem hoisted the rig off me and back onto its wheels. "Are you injured?"

"I don't think so."

He extended a hand, and I latched on.

Back on my feet, I brushed debris off my buckskins, my ego deflated. "Can you, uh, gimme a few pointers on how to drive this thing?"

"You've never driven an ATV?"

I flung up my hands, slapping my thighs on the way down. "Where would I have the opportunity?"

"With Detective Samuels or your friend, Nadine?"

I pressed my lips together. "Can you tell me how to do it or not?"

"Certainly. Please remount the vehicle." He swept a hand toward the ATV, and I hopped on. "Relax your shoulders, elbows slightly bent, hands on the handlebars, knees pointed at the gas tank, feet on the footrests, toes aimed straight ahead."

Somehow, I managed to follow his instructions.

"Good. Keep your back straight, not tense. Muscles loose and flexible."

"Got it."

"As you turn, lean into it, distributing most of your body weight on the outside foot peg."

Man, that was a lot to remember. "Maybe you should take the lead? That way, I can see it in action."

"As you wish."

Ego bruised but not broken—kinda like my legs—we swapped ATVs, and I mimicked his body position as he cornered the enclosure, circled wide, then rolled in front of the pen door. All the wolfdogs sat at *Shicheii's* feet inside, gazing up at him like he held all the answers to life's mysteries.

"How are we doing, Jacy Lee?"

"They're excited about their new adventure."

"Splendid." He swung open the cage door on the back of his ATV, and I did the same on mine. "Whenever you're ready, please bring out the first two brave soldiers."

My grandfather led two wolfdogs out the door. He stopped at the first cage, and the wolfdog jumped in without protest. Same with the second. Unbelievable. Whatever *Shicheii* told them worked. One would think they'd attended six weeks of training camp by their tameness. Love really did conquer all.

Driving the lead ATV, Mr. Mayhem putted down a winding trail through the woods to the power lines. The openness allowed us to accelerate, but the trip still took forever. I maneuvered through some hairy points, too, but the spot he chose at the pinnacle of a mountain was so breathtaking, so awe-inspiring, all the sore muscles were well worth the effort.

Under the moonlight, he and I freed the wolfdogs. They ran and played, rolling around in the vastness. Freedom—it's everything.

Tears of joy wet my lashes. "You couldn't've chosen a more perfect spot."

He slung an arm around my neck. "I'm pleased you approve."

"Look how happy they are. They're free because of you."

Rather than share in the victory, he flipped me a Scooby snack. "This was your plan, not mine."

"Does that mean I passed my first trial?"

"With flying colors."

"Did I earn a handprint?"

Gray eyes squinted down at me. "Handprints signify bravery in hand-to-hand combat. Were you successful in that area?"

"Yeah, about that. You didn't deserve to take the brunt of my bullshit— I mean, baggage. I'm wicked sorry for how I acted."

"Already forgotten, Cat." He focused back on the wolfdogs, running free. "Although, I do appreciate the apology."

"Doesn't seem enough." I kicked the soil. "Wouldn't blame you if you said I failed because of my hissy fit back there."

"Look at me, please." When I raised my chin, he degloved then thumbed off one yellow dot from his collarbone. "This you earned. Where do you want it?"

"Really?"

"Really."

Hope soared like a rainbow after a shower, and I reclined my head. "Next to the other one, below my Apache Tears to remind me of who I represent, what I'm fighting for, and who I want to become."

The touch of his warm thumb against my neck made me emotional, and I folded my lips around my teeth, holding back a tidal wave of tears. "Looks beautiful, Mourning Dove."

"Thanks." In front of us, the wolfdogs frolicked, playful barks tossed back and forth. "Let's get the others, so they can stand beside their family, too."

A slow smile built on his lips. "Your wish is my command, Chief."

"Careful. A girl could get drunk on that kind of power." With an exaggerated wink, I hopped on the ATV, revving the engine.

For hours, Mr. Mayhem and I drove back and forth, transporting the wolfdogs to their new home—away from people who'd harm them. On the final trip, when we crested the pinnacle with puppies on the back, the whole pack galloped toward us, encircling our ATVs, eagerly awaiting their young.

Once the last pup hopped out, Mr. Mayhem and I stayed a few minutes, reveling in their reunion, their freedom. Long, steady bays howled in unison, rejoicing over their fresh start. No more abuse. No more confinement. No more taunting from assholes who weren't even worthy to stand in their shadows.

"Will they make it?" I asked.

"With family by their side, they'll be just fine."

Was he talking about us or the wolfdogs? Didn't matter. The sentiment remained the same.

"As much as I hate to be the bearer of bad news, I'd be remiss if I failed to mention one variable to our current situation."

I was almost afraid to ask. "What is it?"

"Mister Hawthorne was not surprised by our presence tonight. Thus, he may've notified the organization of who we are and where we live."

All contentment petered out in an instant. From here on out, we weren't safe from the Killzme Corporation. No place to run. No place to hide. No idea who'd come for us next, nor how many soldiers they employed.

Aw, man. What'd the future hold?

ABOUT SUE COLETTA

Sue Coletta is an award-winning crime writer and an active member of Mystery Writers of America, Sisters in Crime, and International Thriller Writers. Feedspot and Expertido.org named her Murder Blog as "Best 100 Crime Blogs on the Net." She also blogs at the Kill Zone (Writer's Digest "101 Best Websites for Writers") and Writers Helping Writers.

Sue lives with her husband in the Lakes Region of New Hampshire and writes two psychological thriller series, Mayhem Series (Crow Talons Publishing) and Grafton County Series (Tirgearr Publishing) and true crime/narrative nonfiction (Rowman & Littlefield Group). Sue teaches a virtual course about serial killers for EdAdvance in CT and a condensed version for her fellow Sisters In Crime. She's appeared on the Emmy award-winning true crime series, Storm of Suspicion, and three episodes of A Time to Kill on Investigation Discovery.

Get in touch with Sue:
Website - http://www.suecoletta.com
Facebook - https://www.facebook.com/SueColetta1
Facebook - https://www.facebook.com/SuePhillipsColetta
Twitter - http://www.twitter.com/SueColetta1
Blog - https://suecoletta.com/murder-blog
Blog - https://killzoneblog.com
Goodreads - http://www.goodreads.com/SueColetta
TikTok - https://www.tiktok.com/@suecoletta
StumbleUpon - http://www.stumbleupon.com/stumbler/
SueColetta1
Pinterest - https://www.pinterest.com/suecoletta1/

LinkedIn - https://www.linkedin.com/pub/sue-coletta/a0/1b9/161

BOOKS BY SUE COLETTA
THE MAYHEM SERIES
WINGS OF MAYHEM, #1
Released: March 2023
ISBN: 9798987998014

Shawnee Daniels breaks into the home of Jack Delsin who's accused of embezzling money from his employees' retirement fund. Intent on returning their hard-earned cash, she discovers Jack has secrets worth killing over. A deadly game of cat-and-mouse ensues. Can she outrun the killer, prove she's innocent of murder after Jack sets her up, and protect those she loves before he strikes again?

BLESSED MAYHEM, #2
Released: March 2023
ISBN: 9798987998038

Accompanied by his loyal crow companions, Poe, Allan, and Edgar, Mr. Mayhem's crimes strike fear in the hearts and minds of folks across Massachusetts' North Shore. When Shawnee Daniels–cat burglar extraordinaire and forensic hacker for the police–meets Mayhem in the dark, she piques his curiosity. Sadly for her, she leaves behind an item best left undiscovered. Or is it serendipity by design?

SILENT MAYHEM, #3
Released: March 2023
ISBN: 9798987998052

A madman is decapitating men and women and dumping their headless corpses on two area beaches. Mr. Mayhem—the most prolific

serial killer the North Shore has ever known—claims Shawnee Daniels' life is in danger. He "claims" he wants to help her, but just last year he threatened to murder everyone she loves. Can she find the strength to move forward, or will the truth destroy her?

I AM MAYHEM, #4

Released: March 2023

ISBN: 9798987998076

Serial killer Mr. Mayhem wants Shawnee Daniels dead and threatens to murder everyone she loves, sending Shawnee a severed body part at a time. With crows stalking her every move, Shawnee can barely function. Can she solve his cryptic clues before it's too late? Or will she be the next to die a slow, agonizing death?

UNNATURAL MAYHEM, #5

Released: March 2023

ISBN: 9798987998090

Explosive news of a crow hunt rings out in the White Mountain Region of New Hampshire, and one hundred crows gather to put an end to it. With so many lives at stake—including Poe's—Shawnee and Mayhem must work together to stop the trophy hunters before they obliterate the local murder. Taking on twenty-five experienced hunters armed with shotguns is no small feat. If they fail, Poe may lead his brethren to their death. But what if Shawnee and Mayhem aren't see the full picture? What if these hunters have secrets worth killing over?

RESTLESS MAYHEM, #6

Release: April 26, 2023

Amidst a rising tide of poachers, three unlikely eco-warriors take a stand to save endangered Eastern Gray Wolves—even if it means the slow slaughter of their captors.

Deep in the woods of Jackson, New Hampshire, an ancient evil lurks. Armed poachers patrol a secret enclosure, holding captive a pack of majestic Eastern Gray Wolves. But three unlikely eco-warriors are determined to free the wolves, embarking on a dangerous mission to end their torture. With courage and conviction, Shawnee, Mayhem, and Jacy Lee march onward, even if it means risking their own lives to take down the poachers and restore freedom to the wolves. It's a battle between justice and injustice, and the eco-warriors are determined to win—no matter the cost. But what if something even more evil lurks in those woods? What if Shawnee's not ready to answer the cry for help?

GRAFTON COUNTY SERIES

MARRED, # 1
Released: November 2015
ISBN: 9781311566508

When Sage Quintano barely escapes from a brutal serial killer, husband Niko, a homicide detective, insists they move to rural New Hampshire, where he accepts a position as sheriff. Sage buries secrets from that night—secrets she swears to take to her deathbed. Three years pass and Sage's twin sister goes missing. Is the killer trying to lure Sage into a deadly trap to end his reign of terror?

CLEAVED, # 2
Released: May 2017
ISBN: 9781370387946

Sage Quintano writes about crime. Her husband Niko investigates it. Together they make an unstoppable team. But no one counted on a twisted serial killer, who stalks their sleepy community. Women impaled by deer antlers, bodies encased in oil drums, nursery rhymes, and the Suicide King. What connects these cryptic clues? For Sage and Niko, the truth may be more terrifying than they imagined.

SCATHED, # 3
Released: July 2018
ISBN: 9780463607176

When a brutal murder rocks Alexandria, Sheriff Niko Quintano receives a letter: Paradox vows to kill again if his riddle isn't solved within 24 hours. Niko turns to his crime writer wife, Sage, for help. But she's dealing with her own private nightmare. A phone call from the past threatens her future. Can Niko and Sage solve the riddle in time, or will the killer win this deadly game of survival?

RACKED, #4

RESTLESS MAYHEM

Released: August 2019
ISBN: 9780463275467

Five missing boys and an adult corpse found in the town's water shed was only the beginning for Sage and Niko. After a hooded stranger gives their son, Noah, a stuffed toy—the exact Christmas moose given to all the missing boys days before their abductions—their lives spiral downward into uncertainty. Will Noah be the next boy to go missing? The truth of what they discover blows everyone's mind.

HALOED, #5
Released: October 2022
ISBN: 9781005734039

A string of gruesome murders rocks the small town of Alexandria, New Hampshire, with all the victims staged to resemble dead angels. All the clues point to the Romeo Killer's return. Except one: he died eight years ago. Dead serial killers don't rise from the grave. With only hours left to live, how can Sage convince her Sheriff husband before the sand in her hourglass runs out?

Don't miss out!

Visit the website below and you can sign up to receive emails whenever Sue Coletta publishes a new book. There's no charge and no obligation.

https://books2read.com/r/B-A-DFAW-CUOHC

BOOKS 2 READ

Connecting independent readers to independent writers.

Did you love *Restless Mayhem*? Then you should read *Unnatural Mayhem*[1] by Sue Coletta!

[2]

The Cat Burglar, the Killer, and the Shaman Unite to Fight For Earth's Precious Animals—No Matter the Cost. Explosive news of a crow hunt rings out in the White Mountain Region of New Hampshire, and one hundred crows gather to put an end to it. With so many lives at stake—including Poe's—Shawnee and Mayhem must work together to stop the trophy hunters before they obliterate the local murder.Taking on twenty-five experienced hunters armed with shotguns is no small feat. If they fail, Poe may lead his brethren to their death.No matter what it takes, this group must be stopped.But what if Shawnee and Mayhem aren't seeing the full picture? What if these men have secrets worth killing over?

---

1. https://books2read.com/u/m2QDrO

2. https://books2read.com/u/m2QDrO